MEDICINE

MONEY

AND

MURDER

ANNE PETTIGREW

Copyright

SPARSILE BOOKS LTD

To medical students everywhere

Contents

Prologue

For me, the summer of 1971 was one of shattered misconceptions and mysterious events.

For a start, I discovered life in the United States was nothing like Doris Day's in *Move Over Darling*. For many US citizens, reality didn't involve sweetness, light and apple pie. Democratic access to advancement, prosperity and happiness wasn't automatically a given 'thing.' Instead, many US citizens faced a struggle for survival that left them constantly worrying about money and the costs of healthcare, and open to exploitation.

Secondly, not all doctors were like my TV heartthrob, Dr Kildare, providing altruistic care with their patient's best interests at heart. When money entered the equation, greed could rear its ugly head. Lives could be destroyed. Or ended. Cold-blooded murder might even happen.

Perhaps most importantly, my fear that I was doomed to spend a lifetime battling neurotic anxiety about sin, sex and salvation proved unfounded. I turned out to be stronger than I thought. (And discovered some supposed 'sin' was not so bad...)

The mysterious events I encountered? Well, from the day Laura Ellis and I started as students on work experience at New Jersey's Ellis Memorial Hospital we became aware of peculiar people and odd incidents that we tried to ignore.

But then came one inexplicable occurrence we could not disregard. An intriguing young woman patient called Carmela Gomez simply vanished.

And that changed everything.

Chapter One
The Vanishing Patient

Brunsfield, New Jersey, Monday July 19th, 1971, 8.30 a.m.

There are some patients who stick in your mind once you've seen them, especially those with interesting conditions you have never encountered before. Such a one was Carmela Gomez. Ever since I saw her leave the Emergency Room on Friday evening for transfer to a critical care unit, I had wondered about her fate. By Monday morning I felt that I had to know how she was doing. So, I phoned St Thomas's.

Out in the hall of the Ellis Memorial Hospital Nurses' Home, I hung on for ages as the switchboard girl checked her whereabouts for me. Eventually I replaced the aged phone receiver on the wall feeling frustrated. It was bizarre: the Admissions Clerk at St Thomas's Hospital could find no trace of the very ill patient that had so intrigued me. Yet I had definitely overheard Dr van Lindholm on the telephone arranging her transfer there.

Back in the kitchen, I found Laura looking surprisingly better. Or at least, somewhat less green. Must be powerful stuff, Advil. She'd only taken one as I left to phone and I'd been away for no more than fifteen minutes, but now she even managed to sit up, lift her eyes and look at me expectantly. 'Well, how is she?'

'You won't believe it, but St Thomas's in Westplains have never heard of Carmela.'

'What? But you seemed sure that was where they were taking her. And she went off in an ambulance you saw yourself?'

I nodded and sat down. 'Her daughter and I watched her leave.'

Laura frowned. 'Then are you sure you phoned the right hospital?'

'Yes! The telephone book in the hall lists only one St Thomas's Hospital. The girl I spoke to was really nice. She checked with every department—even the morgue. Horrible word, morgue. Sounds much more ghastly than mortuary, doesn't it? But she could find absolutely no record of a Mrs or Senora Carmela Gomez being admitted for critical care there on Friday night—or for that matter, at any time over the weekend. Carmela wasn't even seen in the Emergency Room. It's weird.'

'But where on earth can she have gone? I mean, I suppose it's possible she might've died enroute—but then, they'd still have had to take her into the ER for a doctor to certify her dead, wouldn't they?' Laura was now sitting pensively, chin on both hands, elbows on the table, the overindulgence of yesterday and hangover of today apparently forgotten.

'Not sure how that works here,' I said, 'but I expect you would still need a doc to pronounce someone dead. I'd be surprised though if she died that quickly. She'd definitely perked up a bit by the time she left. I was hoping a day or two of critical care would've seen her right, and that possibly she'd be in an ordinary ward by today. Though suppose I don't really know. She's the first septicaemic patient I've seen.'

'Surely though, if she did die, her name would still show up on the ER attendance records? I wonder if there's another way to find her? Like, if you could get her home number from our ER records, you could phone the family to ask how she's doing, couldn't you? Though I wonder if it would it be okay ethically to call them up directly. I mean, you're only a medical student, not actually her physician.' Laura bit her lip.

'I'll speak to Randy after the tutorial and see what he thinks or if he knows another hospital I could ring. As a Fifth Year ER Resident he'll know the score. To be honest, I wouldn't like to contact

Carmela's daughter, Elena, to ask how she is in case I upset her. She was lovely. Felt very sorry for the lass, especially when they wouldn't let her go in the ambulance with her mum. I couldn't see why they stopped her. Pretty harsh.'

While I rose to put away our Cheerios cereal packet and milk, Laura rinsed out our dishes, muttering about the dirty dish mountain on the draining board left by our lazy nurse housemates. Drying her hands on the correct 'regulatory' red kitchen towel (as designated by our 'House Mother', the formidable Mrs Heinz) and not the 'regulatory' green (and hardly used) one kept solely for drying dishes, she looked up at the clock.

'Right, we best go get dressed. Seminar's in twenty minutes.'

Laura was still in her PJs but I had changed into my working clothes of navy mini skirt and white blouse. Once in my room, I brushed back my long unruly wavy red hair, crammed it into a bobble with a black bow and donned our regulation white student jacket and name badge. Only moments later, Laura joined me fully dressed, with immaculately applied lipstick and her long shining black hair neatly twisted up into a knot with a clasp. In the few short weeks that we'd been living together in the US, I realised her capacity for springing back to life— even after massive hang-overs—was amazing.

Though only 7.45 am, it was already hot as we walked slowly in silence up the drive to Ellis Memorial Hospital. On the white stone steps at the front door Laura stopped in her tracks and turned to frown at me.

'You know what? I think Carmela didn't make it. Septicaemia's tricky, serious stuff, even with modern antibiotics. I mean, I doubt anyone at home would have dreamed of moving her to another hospital like you say Dr van Lindholm insisted on doing. I bet if she'd had insurance ...' She shrugged and left the thought hanging.

We passed through the cool, spacious lobby with its pale blue walls and lush green plants to walk towards the elevators. I looked around thinking how different this place was from the dark and dated Victorian hospitals we were taught in back home in Glasgow.

Laura echoed my thoughts, looking around appreciatively and saying, 'This place is pretty super, isn't it, Mhairi? It could be a five-star hotel.'

I sighed. 'Och, I wouldn't know, I've never stayed in one. Nor to be honest, in any hotel till the ones in London and New York on the way here.'

'Really?' Laura raised her eyebrows. 'What did you do for holidays?'

'Went to relatives in Lewis. At least, until mum died when I was thirteen. After that we took holiday houses, like in Fife or Millport usually.' I changed the subject unwilling to dwell on my mother and my attendant worries about the circumstances of her death. 'D'you know what this morning's seminar is about? I couldn't find my list.'

The lift arrived. As she stepped in, Laura pulled a crumpled sheet from her pocket. 'It says Kidney Disease Update.'

I feigned horror. 'God, I hope it's not led by Dr Loony van Lindholm!'

She gave a short laugh. 'Though if it is, then I suppose you could always ask him what happened to Carmela!'

Hitting the second-floor button, I made a face at her. The doors glided smoothly shut. No clanking iron gates here. 'Aye, right! But you know, another thing that puzzles me is why they operated on Carmela's to remove her kidney stones in the first place? Maybe that's routine over here but in Scotland, I think we'd be more likely leave them try to see if they'll pass themselves naturally. Well, apart from those huge staghorn ones that clog up your whole kidney and risk giving you renal failure. Passing stones is brutal, though. Watched a guy in casualty once peeing stones. He was writhing in agony. You have to give them pethidine and not morphine if it's bad. Exactly why, I forget.'

The lift dinged our arrival at Level Two. As the doors glided smoothly open, Laura stepped out, shaking her head. 'Well, I don't know about that, but taking out the stones, nephrolithotomy, is an op, isn't it? And here ops earn money for the hospital. And the surgeons.'

'But remember, the daughter said Carmela didn't have full insurance. I got the impression van Lindholm moved her to a charity hospital simply because Ellis Memorial wasn't going to get paid for treating her here in our critical care unit. The one at St Thomas's is seemingly heavily charity funded.'

'It all seems very complicated in the States. Thank God for our NHS. We're lucky.'

'We are. Though, as Elena told me her Mum's kidney surgery was paid for by some charity, I can't understand why it wouldn't fund any complications that followed, like post op infection.'

Laura held the Seminar Room door open for me.

'Thanks. Medicine seems so commercial here, Laura, doesn't it? I mean, no profit? No treatment. Or am I cynical already?'

In the room, her new admirer, Coop, rose to give her a hug. As they drew apart, their eyes locked. I could see things were progressing between them. He was a charming, good-looking chap and they seemed well suited. But then, she was never short of male admirers, albeit often in short lived, intense, romances.

The other students had yet to arrive. Sitting down beside her in silence, I reflected on what she'd just said. It had taken less than two weeks to convince me that Medicine over here was entirely different from home. But mostly, I was still pondering the where-abouts of the very ill, bonny young Mrs Carmela Gomez, lone parent to a vulnerable teenage daughter who'd wept in my arms. People couldn't just vanish. Where had that ambulance spirited her off to? Perhaps I could phone the ambulance service itself? Would they talk to me?

Something niggled me, however, about that ambulance. Normal looking inside, it had the usual two attendants, albeit striking to us with their mahogany skin contrasting sharply with their pristine white uniforms. But it was blue and from a company called MRT, different from the usual white emergency ones we'd seen drawing up at the ER door. Why had they summoned a different company?

Chapter Two
Apples: Big and Otherwise

Two weekends earlier, Saturday July 3rd 1971

Let me rewind to our arrival in the United States, which in itself was not without incident. Minutes after we touched down on
American soil, we found ourselves jerking around in a bus. More
like a cattle truck, it was standing room only all the way to the
terminal at Bangor, which was worse than Stansted, our departure
airport. Though also out in the sticks, it was essentially a bare
aircraft hangar lacking any facilities, even a coffee shop. While
we were standing about, another student from the flight informed
us that this was actually a US Air base. Indeed, looking around I
could see several military planes. I'd been feeling stressed since we
left home but now began to get seriously edgy. Lots of uniformed
men were hustling us into single lines.

'Hey, this isn't on! They're treating us like criminals.' I muttered, nudging Laura.

'Shhh!' She frowned at me, nodding towards a squad of grim-
faced Customs Officers assembling in front of the six lines we'd
been mustered into, each of which held forty odd students if my
numbers were right. (While taking a walk to stretch my legs on
the flight I'd counted 274 of us. I like knowing details).

It had been a rough trip so far. A rotten sleepless night in a
seedy (Student Travel assigned) London hotel, not helped by the
troubling information my father had dumped on me the night before. Hanging about in the city for an eight-hour delay in departure
due to 'Technical Difficulties'. Eventually leaving from Stansted (in

15

Essex, not Gatwick as planned), and in an old plane with a different carrier, Delta Airlines, not United. Still, we'd only paid £98 return to Student Travel so perhaps we couldn't complain.

Bangor wasn't offering us a warm welcome to the States. The temperature was as chilly as the officials' expressions. The stiff breeze blowing through the hangar made me regret I'd bagged my cardigan. Zipping up my summer anorak and shoving my cold hands into its pockets, I worried we'd badly misjudged the warmth of eastern US summers. Laura had made me buy flimsy cotton dresses and thin shirts. I whispered, 'I think we've brought all the wrong clothes.'

Laura disagreed. 'This cold is probably exceptional. But nonetheless, it's hardly stormy enough weather to justify changing to land here. Did we really have to stop in Maine? Is it just an excuse for taking a break or what?'

The well-informed student companion behind us again butted in. 'Defo an excuse, ladies. I had the same last year. Loads of charter flights land at Bangor for customs clearance. I think it might let them arrive in New York at the cheaper Newark domestic terminal.'

Laura nudged me to turn around. The line had moved and we had reached the front of the queue.

'Anything to declare?' snapped a podgy pale-faced officer. A long, small print list was thrust in my face. I couldn't read it, having taken out my contact lenses to try (unsuccessfully) to sleep on the plane, and hadn't found my specs when we landed. My squint was obviously taken as an admission of guilt. 'Search!' growled Podge to a female officer hovering behind him at a metal table.

The muscular woman stepped forward, wordlessly pointing at my big red case then gesticulating up to her table. I hauled up my beautiful new Antler suitcase, a present from my Aunt Sheona.

The officer opened it, stared and started to laugh. I almost did too: it was extraordinary. The weekend before we left, my aunt had come down from Stornoway to wish me luck on what she called

'My Big Adventure'. I'd spent ages trying to pack and panicked when I couldn't shut the case. She'd shooed me away and redid my packing, instructing me not to open it until I arrived in the States. The packing was a testimony to her youth spent as maid to the lady in the 'Big House'. It comprised exquisitely folded clothes sandwiched between layers of tissue paper.

My dour customs officer was now chuckling. 'That sure is a beaut! Never seen a case packed like that, honey! Have a nice holiday.' She closed it. Easily. Giving me a pang of anxiety: what had Sheona left out? But at least it had given the custom's officer a chance to show her human side. Perhaps not all Americans were querulous and officious.

That assumption didn't last long. At the next table, a furious argument arose between a young Customs guy, whose uniform was at least two sizes too big, and Deirdre from Dublin whom I'd met on my walkabout. A softspoken convent-educated girl (as she'd disclosed waving a double vodka at me), her nuns might not have approved of the torrent of abuse she let fly at the boy.

'It's only a bloody apple, for Christ's sake! It's my breakfast. Have you ever eaten Delta's food? It's shite!'

The boy went red as he raised his voice. 'Ma'am you cannot bring fruit or vegetables into the United States under any circumstances, not even for personal consumption.' He pointed at a large sign saying so. 'I'm afraid I will have to confiscate it.'

'In that case I'll have my breakfast now!' At that, Deirdre clamped her jaw violently round the apple on four sides in quick succession and dropped the soggy core into the boy's outstretched hand. A cheer went up breaking the silence that had grown while everyone listened to the exchange. Despite her bulging cheeks, Deirdre looked triumphant as she chomped noisily, trying to masticate her big bites of fruit without spitting any out. I'd have choked. At the very least Deirdre was going to have violent indigestion. I suspect she thought her Guinness World Record attempt at Speedy Apple Eating was worth it for the look on the boy's face.

After this altercation, a hubbub of support arose from the throng of milling students. The temperature of the place was palpably rising. Grumbling came from several quarters. The Customs staff quickly conferred before deciding, I suspect, that it wasn't worth risking any further loss of face and dignity by continuing to be over-thorough with us, a throng of young, fit—largely male—students whose numbers far outweighed theirs. And in any case, so far their searches had been fruitless. Apart from the illegal apple, of course.

They started waving people through. Thank God. My watch made it almost four a.m.

The luggage onboard again, we re-joined the plane. As Deirdre walked down the aisle to her seat, there were whistles and cheers. Once in mine, I was relieved to find my spec case in the seat pocket. Before we took off, an announcement confirmed we'd be landing in Newark in thirty minutes. Laura nudged me.

'You know, when they singled you out, I thought you'd be the one to create a fuss.'

'Oh, no. It's never worth arguing with authority. Those guys were right 'jobsworths' like you see on *That's Life*. It's a wonder they didn't arrest Deirdre.'

'Honestly, all that fuss over a wee apple!' Laura tutted then looked puzzled when I started laughing. 'What's so funny?'

'I was just thinking about another international food drama. I bet you've heard of *The Boston Tea Party*, but do you know about the *Naval Battle of the Cheese* in 1867?'

'God, where do you get your weird stories from, Mhairi?'

'We had a brilliant history teacher, full of mad facts. Seems the Uruguayan Navy ran out of cannonballs fighting the Brazilians and used mouldy Dutch cheese balls instead. They sank a boat and won.'

'You're kidding? Anyway, stop talking about food. I'm hungry!'

'Oh, I have something you can have!' Diving to the bottom of my bag, I produced two bananas. 'Have one of these from Gran's picnic yesterday. Or was it the day before?'

'God, girl, lucky they didn't look in your holdall!'

'I forgot about them. They're a bit speckled but still edible. We better eat them in case they cause another international incident at Newark!'

~~~

The Domestic Terminal in Newark was more like my idea of an airport, although we had to wait ages for our luggage to come round on the rubber conveyor belt. Thankfully, there were no more Customs to negotiate, but on the concourse we met chaotic crowds. Eventually we found a man with a BUNAC (British Universities North America Club) flag trying to muster those of us who'd booked onward arrangements with them. After numerous head counts, he set off with his phalanx of tired students towards a waiting bus.

We'd taken advantage of a stop-over package in New York with transfer into the city and a hotel overnight, planning to do some sightseeing. But the change of plane, the delays in London and the Customs stop at Bangor were going to seriously cut into our free time in the Big Apple.

Once in the city, we had a long walk to the hotel from where the bus was allowed to park. Hauling my big suitcase with one arm while balancing my overnight bag on my other shoulder was hard going. By the time we reached the hotel, I felt like a lopsided gorilla with one arm longer than the other.

The City Fare Hotel was just off Times Square and much better than the London one. Laura was delighted to find a note at reception from her Uncle Vincent, apologising that he was away for the holiday weekend but listing various numbers in case we needed anything. I was keen to meet him as I credited him with my father's eventual acquiescence to our trip. I couldn't have come without his financial support but as he stressed out if I took a bus instead of a taxi coming home late from University functions, the idea of me traipsing across the Atlantic for three months had filled him with horror. It was Laura's mother's assurance of the support we would have from her New York-based brother, Vincent and his credentials as a member of the Board of Chase Manhattan, that finally crumbled Dad's opposition. Good old Vincent.

We lugged the luggage to the elevator and along the endless sixth floor corridor to our room where I immediately flopped onto the nearest bed and slept for a couple of hours before sitting up with a start. 'What was that noise? Is there a fire?'

Laura was sitting in a chair at the window, reading. 'Which noise do you mean?' As she leaned over to open the window further, the volume of the "Honk, Honk, Honks" and screaming sirens I'd heard grew even louder.

'God, New York's noisy.' I yawned.

Laura shrugged. 'The honks and toots come from the yellow cab taxis. The sirens are police cars. We're just off Times Square, remember. It's dead busy even at this time in the morning!'

I took my watch from the bedside table. 'But it's nine now. Surely the commuters have been arriving for a couple of hours? Funny it's still dark.'

'No, it's four in the morning, silly! Look at that hotel alarm clock beside you. We're five hours behind now.' She took my watch and re-adjusted it to New York time.

I strapped it back on, feeling an idiot. 'Of course! I thought those Customs folk were pissed off because they'd been wakened up for us. But they were on an evening shift!'

'I suspect they behave the same whatever time of day it is.'

I lay back down. 'Can't get a handle on time differences. Why we're forward, they're back...' I stared at the ceiling but it didn't improve my thought processes.

'Think of it as the sun here has come from the UK and taken five hours.'

'Not sure that helps.' I tried sitting up to look around the room properly. 'Oh, that's good. There's a kettle on the dressing table! Let's have some tea.'

'Right, I'll make a cuppa. God, I'm hungry. Doubt anything will be open yet, though.' Laura lifted the kettle. Returning from the bathroom to plug it in, she opened a wooden box placed beside the socket. 'Hey, we've got teabags, coffee sachets—and biscuits!'

'Great! Better call them cookies here though, start thinking American!'

I looked out of our window. There were few folk on the pavements but plenty of cabs on the road. Or should that have been sidewalk and pavement? Through the thinning darkness, neon lights flashed brightly as edging on signs and pictures in ads. A maelstrom of confused visual signals stressed my sleepy brain. All greens were violently lime, all yellows searing citrus and the many flashing reds triggered unease. Now, why had red become a sign of danger, I wondered. Because it was the colour of blood maybe? Hardly relevant at present, but as I've said already, I like knowing details. My brain frequently operates at tangents. Somewhere a phone rang. Its long r-r-r-r-rings, each followed by a few seconds of silence, were quite unlike our barely separated ring-ring-rings at home. This, indeed, was America, looking and sounding just like in the movies.

We drank instant coffee made from paper packets, adding little pots of a sickly artificial creamer milk substitute that obviously didn't need a fridge. I still felt daring drinking coffee. It was one of my Gran Una's prohibited foods considered "too stimulant", although I was pretty sure coffee never featured in the Old Testament. God knows what she'd say if she knew I'd had two Martinis on the plane coming over! At home, the most I'd risked on a night out was a Babysham. Una's pious alcohol taboo was also rubbish: Jesus drank wine.

We took our time showering and changed into short summer dresses. Gran hadn't seen my summer wardrobe, assembled by Laura hiding me in cubicles at Marks and Spencers and C&A bringing me stuff to try on. A tried and tested system she had acquired with her mother. There was much I had missed by losing my mother early. She was more on my mind than ever after Dad's revelation before I left.

By eight we could wait no more and headed out for breakfast.

The streets proved quite stressful. Water dripped down from overhead aircon units and steam rose up from the many road drain covers. We got screamed at by a taxi driver for crossing the road in front of him and were chastised for 'jaywalking' by a nearby elderly Irish cop who informed us cars can turn right on a red light in America and it was against the law to cross the road if the lights flashed 'Don't Walk!' Laura later admitted she actually knew this but was so tired and hungry and hellbent on crossing the road to a diner that she forgot.

We were pretty much in a daze as we ordered a hamburger, perhaps not the best thing for breakfast being massive and greasy, before wandering around New York. We made it up to the top of the Empire State building and saw a few other sights listed in my guidebook, but after a few hours, the heat and fatigue got to us and we stopped for a drink and some more food. This meal, my first ever pizza, turned out to be even more gigantic. I barely ate half. The waitress cleared the table, then returned with my uneaten portion in a box Laura pronounced as a 'doggie bag.' Despite suspecting few of these ever fed dogs, I thought this a great idea and took it back to the hotel for later.

Laura had a purse full of dollars and insisted on paying for everything. I felt bad. Though I had travellers cheques, I had brought no cash with me. I reflected on one recent discovery I had made; I had stacks of money in a bank. It had been the only bit of comforting news amongst otherwise disturbing disclosures at home.

But well-heeled as she was, Laura didn't waste money. She insisted we call our destination hospital to tell them we'd arrived from the hotel foyer phone and not our rooms which she declared would be much more expensive. Getting the Brunsfield area code from the receptionist, I dialled several times but found the number constantly engaged. The public phone flummoxed me. It had no dial, only pushbuttons. But unlike in the UK, had no button B to get your money returned if you didn't connect. When I was almost out of the dimes Laura had exchanged for dollars at the desk, she snatched the phone from me.

'I don't believe a hospital switchboard can be engaged all that time!' Firmly pushing the buttons again, she held out the receiver so we could both hear.

'There, it's engaged. I told you!' My triumph was short-lived.

'No, that's the US ringing tone, you twit!' This time Laura held on for the switchboard. 'Hello, could I speak to Dr Carlton Harper's secretary, please?'

'I'm sorry, no. It's Saturday.' God, we were idiots not even knowing what day of the week it was! The woman added helpfully. 'It's the Fourth of July weekend anyway. Hardly anyone's in. Can I take a message?'

Laura replied,' We just wanted to confirm that we had arrived in New York and wonder how best to get from Brunsfield train station to the hospital?'

'Say, are you one of the Scottish medical students we're expecting?'

'Yes. I'm Laura Ellis. We're in New York. Coming over tomorrow.'

'Oh, hi! Get a taxi right up here. Charge it to us. That'll be OK, for sure!'

Still feeling foolish, we then consulted the City Fare reception desk about which station had trains to Brunsfield and where we could get a timetable. The receptionist thought the service would be much reduced for the holiday weekend and suggested Greyhound buses might be better. Giving us a New Jersey bus route map and timetable, she marked the way to the bus station on a city map. We were all set.

Once up in bed, I relaxed a little. At last, Laura and I were finally in the United States of America. Despite my general anxiety and pre-occupation with family troubles, I was looking forward to some freedom.

I had three months to do exactly as I pleased, drink what I wanted, come home late if I wished and be free from nagging reminders for church and prayers. Time for some fun after a tough year of late-night studying and exams. I had a pang thinking about my lovely Roddy, a romance kindled some months ago after Laura dragged me to a Union dance. But three months away was a long time. Anyway he'd likely find someone else while I was away.

I now had a chance to let my hair down. Which would include getting it cut! Gran Una's belief that scripture forbade the cutting of cutting women's hair was ridiculous. My wavy, thick, almost waist length tresses were a time-consuming nonsense. For goodness sake, the men of the Free Presbyterian Church could have their hair cut, yet Jesus was always shown with long hair.

Turning over, I curled up in bed. How I was looking forward to this summer of freedom and liberation. Bound to be exciting.

It was. And then some.

Chapter Three
A Tale of Two Waitresses

Next morning was Sunday the Fourth of July, American Independence Day. We rose at half seven and went to breakfast in the hotel restaurant. There we were confronted by a buxom waitress with a messy French plait hairdo exuding haphazard pins who looked like one of TV comedian Dick Emery's female drag character but wasn't funny. She slopped down two tepid coffees without asking, rattled off a bewildering choice of egg dishes then left without taking an order.

We helped ourselves to cereal, juice, rolls and pastries, scoffing four each before heading off. At the door, I glanced back and saw the waitress had finally returned and was theatrically raising our abandoned plates and peering under them. Looking up, she shouted over, 'No tip? Thanks a bunch girls! Fifteen per cent is usual here, you know!' Sticking up a rude forefinger towards us she finished off with, 'Sure and it's right what they say—the Scots are real mean!' Every head turned towards us.

Sensing a scarlet Laura was ready for a fight, I hissed, 'Don't waste your energy! Think she's just an unhappy woman with a job she hates. Let's go. We've got a bus to catch.'

Wheeling Laura round, I steered her out. She muttered, 'Bloody cheeky bitch!' and seethed until we got on the bus an hour later. I did sympathise with her. We'd had aggro from Customs, a belligerent taxi driver and now an angry waitress. It wasn't a good start. But I was convinced our hospital posts would be more congenial than my last summer job: refereeing unruly children at a Woolworths' sweetie counter.

~~~

The Greyhound bus trip was slow. For once I didn't let Laura sleep. She had dozed off within minutes on every form of transport we'd used since leaving home. I decided I had to tell her why I'd been so worried. This bus journey was as good a time as any to get things off my chest. I think travelling lends itself to 'heart-to-hearts'. It is easier to discuss emotional things while sitting side by side with someone looking out of a window. It's almost like talking to yourself.

I'd already told Laura that while looking for my birth certificate to make my passport application I'd found my mother's death certificate. Strangely, it had recorded her as dying of heart failure, not the head injury caused by falling downstairs that my father had previously claimed. I'd also previously said that, after finding the certificate, I'd confronted our family GP, Dr Emanuel Cosgrove who'd issued it. He insisted her heart had failed, likely from a heart rhythm problem. But he'd been cagey. I suspected it wasn't the whole truth.

Once we were driving out through the New York suburbs, I took a deep breath and turned to Laura. 'I'd like to tell you something.'

'What?'

'It's about Mum. The night before we came away, Dad spoke again about her death.' I bit my lip. It was hard, but I had to talk about it or go mad. 'He said she didn't die of a fall, like he said years ago, nor of heart failure as certified.'

'So, what was it?' Laura asked quietly, glancing around the almost empty bus. To the rear, there were several older black travellers and a youth but there was no one within earshot.

'He said she took an overdose.'

'You mean she committed suicide?' Laura looked startled.

'Well, she didn't leave a note. He said he thought that she only wanted to get to sleep and took some extra antidepressant pills in the early hours topped up by some of his sneaky sideboard whisky. He maintains he didn't hear her get up, only found her dead on the sofa when he tried to wake her in the morning.'

'But why tell you that just before you were leaving? Bit cruel, wasn't it?'

'Oh, I expect he had a crisis of conscience or something. Needed to confess. Wish he hadn't bothered. Dr Cosgrove had phoned to tell him I'd found the death certificate and Dad said Cosgrove suggested 'heart failure' as it was what likely what happened anyway since tricyclic antidepressants can cause erratic heart beats and death. I don't know what to believe, but since I came away I'm obsessed by memories I think I must've suppressed. Like shouting matches where Dad told Mum he'd had enough, couldn't take it anymore. Makes me wonder. Did he drive her to it? Or even help her...'

'You mean murder her? Oh Mhairi, surely not?' Laura looked appalled.

'Apart from maybe wanting to silence her for peace, there's the money. You do know if a death is from suicide you can't claim life insurance? Well, he got a huge life insurance payout after she died. I wonder when he took out the policy?'

Laura sat silent as I looked out of the window at two laughing dog-walkers ambling along. Carefree folk going about their everyday business. Happy. I felt I'd never be happy again. Tears welled.

'Och, it's awful.' Laura squeezed my hand.

I felt my jaw tighten. 'Och, all Dad's "Holier than Thou" stuff, pretending to be pious. He's a bloody hypocrite! Whisky in the sideboard. Breaking commandments right left and centre. Lying. Profiting from Mum's death. You have to admit it's all a bit suspicious.'

'About the money, have you always known it about it?'

'No, not until I found bank books when looking for my birth certificate. Looks like most of it's in trust for my young brother Archie and I.'

'But still, I don't get it. Why tell you in the first place that she died in a fall?'

'God knows. Maybe hoping Gran Una wouldn't twig she'd been depressed and overdosed in case she wouldn't come down to help with us? Dad did say she already disapproved of Mum, because they'd "Got ahead of their wedding night" as he quaintly put it. Knew that anyway from seeing their marriage certificate. I couldn't possibly have survived at five months premature. And another thing: if she had been certified as a suicide, she couldn't have been buried in the churchyard at Uig, especially in the Free Presbyterian Church of Scotland. We're Wee Frees, you know.'.'

'I sort of gathered that. But gosh. What a lot to take in.'

'That's not all. His final blow was telling me that Mum gave up studying medicine 'cos she was pregnant with me.'

'Really? How cruel.' Laura now looked so concerned that my eyes filled.

'God, it feels as if I can't win. After speaking to our GP, I was worried I'd inherit some heart thing. Now I worry Dad might have killed Mum or she killed herself as she couldn't face living with us. Plus, I'm wracked with guilt that I ruined her life.' My contact lenses were swimming in the tears now overflowing onto my cheeks.

'Oh, nonsense! She went on to have your brother, Archie, too, didn't she? I'm sure she loved you both. It's horrendously sad, but all you can do is qualify well and make her proud. You have to put it behind you.'

'But what if I get mentally ill like Mum? I mean, after she went, I had to go to the doctor for ages with depression. I feel I'm a basket case already!'

'Don't be ridiculous! Listen, you can't bring back your poor mum but at least now you know the truth that she died because of extra tablets, however that happened. I'm glad you've told me about what your Dad said, but you have to put this behind you and try to have a stupendous summer.' She nodded outside. 'Look, here's Brunsfield. Up you get! Let's fetch the cases and go a find taxi.'

I had to admit I felt better after my outpouring. I knew that now there was nothing for it but to tackle full-on the challenges we were about to encounter, which would include querying the causes of other deaths. And some of them would definitely turn out to be murder.

~~~

Our destination appeared to be a pleasant town. Outside the bus station, we easily found a taxi to take us to the hospital entrance. Inside, a receptionist called for someone to take us down to our residence for the next three months, the Nurses' Home.

While waiting for this housekeeping person, we asked the girl where we might get a late lunch. Telling us the Dining Room would have finished serving and the hospital Coffee Shop was closed for the holiday, she suggested a restaurant in town called Bohemia, likely the only one that would be open. It was about twenty minutes' walk away so she offered to get us a taxi, which we declined. A walk would do us good.

The hospital brochure had informed us Brunsfield had 20,000 residents but on our first walk into town we saw none. It was hot and steamy as we passed through tree-lined streets past smart substantial houses with two-car driveways and well-tended gardens.

Further into downtown Brunsfield, the houses became less prosperous and blocks of flats more predominant, though no building was more than three storeys high. The streets were wide, most offering welcome shade from a variety of trees. It was quiet compared to New York: no congested streets, no honking taxis, more my idea of what I'd heard called 'small town America'—neat, clean, ordered. Almost idyllic. But as we walked, the silence became eerie. Brunsfield was like a ghost town: no soul walked its streets, no dog barked, no car passed. Traffic lights suspended on high wires swayed in the breeze at junctions while constantly flashing amber. What was their point if they never went red to stop traffic? Nearer the town centre, the odd car passed, each longer, leaner and meaner than a UK vehicle. No stubby Morris Minors or Ford Escorts here!

'Wonder why these cars need such long bonnets? I mean, you can get car engines into bonnets half that size, can't you?' I pointed across the road at one particular big green, shiny, be-finned car with polished chrome hubcaps.

'Not bonnets, darling, its 'hoods' in the States. My brother James reckons the Yanks have 'Small Dick Syndrome' and need an aggressive-looking car to show they've really got big willies! But, of course, he has a Jag, so he's one to talk. Getting too big for his boots is my brother. Fancies himself as a judge before he's forty. As if!'

I'd heard Laura make digs about her lawyer brother before, feeling that he was her father's favourite though I'd seen nothing supporting this. It was comforting to know all families had problems. I chided her a little. 'Och, you never know, he might end up on the bench. He is very bright, isn't he?'

Laura ignored my question. 'I've heard Mum talking similarly about red sports cars at home. Thinks they're a sign of male mid-life crisis or inadequacy in the bedroom department!'

I couldn't imagine Grace, her cool sophisticated Mum, talking to her daughter about sex. Certainly, no one ever mentioned it in my house. It was a source of wonder how my pious grandmother had ever consummated a marriage to produce my father. I countered with, 'Och, maybe it's not just about sex, rather about showing off generally, like, "My car's bigger than yours", kind of thing? These long cars must be terribly difficult to park. Not that I've ever tried parking myself.'

'Well, I've passed my test but I'm still hopeless! Shouldn't think it's a big deal here. There are loads of roomy lots to park in. But you're right, it's all about show. The Yanks like symbols of prosperity.' Laura crossed the road. 'Must say, I'm surprised there's no one about. I expected Fourth of July celebrations, fireworks and star-spangled banners.'

'Maybe they'll come out tonight when its cooler?' I suggested.

Laura took off her straw hat and wiped her brow.

'God it's hot! The heat seems to radiate up from these pavements. Not surprised we don't see any dog walkers about. This tarmac would singe poor wee paws.'

'Never thought of that. But I do think this new crocheted tank top of mine is too tight in this heat. Bell bottoms aren't bad though, are they? They kind of flap as you walk, create a bit of a draft round the legs!'

'I'm just glad of my short skirt. Minis are the thing!' Laura laughed.

I checked the time. 'It's almost three. I'm starving. Where's this *Bohemia* restaurant?'

'Main Steet,' said Laura looking about. 'We are on it now.'

Every shop we'd passed had its shutters down or blinds drawn. Even the drug store. Up ahead on the opposite side of the road, I spied a women coming out of a glass door while calling back inside, 'Swell lunch—see you next week!'

I pointed. 'There! That must be the *Bohemia*!'

Just then, a silver car cruising past slowed to a halt at the kerb beside Laura. From its nearside window loomed a dark face in a trilby hat and fine trimmed beard.

'Say ladies, need a ride somewhere?' His hair was oily, his leer accompanied by suggestive lip licking. Across in the driving seat was another, bigger, guy. I became uneasy. Looking around, I saw the street was completely deserted. Even the woman from the restaurant had disappeared.

Laura was quick. 'In your dreams, boyo!' Grabbing my arm, she shoved us behind the car and across the road to the restaurant. The battered car sped off throatily.

Just inside the restaurant door stood a tall blonde girl with ornately plaited hair. She looked concerned and nodded out towards the street behind us.

'Everything all right out there? That Cadillac sure drove off fast.' She had an accent I couldn't place.

'Yes. We're fine.' The catch in Laura's voice showed that she'd been unsettled.

'I saw it stop. Were they hitting on you?'

'Just some low life chancing his arm.' Laura shrugged.

'Did you get the plate? I could phone the cops.'

'No. Never mind. It's okay. Can we have a table for lunch? Hope we're not too late.'

'Of course. My name is Gretel and I'll be your hostess for today. Come this way.'

Her pronunciation of 'way' as 'vay' suggested to me she might be German. Or Austrian, I supposed. She led us away from the window past potted palms to a table that bore a pristine white linen cloth, polished cutlery, sparkling wine glasses and a small vase of fresh flowers. All very European, cool and smart. Sinking into a padded velvet seat, Laura looked round, commenting, 'Nice!'

Gretel looked delighted. 'Here is the menu. Of course, today roast turkey is the dish of the day and key lime pie is the dessert. What will you be drinking?'

'A Coke please.' I said, flicking through the large menu.

'And I'll have a glass of Californian white, please. And the specials.' Laura nodded at me. 'Mhairi?'

'Okay, I'll have that too.' I was beyond making any decision for myself.

'Hope that you are hungry, guys!' Gretel retrieved her menus and moved off.

Laura sat back. 'Since we're late and starving think it's sensible to have the specials; they'll be ready to go.'

'Never thought of that. You're so worldly-wise, Laura. And I'm thinking maybe we should get a taxi back up to the hospital? Apart from it being scorchingly hot, those guys were a bit scary. There aren't many people about.'

'Sure. Good idea.'

The meal was delicious. And huge. I surprised myself by eating more than half and decided we could take some home in a 'doggie bag' now that we'd have access to a fridge. (And I knew what a 'doggie bag' was).

After the last of the largely solo diners had drifted off, the hostess sat with us over coffee. Gretel Neuberger was extremely attractive. She was twenty-five, from Nuremburg in Germany and had been in Brunsfield for four years having followed out an American lad she'd met when he'd been on a university exchange. The engagement had foundered but she'd no plans to return to Germany. 'My parents were against Des. Can't face going home to hear them say, "We told you so!" Well, I did have someone else for a while, but he was another rat. I'm off men now. Who needs them?' She pouted. 'What are you girls doing over here?'

She was surprised that we were doctors in training.

'I have not met any women doctors. In fact, I have a poor opinion of the male ones I have met, especially here. I am sure you will be much better than any of them!'

Gretel had a lovely gentle laugh. The guys who'd dumped her obviously had no taste. But there was a sadness in her eyes; they didn't laugh when she did. Moving off the topic of men, she went on to extol the virtues of New York.

'You must let me take you to New York City when I have a weekend off!'

'That would be really kind, Gretel.' I was touched.

'I'll give you the restaurant telephone number. You'll find me here more often than in my flat.' She scribbled it on a piece of paper that Laura put it in her bag.

Laura paid the bill and said, 'Great. Now I think we should be off.'

Gretel jumped up. 'Shall I call you a cab?'

We had to wait some time for one. Gretel suggested they'd be busy transporting people home from family lunches. The 'cab' was actually a black limo. I sank into the back seat with an appreciative stroke of its leather. Laura gave the driver instructions before sitting back and saying, 'Was really nice of Gretel to offer to show us around, wasn't it?'

'Yes, but mibbe she's a bit lonely. I mean, she seemed very keen to meet up, didn't she?'

Laura agreed. As we drove, I found myself looking up every street we passed. 'Have you noticed there are no bus stops? You must need a car to get around here.'

'Probably. I know in New York my family drive or take cabs, never public transport. Well, maybe the Metro. But never at night. Buses are for the poor, particularly Black folk. You saw that in the Greyhound Bus Station. White faces were in a minority.'

At the Nurses' Home, the fare turned out to be more than I'd expected but Laura proffered a wad of notes, telling the friendly driver to keep the change. Generous tipper was Laura. (Apart from to surly waitresses).

American travel was tiring. After unwinding some tissue paper and unpacking a bit, I lay down and slept. Around eight, we ate our turkey and key lime pie doggie bag and made cuppas with some tea bags we found in the cupboard and splodges of someone's milk from the fridge. Lounging on the squishy chintz sofas in the old-fashioned lounge, we watched I Love Lucy, laughing at the frequently interspersed ads for Ivory Soap which apparently floated. Exactly why that was a marketing advantage was not disclosed. By ten we had collapsed into our comfy single beds. And I hit blissful oblivion for the first time since leaving home. Without any nightmares about murderous fathers.

Chapter Four
Jess, Mrs Heinz & Kitty

Early next morning, I woke parched. In the kitchen I found a young blonde woman in Bugs Bunny baby doll PJs sitting at the table reading. On our arrival, we hadn't met any nurses. The Nurses' Home had been as deserted as the streets. A hospital clerk had simply let us in and left us to it. To my surprise, this jolly-looking girl suddenly leapt up to hug me.

'Hi, Mahari—great to meet you!'

'Oh, hello! How on earth do you know my name?'

'From the photos they've had up on the notice boards for weeks. Welcome to Ellis Memorial! I'm Jessica Heffernan, but everyone calls me Jess. I'm a final year RN. That's a Registered Nurse,' she added helpfully.

'Pleased to meet you. By the way, my name's pronounced 'Vary', it's Gaelic.'

'Oh, how cool!'

I filled the kettle at one of the two sinks. 'What happens about food in here, by the way? We only got in yesterday and don't have any.'

'Well, you're welcome to use some of mine today, second shelf in there.' She pointed at one of two giant fridges. 'And I finish at six, so I could maybe take you tonight to the store to get what you need? Most of us keep food in the kitchen. Label anything in the refrigerator though. There's sneaky folks about. You can get all your meals in the dining room but in the morning most of us like having toast or cereal for breakfast in the Home before getting dressed.'

'Sounds a good idea.' Rummaging through cupboards, I located two mugs. Jess gave me teabags. Laura appeared and received the same effusive greeting. We sat chatting while consuming tea and toast slathered with Jess's Nutella. Like Marmite, I wouldn't rave about it, but it was kind of her to offer some. And we were hungry.

Jess put her dishes in the sink. 'Hey guys, why not meet me here around six-thirty and I'll drive you to the store?' She sped off to get ready for work, plaiting her long hair as she went.

Almost immediately we were joined by someone much less effusive. A woman let herself in the front door and marched straight into the kitchen. She was in her fifties sporting brillo-pad hair (defo excess hair lacquer) and a fixed attempt at a smile that fooled no one. God, another Dick Emery to be reckoned with! Noting a bare left ring finger, I wasn't surprised. It would be a bold fellow who'd propose to this stern lady. Gosh, here I was, miles from home, not only meeting new folk without panicking but making snap judgements on them. I could do this.

'Good morning, girls. I hope you have recovered from your long journey?'

Laura stood to answer. 'Yes, thank you. I'm sorry, but who are you?'

'I am Mrs Adela Heinz, Nursing Home Supervisor.'

I smiled to myself. Mrs! So, there must be brave men in America.

'Please read these Home Rules and Regulations.' She handed over two sheets of closely typewritten paper. The top listed dozens of "Do nots", the one beneath a shorter list headed of "We Encourage You To".

I smiled. 'Thank you.'

She patted her crisp hair. 'Now, you will see a telephone number written beside the hall phone in case of emergency. I live in for much of the week but do not expect to be disturbed unless it is something drastic.' Her eyelids narrowed and her eyes darted from Jess to me and back. 'There are notices in the kitchen and on the back of your room doors about what to do in the event of a fire. Please familiarise yourself with them. And I must emphasise one very strictly enforced rule; there must be no male company entertained in any room apart from the sitting room. Male guests may meet you in the public lounge after 2 p.m. but all must leave before 11 p.m. Is that understood?'

'Of course, Mrs Heinz.' Laura had assumed an uncharacteristic obedient schoolgirl look. Demurely, she tucked a loose hair strand behind an ear.

I only said, 'Yes, Mrs Heinz.'

The woman nodded. 'That's all, girls. Enjoy your stay. And here you are. This is from Dr Harper's Secretary.' She handed Laura a long white envelope.

As she left, we both sat down and looked at one another. Laura blew out through puckered lips. 'God, wasn't she something else? That felt like a Gestapo briefing!'

'Wouldn't like to cross her. Wonder what her background is?'

'Alcatraz?' Laura raised an eyebrow. 'Right, no men in your room, Mhairi MacLean. Got it?

'The thought has never crossed my mind! Don't worry, love affairs aren't on my agenda. Remember I have sweet Roddy waiting at home in any case!'

'Darling, he's miles away. You've got all summer to play the field!' She turned over the envelope in her hand and ripped it open.

'What does it say?' I stretched up my arms and yawned.

'It's from a Mrs Caraciola telling us today's a public holiday so we should take it easy and appear tomorrow at ten in some second-floor seminar room for 'Orientation'.

I was delighted. 'Great, our first day's a holiday! Let's wander into the town and see if we can find a shop to get some food for the fridge so we don't need to bother Jess later. Then I would't mind an afternoon nap to be honest. I'm still knackered.'

'Don't fancy walking miles in this heat. Maybe we could call a cab to go downtown for an early lunch and then find a supermarket?'

'Och, let's just slap on some suncream and walk in now. I bought some Boots' own. I've never used it much before but the sun here seems very strong.'

'I think we need our sunhats too if we're walking,' Laura asserted, mothering as ever.

~~~

After walking for a good twenty minutes, we found an open A & P supermarket and picked up an assortment of breakfast goodies and snacks. Laura wanted to buy wine to celebrate our arrival and was surprised to discover they didn't sell it.

The checkout assistant laughed. 'No can do, guys. You'll need to go across town to the liquor store on Madison Street for that. And you'll need ID. You over twenty-one?'

'Yes,' replied Laura. 'You know I've never bought alcohol when I've been visiting before, didn't have to. Back home we can buy wine in off licences at eighteen.'

'You don't say? Think it's even twenty-five in some States here. I've got cousins in a Methodist town in Massachusetts. There it's as bad as the Prohibition—you can't buy liquor at all.' Pausing in her tap, tap, tapping of prices on the cash register as she flipped each item from our basket to the side, she asked, 'You guys got somethin' to put this into? Or you need a bag?'

Laura frowned. 'Oh. Yes. I mean, no. We're a bit-jetlagged! Bag please!'

'You guys Irish?'

'No, Scottish.' A reply I repeated all summer.

'That's a gas!' She smiled and produced a flat brown bag from under her counter which she dexterously flipped open one-handedly before packing in our milk, cereal, bread, eggs, cheese, bananas, crisps and chocolate bars. At the crisps she paused. 'Say, you'd be better with one of those multipacks of potato chips.' She pointed at a display stand. 'You'll get six for less than the cost of these four individuals.'

Laura fetched a 'multibuy pack'. Kitty, as she'd introduced herself, threw our single ones into a basket of discards at her feet. The big new pack's brand declared it to be 'Lays' potato chips. Made me smile. Who'd name a brand after sex? Made our *Golden Wonder* and *Smiths* seemed positively boring.

'Cash or credit?'

Laura took out a Barclays bank card and paid. I was impressed. A card! Sophistication. I doubted Dad would allow me one. Though could he stop me now that I was twenty-one, and knew I had my own money? I planned a trip to a bank when I got home to access it. Not one of Dad's branches. But for the present, my traveller's cheques needed cashed—and all the banks we'd passed had been closed. I had a thought.

'Say, Kitty, do you take travellers cheques in here? I mean, do shops take them or must I take them to the bank? And will I get change if they are for more than I've spent?'

'Sure, we get them all the time, American Express especially. Some stores have minimum spends, like ten dollars. You'll need ID though.' She handed Laura a till receipt, flashing an American smile of beautiful big, even, white teeth. It was a striking feature of Jess's face too. 'You got driving licences with you for the liquor store?'

To Kitty's surprise, I had to admit that I didn't have a licence. 'I suppose a passport would do?'

She nodded, handing me the brown paper shopping bag bearing the Atlantic and Pacific logo., I had to cradle it like a baby. It wasn't a great design: no handles. I made a face. 'Not sure I'd like to carry my passport around with me unless I have to, though.'

Kitty smiled widely. 'Hey, gals, no worries- you can breathe easy here. This is a real safe town. Nothing ever happens! Great to meet you folks. You all have a nice day—come again.'

When we returned some weeks later, blonde and bubbly Kitty wasn't there. And when I did finally see her, I concluded that Brunsfield wasn't a 'real safe town' after all.

Chapter Five
Getting Started

Tuesday July 6th, 1971, was our first working morning as student summer 'externs' in the hospital. 'Interns' we knew were junior US doctors, qualified but still in specialist training. Us externs, on the other hand, were medical students from out of the area that American hospitals hosted in summer programmes while providing board and lodging, clinical experience and a nominal pocket money stipend towards expenses. We'd applied to several and felt ourselves lucky to have been accepted by this great hospital.

As we came out of our air-conditioned Nurses' Home lodgings to walk up to the main hospital building, the heat was intense even that early in the morning. Toiling up the long curved driveway, Laura moaned about us being stuck at the bottom of the hill in the Nurses' Home when we'd learned that our male student colleagues were billeted in the Doctor's Residency on the top floor of the hospital. With no female junior doctors on Ellis Memorial's staff and us being their first-ever female medical students, we'd been lumped in with the nurses.

Walking along, there was some light relief in the form of the spray from sprinklers sitting amongst the shrubs at the side of the drive. Though the verges were green, the rose bushes were spare, scraggy and spindly compared to ours in Scotland. But other, presumably more drought-tolerant shrubs, had exotic looking blooms wafting sweet scent in the occasional light breeze.

From the outside, Ellis Memorial Hospital looked impressive. We'd been sent a leaflet extolling its excellent record of care, ensuite bedroom numbers, specialities and the prosperous district it served. Only ten years old, it was a sleek purpose-built six-storey structure of white stone with extensive windows now reflecting the glory of the clear blue sky. We thought patients were very fortunate being treated in this comfortable modern facility compared to our big Glasgow twenty-bed Nightingale wards with their communal facilities and Victorian décor of linoleum floors and cold wall tiles.

Pulling open the heavy front door of the hospital, I half-turned to look down at the tree-lined streets of the town of Brunsfield below and thought that we could have made a worse choice for summer placement. It was a pleasant, peaceful town. And this was, on the face of it, a well-run, state of the art hospital that its residents could be proud of.

The huge reception area boasted blue deep-pile carpets, modern upholstered chairs and magazine-strewn coffee tables. To the right lay an open plan coffee shop. Above our heads, a plethora of pale blue hanging signs gave directions to departments. To the left was a large open reception desk. Mounted on the wall beside it was a hospital directory. Noting our Seminar Room destination was listed as being on the second floor, I led the way to the bank of elevators on the rear wall, still feeling too tired from our journey to contemplate tackling stairs.

In the shiny lift I pressed the button for Floor Two and remarked, 'Hey, there's no button for ground floor. Not even a zero!'

Laura laughed. 'They don't have one. Here, ground floor is first and first is second. You'll need to press the button for one if you are coming down to the lobby.'

I sighed. Laura was so full of useful US facts. With relatives in New York, she'd often been over in the States and had travelled extensively with her wealthy family. Her father was an advocate and her mother had been a debutante. Mine was Bank Manager and we were not exactly penniless, but I hadn't travelled. My grandmother saw no merit in leaving the country where the Good Lord had seen fit to place us at birth. Everything I knew about the

States had been gleaned from books and films, where the absence of ground floors had never been mentioned...

Upstairs, the seminar room was windowless, white-walled and spacious. More plush dark blue carpet. Half a dozen turquoise padded chairs with arm rests were set out in an arc. Each had a small drop-down writing table hanging from one arm. Neat.

It was splendidly organised. Opposite the seats a large white-board was hanging on the wall with a rolled-up projector screen positioned above it. Below stood a table set with two chairs, two glasses and a jug of water. To one side was a water dispenser with plastic cups. At the other side was a tall, mobile, shelved unit that housed various electronic gadgets including a projector. Sorry, I know I obsess about details, the product of my father's exhortations to carefully observe your surroundings so that in times of trouble (unspecified) there will be fewer surprises. If I felt 'imperilled, I should remember something notable about any assailant to tell the police. I always thought him far too overprotective, likely because he was a lone parent. Yet I was soon to see he was right; you can't trust everyone in the world. My grandmother was even worse, seeing the Devil around every corner. I was more fortunate: it took me twenty-one years to meet him.

But back in the seminar room, we were not imperilled by any evil, only faced by the arc of six chairs, three of which held neat stacks of papers and three which held young men.

The first tall, athletic lad leaped up and towards us with a wide smile. As he flung his arms out and leaned in, I stepped back, worried he might bowl me over. But he simply clasped my right hand firmly in both of his.

'Welcome to the US of A, girls. I'm John Coulter, one of the summer externs.'

When I looked up at his face, I was disappointed that I hadn't received a bear hug. This was an exceedingly good looking hunk of

44

manhood. John Coulter was over six feet, muscular, with a shock of thick blonde hair. Warm blue eyes shone in his suntanned face.

I felt my knees sagging slightly but managed to summon my voice to audible pitch. 'Thanks. It's great to be here. I'm Mhairi MacLean. But it's spelled the Gaelic way, with an 'M' and an 'H' which is pronounced Vary.' Becoming aware that I was burbling and likely grinning inanely, I tore my eyes away from John's film star face to address the other boys. 'And are you all externs too?'

They nodded while John continued speaking.

'I'm from New York City, studying at the University of Virginia Med School. Came over last week. And yes, these guys are on our program too.' He waved at them before moving to shake hands with Laura and sitting back down.

As I approached these boys, the first stood, smiled and shook my hand firmly. Not quite as tall as John, he too was deeply suntanned. Strikingly brown-eyed, he had neat short sideburns and long dark hair curling over the collar of his white shirt.

'Hi, I'm Coop, at the same college as John. But I'm not staying in the Residency. My dad's a cardiologist on staff in the hospital, Dr Michael Mayfield. We live out on the west side of town.'

'Coop? That's an unusual name...'

'Yeh, short for Cooper, after my grandfather.' He grinned. 'So, where are you guys from?' He looked from me to Laura who stood with her mouth fixed open as if she were about to speak but nothing came out as she gazed at Coop in a way I recognised, already rapt. She fell for boys at the drop of a hat. Frequently and usually disastrously. I replied for us both.

'We go to the University of Glasgow, in the west of Scotland.'

'Hey, I've been to Edinburgh, that near?' Coop was now staring back at Laura.

'Sort of,' I answered, thinking the Edinburgh to Glasgow distance was chicken feed to an American, considering the vastness of their country. I also didn't correct his pronunciation of the silent 'g' in Edinburgh. What did it matter that in Scotland we said 'Edinburra'?

The last student only half rose to shake our hands. He was a pale-skinned, sad-eyed boy with a shy smile and centre-parted long brown hair.

'Nat Pitt,' he said softly, offering a slender, manicured (?!) hand. He didn't disclose where he was studying.

Laura suddenly spoke. 'Sorry, I didn't introduce myself. I'm Laura Ellis.'

At this point, another boy arrived who looked like Elvis in his days of excess: puffy, sweaty, overweight and short of breath. Trousers a size too small. Substantial tummy overhang. Poor thing, I shouldn't have been so critical, but he was very large for being so young. He sat down with a cursory wave of his right hand. 'Hi girls, I'm Frankie. Sunday name is Francis Cooke Junior.'

'Where are you from?' asked Laura.

'I'm from New England, Hyannis to be exact.'

'And where do you study?' I asked.

'I'm at the good ol' University of Monterrey, Guadalajara—in Mehico. Over in Jersey for the summer. Came last week. Second year in a row, in fact. Asked back.' His smile was smug. 'Need to know anythin'? Just ask!' He clicked his tongue, nodded his head forty-five degrees sideways, and winked. I reserved judgement on Frankie. The others all seemed very personable. I relaxed.

Introductions over, Laura and I took the vacant seats at the end of the row nearest the door. I looked along the line up trying to memorise their names. I always need mnemonics or tags to remember people. John? Hmm. Hunky, Paul Newman-ish. Coop? With his sideburns and craggier looks, more Clint Eastwood. Frankie? Elvis, hands down. Nat? Oscar Wilde came to mind. Odd since I'd only once seen a photo of him.

I noted they all wore short white jackets with lapel name badges and assumed we'd be issued with these too. In fact, I realised that must have been why we had been asked our dress sizes. At the time, I'd thought it odd, though Laura said at least they weren't after our vital statistics! The photos they'd also requested had caused my father to wonder if they'd wanted to ensure we weren't coloured, but the reason was simpler; they requested them to display on a noticeboard before our arrival as Jess had told us. Anyway, these jackets looked cooler and more stylish than our own white coats.

I found myself yawning. Since leaving home, I'd had precious little sleep. The first night in a London hotel had been dire, the second had been on a shoogly old plane and the third in our New York Times Square hotel was very noisy. And as for the last two nights in the Home? Jet lag had knocked me out only to be woken in a sweat from nightmares. On the Sunday I was on a plane crashing into a lake and last night I found myself looking down on own funeral with six strange mourners at the graveside, even my father wasn't present. When I pronounced the nightmares a sure-fire sign of insanity, Laura had found it hilarious and gave me a hug. Her laughter was curiously comforting.

The door opened to admit a silver-haired man in a sharply tailored grey suit. The chatter in the room subsided. He set down a holdall on the floor before taking a seat at the table beside a younger Latino man in blue scrubs who'd accompanied him.

'Good morning, ladies and gentlemen, I'm Dr Carlton Harper, Chief of Medical Staff in Ellis Memorial Hospital. Welcome to our award-winning Community Hospital in Fraser County, New Jersey. Now I am aware some of you have been having a look round for a few days already, but this week we start official. Hope y'all enjoyed your Fourth of July holiday but for the rest of this week you'll be rotated to different departments so you can get a flavour of how we work. Monday, we'll meet you each individually and if we can, we'll place you where you might best find the experience you need. I think that—'

He was interrupted by a loud squeak. As the door beside me opened abruptly, everyone turned. Framed in the doorway was a six-foot, white-coated figure with a craggy face, shoulder-length blond hair and generous moustache. He was waving a brown folder as he called out, 'Carl, a word!'

'I'm busy, Elias. Can it wait? My office in ten?' Dr Harper raised a hand, palm out.

'No. These kindergarten docs can spare you a minute. I need to give you something. Now!'

With obvious (and I thought justifiable) irritation, the Medical Chief walked briskly over to the intruder. Being the one nearest the half-closed the door at his back, I could still hear the exchange.

'Here. Take this and fix it. These two, on the payroll by next Monday.'

'You know, Elias, these things have to go through the Board and HR—'

'No excuses, Carlo my boy. I've vetted them. Get it done. Juan needs these two. You know the score. What I need is what I—'

'Okay, Okay!'

The door opened enough for me to see out of the corner of my eye that 'Carlo' was snatching the folder even he was starting to close the door firmly in Elias's face.

Everyone had politely turned their faces away from the encounter but the mood in the room had changed. Dr Harper looked unsettled. John was muttering about the rudeness of the intruder. Frankie sat grinning in a self-satisfied way, God knows why.

The Medical Chief started explaining about the papers we'd been given with guidelines on conduct, lists of staff names and numbers to phone should we have problems. He reminded us we were duty bound to turn up where directed or our contract would be terminated. After detailing a few housekeeping points, like how we'd be paid and where to collect 'chitties' to exchange for food in the dining room, he nodded. 'Right, that's it. OK. Good luck!'

I felt a bit cheated that our orientation had been cut short, having expected we'd have been given time for some questions. Dr Harper quickly came forward, shook everyone's hands, gave a weak smile and a curt nod then shot off, taking his holdall with him. The scrub-clad chap he'd left at the table stood up to announce that he was a Fifth Year ER Resident, now in his last year of specialist training, and that he was supervising us summer students. He came over to Laura and me first.

'Hi girls, I'm Randy.'

Laura gave a guffaw of laughter. I suppressed a giggle.

'Something wrong?' He looked puzzled.

'No, it's just that in the UK, if you're 'randy' it means you, well...you want sex. Sorry.' Laura bit her lip. Possibly to deter more laughing.

He blushed. 'You're kiddin' me? That's called being 'horny' in the States, by the way. OK, then if you want you can call me Randolph Ortez, though only my grandmother ever called me that!' Laughing at himself, he moved on to introduce himself to Coop.

'Hi, Mayfield? Good to meet you today. Know your father well. Hope you have a good summer here.'

He nodded at John and Nat, whom I assumed he'd already met in the Residency, but completely ignored Frankie, who turned away as he passed. What was that about? They should have know one another from last year.

As Randy approached the door, Laura boldly called after him, 'Sorry, Dr Ortez, can I ask you who that chap at the door was?'

'Ah, that's Dr Elias van Lindholm. He's a senior attending Renal Specialist.'

'Looks to me like he runs the place!' said John, who'd come to our side while the others were gathering up their papers from the floor.

Randy smiled without commenting and merely looked around before saying, 'Why don't you folks go to the Coffee Shop and get acquainted? Then, after lunch, you need to be at your first given attachment by two. Details in top set of papers. And girls, as you're in ER with me, I'll bring your jackets and name badges down there when I come. Carlton seems to have gotten distracted and taken them back to his office.'

After he left, John stood back to let me go through the door first.

I bowed. 'Thank you, kind sir.' His wide smile was disarming. 'Er, so where is this coffee shop, John?' As I said this, I wondered again at my sanity. I knew fine well where it was as we'd passed it on the way in. John was grinning. I'd never met a brain addling smile before.

'First Floor. I'll show you.' I felt his arm across my back chivvying me along, but I didn't mind. Glancing behind, I caught Laura's eye. She winked and nodded at John's back while pouting a kiss. Impossible woman. Seeing a door labelled 'Stairs', I put my hand on it to push. But John pulled me back.

'Hey, here's the elevator. Come on!' he ushered in Laura as Coop, Nat and Frankie took the stairs. The rest of us piled in the lift.

Inside John addressed us both. 'By the way, that Dr Elias van Lindholm is one of the oddballs about this place. The other's a Dr Juan Mendoza, who creeps around mostly at weekends.'

'Ah, I heard van Lindholm mention a 'Juan'. That must be him. Why is Dr Mendoza only in at the weekends?' I asked as the lift doors opened.

'No idea,' John shrugged as the doors opened.

We headed across the foyer towards the Coffee Shop. The boys walking in front. Behind, Laura nudged me. 'Looks a piece of work, that van Lindholm. Wonder what that interruption was all about? Did you hear what he said?'

'Yes. Wanted two people put on staff. Demanded actually. Harper seemed afraid of him. Yet he's the big boss, isn't he? Very curious...'

'Ah, a little bit of mystery to work on! Let's grill Frankie later. He was here last year and should know. You did good at the intros. Defo coming out of your shell. Way to go girl!'

I punched her on the arm.

Chapter Six

Dr Pacemaker, Ellie May & Makkonen

The hospital Coffee Shop was like a smart English tearoom. It had polished wooden tables and padded chairs: much more upmarket than the metal seats and Formica tables in our hospital eateries. Posies of fresh flowers graced each table. Watercolour paintings "Donated by Brunsfield Rotary Club" hung on the walls. We didn't have those either.

Laura and I sat down opposite John and Coop at one table, Frankie and Nat at an adjacent one. A waitress arrived. My request for a coffee produced a list of choices rattled off at speed, similar to the bewildering egg menu we'd been offered in New York. Recalling it, I resolved to ask John what an 'Easy Over' egg might be. For today's list of choices, however, he jumped to my rescue immediately.

'How about a flat white?'

'Fine,' I replied, hoping for a non-frothy coffee with milk. The waitress departed.

'Ok guys, tell us. Why did you come to Brunsfield? Any particular reason?' John asked.

'We stuck a pin in a hospital directory.' I smiled at him, having already decided he was completely charming and our pin had served us well.

'No way? You kiddin' me?' John looked across at us wide-eyed.

I related to him our scientific application process which had consisted of sitting down on a sofa in the Medical Faculty Office with a large directory of US hospitals, closing our eyes and stabbing at pages with a straightened-out paperclip provided by the secretary.

Laura chipped in. 'Since I've got relatives in Boston and New York, we decided to apply to East Coast hospitals. Seemed as good a criterion as any. We had other offers but the letter from Dr Carlton Harper was the friendliest and with the hospital having my surname...' She laughed. 'To be honest, we didn't think it mattered much where we went. All the hospitals looked pretty high standard and well-regulated. Anyway, we accepted Ellis Memorial, the hospital applied for our work permits, we booked flights, got visas—and so, here we are. Mind you the US Consulate in Edinburgh were difficult to get past for the visa. Some tricky questions.'

'Oh, like what?' asked Coop.

'We had to declare we weren't insane or suffering from venereal disease!'

Coop hooted. 'As if anyone would admit either!'

The boys looked even more amused when Laura added, 'And anyway, we had to come to Ellis Memorial. It was fate. Carlton's letter came on the seventeenth of January and 17.1.71 is a dead auspicious date! I mean, a palindrome with sevens? It's the number indicating 'path to spiritual growth.'

John looked bemused. Coop entranced.

I burst the bubble by rolling my eyes. 'Sorry boys. That's nuts, obviously. Still, no harm in a bit of spiritual growth if it's on offer, is there?'

The boys laughed. Laura folded her arms indignantly as the waitress arrived with laden tray.

'Anyway, this hospital is an excellent choice,' wheezed Frankie, leaning over to snatch his Coke from the waitress. Declining her proffered glass he slugged from the bottle.

Sipping my 'flat white', I found it incredibly strong and bitter and reached for two packets of sugar.

Laura genteelly decanted her Coke into a glass. 'So, anyway, what's with that Doctor van Lindholm? He was pretty rude to Dr Harper, I thought.'

Frankie shook his head rapidly. 'It's just his way. Maybe sometimes he acts the bad ass, but he's a guy that gets things done and no mistake. Real clever. Done great research in renal disease. Should be moving on to the Mayo Clinic or somewhere like that soon. I respect him.'

John raised an eyebrow. 'You do? That's only the second time I've seen him but I think he's a bit of a pig, Frankie. You shouldn't talk to colleagues like he did to Harper, especially with students around.'

'It's a dog-eat-dog world, Johnnie boy!' Frank reached over to slap John on the back then drained the rest of his Coke, banged the bottle onto the table in front of him and burped before standing. 'See you guys. Places to go, people to see! Ciao!'

He left with a desultory wave of a hip-level hand and was just out the door when John slapped the table. 'There. He's done it again, Coop!'

'Done what? Burped loudly?' Laura's attempt at being funny was lost on John, who was genuinely annoyed.

'Gone without paying a cent. That's several times now he's left us to pick up his tab. What a user!' John hissed through clenched teeth.

'I'll sort that! Let me get the server.' Coop called the girl over. 'Can we have the check please? I'm afraid he...' At this he pointed to Frank's recently vacated chair. '...had to leave in a hurry and said to put his on a tab. Can you do that?' He gave her a big smile.

She returned in minutes with a bill for us and a notepad on which Coop wrote Frankie's name in full, his Residency room number and a florid curly 'FCJ' signature.

'That's you sorted, Francis Cooke Junior!' Coop settled the rest of the bill—or 'check' as he called it. 'This is on me today!'

John turned to grip Coop's upper arm. 'Thanks, buddy. And that was good thinking on the tab, Batman!'

Coop sighed and smiled wanly, staring into the distance. 'Christ, Batman! How I loved him. You guys seen the Batman series on TV across the Pond, girls?'

I assumed he meant 'in the UK' but since my TV knowledge was limited by my Gran's largely weekend-only family viewing restrictions, I had to admit I wasn't sure. I was too embarrassed to tell Coop she regarded television (and most other enjoyable pursuits like music and dancing) as potentially blasphemous but I did say, 'We have the comics. My young brother Archie loves Batman ones.'

'Yeah! Way to go! But there's another great series comin' out I'm itchin' for. You guys seen that movie M*A*S*H?' John nodded. Nat shook his head. 'Heard we'll soon be seeing a spin off TV series. Should be a gas.' Coop talked like an eager little boy. Throughout Laura sat hand on chin, gazing directly at him, transfixed.

'What's M*A*S*H about?' I asked.

'Stands for Mobile Army Surgical Hospital. The film's from a book by a guy called Hooker. It's about Army medics in the Korean War,' said Coop.

'Sounds gory.' I shivered.

'The film was a bit bloody at times but it's mostly a kind of crazy black comedy. Lots of laughs. Mind you, the current war in Vietnam's more like a bad joke.' John looked angry again. 'We should never have gotten involved.'

Laura looked pensive. 'Afraid we don't know much about it. We only see news bulletins of helicopters and pics of bombed villages, injured kids and other horrors. But I know one of my New York cousins was delighted his asthma made him medically unfit for the forces. My understanding is that it's a fight against communism. But it's a heck of a long way away to be waging a war, isn't it?'

John exhaled forcefully. 'Sure is. Crazy. If we weren't med students, we'd probably all be drafted by now. By the way, don't ever get Frankie onto the subject of the War whatever you do! He'll bore you to death with its justification for 'nuking' commies. Bet it'd have been a different story if his Senator dad hadn't managed to get him into Mexican med school so he could claim deferment from the draft. He'd applied unsuccessfully for dozens of US courses. But on the other hand, we've got some crazies here who want to fight. Two of my idiot schoolfriends chose to volunteer before they were called up and went into the army instead of going to college. One's dead already and one's lost a leg. Hellish.' John rubbed his nose with his palm. 'Anyway, guys, you want proper lunch?' He looked at us and nodded up to the ceiling. They just do snacks here in the Coffee Shop.' He looked at his watch. 'Plenty of time.'

'I'm starving!' Laura always was.

Coop stood up and held out his hand to her. 'Then let me show you to the hospital staff dining room, Laura. It's up on Second. Best get something into you if it's ER you're bound for! It's may not be as crazy as a M*A*S*H Unit but it can be hectic and bloody. In fact, I saw a couple of gunshot wounds last week. One of the guys had almost half his head blown off. Didn't make it, though they took him to surgery anyway. Expect they thought it worth a go for the insurance.'

Coop's last remark made me feel squeamish. Why prolong a family's agony and give false hope by attempting impossible surgery? For money? Anxiety in me never far away, tension tightened round my chest. I wasn't sure I could face blood and gore in the ER on a full stomach. But I trotted after the others. Maybe the dining room did small salads.

Heading into the lift, I realised Nat was still with us though he hadn't said a thing all morning. He was a bit creepy, especially in his black shirt and grey tie. I'd never seen anyone wear such a combination. I smiled over at him but he immediately looked to the floor and shot out of the lift first when it stopped. What was the story there?

We had pizza and salad before dividing up into our assigned postings.

~~~

The Emergency Room (ER), our Casualty equivalent, was down on the First Floor to the rear of the hospital where ambulances could easily draw into a designated entrance. Laura and I presented ourselves at its reception desk fifteen minutes before our due time.

The place was quietly bustling. The waiting room held ten patients who looked to be waiting for attention. Two more were tackling a drink and sweet dispenser which apparently needed kicking to work. At the far side, an elderly Black gentleman was shouting into a public wall phone and near us, a crying child was hitting its disinterested mother with a toy car as she sat attempting to read a magazine. There were far fewer customers than our Casualty back home, though I still experienced that fluttering of anxiety I always got when shadowing staff in Accident and Emergency Departments. You never knew what drama might unfold in the blink of an eye. But in my wildest dreams I never expected to witness a murder. That would cause more than a flutter...Another day.

As if on cue, a blue flashing light came to a stop at the wide entrance beside us. Within seconds, the automatic doors flew open and an unconscious patient on a trolley was rushed past propelled by two attendants, one pumping an Ambu ventilation bag that was placed over a woman's face in an attempt to pump air into her lungs, the other holding aloft a drip bottle connected to a cannula inserted into her arm. As they ran along, they were joined by two white-unformed, white-stockinged ER nurses to whom they shouted out details of the patient's condition. When the trolley passed within inches of us, we noted the spreading dark ruby stain on the green sheet over the blonde casualty's chest. I suspected she'd been shot or stabbed. Unlikely to be a road accident. Traumatic for staff to deal with. I'd never seen a gunshot wound in Glasgow, but I had seen several stabbings, some of whom hadn't survived.

Overhead, a public address system was endlessly repeating 'Doctor Pacemaker to Trauma Two.' A male figure in blue scrubs appeared from a side room to scurry after the casualty. Then out of the elevator burst Dr Randy Ortez from our Seminar briefing. Nodding at us, he tossed his bag down on the reception desk and ran towards the room that had received the casualty; I presumed Trauma Room Two. A woman in 'civilian' navy skirt, white blouse and huge pearl earrings, clutching a pen and clipboard, emerged from the offices behind the reception and followed Randy in.

We turned our attention to the young blonde sitting demurely behind the reception desk. She wore an old-fashioned-looking pink-striped dress with a white Peter Pan collar much reminiscent of the summer dresses from my early fifties childhood. I'd already noted the uniform of nurses (white dresses, white tights, laced white shoes), of doctors (cotton twill pyjama-like scrub suits in blue or green for interns, white coats over shirts and ties for specialists) and the office staff like the clipboard lady (navy skirts and white blouses). But I couldn't work out who this quaintly attired girl could be. First I had to ask, 'Who's Doctor Pacemaker?'

'There isn't a Doctor Pacemaker. It's the call they use for help at a cardiac arrest. S'pose it'd upset people if they shouted out, 'Cardiac arrest! All on-call docs to Trauma Two!' That's the main resus room, by the way, Trauma Two. The ambulance called in that woman ten minutes ago. Domestic violence victim. We've been expecting her. Be police officers here soon, I expect.'

Laura was squinting at the girl's badge, angled downwards and of small print.

Looking from her to me, the girl asked politely, 'Can I help you ladies? I'm Ellie May, one of the Candy-stripers.'

'Candy-stripers?' My mind boggled. Why would Casualty need someone to stripe candy? I saw no sweetie counter and doubted they had seaside rock or Everton mints on sale.

The girl was heavily made up. Her lips were a pale candy pink, her eyebrows symmetrically plucked and pencilled and her lashes thick and dark a la Dusty Springfield. When she suddenly made wide eyes at me, I blushed, embarrassed that I'd been caught staring. But her surprised expression was caused by her suddenly twigging who we were.

'Oh, hey, you're the Scotch students, aren't you? Wicked! Right, course you won't know what Candy-stripers are! We're hospital volunteers. Corny name but we get it from these dresses. Candy-stripers were founded in a high-school Civics Class project in East Orange, New Jersey, way back in the Forties. The first uniforms were made from this kinda stuff.' She pinched a fold of her puff sleeve. 'Still usin' it, so, we're forever Candy-stripers! I'm volunteering during college vacation. This week I'm filing and generally being useful in ER but I rotate to the Floors and Coffee Shop as needed.'

'Oh, that's a great thing to do. Do you know where we're supposed to be, Ellie?' I asked. 'The info just said, 'Report to ER.'

'Why don't ya sit beside me till the drama's over in Two? Or s'pose you could look at some of the patient files over there?' She pointed at a long trolley with vertically hung metal clipboards. We had just taken one out when a nurse appeared.

'Hello. I presume you are the new externs.' She looked us up and down critically. 'Where are your name badges?' No warmth radiated from this very slim pale woman who looked like a ghost in her stiff white hat, white dress and clumpy white clogs. As she tutted, I wondered what her position was? Or her name. I noticed *she* wasn't wearing a name badge!

'Possibly in that?' I pointed at the bag Randy had tossed down on the countertop. It looked like the one Harper had taken away earlier on his rapid departure from the Orientation in the Seminar Room. Opening it gingerly, I found four white jackets and two name badges. As Laura tried her jacket on, I wondered why they'd bothered asking us our dress sizes. It swamped her. Our coolly critical nurse moved off, seemingly disinterested.

'This doesn't look like a size ten! It's massive!' Laura turned up the sleeves and wrapped the edges of the jacket across her chest. They reached to her opposite armpit on each side.

Ellie looked perturbed. 'Oh, my! I reckon our US sizes are different to yours. Maybe they can find you smaller ones later?'

We put them on anyway, pinned our name badges to the lapels, and rolled up our coats behind the desk with the holdall just as there was an exodus of staff from Trauma Two. The faces of the nurses told us there was no longer any need for a Dr Pacemaker. Randy came out last and walked to the desk.

'Well, you can't win them all. If only someone would repeal the Second Amendment our life would be a lot easier.'

'The Second Amendment?' asked Laura.

'The Right to Bear Arms. Belongs in the Wild West. Mind you, Puerto Rico, where I came from, is as bad. Okay, girls, let's go to the doctor's room and decide what we're doing with you.'

In the tiny room he regarded us thoughtfully. 'Many women do medicine in Scotland?'

''Around twenty-five per cent of our class of two hundred. Why? Don't girls do it over here?'

'Very few. None in Ellis Memorial past or present, as far as I know.'

'Really?' I remembered the boy at home last autumn, Simon Winters, who'd put me up to this US summer challenge at a tutorial group night out. He'd said I wouldn't believe how much there was to learn about the United States. I was beginning to understand what he meant. A myriad of differences in language, history and culture were already obvious, not to mention wonky different dress sizes and there being no women in medicine! He'd also advised that I 'get laid' for my next stage of professional development, but I didn't mention this to Randy. I only complained, 'I don't see why there shouldn't be more women in medicine.'

'Me neither. Right, what stage are you at? Have you seen many patients?' Randy asked.

'Of course, we've just finished Third Year!' Laura sounded indignant.

'Cool. It's just some guys come here with no patient experience, especially from Mexican med schools. You able to take a history?' He looked at us quizzically.

'Of course!' It was my turn to be a bit iffy.

'Right. Let's split you.' He looked at my name badge. Perhaps wary of my odd first name he addressed me by my surname.

'So, MacLean, with me. And I'll get our Second Year Resident, Hiro, to come take Laura. This afternoon you can shadow us in the consults. Tomorrow you can clerk in patients if we find you're up to it. It's busy. Don't forget to take drinks and eat when you can. The Coffee Shop will let you bring out cookies and sandwiches—but no eating anything in clinical areas where patients can see, okay?'

He left to return with a Japanese doctor whose name badge pronounced him to be Dr Hirohito Wantanabe. Smiling broadly, his eyes twinkled behind his thin-rimmed gold glasses as he gave us a brisk short bow and said, 'Please call me Hiro' (pronouncing it as "Hero") Laura went off with him and I followed Randy. Our clinical experience Stateside was about to begin. It was quite a culture shock.

Chapter Seven
Sparrows & Hummingbirds

The first patient I saw with Randy was a twelve-year-old boy, Tyler Consett, whom we found sitting hunched, head in hands and eyes closed as his worried mother clucked beside him. Randy addressed her.

'Good morning, Mrs Consett, Miss MacLean here will take Tyler's history, and I'll be back to assess him momentarily.'

'Thanks, doctor. We're so worried. He's had Tylenol but the headache's worse.'

I sat asking questions as taught. Where was the site of pain? What did it feel like? How long had he had it? Did anything make it worse or better? Past history? He had asthma and allergies. Medication history was trickier. I had to ask the attendant nurse the chemical names of Tyler's brand name medicines, or 'meds' as his mum called them. His Ventolin inhaler I recognised. Tylenol I didn't. It was paracetamol. The nurse in attendance was the abrupt one who'd challenged us at reception. She now wore a badge. Nurse Freja Makkonen was monosyllabic with me but kind with Tyler, helping him undress to his undershorts and mount the couch. She swiftly covered him in a sheet and took his temperature, pulse and blood pressure.

When Randy reappeared, I recited Tyler's story. 'This twelve-year-old boy woke with a severe one-sided headache and visual upset. One previous less severe episode. Photosensitive, feels sick, tummy pain, vomited. Last night had two cheese pizzas and a lot of Coca Cola at a birthday party. Bed late. History of atopy but allergies and asthma well controlled. Sees a paediatrician regularly. His father has migraines.'

To my surprise, Randy didn't examine Tyler or even look at the back of his eyes in case he had raised intracranial pressure but waved at him to get up and dressed. He addressed his mother. 'Right, no point in hanging about, Mrs Consett.' He turned to Nurse Makkonen. 'Let's get a brain scan stat. Abdo too. Full blood screen.' Patting the mother on the shoulder he added, 'See you later with the results.'

'So, what do you think's wrong, doctor? You don't think it's a brain tumour. do you?'

'Let's not jump the gun but make that judgement when we have the results.' He backed out, indicating I should follow.

'Good history, MacLean. Write it up in the charts following the format there and I'll sign it.'

'But why does he need a scan? It's obviously a migraine. He needs Caffergot.'

Randy stopped in his tracks and turned. 'First thing to learn in medicine, MacLean. Diagnoses can be hummingbirds or sparrows. Missing a hummingbird will get your ass sued off. Exclude them first, then accept it's a sparrow.'

'Back home we don't refer for scans unless clinical signs suggest a tumour or stroke. They're expensive. And I should think we have less scanners than you have.'

'We have two. The Consetts have high end insurance. Anyway, scans help revenues.' He shrugged. 'Means we can afford more scanners, everyone wins.'

I followed him into the next case thinking that the poor distraught mother he'd left worrying needlessly that her son might have a brain tumour hadn't won anything. And the boy had overheard everything.

Our next patient was a dishevelled old man who was struggling with a slight nurse trying to take his BP. She stopped to speak. 'This is Patrick Donovan. He's deaf and confused.'

Randy approached him, speaking loudly. 'What's the problem, Patrick?'

'Nuthin'!' he declared, before addressing someone non-existent in the corner.

The man was in serious need of a haircut. And a bath.

'Who brought him in, Thelma?'

'Police,' answered the nurse.

'No! These guys new on the block?'

She handed him a chart and smiled. 'Yep, fresh outta cop school.'

Making a face, he handed back the papers. 'Waste of our time.'

This man made me think of another Patrick (Paddy) I'd seen back in Glasgow one night, although this Paddy was still on his feet and less ill.

Randy sighed. 'Suppose we'll have to ask for a Psych consult and phone Social. But he's a drunk. It's his lifestyle. His choice.' Randy looked resigned. 'Next?'

'See Shelley in Room Five.' The girl picked up the desk phone.

I had to break off for the loo where I stayed longer than necessary, reflecting on the story of my Glasgow Paddy.

~~~

The previous year, I'd spent Saturday nights in Casualty at my local hospital as advised by my tutor for acquiring extra clinical skills. One evening, my mentor, Sister Mary MacKinnon, had me dressed in protective apron, gloves, hat and mask in an isolation room. A drowsy muttering patient lay on a bare rubber mattress atop a steel trolley. The air was foetid.

'This is Patrick McConaghy. Not been in for a while. Comments, Mhairi?'

'ER, man in his fifties? Ragged clothes, holey boot soles. Un-washed. Smelly. A tramp?' Moving nearer, I added, 'Has nits and lice.'

'What else?'

'Yellow, jaundiced, swollen abdomen, twitchy. Liver failure?'

'Full marks!'

We'd rolled him about to remove his tatty clothing. Mary washed him tenderly with disinfectant and sealed his clothes in a biohazards bag. She'd exposed bruises and scabies sores plus a fulminating stinking leg ulcer she covered with a loose dressing. 'Remember that smell, Mhairi. Anaerobic bacteria of gangrene. Poor Paddy.'

He also stank of a cheap, bulk-bought hair lacquer, Belair, that alcoholics used as a last resort. I recalled her kindly look at the sorry soul on the trolley, Highland lilt recurring while re-counting his story: an accountant convicted of fraud, divorced, lost everything and ended up on the road. 'The Polis keep bringing him in but he's never kept up with any social support. Remember Mhairi, patients are all God's children. Aye, like in Matthew, 7:12. "*Do unto others*..."' She'd patted Paddy. 'No matter who they are, we mustn't judge. And every day we should give thanks for Nye Bevan, the great Minister of Health after the War. His NHS is a perfect example of Christian compassion, treat everyone free and equally. You've no idea what it was like before.'

The on-call registrar had come along to diagnose Hepatic Encephalopathy and had let me take my first blood sample, insert a drip and inject antibiotics. I'm not sure whether Patrick McCo-naghy made it in the end. But they'd tried.

Washing my hands in the Ellis Memorial toilet, I surmised our Brunsfield Paddy wasn't yet as bad as my Glasgow Paddy had been, but Randy had already judged him unworthy of saving. And I felt desperately sad.

Back with Randy, the afternoon flew by with a dog bite, a heart attack despatched to Coronary Care, a fractured femur sent to Orthopaedics for surgery, a whiplash suffering driver needing neck X-rays (and copies for his car insurers), a cook with a severed thumb needing Plastic and Vascular surgeons plus a few 'worried well' who didn't need sent on to anyone as they had nothing wrong with them. Most got physical examinations, a battery of tests (especially if insured) and many were allowed to call in a specialist of their choice. Since we had in-house ones, I couldn't see the point of phoning in other doctors and clogging up a room for hours. But if someone wanted their own physician, they had that right.

By six I was wilting. Randy suggested Laura and I had done enough for the day and despatched us for tea. He was on duty till nine and had been since seven a.m. yet showed no sign of tiring. He hadn't even had a holiday in two years! You obviously had to be tough to 'get on' in US medicine. Not sure I could have hacked it.

Laura and I decided we were too tired to head up to the dining room so had bagels and coffee and an ice cream in the Coffee Shop. We saw Frank and van Lindholm cosily tête-à-tête in a corner. But didn't speak to them. Our Lox (aka smoked salmon) and cream cheese bagels weren't bad, but I thought it would be easier to have some proper food of our own down in the Nurses' Home. 'Think we should accept that nice nurse Jess's offer to take us to a supermarket soon.'

'Good idea,' said Laura. 'By the way, how was your day?' We'd barely seen one another.

'Very different from home.'

Without me expanding, she hit the nail on the head. 'Yep. Funny how much clinical practice changes when money comes into it.'

'Doesn't it? Randy said a funny thing this morning. He thinks medicine is all about Hummingbirds and Sparrows. Look for the rare Hummers first in case you get sued. And when I asked him what happens to the folk who don't have money for insurance and get sick, he just shrugged and said, "Well, you'll probably will get immediate care but then when the bills run up, you get into debt and have to deal with it.'"

Laura frowned. 'Bit harsh, isn't it? Like this morning, I saw an old man with pneumonia needing ventilated but the family decided against it after Hiro spelled out ongoing costs. We'd have been given him a go in the NHS. Can't get his face out of my mind. He was so like my grandpa. With no intercurrent illness he'd have had a good chance of recovering.'

As we walked back to the Nurses' Home I told her about my two tramp Patricks and got even more depressed. Inside, as we passed the kitchen, a cheerful Jess shot out.

'Hi girls! You wanna come to the movies? We're going to the drive-in at Maryville. Teddy says you don't have them in England, so we thought you'd like it.'

'Gosh, Jess, that's very sweet but it's been a long day and I'm knackered. Sorry.'

She hadn't mentioned Teddy, but I assumed he was a boyfriend.

'Me too,' added Laura.

'That's Okay. You're here a few months more. We can take a rain check.'

'A rain check?' I had to ask.

'Yeh, you know, when you've paid for a baseball ticket and the game's rained off? You get a rain check to come back free next time!'

'Okay, it's a rain check then.' I grinned. Logical. Like Floor One, Two, Three.

'Hey, did you see Teddy's new Ford Mustang outside? It's a great ride. Kinda like him!' With this last throwaway line and a wink, she wiggled off seductively to her room, doubtless to change into something sexy for her hot date.

Watching Jess go, I shook my head. 'They're very open about sex over here, aren't they? I mean, some of Frankie's comments at lunch today about his conquests were near the knuckle. It was like he forgot we were there.'

Laura pursed her lips. 'Och, Mhairi, they aren't used to having any female medics around. And anyway, I think sex is on guys' minds all the time everywhere. But maybe American females are less inhibited than Scots girls when it comes to the subject. I saw a patient today who spontaneously started asking about the best sex positions she could adopt to avoid problems with her prolapse! Never seen a patient bring up that kind of thing at home. But I don't know, is it such a bad thing to be less buttoned up about it?'

We made a cup of tea and spent the evening lounging on the sitting room, eating stringy cheese and chomping on Lays crisps while watching mindless TV programmes peppered by hilarious ads exhorting that we, "Please, please don't squeeze the Charmin". Apparently, it was a brand of irresistibly squeezable toilet roll. Some things Stateside defied explanation.

Channel searching, we found an old Ealing Studios comedy that was wincingly not funny at all but then a Bugs Bunny cartoon that was. Then came a late night News programme showing horrendous plane crash pictures that was suddenly interrupted by "A message from our sponsors" which entailed two well-scrubbed young boys chanting, "This programme is brought to you by Juicee Juice!" followed by a facile ditty extolling its health-giving qualities at breakfast. Apart from it being late evening, I thought this bizarre, especially when the screen seamlessly returned to macabre news footage of scattered possessions and bodies at the crash scene. Worse, somehow, was the newscaster. No sober-suited, collar-and-tie BBC news reader on the box here in Brunsfield, but a girl in a short red dress with a dishmop perm delivering all news items, whether serious or light, in a similar chatty style.

"Police say gun crime in the city this quarter is up by 25 percent," was offered as cheerily as the New York Yankees latest baseball results. Suddenly mid flow she piped up, "We'll be right back!" and gave way to a cartoon ad for car hire discount. I found this assault on the senses incompatible with my persisting jet lag sensitivity and switched off.

'God, the news is presented weirdly, even callously.'

'Mhairi darling, everything's sponsored in America. Ads dominate TV. This may be the Home of the Brave and Land of the Free but it's also home of Big Business.'

I remained indignant. 'But surely it's bad taste to interrupt a human tragedy story with banality? And have newsreaders read out their stuff like everything's a joke?'

Laura leaned forward, unpinning her hair from the plait at the back of her head and shaking it free. 'Think you'll need to take them as you find them, Mhairi. Why not stop analysing everything and turn in for an early night? It's been a long day.'

~~~

Wednesday I sat with Jess toying with a breakfast cereal I'd randomly picked up in the A&P which consisted of unchewable grains and dried fruit lumps. The milk too was weird, tasting vaguely like Carnation, only sickly. Jess laughed.

'UHT is great. It last for ages, doesn't go off!'

She laughed again when I said I didn't care if it was immortal, and offered me some salami for a sandwich instead. I took the meat gratefully. I'd enjoyed it for the first time in a New York deli. Laura arrived to make a face.

'Salami for breakfast? Yuk! It's like pink plastic.'

'Och no, it's nice. It's salty and kind of picklish. We never had it at home.' I munched on with occasional orange juice slurps. It was the only thing we'd bought that was OK.

Laura poured out some of the cereal and milk and stoically tucked into a plateful. 'You mean you don't have any cold meats or just not foreign ones? Or is it a pork thing?'

'No idea! Probably 'cos it's not mentioned in the Bible.'

'But neither are mince and marmalade. And I bet fish and chips aren't in Paul's Epistle to the Ephesians, either.' Laura chuckled, waving her spoon and rolling her eyes heavenward as if seeking guidance.

Jess rose to go and finish getting ready for work, promising to take us to a supermarket at six after she finished.

Washing my dirty plate and juice glass, I quickly dried them with the correct Mrs Heinz green towel and my hands with the red one. 'God, look at the time! It's ten to eight. Randy's hot on punctuality.'

'Pity about his name, but he is nice.' Laura drank the last of the milk out of her bowl. I thought of my gran seeing that...Funny how I couldn't get home out of my mind.

'Yes. I'm glad we're still with Randy today. And it's Surgery tomorrow and Cardiology on Friday, that right?'

'Yep. We've got Coop's Dad in fact, on Friday. Wonder what he's like.' Laura linked arms as we left. 'Coop's a bit of all right, too, isn't he?'

I couldn't disagree.

Chapter Eight

Angelina, van Lindholm & Biohazards

In ER, we found Wednesday morning less hectic than Tuesday afternoon but still saw a steady stream of patients; an elderly lady who'd broken her collar bone falling over a cat: an irate lawyer with a retention of urine. Randy suspected he had prostate cancer. He relieved his pain by catheterising him and called for a 'Uro consult.' I was picking up the lingo. At noon came another urological problem.

Paramedics wheeled a distressed woman into Room Four where Randy and I found her violently throwing up. The stiletto clipboard finance woman had clopped into the room ahead of us to confirm the patient's insurance status, vital information required before treatment unless the patient was unconscious. The girl's anxious young husband was holding back her long black hair as she filled a sick bowl. Randy nodded at the clipboard woman as she left before speaking directly to the husband.

'Hi. Back again, I see, Mr Martinez. First things first. Let's get an i.v. . Then I'll call your wife's specialist. Meanwhile, to save time, Miss MacLean, my clerk, will take a history of what's been happening today.

A nurse was assembling a trolley with the sterile needles and tube needed for the drip as Randy nodded at me and then the door saying, 'A minute, MacLean?' Touching my arm, he led the way out into the corridor where he was succinct.

'OK, this is Angelina Martinez, age 26. A frequent attender upstairs for dialysis. Has congenital Polycystic Kidney Disease and deteriorating renal function. Her specialist is Dr van Lindholm.'

He raised an eyebrow, looked up and down the corridor and whispered, 'A warning, he can be trouble—though I never told you that. Just be brief, ignore his rudeness and largely stay out of his way if you can while doing whatever he asks. But take my advice and don't let yourself end up in a room alone with him—you get me?' Both his eyebrows disappeared up into his fringe.

I was dismayed, intrigued and completely clueless all at once; what exactly was Randy on about? Who would try on anything in a busy casualty department? Was van Lindholm a sex maniac? Randy shot back to reception and I stopped staring into space with my mouth open and returned to Angelina.

The poor girl had stopped being sick but was lying back exhausted on the couch. Her closed eyes were circled by dark puffy rings, her face was a pasty lemon colour and her hands and feet looked markedly swollen. Mr Martinez was now holding Angelina's hand and the bustling Nurse Makkonen was in attendance. Ignoring me, she gave the husband a new sick bowl and looped up a bottle of saline on the stand as a phlebotomist girl came in.

I approached Angelina's husband. 'Good morning Mr...'

I'd barely hesitated before he replied, 'It's Martinez, Rico.' His eyes were dark and soulful. He was probably a little older than his wife, impeccably dressed, gold watch on his left wrist, thick gold chain bracelet on his right. Serious disease is no respecter of wealth.

'So, can you tell me what's been happening with your wife today?'

The story was she'd been vomiting on and off overnight before collapsing this morning and becoming rambling and confused. He'd called 911, which I knew from US TV shows was the US Emergency number. Being well versed in what was needed on hospital visits, Mr Martinez handed me a typed sheet of Angelina's history, admission dates and meds. It was long. Rico told me sadly Angelina and her sister had inherited polycystic kidneys from their father, now dead. The young man looked worn out and grief-stricken. Rubbing his eyes, he looked at Angelina with a look of devotion that made my throat close over before turning back to me, sighing. 'The dialysis doesn't seem to be helping now. I'd do anything for her, but it seems sadly, I can't give her a kidney. My blood is the wrong type—and since her sister died, she has no family.'

Asking sulky Nurse Makkonen to give me Angelina's stats brought forth staccato bullets of information too rapid to write down. As I reached instead for the nursing chart I'd seen her fill in, brisk footsteps approached and the door opened at my side. Quick as a flash, Makkonen rushed to the head of the exam couch where she assumed a stiff stylised pose, hands clasped in front at waist level, chin up, facing the door and looking like a kind of histrionic heroine in a movie clip. Ye Gods, the woman was off her trolley!

In strode Dr Elias van Lindholm. Ignoring Makkonen and me, he went straight to Rico and shook his hand. At the head of the bed, my blonde nursing companion remained posing like a lovesick schoolgirl. Yet, he looked oblivious. She then bustled over and attempted to stand between the doctor and me. But he still ignored her, merely barking over her shoulder to me, 'So, child, what's the story?'

Ignoring Makkonen's looming presence, I recited the history I'd gleaned, but a few seconds into my spiel, his left hand rose, with outward palm held inches from my face. Realising my part was considered over, I stopped. He turned to address Rico dramatically, arms waving and tone grave.

'This is serious, Mr Martinez. I think we have another critical infection on our hands.' I was glad Angelina looked as though she was sleeping when he continued, 'It's not looking good. The pyrexia, the vomiting...' He shook his head. 'Probably urinary infection which will only exacerbate the renal failure. We'll have to hit it and hit hard before next dialysis.' He barked side on at Nurse Makkonen, his head barely inclined, making no eye contact. 'Bloods done nurse? Catheter specimen of urine off?'

'Yes, doctor,' Nurse Makkonen replied breathily. I stood flummoxed. She was like one of those silly *Carry on Doctor* film nurses, coquettishly showing him a urine sample in a plastic poke and handing him a request form to sign.

'Catheter left in?'

Looking angst-ridden, Makkonen shook her head. 'Sorry, Doctor, no. But I'll replace it if you want. A fluid balance chart is ready.'

At this, Angelina seemed to rouse and tried to push herself up on the bed only to wearily sink back. Dr van Lindholm smiled grimly at her. 'Take it easy Mrs Martinez.' Turning his back on his patient, he at least did lower his voice as he said to Rico. 'I don't mind telling you, Mr Martinez, we're Big League now. Transplant's the only hope. You'll need to speak to your provider stat. If they won't cover it all, we have Hospital Plans that can help. Hey, Makkonen, keep that i.v. slow till we get the bloods. Nil by mouth till half an hour after promethazine i.m. for the puking then let's get her upstairs.'

He snatched Angelina's chart from me, scribbled a few lines, added the meds to a prescription form and signed both floridly. 'Fine, that's it for now.' He shook hands with Rico and fired orders at me. 'Bed upstairs immediately. Demand workup results back stat, no, yesterday and get them faxed up to the Unit, comprende?'

He exited, waving me out with him. In the corridor he paused. 'You're one of the Scotch med students, aren't you?' I nodded, restraining myself from saying only whisky is "Scotch", people are Scottish. 'You seem to speak decent English, girl. Got any Spanish?'

I stared, mouth open. What the hell did he think Scotland was—a backward land of Gaelic-speaking peasants? Doubting my O-level Spanish would pass muster, I shook my head. In any case, he was speaking without pause, nodding frequently like one of the little dogs folk place in car rear windows. 'No matter. Must say I'm surprised Harper's taken you girlies. No future for you in Medicine. It's not a job for a woman. What'll you do when you have kids?' Laughing peculiarly unpleasantly, he left muttering under his breath.

His long dirty blonde hair was unbrushed, his white coat flapped open and his unused stethoscope was draped carelessly round the back of his neck. I wondered if he ever used it. He hadn't even laid a hand on the patient.

Blushing from his tirade, I headed to the desk where Randy was writing up a case sheet. Sliding it vertically home into the trolley he asked, 'So, what did the great VL decide?'

'I've to send her up to the 'Unit'—I presume he means Renal or Dialysis? And he told me I shouldn't bother doing Medicine as it wasn't a job for a girl.'

'It probably isn't, you know, MacLean. But if you want to do it that's your business, not his. Marion will get you the number for upstairs.' He tapped the upper arm of the receptionist beside us. 'Renal and Dialysis are the same ward anyway. Give them the story—which I bet he never listened to, did he?' I shook my head. He nodded, looking not a whit surprised. 'Then write it up in the notes for posterity, take a break for ten and then come get me.' He patted my shoulder. 'Well done. Few come out of a first encounter with Dr Elias van Lindholm unscathed. You got off lightly!' He gave me a thumbs up and dashed away.

Marion, today's receptionist, dialled Renal and handed me the phone to offload Angelina's story before I called to arrange for a porter to take her to the ward. I was beginning to feel like a real doctor, although admittedly I'd no idea what was actually involved in dialysing patients. Perhaps I should take a look in up there. Thinking about the desperately sick and passionately loved young Angelina, my thoughts went back to another patient I'd seen at home whom I'd feared was being used as a corpse to be plundered for its organs. But here was the other side of the equation: without a new kidney, Angelina's only option was death. I wrote up the notes then took myself off for a break.

Stirring sugar into my coffee, I recalled the boy who'd become a donor. Last term had been my first brush with Intensive Care, an unsettling place where patients hovered between life and death. It's young Registrar, Dr Jonathon Baker, had given me important advice, warning to take care what you say around unconscious patients; hearing is the last sense to go. And always be as positive as you can for hope is a powerful medicine.

The patient had been Sandy Lauder, a handsome lad. Blond head partially swathed in gauze, he lay immobile, tracheostomy tube in-situ, ventilator wheezing at his side. He was a twenty-five-year-old PhD student and junior golf champion, felled by a speeding West End van. In the duty room, Jon Baker had made us coffee (Nescafe) without milk (off) or sugar (finished) before asking me to sit in while he spoke to Sandy's parents. 'This interview will be as bad as you'll get. I've to tell them Neuro was in and pronounced Sandy brain dead. No hope. But we'd like his kidneys. Here's his notes. Read them while I go get the forms.'

Half an hour later in the Western Infirmary Intensive Care Doctors' Room, Sandy's businessman father resignedly accepted there was no one else to 'buy in' for a second opinion. Sister brought tea. Mr Lauder signed forms. Mrs Lauder folded a handkerchief into tiny squares and said, 'At least someone will benefit from his death,' and wept.

The driver had been caught. Little consolation. Sandy's parents went to sit at the bedside while Jon tee'd up the theatre to chop up the lad. I'd considered it gruesome and desperately sad. But seeing Angelina, there was another side to the transplant story. And knew if she was my brother, Archie, I'd do anything to save him.

Angelina's transfer arranged, I headed for the loo before resuming my work. The ladies was inconveniently situated down the corridor leading to the labs. Turning into it, I stopped in my tracks. Halfway down was the young phlebotomist. Carrie, who'd just bled Angelina. Her progress back to the lab was being impeded by the arm of the stroppy Dr Elias van Lindholm who was leaning across her, hand pressed on the wall. Despite him being over six foot and Carrie being barely five four, his face was down level with hers. His body language suggested this was no chat-up situation, more an intimidating pep-talk. She was looking down at the floor, nodding and looking cowed. I shrank back for a moment but decided it was ridiculous to wait till they were done. My need was too great. I strode out nonchalantly.

Noticing me, "VL" as many called him, sprang away from the wall, lobbed a final remark into Carrie's ear, and rushed past me back up the corridor towards the ER. A pink and embarrassed Carrie hurried on down towards the laboratories.

I made it into the loo. Just. (A frequent occurrence for medics).

Later, Randy sent me to fetch an antibiotic injection from the pharmacy which was situated in a room next door to the labs. There, I found Carrie placing a box in the fridge. Hastily jumping back, she set flying her work tray of needles, vacuum vials for taking blood samples, rubber gloves and gauze swabs. I rushed to help retrieve the debris but, ignoring the stuff on the floor, she swiftly picked up her depleted tray by its top handle and fled without a word.

Sighing, I went into the fridge to take out the Magnapen antibiotic vial I needed and looked at the box she'd left. It was green, the size of a tea caddy, with two labels: one, yellow, proclaimed it a "Biohazard", the other was white and scrawled unevenly, with a warning, "Do not open. Property of Dr E. van Lindholm". What was that all about? I certainly wasn't going to open it and see. My God, that van Lindholm guy was freaky. He was so rude. How come he hadn't been 'given his jotters' as my gran would have said? And that Makkonen woman was plainly a love-sick nut. Poor wee Carrie looked a bit neurotic, if not bonkers. However, I had no time to ponder the peculiar staff at Ellis Memorial. I had a patient needing treatment.

Returning to Exam Room Five, Randy allowed me to lance an abscess. Satisfying for the patient, whose pain immediately reduced as I released the pressure. But for me, the incisor? Not so happy. I returned to the Nurses' Home for a quick change from my pus-sprinkled jacket. Point to note for the future? This procedure might be best performed wearing goggles and a protective apron.

Chapter Nine
Fridges, Sponges & Pickups

At lunch, Laura and I met up with John and Coop in the dining room. Sitting down with our laden trays, I again spied Frankie at the far side sitting with Dr van Lindholm. God, he was welcome! Frankie handed VL a bundle of yellow papers which the specialist worked through, tapping some which he'd add to a pile at his side, while others he'd discard back across the table with a head shake. Nearby, I saw Nat sitting with our bubbly ER Candy-striper, young Ellie May, their heads together, laughing conspiratorially. I was pleased. I'd worried he was a solitary, unhappy fellow.

While eating massive plates of Spaghetti Bolognese, Laura and I compared notes with the boys about our mornings. We seemed to have been the luckiest so far, having had an interesting and varied time in ER. Coop, on General Medical Floor, had been resigned to reading case sheets and chatting to nurses; his resident hadn't engaged with him. Word on the Floor was that the young doc been dumped by his girlfriend and gone all moody. On the Surgical Floor, John had only managed a short Resident's round then drunk coffee with staff.

John insisted on fetching us dessert: muffins. Massive muffins I couldn't contemplate eating. He laughed, took a huge bite, licked his lips and grinned. 'You don't know what you're missing, babe!'

No one had ever called me that before...But Coop was speaking. 'OK, girls. This weekend, what are you up to?'

'No plans,' said Laura. 'Why?'

'Good. We thought Saturday we'd throw you a welcome party at the Residency.'

'Is that allowed?' Laura looked surprised.

'Sure, as long as we don't make too much ruckus and burn the place down with candles 'n stuff. Randy told me they were forbidden after an incident last year.' Swallowing the last of his muffin, Coop added, 'We've got more stuff planned. Like a party at my house next month when my folks are upstate.'

'Gosh, won't your parents mind you having a party when they're away?' I asked.

'Nah, I've had them before. My sister Suzi will be upstairs reading her poetry and playing goody two shoes. She'd be on to my parents in a flash if things got out of hand. Reckon she shoulda been a nun!' He chuckled and stood up.

John followed suit. 'Okay. Eight on Saturday night. You know the Residency's on the top floor. If the door's shut, buzz and we'll let you in. And when we have the shindig at Coop's, don't worry about getting there. I've got a car and we can share a cab back if we get wasted!'

The afternoon held nothing memorable. No one acted weird. Almost disappointing. In the evening, we walked into town to stroll through a park behind the town hall. On the way we had three offers of a lift by people we'd met. Obviously, people didn't go for walks in New Jersey. As we returned home up the hill, I remarked to Laura, 'You know, I almost got into that last car.'

'Why, you still tired?' Laura stopped.

'No. It was Carrie, the blood-letting girl from ER. I'd have liked to ask her what van Lindholm was on about when he pinned her down in the corridor. And what was in a weird box of his that she put in the side room fridge.'

'What box?'

I explained but she looked disinterested. 'Oh, forget it. Marion on ER reception says Dr van Lindholm's doing some dodgy research. More worryingly, he's a big-time womaniser, apparently been reported several times but Harper does nothing. She thinks three nurses have quit because of him. Her take on it is that he gets off with anything as he's a big money spinner for them.'

'Or has VL got something on Dr Harper?' I stopped to think. 'That first day incident...I mean, Harper acted as if he was almost scared of van Lindholm, yet he's the boss.'

'Oh, Laura, stop making this trip into a mystery thriller. Come on, I need a drink!'

'Och, I'm not! But I did see a murder today. Well, a victim, a stabbed shopkeeper. The ER Crash team was impressive, but the knife had nicked his left ventricle. Blood bath. Had no chance.'

'Enough.' Laura tapped in our door code and pushed me into the Home.

~~~

Next day I was very much looking forward to our surgical attachment. According to the printed *Week One Rota*, we'd to assist gastro-intestinal surgeon Dr Bobby Newman operate in the morning and on a ward round in the afternoon. We were together for once, which was nice.

Well in time for our eight a.m. start, we were up, out and ready. Jet lag had finally worn off. John had informed us physiologists reckoned it took a day for every hour time difference. Day 5, my body clock agreed.

But up in the foyer of the hospital we were stymied. Despite scanning every sign and the Hospital Directory, we couldn't locate the Surgical Theatres.

'Likely they'll be on the top floor,' suggested Laura helpfully, 'like at home.'

'I'd rather know exactly where and not just go wandering around. We don't want to be late.' I approached the girl at the desk. We hadn't met this one before. She was very young, almost doll-like, with heavy Pan-stick make-up, smoky lashes and pale lips.

I leaned on the counter. 'Hi!'

She sat back from her Hollywood magazine looking bored. Granted it was only half-seven and very quiet.

'Yes?' This receptionist didn't fling her arms round us. I was almost disappointed.

'We wondered if you could help? We're looking for the theatre to find a Dr Newman but there's nothing on our info sheet or the Directory Sign to say where the theatres are.'

'Theatres?' Her pretty nose wrinkled. 'Like, for Shakespeare and all?'

I was thrown for a second at this daftness before she suddenly brightened, eyes enlarging as if a bell had gone off in her head. It was our turn to look stupid.

'Dr Bobby Newman, the surgeon? Oh, you want the OR!' Folding her arms, she looked triumphantly at me as though she'd solved the riddle of the universe.

'OR!' Laura exclaimed. 'Of course, we are daft. It's the Operating Room in Dr Kildare!'

The girl hooted with laughter. Loudly. Some new arrivals looked over. 'You sure have made my day. Sixth Floor, ladies. Residency to the right, OR to the left out of the elevator. Have a nice one.' We crept away.

~~~

Dr Newman was a friendly chap in his early sixties and was already in scrubs and waiting at the OR door chatting to a senior nurse.

'Ah, here you are. Welcome.' He shook hands with us both vigorously.

After learning which of us was which, he told us he loved London, having worked in England in the sixties. We quickly learned he had a daughter our age in an overseas aid programme and a son at Harvard doing Law. Having assured himself that we'd already assisted in surgery at home, he sent us off to scrub up supervised by his accompanying nurse, Kathy Martin. She was thorough and finicky. My hands were sore by the time she led us, suitably scrubbed, gowned, hatted, masked and gloved, into the operating room where the anaesthetist was just pronouncing the patient as 'under'.

Newman nodded at our tormentor. 'Thanks, Kathy. Now, girls, come meet Dave, my anaesthesiologist for today.' He waved towards the patient's head to the man sitting beside the machines of his trade.

Anaesthesiologist. Another different medical word, but one that defied Laura's theory that Americans changed UK words to simplify them. 'Anaesthesiologist' was much more complicated than 'anaesthetist'.

Newman waved at the intubated, silent patient lying covered in surgical drapes. 'Right, people. This is Mahalia who has a nasty gall bladder to come out. Mhairi, perhaps you could go opposite me for this one and hold the retractor when necessary? Laura, would you like to assist Nurse Martin and hand me equipment as I need it?'

As we moved to our designated positions, Newman cheerily greeted a newcomer sporting a Mickey Mouse cap and mask. He looked in his thirties, stocky, with round gold-rimmed glasses. 'Hey, it's real busy in OR today!' he exclaimed.

'Hi Sean. These are the gals over from Scotland for the summer. Laura and Mhairi, meet Sean, a Fifth Year Resident about to take his Surgical Boards.

'Boards?' asked Laura.

Sean stood, gloved hands held up either side of his head to avoid contamination.

'Yep. American Board of Surgery Exams. Written, then Oral. Stateside, we have surgical colleges like yours, but they don't do the exams. Each State has a Board of Examiners setting speciality exams. And even after you've passed you have to keep resitting them throughout your career.' Sean shrugged. 'It's a hard life being a surgeon in the US. But I love it. Nothing like seeing a problem then working out how to go fix it.'

'Gosh,' I said, thankful to be doing medicine in the UK.

'Anyhow, it's time for a right subcostal incision.' Newman took a scalpel from the tray of instruments beside him and made an incision in the woman's upper abdomen in the area framed by the clipped green surgical drapes. As he progressed, Sean stepped forward occasionally to cauterise bleeding vessels. It took some time for his boss to cut through the thick abdominal wall. Once she was opened up, Newman gave me a retractor to hold the wound apart and Sean 'set to' inside her abdomen. Newman allowed him to dissect while giving us a running commentary of his junior's knife work and occasionally asking us questions.

'So, girls, what predisposes a patient to gall bladder disease?'

Thankfully, this medical term was unchanged across the Atlantic. Laura reeled off 'Fair, fat, forty, female and fertile,' as our exam mnemonic went. Newman laughed.

'Yeh, well, she is heavy, and forty-two with five kids but I don't think we can call her fair. Not sure how many you see in Scotland, but never be too critical of heavy Black patients. Research shows they've got different metabolism to ours and are more prone to weight gain, diabetes and heart attacks. Never diss them about obesity. They find it harder to get thin.'

Sean was now requesting instruments from the tray beside Laura. But each time, before she could help, Nurse Martin handed them over until Newman waved his hand.

'Come on, Laura. Time for you to be the handmaiden.'

I could sense Laura bristle. She was no one's handmaiden. But she said nothing.

Sean nodded at her. 'You got a pickup?'

Laura looked at the instruments laid out on their green sterile sheet atop a gleaming stainless-steel tray and frowned. She glanced at me but I didn't know what a 'pick up' was either. Thinking laterally, she decided it was a social question. To my surprise she suddenly announced, 'Er, well, yes, I do have a boyfriend. He's called Greg.'

It's funny watching people in theatre when you can only see their eyes. But I knew Newman was suppressing laughter as he blinked to contain the tears he had forming. Sean did laugh. 'Right, that's great, but I still need a pickup!'

The stony-faced nurse whom I suspected resented our presence in her domain, reached out and with a flourish, handed Sean an instrument that appeared to be forceps. 'Your pickup, doctor.'

Poor Laura was now blushing. Sean reassured her. 'No worries. It'll go down in OR lore, Laura. Let's have a sponge now.'

There was a look of panic before she admitted, 'Sorry I can't see one.'

Nurse Martin leaned over to pick up a wad of gauze swabs. I swear her eyes smirked.

'Ah, those!' said Laura. 'I was looking for something like a wee sea sponge and wondering how you could be sure such a thing was sterile?'

'Well, you couldn't, I guess.' Dr Newman looked kindly at Laura, who said, 'Actually, might it not be safer if I just watched for now?'

The two surgeons then led us through a list of US surgical instrument names. Scalpels were still 'scalpels' and referred to by size, a number eleven being good for fine dissection. Forceps were 'pickups,' with many forms like Russian and Adson. Our 'clamps' were called 'locking forceps' in the States, not locking pickups. But some forceps had teeth. Confusing.

I tried to equalise things a bit by relating our amusement at Randy's first greeting. That went down well with the boys. The nurse glared. One reason might've been that Sean was subtly flirting with Laura. I'd noticed the nurse's large expressive eyes had hardly left Sean's face all morning, though she was less blatant in her flirting than Makkonen in ER. Mind you, Sean was personable, and witty and attractive. More than could be said about Dr van Lindholm.

But mostly I was concentrating on observing the surgical skill and rapport between two craftsmen at work. When Mahalia went to recovery, the next patient was a man in his forties with a colonic adenocarcinoma whose removal meant he'd not have enough bowel for reconnection, necessitating an external abdominal stoma with a bag for collecting stool. Life-changing surgery. Eventually, his drapes were removed, the anaesthetist began to lighten his coma. We came out to change.

Newman took us into the OR doctor's room for coffee while Sean wrote up the surgical notes. He re-appeared maskless, looking younger and with long loose blond curls. He smiled as he sipped his coffee.

'Gee, I didn't realise we spoke such a different surgical language over here. D'you think Boss, we should make a list of instrument names for our foreign interns and residents? I mean, they're from all over, like the Philippines, Japan...'

Newman nodded. 'Sure. A few years back I did a translation list for US names for body parts and slang. You might find it fun, girls. Ask Carlton's secretary for one—though I'm sure you know 'belly' is abdomen and 'ass' is backside!"

We chatted about our trip so far but when we talked of our time in New York, Newman was aghast. 'You walked round Times Square alone? And at night? Jesus, girls! You were taking a chance. I'd murder my Ashley if she did that!'

Just like my father. We hadn't felt threatened but might be best never to tell him about Times Square. Whenever I got around to writing one of my promised letters.

Newman and Sean headed back to scrub up for another case but let us go. With a sigh of relief, we went to change. Tossing our discarded pink scrubs into the linen basket, I realised that there were no female versions of the blue doctors' ones. Obviously, they weren't needed.

A glance in the changing room mirror horrified me. Cramming my long thick hair under the theatre cap had been a nightmare. Now it was a completely tangled, bushy mess. My next rebellious act would have to be a haircut. Soon.

'I must ask Jess where she gets her hair cut. I badly need one.' I re-attached my elastic bow onto a tightly rotated but still tangled, fat, ponytail.

Laura was combing her sleek tresses. 'Good idea. I couldn't be doing with your mop. It takes far too long to dry!' She donned her jacket, slipped her comb into the pocket, smoothed down her skirt and turned in front of the mirror to check her ponytail was neat. 'Thank goodness they got us smaller jackets!' She turned to me. 'Yes, defo do go get a haircut. Life's too short for waist length hair! How short will you take it?'

I shrugged. 'Shoulder length to start?'

'I've made a decision too, Mhairi. That three hours today is the longest I've been in a theatre. Apart from getting tired standing and the stress of maybe slipping the knife, I think surgery is not for me after all. Oh, the smell when we were so long inside that poor stoma guy? Blood I can take, but faeces? Yeugh! Pity. I loved the idea of being a pioneering surgical diva. I hadn't really considered the brutal reality. Anyway, where do you want to go for lunch?'

That's Laura. Decisive, confident, rapidly moving on from adversity.

In the Coffee Shop we had bagels again, this time with bland cream cheese, nothing meaty or odorous. Today's server was Candy-striper Ellie May who urged us to try a different soda than our usual Coke. (We'd gathered 'soda' here wasn't related to our Scots syphon stuff used for whisky but encompassed any fizzy drink). Today's suggested Sarsaparilla proved awful, a cross between liquorice and liquid Germolene (not that I've tried liquid antiseptic). It was quiet so Ellie May paused for a chat but when Laura mentioned the theatre nurse making eyes at Sean and how I'd seen Makkonen in ER swooning at van Lindholm, she turned tight-lipped and left.

Laura stared after her as she disappeared into the kitchen. 'What did I say?'

'Och, maybe she remembered something she forgot to do in the back? But then lots of folk act funny in Ellis Memorial. Maybe it's the heat.' I started blinking madly. 'Help, there's something in my eye.'

Laura peered at it. 'Can't see anything. But while we're on the subject of flirting, have you seen how John looks at you? He's got it bad...' She leaned back in her chair with a stupid grin. 'What are you going to do about it?'

'Nothing,' I said. Dabbing my watering eye, I headed for the loo to take my lenses out.

~~~

That afternoon we trotted round surgical in-patients with Bobby Newman and Sean hearing patients' stories and learning about surgical treatments and complications. Newman's bedside manner was such a contrast to van Lindholm's. He sat on beds, invited questions, implied he'd all the time in the world, shook everyone's hand. My kind of doctor. Between patients he'd give us background notes on folk we'd seen. He knew his patients and their circumstances inside and out, even worrying about how one women might not return for follow-up because of costs. At the inevitable coffee break, Laura asked what happened if you had no insurance. We had trouble getting our head around the US system. Newman put us right.

'Medicare and Medicaid were Bills passed in 1965 by President Lyndon B Johnson. Not perfect, but Medicare improved access to medical care for citizens over sixty-five and Medicaid for the blind, disabled, and families with dependent children, although single able-bodied adults aren't eligible no matter how poor they are. Each State can decide on its own Medicaid program. That means many States in the South or Southwest, like Mississippi, have no programmes like we have in Jersey. But even round here, the elderly can end up with debts since they're still responsible for 20% of hospital bills. People lose their homes to raise it.'

'Gosh,' was my only comment. It sounded quite a lottery.

'But believe me, it's better than nothing. You cannot imagine what it was like before.' How ironic that he should mirror Sister MacKinnon's very words from the day I saw Glasgow Paddy. 'There was no help if you didn't have private insurance. We got a bit more social security help too from Johnson when in office. He was a clever sod. Had to be. The AMA and the Republicans were tough opponents. It was quite a battle to get his Bills through. You girls don't know how lucky you are, living in England.'

Well, we didn't live in England but I saw no point in correcting this assumption: I realised that Americans didn't understand that the United Kingdom was a united nation comprised of different countries. Then again, I didn't really understand how their federal system worked either. Or that different States might have Medical Boards that didn't communicate with one another. Which might have fatal consequences.

Chapter Ten
Pizza & Pigtails

Back on the Surgical Floor, the last two patients of Newman's that we saw required only short chats as they were being discharged. In the first room, a young woman, presumably the patient's daughter, received carrier bags containing drugs and dressings from a nurse and paperwork from a lady whose badge identified her as "Helga, Finance Department". She was briskly efficient in her blue-striped blouse and short navy skirt as she clutched two multilayered clipboards, proffering one to Newman to sign before she'd tear off a top sheet of paper, fold it and insert it into an envelope to hand to the patient. My supposition that this was a bill was confirmed when Newman said gently to the patient, 'There'll be more invoices from my office later, Kathy, but don't worry about the settlement yet. I'll see you in my office at ten on Tuesday, check the wound and see where we go from here. The Path report will go direct to your oncologist.'

'Thanks, doctor, I owe you.'

The woman was assisted to her feet and unsteadily supported out of the room by her daughter who balanced a small suitcase and flowers as well as the carrier bags. They progressed slowly along the corridor, an empty-handed nurse walking at their side. Meanwhile, Helga shot out past the trio, called the elevator, darted in and took off without a backward glance, leaving the patient and her carer standing.

From the room door, we watched the floor number light above the lift door indicate its descent to Level Two, home of Admin

leaving quite a bit on my plate wouldn't attract comment. But while thinking this, I had a startling revelation: I hadn't felt the need to leave much food on a plate since I'd left Scotland. Well, unless the portion had been gargantuan.

More astonishing than my healthy appetite though, was Jess's revelation on the way to the A & P tonight about the charming, pig-tailed, bubbly child currently at our table, eating a Pepperoni Pizza twice the size of her head while smearing tomato sauce everywhere.

Before going to the Pizza parlour, we had shopped at an A&P supermarket, a giant one easily three times the size of a Safeway's at home. Its variety and choice in every category was ludicrously immense. Did we really need a whole aisle with 101 types of cooking oil? Wanting to avoid US cereals after my last disastrous buy, I picked up standard Cornflakes and, persuaded by Jess, some Cheerios. Laura bought some 'ready meals' for the freezer: a lasagne and crispy chicken things. We'd then visited an off licence (liquor shop) for beer and two bottles of wine for which I used some of my American Express traveller's cheques. Kitty was right: I needed my passport both to cash the cheques and to prove my age for legally buying booze. Jess bought some Tennessee Whiskey to show us it was, 'Better than Scotch any day!' Wouldn't be hard for me. I hated whisky.

Back at the Nurses' Home, the food we stashed into our newly labelled freezer drawer and cupboard, but the alcohol we put into our wardrobes on the advice of Jess who warned that occasionally 'Hitler' Heinz, the strict Nurses' Home Supervisor, made snap inspections of the kitchen and confiscated alcohol although it wasn't on the official list of 'Don'ts.' Jess suspected she drank it herself despite professing to be a stout Methodist. No one ever challenged Mrs Heinz, not even the hospital Admin staff. She had the final word on who could stay in the Nurses' Home. With any other rental accommodation in the area prohibitively expensive, the girls all kowtowed. I told Jess that Heinz reminded me of my Grandmother Una with all her rules. She laughed.

'Huh, you know what I mean, then. We do anything for peace!' I did know.

With a cursory hair comb and splodge of lipstick, we'd set off again in Jess's old Ford. Disconcertingly, she talked as she drove, lifting both hands off the wheel to emphasise points. I was delighted when we finally halted, but when I opened my eyes I'd no idea where we were. Looking around I saw only leafy suburbia.

'Where's the pizza place?' I asked.

'Oh, it's a coupla blocks away but we're picking up someone first. You'll love Barbara. She's a doll. My mom takes great care of her but I see her as much as I can on free evenings and weekends.'

'Barbara?' I questioned, thinking I'd missed something during the erratic car ride.

'My girl. She's five, thinks I'm her big sis but actually, I'm really her mom. I'll tell her one day but at present, it is as it is. Pops thought it best. I was only eighteen and he thought they might not take me into nursing school if they knew I had a kid. By the way, haven't told anyone in the Home about Babs, so I'd appreciate it if you didn't say to anyone.' With this bombshell, she got out of the car to walk up the short drive of a pleasant small detached house with green lawn and geranium tubs by the door. A curtain twitched, the door opened and a small girl ran out to throw her arms around Jess. I felt emotional. This was a child who, like me, was going to know when she was older that she'd been lied to. Even if it was for a specific noble end—to help her mother build a career—was it ever justified? As we set off, Barbara sat in the back, telling me "Pizzas were her favourite food, in all the world". She rattled off the choices available. Always choices. Nothing Stateside came simply in one variety.

We had a relaxed entertaining tea in Pizza King with a lot of laughter. I stuck to Coke and a plain cheese and tomato pizza of which I managed about seventy-five per cent. Barbara made me taste a bit of her Pepperoni and regarded me with the kind of fascinated, intent stare that only five-year-olds can manage. 'You sure talk funny, Your name's funny, too. Where you from again?'

I explained about Scotland being far away across the ocean.

Jess winked at me before telling her, 'It's a funny place, Babs. It's cold but the men wear skirts called kilts and their music comes from squeaky bagpipes.'

I added, 'Kids can wear kilts too. I had one for school. There's different ones depending on your family name. Ours was red with darker checks over it. But nowadays mostly it's only men, like in pipe bands or at weddings, who wear them.'

My explanation didn't stop Babs rolling around in laughter. The tomato sauce overspill had now tracked from her white Minnie Mouse T-shirt down onto her dungaree shorts. After she'd pushed back her plate, surprisingly empty when we considered the size of her stomach, Jess took her hand and got up.

'Time for the washroom, girl. What a mess you've made!'

Watching them go, I asked Laura, 'What d'you think about Babs being told Jess is her sister?'

'It's not for us to say, is it? Jess is doing what she thinks is best. Wonder who the dad is. Funny she doesn't mention him.'

'Obviously, a rat who didn't stand by her. Don't think that's our business though, is it? I wouldn't ask. But likely he'll have been blond, possibly tall. Babs is big for a five year old. And Jess is more mesomorphic...'

'Mesomorphic? My, how technical, Miss MacLean! Och, you're right, we can't ask. Anyway, Babs has Jess's rosy cheeks and smile. I wonder what they'll do when she starts school? We had to produce birth certificates then, didn't we? I wonder what hers says under 'Father'?'

'Who knows? I'm off the subject of birth certificates.'

'Sorry, Var, I know. Here they come again.'

I noticed Laura was adopting the US tendency to shorten everyone's name. A skipping, slightly cleaner, Barbara approached followed by Jess, who didn't sit down.

'That's us. All fixed! Shall we head off? Mustn't be too late. Kindergarten tomorrow for this little one.' She tickled Babs in the tummy and the child squealed in delight.

I thought what bliss it was to be five but had to ask, 'You said Babs is five, didn't you? Isn't she at school already?'

'Oh, we start at six. No real serious stuff like reading and writing till then.'

Babs sang all the way back to the Heffernan house. We all got a hug from her before she was tickled and covered in kisses and hugs by Jess. At the door, as her gran stood to wave us off, Babs was laughing, her arms curled around the woman's waist. 'It's a lovely house your parents have,' I commented, bravely sitting on the return journey with my eyes open all the way, having decided Jess was, on the whole, driving safely, but mainly because I get carsick if I can't see where I'm going and am full of food.

'Yes, it's better than our old one. We got it after Babs was born when...' she paused, took a deep breath and said, '...I came into some money. It was a bargain. Needed a lot of work but Pop's a carpenter, great at DIY. Mum's a homemaker. She had me at eighteen so she never went to college. She's only ever worked part-time in a bakery. Makes mean cakes.'

Laura commented on the fact that all American TV shows we'd seen only depicted women as housewives, never in professions unless maybe as secretaries. 'Don't women work much outside the home in the States? I mean, out here we see there are no women medics but in Glasgow, about a quarter of our year are female. Is it not acceptable for women to work outside the home? I got mad today hearing someone call me a 'handmaiden'—like it's our place to be subservient. Don't you think it's terrible for women to be treated as second-class citizens like that or pushed into stereotypes of permitted behaviour?'

Jess agreed. 'I think the United States is behind in equal rights. Over here even a lot of women think marriage and kids is 'all'. I don't think the woman's movement has had much effect, to be honest. It's still all 'Mr Daddy-Breadwinner' and 'Mrs Pretty Stay-at-Home Momma' unless you are a single woman who chooses a handmaiden kinda career like nursing or secretarial. Or of course, teaching. But you have to give up once you've got your man. Not my idea of a life.'

'Are you against marriage?' I hadn't formed the impression that she was against the opposite sex, even if the 'good ride' Teddy had obviously not come up to scratch.

'Pretty much. My attitude is to get like the men and use the opposite sex for pleasure. Given up thinking I'll find a soulmate. Anyway, back to equal rights. You guys read about Gloria Steinem?'

'No, who's she?' Laura asked.

'Awesome woman. She sure had a hard life. Brought up in a trailer by a psychotic mom. But she's trying to change things, at least in politics. There's a big Convention this weekend in Washington DC for something called the *National Women's Political Caucus*. Betty Friedan's another one of them. You read her *The Feminine Mystique?* They're trying to push for more women in the legislature, get laws changed, end discrimination and force through equality. I hear a hell of a lot of folk are going to the Convention. Would love to be there. It'd be my dream to be a senator. But you never get elected unless you're filthy rich so I can forget it.'

We swung into the Nurses' Home carpark and Jess backed effortlessly into a free space. The rest of the evening involved percolated coffee and more chat on the slow progress of women's liberation. Jess suggested a reading list for Laura and even fetched a copy of Friedan's book from her room. 'Hey, Laura. Try this. Let me know what you think.'

I went to my bedroom at that juncture but stayed up for a bit drafting a letter home to Dad, mainly listing the specialities we'd been attached to and saying how nice everyone was. I made no mention of sexy comments encountered nor van Lindholm's insults about women in medicine. I slept fitfully. Probably the late coffee. My vivid dream of spinning pizzas and children leaping to catch them was likely triggered by Jess's promise to play Frisbee with Barbara at the weekend. Another new word. My brain was likely jumbled after all that pizza cheese. Una always warned against too much cheese in the evening.

~~~

Next morning, I realised we'd only been away from home a week though it seemed much longer. Our attachment for Friday July 9th was with Coop's cardiology Dad, Dr Michael Mayfield. I found him as charming and welcoming as Dr Newman. Despite Dr Mayfield suggesting we could call him "Micky", neither of us could bring ourselves to call him anything other than "Doctor." He shepherded us around several patients, mostly post heart attack, stressed, overweight, bourbon-drinking, chain-smoking businessmen who were adamant that now they were going to make serious lifestyle changes though I wondered whether the diet and exercise sheets that they were handed would be followed for more than a few weeks. Habits are hard to break.

After the first patient, Dr Mayfield looked at us sternly. 'You girls smoke?' We shook our heads. 'No? Good. They're nothing but coffin sticks, cigarettes. If you ask me, the tobacco lobby has too much power in this country. I'd ban smoking in restaurants for a start. And all those TV ads. Fancy calling a brand Luckies. They're anything but. Have killed as many folk as bullets in the US, yet our National Legislature seems unable to curb them. Mind you, they've done nothing about guns either. Ridiculous.'

It was only the second time I'd heard the word "Legislature'" Like "anaesthesiology", a word much more complex than our UK equivalent, 'government'.

In the afternoon, Dr Mayfield ran a Cardiology Seminar with his Third Year Resident, Dr Clayton Randall. On the drop-down white wall screen, Clayton ran through some projected slides of the detailed images they were getting from the new technique of angiocardiography, where injected dye showed up blocked heart arteries. He also showed diagrams demonstrating the different areas of the heart that 'died' after blood clots blocked particular arteries and matched them up with their corresponding "EKGs". It took me a wee while to realise his EKGs were what we called ECGs, electrocardiographs, in the UK.

When he moved on to discuss arrhythmias, different types of irregular heartbeat, I was delighted not to feel anxious. Back in Glasgow I had had a serious panic attack at an arrhythmia tutorial after our GP had told me Mum had died from heart rhythm problems. Although that class hadn't been pushing any idea that rhythm problems were hereditary, I'd rushed off to hyperventilate in the loo, fearing my own imminent cardiac arrest. But now I knew faulty heartbeats hadn't killed her. Well, if she'd had them, they were iatrogenic i.e., medically induced by drugs. Taking a deep breath, I steadied myself, vowing not to brood any more on my mother's final hours. Whether she'd died by accident or purposefully by her own hand or been murdered by my father feeding her pills was impossible to know. But she was dead. I had to move on.

Back in the present, I was losing the thread of Clayton's talk. He was going on about 'PVCs.' I thought of Polyvinyl Chloride, the plastic material popularised by Mary Quant for white boots and black shiny coats. Only when someone expanded the initials to 'Premature Ventricular Contractions' and pointed them out on an EKG, did I twig that PVCs were what we called extrasystoles, extra irregular heartbeats! Clayton was an interesting speaker and I soon forgot my previous resolve to avoid cardiology wherever possible. I even took notes on some useful new drugs, though suspected they'd have different names at home. The talk of new possible treatments like electrical 'pacing' was encouraging. I turned to whisper this to Laura at my side but it was pointless: she was fast asleep. Luckily, the lights were off. I nudged her awake as the lights went on at the end.

~~~

After a homecooked meal (well, a heated-up one previously prepared by A&P stores), we walked down again into the park to sit on a bench in the shade of a tree. The sun hadn't yet set. I'd noted it got dark much quicker in summer Brunsfield than Glasgow and reckoned we only had about another three quarters of an hour of daylight. We made the most of it.

'Nice of Doctor Mayfield to ask us to go and visit his country club, wasn't it?' I said.

Laura nodded. 'Coop's already suggested we go next weekend. But first, this weekend we've got the party in the Residency. Should be fun. They've asked a lot of the nurses too. Are you looking forward to it?'

'Yes!' I didn't say, but the main factor in my keenness was John. After Laura's comment, I had started to notice, like after today's seminar, that he did spend more time seeking me out and talking with me specifically. A little pang of guilt about Roddy flashed up, but he was far away. And it wasn't as if we were engaged or anything. Besides, my new philosophy was to be open to new opportunities. If that meant getting to know John, so be it...

Before bed, I rewrote my bland letter to Dad on one of the thin, pre-paid, blue airmail letters Jess had given me. Much cheaper than using ordinary paper, an envelope and stamps, she had them for writing to her younger brother overseas in the military. Then I penned an uncensored letter to Roddy which made me realise how much I'd learned about the US already. In bed, I stayed up late reading about St Luke. On the plane I'd started *Dear and Glorious Physician*, a present from my grandmother who'd obviously thought it was a suitably soul-improving religious book about St Luke. In fact, Taylor Caldwell's novel was a raunchy and entertaining romp set in biblical times. Her St Luke sounded a fine supporter of women, underdogs and those on hard times. And a compassionate doctor. It never occurred to me a doctor might be anything else. Then.

Laura had brought an Agatha Christie away with her, joking, 'Nothing like a bit of murder on holiday, is there?' Later I'd tease her about tempting fate. But after two pages on the plane, she'd fallen sleep and I hadn't seen it since.

~~~

Next morning, I regretted not putting out my light earlier. I'd forgotten I had a hair appointment. I hate getting up early, especially so on Saturdays but Jess was at my door at 7.45 a.m. Sleepily, I dressed and cleaned my teeth with Jess chivvying me on.

'Hurry up. We can't be late. Sabrina's doing this as a favour.'

It was good of her to fit me in. When Jess had phoned her earlier in the week, this was the only slot she could offer. Laura thought going early wasn't a bad idea, up and out with no time to change my mind. But I knew she wouldn't be coming along for support. Laura was not a morning person.

Having not had time to even drag a brush through my immense hair I viewed my reflection in Jess's sun visor mirror with horror. Sabrina would have her work cut out.

Chapter Eleven
Parties & Politics

Sabrina had large eyes with sclera so white they sparked like snow in her dark face. A woman in her early twenties, she was stunningly beautiful, with hair wound tightly in tiny plaits and piled high on her head. She hugged Jess and then me.

Back home in Glasgow, I'd only ever had my 'ends' trimmed in an old-fashioned dark salon in Cathcart Road. But *Sabrina's Hair and Beauty Salon* was glamorous, bright, modern and shiny. Big mirrors hung in front of padded scarlet chairs. Gleaming white basins along the back wall had semi-circular holes cut out of their front edges. I'd never seen rear-wash basins.

After an introductory chat, mainly centring on her amazement that I'd put up with my thick, wavy, frizzy, waist-length hair for so long, I was shampooed and 'conditioned.' Sabrina was aghast when I asked what that was.

'You've never heard of conditioner?'

The difference it made was extraordinary: her brush sailed through my hair! We'd decided on shoulder length, leaving enough to tie back when in the wards but making for shorter drying time. She showed me how to style it with a large circular brush. The result was a gentle-waved, shinier head of hair than I'd ever dreamed of!

'Sabrina, you're a genius!'

By this time, her beautician had arrived. The telephone rang. After answering it, the girl cursed and threw down the receiver. Her first customer had cancelled.

Sabrina nodded at me in the mirror. 'Say, Mhairi, why not get your nails done? Alissa's got no one till ten now.'

I could hear Una's voice saying, "Painted nails are the sign of a Jezebel!" But when the chips were down, who could it harm? 'I've never had them manicured,' I admitted, looking to Jess for support. 'What do you think?'

Jess gave a thumbs up. 'Go for it, babe! Party time tonight remember!'

Just after ten, I left the salon with a gleaming head, shiny peach nails and a carrier bag containing shampoo, conditioner and a new circular brush. We went to a diner and celebrated with blueberry pancakes for brunch. A new Mhairi was born.

~~~

That evening, I was putty in Jess's hands. It was almost as bad as Laura dressing me for my first dance at the Men's Union in the spring when I'd 'got off' with Roddy.

Determined that I needed to socialise more before setting off on our trip in the summer, she'd zoomed over to my Mount Florida home in her mother's Mercedes, whisked me back to the Ellis's Pollokshields house and dressed me like a marionette. After her ministrations, I'd had trouble recognising myself in the mirror: upswept hair, black lashes, pale lipstick, short purple crochet mini dress and white tights. Laura's Dad then drove us across the city to the Men's Union at the University and we promised to get a taxi home to the Southside. It had been decided that I would stay over to ensure my dad wouldn't know how late home we were. Laura's mum had even promised to drive me to our West End Church next morning to get him to agree. But here in Brunsfield we only had to walk up the drive to this party and no one would care what time we returned. Pretty exciting, I thought. God, I was so naïve.

Jess was no less exacting than Laura, having me try on umpteen outfits and experiment with multiple cosmetics from her large beauty case. I went along with it knowing she was upset at being denied her usual day with Barbara who'd been taken to see her great-grandmother, a Una-like figure who had tolerated Jess staying at the upstate family farmhouse during Bab's pregnancy, but now didn't acknowledge her, she being a fallen woman.

From my limited wardrobe, Jess chose a pale green mini dress with blouson sleeves. She was wearing a cream-striped blouse and black miniskirt while Laura had on a little blue number she'd bought in Fraser's department store at eye-watering cost. Around eight, we walked up to the hospital and a low white ambulance drove past, lights flashing. It disappeared round the back towards the ER entrance.

'Work for someone!' declared Jess. 'Luckily not us tonight!'

'Do the hospitals each own their own ambulances?' I asked out of curiosity.

'Most are community funded, I think, but there're some private companies too. Not sure how 911 chooses who to send. A rota maybe?'

'Suppose medical insurance pays for them too?'

'Sure. Patients get billed.' Jess shrugged.

Another ambulance passed and I shook my head at it. 'I don't understand why the American Medical Association and these ambulance companies use that symbol.' I pointed at the ambulance logo of a staff bearing two symmetrically entwined snakes. 'That's actually the Caduceus of Hermes, Messenger of the Gods. The actual God of *Medicine* was Aesculapius. His emblem is a staff with *one* snake, suppose because snake venom was good medicine.'

'You don't say? My, Mhairi, you're so clever! We didn't learn anything like that at my High School. Guess the guys just liked the look of the symbol and didn't realise it was wrong?' An ambulance is an ambulance!' She shrugged. 'They're all the same.'

But they weren't.

~~~

Up on Sixth Floor music blared out of the open Residency door. The boys' sitting room was twice the size of ours, albeit for half the number of occupants. Off to one side was a kitchen, off the other a dining room and at the back was a door leading into a corridor with bedrooms. John appeared to greet us with hugs.

Drinks on offer were beer, Coke, other 'sodas' and wine. Crisps (aka potato chips) and popcorn had been decanted into paper dishes. Jess put down our wine contribution, although she'd said that here it wasn't usual to take drink to a party. Lifting two beers, she expertly flipped off their caps with an opener and handed me one. Laura went for wine. Swigging out of a bottle like Jess didn't appeal so I looked around for a glass. I found one in the cupboard but when I started pouring, produced a mess of overflowing froth. Laughing, John took it off me, demonstrating the technique of pouring it down the side to keep it in the glass.

'You never poured a beer before, girl?'

I hadn't but didn't admit it. More folk had arrived and the kitchen was becoming crowded. We moved into the sitting room and sat on a group of low seats that had been pushed into the corner. Laura, Coop and Jess joined us. Nearby, Hiro was discussing the merits of a pile of records with the Cardiology Resident of the mysterious PVCs and EKGs, Clayton. When the last Beach Boys track came to its end, Coop got up to exchange the stack of LPs for a new one. The record player was a fancy General Electric machine with speakers attached at each side. I'd never seen anything like it, nor heard the quality of the music filling the room.

'Amazing sound!' I looked at the machine in wonder. 'Sounds like a cinema.'

John nodded. 'Yep. It belongs to Coop's dad.'

Coop took Laura up to dance. I sipped my *Budweiser* beer thinking it didn't measure up to its ad hype on TV. John nodded at the record player.

'I'm supposed to watch no one fucks it up or walks off with it.'

'Surely no one in here would? I mean, docs don't need to steal stuff, surely?'

'They're not all lily white.' John stood up to greet Randy, who swigged his beer and sat down beside us.

'Who're not all lily white?' he asked.

'Oh, Mhairi doesn't believe docs break the law,' John poked me. I didn't mind.

'Yeh, wish I believed that! But you know, if they do, I reckon most are clever enough to avoid being caught.' Randy nodded to the door. 'Take him. He's out to get anything he wants. By any means, legally or otherwise.' He gulped some beer. 'Thinks he's above the law, does Dr Elias van Lindholm. Acts like a Nazi, though his family's Swedish, I believe.'

John waved his empty bottle. 'Lots of Swedes were Nazis, you know, even though Sweden as a country professed to be neutral. They let Hitler transport iron ore and fuel through the country. Amongst other things. Did you know the word Nazi name came from shortening the "National Socialist Party"? I've learned a lot reading a book about a Swedish guy called Eric van Rosen whose wife's sister married Hermann Göring. A big cheese was Eric, a Swedish Socialist Party leader. They say he adopted swastikas before Hitler did. Dunno why, but van Lindholm seems a bit fascist to me.'

Randy only said, 'Huh!' and took John's bottle to get a replacement.

The object of their interest was advancing through the room cradling a case of beer in his left arm: so much for not bringing booze to a party. Dr van Lindholm was shaking hands as he went with the junior doctors and students. The males. He didn't speak to any nurses or the wives or girlfriends of the junior doctors. Having heard he wasn't universally liked and there were few seniors here, I was surprised he'd been asked. The specialist went into the kitchen. Frankie Cooke on his tail.

'Frankie is always very pally with Lindholm.' I watched through the open door as they talked with much nodding and smiling. 'More than you'd expect from the usual student-teacher interaction. I don't get it.'

John chuckled, giving an expressive downturn smile. 'Frankie says he's doing research and van Lindholm's helping. But I wouldn't fancy him helping me.'

Randy returned to sit, saying, 'Do you know Frankie's the first student extern we've had return? And at the personal invite of VL, I'm told. But tell me, John, what student goes out to interview patients at home?'

'At home? None I should think. Why?'

Randy rolled his bottle between palms. 'Yesterday, though he's not assigned to us, Frankie was in ER talking with one of Lindholm's patients. Way she spoke, seems like Frankie had visited her at home. She told him to "Call again, anytime!"'

'Do docs do house calls here? From TV programmes I've seen, I thought they didn't.' I made a face, partly from the sour taste of the Budweiser. Definitely time for wine.

'Not as a rule,' said Randy. 'But you know, Mhairi, when I said you'd best keep your distance from him?' He pointed at van Lindholm, now walking out of the door after the shortest visit to a party I'd ever seen. 'I meant it. He's bad news. Not only weird but a womaniser and a user. And he's got something on Harper.'

John looked surprised. 'Carlton? The Chief of Med Staff?'

'You must have seen how he snaps his fingers and Harper jumps? It's maybe closet stuff. Rumour has it Carlton likes a hug with the pretty boys. Ask Nat.' Randy left for the kitchen.

John looked after him. 'Phew, bit heavy, all that. Hate internal politics, don't you? Let's go dance.' He hauled me up to drag me to the middle of the room where several people were already dancing to Stevie Wonders' 'Signed, Sealed, Delivered, I'm Yours.' How curious: the first song I'd danced to with Roddy in the Union. I suppressed the memory.

John was a great dancer. I was twirled, hugged and swung about. Exhilarating. Gyrating and waving my arms about seemed natural, obliterating everything but the moment. By eleven, the lights dimmed, scented candles were lit. Obviously the 'no candle' rule didn't hold. For once my thoughts were on romance, not fire risks. But there was more smoke than usual with candles. I coughed. The gathering cigarette fug was annoying. And smelled unusual. Sitting out for a bit with a glass of red wine, I asked John, 'What's burning? It's a sort of earthy, woody smell...'

He laughed. 'Why, babe that's cannabis! You not tried it? Makes you mellow.' He leaned over to kiss me. That first kiss was extraordinary, like mini electric shocks. Worrying I was drunk and making a fool of myself, I pulled back, trying to sound serious. 'Oh, right, yes. Of course. I've smelled it before at parties.' Not that I'd been at many.

'Everyone does it here. But don't let the cops get you—a conviction can finish a career. You know, Frankie boasts his dad got him off last summer? He got chiefed at some barbecue in a park and threw wieners at some cop trying to move them on!'

'Chiefed? Wieners?' This was like Double Dutch to me.

John laughed loudly. 'Got high! Threw hot dogs! You want to try a joint?'

'Oh, no. I'd rather not.' Definitely a step too far in my emancipation.

Our conversation was halted as Hiro appeared with his guitar. I'd heard already that he'd wanted to be a professional musician but his father had decreed his eldest son would be a lawyer, and his second, Hiro, had to be a medic. I'd commiserated with him on the problems of complying with family expectations. As he played, it was obvious Hiro was a talented musician. He played brilliantly. Shame he couldn't follow his dream.

As Hiro took a rest, Coop stacked up some slow music. Carole King's *Tapestry* was first. Moving, poignant. 'Needs the bass turned up,' said Coop, fiddling with the dials.

John held me close. I won't say, 'The Earth Moved Under my Feet', as Carole sings, but as I danced with him, I concluded that I was already 'mellow'. Who needed weed? John didn't either by the feel of him. The passionate kissing was unlike any I'd previously encountered. We retired to a corner sofa where, oblivious to our surroundings, we didn't do much talking.

Later, going to the loo, I passed Ellie May coming out looking curiously pleased with herself. Seeing me, she stuffed a piece of paper into her minuscule handbag and beamed a smile from a newly made-up face.

'Cool party, eh?' she said, which puzzled me: as far as I could see she had spent the entire night so far sitting mute alongside Nat and another lad. Mind you, her eyes looked unfocused. Perhaps she'd had a joint?

Coming back from the loo to the sitting room I next passed Jess in the corridor. She wasn't looking vacant as she animatedly chatted and smiled up close with Randy. Now, they'd make a good pair...

Back in the party proper, Laura was enjoying herself on another sofa, sitting with (no, sitting *on*) Coop, and seriously 'making out'. Even in the dim light Coop's lips looked like they were wearing as much Elizabeth Arden *Summer Pink* lipstick as Laura's. Coop appeared out of it, though whether from the effect of Laura or additional botanicals, who could say?

As the party thinned, around two o'clock, John sent out for pizzas. They were, I decided, an ideal party snack; no need for plates or cutlery or washing up. Wary from my previous pizza cheesy dreams, I only ate half. I have no idea what time we got home, though it was definitely Sunday.

It was perhaps around four when I went to bed feeling very mellow and content without the need to be 'chiefed'. There were no nightmares. I still rose at eight and luxuriated in a bubble bath contemplating life and love. I was sorry John wasn't coming out with us later. Laura didn't surface until noon.

We had a Sunday 'brunch' with some of her wee, frozen, crispy chicken things and lazed about until Coop collected us at four to go for dinner with his family. Not that it matters especially what time we did anything except that I was aware of the day being my own, unregulated by the set prayer times and Church services of Una's Sabbath.

~~~

Coop's mother was Swedish. Contrary to my stereotype of Scandinavians, Brigitte Mayfield was diminutive, dark-haired and hilarious. Coming over on a year's scholarship to Yale, she'd met Michael, married and settled permanently in the US. Currently she was 'Head of Legal' at Ellis Memorial. I wondered if our UK hospitals had 'Heads of Legal' but doubted it.

The Mayfields were hospitable and entertaining. I ate every scrap of our dinner. After prawns, steak and strawberry tart with ice cream, we enjoyed an evening of music. Michael played piano, accompanying Brigitte and his sister Suzi as they sang old pop classics. Hearing I could play, I was coaxed forward and managed an old, short, Mozart exam piece. Wine flowed. I had to cover my glass with my hand more than once. Coop moved on to play blues on an electric guitar. One song, 'Move on Up', he maintained needed a trumpet and drums accompaniment, but it sounded great. It was from an album by a new coloured singer, Curtis Mayfield, no relation. Coop felt it epitomised the current political drive towards equality. Many other songs Laura and I had never heard of were discussed before the conversation turned to US politics.

The Mayfields were Democrats. The current government under Nixon was Republican. For Michael, the only good thing they'd done was the recent July 5th ratification of the 26th Amendment to the United States Constitution, lowering the voting age. He waved his glass around and shrugged. 'I mean, how could they justify asking kids to die in Vietnam but deny them a vote till they were twenty-one? It had to happen.'

I'd never discussed politics before and felt quite ignorant, but Laura engaged with Brigitte in a long discourse on human rights and the current UK political situation. I was clueless about the basis of the Irish Troubles or the political aims of our Prime Minister, Ted Heath: any spare moment in our house was given to religion. Coop and sixteen-year-old Suzi were fully in there at every juncture—giving their views, being listened to. I chilled out of the conversation to stare through the open French doors at the lovely garden of this impeccable five-bedroomed house complete with tennis court. At home, we owned a smart house in a south Glasgow suburb but Coop's home was a mansion. I found myself envying this family. Not for their wealth, but for their relationships, sense of balance, openness to discussion and consideration of everyone's point of view. I experienced a pang of sadness and loss, not just about my dead mother but about how different family life could be.

Coop dropped us off late. Although I dashed out to the front step the minute we arrived to give him and Laura time on their own, I hadn't even reached the steps before I saw they were in a passionate clinch. Had she written to her Greg, I wondered? I'd finished a pretty brief scribble to Roddy earlier in the day, hoping he was enjoying his summer—without spelling out exactly how much I was, or why. I'd never 'chucked' a boy in my life and anyway, felt surely doing it in a letter was a bit mean? In the war they called them, 'Dear John' letters. How could I say I'd fallen for someone else after only a week?

Lying in bed, I tried distracting myself from an unusual and disturbing emotion that I realised was a longing for John, by considering where I might like to be attached for the next weeks of our summer clerkship. What might best help my career? But I couldn't concentrate and soon fell asleep.

~~~

By ten o'clock next morning, we were outside Dr Harper's Office where six seats had helpfully been lined up. I was the first one called in to find the Chief of Medical Staff, Dr Carlton Harper, sitting with Randy.

'So, Mhairi, what would you like to do in the time you have with us—do you have a career in mind?'

'Not sure, to be honest, maybe General Practice or Psychiatry?'

The Chief shook his head. 'I'm afraid we have no Psych Floor here and I don't think there's time for us to arrange for you to go to another Facility who have one, but how about some Internal Medicine and spells in ER? We often see Psych cases there and call in shrinks for consults.'

I nodded. 'Sounds good. I don't mind doing some surgery too.'

Randy looked down at his papers. 'How about some OBGYN and Paeds? I see you haven't done them yet.'

I said, 'Fine,' biting back some anxiety that I might have to do some studying.

Randy scribbled notes. 'Okay, let's see you back around twelve to collect a schedule'

On the way out I passed Laura and whispered, 'See you in the Coffee Shop.'

She nodded and went on in to greet Harper with her usual cheery, 'Good morning.'

Chapter Twelve
The Sunday Patients

At quarter past ten, the Coffee Shop was pretty empty. I got a flat white, served by Ellie May. As it was quiet, she lingered for a few minutes chatting, before shooting off suddenly towards the door.

Dr van Lindholm had appeared at the entrance. He paused to speak to Ellie, smiling and nodding briefly, though I noticed he started walking away while she was still speaking to him. Rude as ever! She looked momentarily upset but pasted on a smile and moved over to speak to a fellow server. For distraction, I turned to a discarded *Brunsfield Free Press* newspaper on the table. On its front page was an article telling of a serious dog fouling incident in the park for which a young man was to appear in court. Not a lot happened in Brunsfield, I guessed. I emptied my coffee cup as Laura arrived.

She announced she'd asked to rotate through Medical and Surgical Floors, ER and OBGYN. Ellie May reappeared, less bubbly than usual, to take our order for coffees and a chocolate chip muffin to share.

Soon after, Coop rushed in, not to tell us where he'd wanted assigned, but with the news that there'd been a horrendous hit and run over the weekend in the early hours of the morning and a girl was fighting for her life. The hospital was abuzz with the news of the dreadful case, especially that the surgeons had been unable to save her leg.

At that point, Frankie ambled up to nod at Coop. 'You talkin about that stupid broad? I mean, what was she doin' walking past a park in the middle of the night? Probably a whore.'

Nat arrived last and for once was eager to talk. 'Hey, I just got some gen from a young cop out in the front hall. Says they've arrested the hit and run woman's boyfriend. Story is, they went to see him since he was listed in her purse as next of kin but when they were leaving, a neighbour came over to tell of a humdinger of a row they'd had in the middle of the night and hinted that drug dealing was involved. The police have towed away his car for examination. Her injuries were real bad. Reckon the car must be covered in blood.'

I was about to say, 'Poor girl, how will she manage with an artificial leg?' but was overtaken by Frankie's loud interjection.

'Say, what kinda damages d'ya think she'll get? What's the goin' rate for a leg anyone know?'

Nat and he started an animated discussion on how such things were calculated.

I left, incensed at their callous money-oriented attitude towards the poor accident victim and went for a brisk walk in the grounds to clear my head before going to pick up my timetable of assignments. But I was still cross. As if money could ever compensate a young women for losing a leg?

~~~

In the afternoon, my first assigned shift was to the Laboratories. Laura, I'd gathered, was off to Physiotherapy, Coop to Radiology and John and Nat to Admin and Finance. Frankie hadn't said where he was heading and I hadn't waited to ask. We'd been told we would all to be rotated for odd afternoons in these, and other, smaller departments but would spend weeks at a time in other main specialities. I was keen to understand how the labs functioned as I had no idea how they tested specimens, however, I learned other things in there which provided more questions than answers. Later, though, they did fit into a jigsaw we assembled that proved this 'award winning' hospital wasn't a complete bastion of compassion and altruism.

As I opened the heavy door to enter the laboratory wing, Dr Elias van Lindholm appeared out of nowhere to barge past me at speed, elbows out and coat flapping behind. He pushed the door so hard that its strong spring hinges caused it to rebound into my face. I managed to catch it, just. It missed my nose by millimetres and gave me quite a fright. I stepped through it gingerly, to be greeted almost immediately by a substantial cheery man coming out of his office whose badge declared him to be Dr C. Caldicott, Laboratory Chief.

'Hello, are you Mhairi?' he asked.

'Yes, I am.'

Caldicott shook my hand firmly. 'Welcome to Ellis Memorial Hospital Laboratories. Dr Harper wants all you good young people to have a little tour of our facilities and for me to tell you how we work here. Now, Mhairi, have you been in any hospital laboratories before?'

'No. Well, only briefly at home in Scotland when handing in blood samples from patients.'

'Right. OK. Let's start first with Haematology—my domain!'

The Haematology Department was essentially a huge room divided into sections by glass-walled partitions. Centrifuges whirred noisily. Half a dozen white-coated staff in goggles were pipetting serum off samples that had been spun in the centrifuges. The serum was then being decanted into other tubes to be fed into analysers from whence broad 'ticker tapes' came out. These were spirited off to two typists in an adjacent glass-fronted room. Along the other wall of the main lab sat a series of microscopes on desks. Here, on high stools, sat white-coated technicians peering down the lenses, some alternately looking and logging results on forms, others with eyes locked on the microscopes gazing at slides while clicking number crunchers like those I'd seen Clyde Ferry seamen using to count passengers aboard.

Caldicott showed me their work system. Samples were logged into a book at reception, assigned a number then provided with stickers bearing that number which were put on both the sample and its accompanying form. The requesting doctor's name was recorded, along with the degree of urgency required. I noted most under van Lindholm's name were labelled 'Stat' that I knew meant 'do immediately'. Didn't surprise me. He had the appearance of a very impatient man although I doubted his patients were more critically ill than anyone else's.

One far corner was sectioned off and assigned to grouping and cross-matching blood. I did understand all about that, but patiently listened as Caldicott outlined the steps for ascertaining a patient's blood group to match them to suitable units for transfusion that could be released from the refrigerated store. One thing that did surprise me was the information that they bought in all the blood they used. All donors were paid in the U.S., including prisoners, whom he said were often generous donors as it earned them privileges as well as money. He couldn't understand how the UK could manage with only voluntary donations nor indeed, why anyone would donate blood free. Altruism seemed an alien concept. With a pint of whole blood having a shelf life of only twenty-one days and packed red cells (often used in emergencies) having only forty-two, maintaining supplies could be a headache.

Caldicott added, 'We are fortunate to have the excellent Medical Laboratories Services company in New York to provide us with what we need. Dr van Lindholm is associated with MLS and they are very reliable, even sending blood products at short notice.'

I wondered if that was the reason van Lindholm was a law unto himself in Ellis Memorial—his labs collected vital blood for them. Likely he profited well, charging more for someone's life-blood than he'd paid for it. But somehow the system felt unsavoury. Different cultural viewpoints, I supposed.

Once we had walked through much of the lab, we found ourselves almost at the edge of the transfusion area where a minor altercation was taking place. Dr van Lindholm was raising his voice at a young woman who looked on the verge of tears. The tall renal specialist loomed over her slight frame just as he had over Carrie. 'Looming' seemed to be one of his specialities. Flicking angrily at a sheet of yellow paper in his hand, he rummaged along benches checking sample labels before finally removing two vials and storming out past us.

The Chief of Labs shook his head. 'Dr van Lindholm likes some patient serum samples to be sent for additional diagnostics to MLS. I fear one of our new lab assistants didn't notice the annotation on the specimen form. Dr van Lindholm has his own ways.'

Which obviously included being rude and arrogant. Yet Dr Caldicott accepted it like Dr Harper did. I thought it outrageous, blood supplier or not.

The Lab Chief next guided me to the microscope bench and beckoned me to look down at some blood film slides. The first showed the numerous and widely varying, undifferentiated white cells of leukaemia. A second offered dense clumps of red cells in a case of sickle cell anaemia. I then had a whistle-stop tour of the hospital's Biochemistry and Pathology departments, followed by Microbiology and Virology. In Microbiology an excited young technician called over Caldicott to look at a slide under his microscope. When I peered down the eyepiece following Caldicott, I saw a slide teeming with tiny bacteria.

The technician looked pleased with himself. 'Treponema pallidum, sir. Syphilis if I'm not mistaken?'

The Lab Chief agreed. 'Yes, indeed. We don't see it as much nowadays, thanks to Penicillin. But it's still about.'

As we moved on, I heard the young man turned to chortle to his neighbour. 'This'll be from a Black whore I bet!' Lifting a lab form, he read out clinical details, ' "Query Syphilitic chancre of vulva". Yep, I'm right. Sample is from one Nida Hardman. Great name for a hooker!' While jerking back in his chair laughing, he almost overbalanced. I wished he had.

'Thomas!' The Chief spun round to glare. 'This isn't a bar! Do not comment on things you know nothing about. She could have got it from a philandering husband for all you know. If you can't be professional this may not be the career for you.'

The boy went crimson. I was shocked at his comments but they weren't the only racial (and misogynistic) slurs I would hear in my time at Ellis Memorial.

We retired to a sitting room just off the office for coffee, that essential episodic stimulant for medics of all kinds. Caldicott re-counted the US career path to becoming a Haematologist or Bio-chemist. As the Senior Lab medics all needed both medical *and* scientific qualifications, the length of training was brutal. One to cross off my list.

Caldicott talked of the problems of running labs, highlighting cost control and the importance of gaining income from tests gen-erated outside the hospital, especially by processing samples from private medical and surgical offices. As well as insurers, Medicaid paid for tests but he was of the view that the system was poorly policed and could lead doctors to order 'blood panels' (i.e., bat-teries of tests) which were often unnecessary. I thought more of him for saying this, as more tests meant more money for his lab. He also complained about the risk of 'double billing' which I didn't exactly understand but whose existence had caused the hospital to be involved in a damaging government investigation. Thankfully, no evidence of wrongdoing on the part of Ellis Memorial had been discovered. He also told me the labs were open from 7 a.m. to midnight, seven days a week. The hours that staff worked seemed onerous. The Lab Chief himself was always on call and individual specialists were responsible for their divisions. It was especially hectic first thing in the morning when the routine bloods arrived from the different hospital Floors and around 3 p.m. when private physicians' offices closed and couriered in their samples. Caldicott said staffing was lighter on weekends. 'Though we always have some people in on Sunday mornings for Dr Mendoza's patients.'

I never asked then why one particular doctor had Sunday morning patients. I was up to my ears in data and needed fresh air. Eventually, just before five, Caldicott shook my hand, I thanked him profusely for his time, and returned to the Nurses' Home.

Later I wished I'd asked what his take was on Mendoza's Sunday morning surgery sessions. And enquired what type of extra diagnostic tests van Lindholm needed from another lab? Might have saved a lot of time and angst. But it's easy to be wise after events.

~~~

Next morning, Tuesday, my rota had me assigned to a Surgical Floor. In Ellis Memorial there were no 'wards', only Floors. I found myself following Hiro, our Japanese guitarist. His rotation involved ER and the Surgical Floor. The lad was affable and amiable, although his sense of humour took some getting used to. He laughed at his own jokes which I often didn't get. Neither did most of the patients but I thought they appreciated his efforts. He did try very hard.

After letting me clerk in a couple of pre-op patients, he critiqued my efforts kindly, highlighting omissions, then suggested I just go to chat with some of the post-op ones while he assisted at a procedure. I gladly went, not fancying any more time in the operating room.

Working my way along the rooms, I saw each patient for a quarter of an hour or so, looking at their charts and asking about their illnesses and surgery. Everyone seemed pleased to talk with me. Hospital can be boring. I noted some patients had TVs, others not. I surmised they might involve an extra charge not covered by Medicaid. There was also a differentiation in garb: non-TV patients were more likely to be in hospital gowns than silk pyjamas.

In the last room I found a young woman lying back on two pillows. Her brow was damp and her thick wavy blue-black hair was in need of a brush. Breathing through dilated nostrils, she had her eyes closed and was obviously in great discomfort. I lifted her chart to find her name, intending to go fetch a nurse to see if she was written up for analgesics but as I was about to open the door it swung inwardly at me to admit a small, deeply tanned man in his late forties or early fifties. His skin was oddly taut over his cheeks, his eyes deep set, his hair dark, possibly oiled, and his beard was a small central, tufty affair. He drew to mind a portrait I'd once seen of Christopher Columbus, although obviously this chap didn't have a frilly ruff under his chin. His fashionably long-collared shirt sat open to expose a gold medallion on a hairy chest and his white coat was curiously styled and fitted, unlike the usual unstructured US doctors' ones. He approached the girl and looked at the bottom of her bed then around the room, presumably in search of her chart which I was holding in my hand. Seeing me standing behind the door, he looked surprised, then annoyed. He abruptly snatched the clipboard from my grasp.

'How did you get in here? No one speaks to my patients except my nurses. You're one of those foreign clerks Harper's taken on, aren't you?'

I nodded dumbly.

He turned to the patient. 'Carmela, so, are we happy?'

The woman looked anything but, for some reason said nothing, though I thought her jaw did move as if contemplating speech. She was anxiously wringing a paper tissue in her right hand.

I butted in. 'She's in a lot of pain.'

He shrugged. 'It's to be expected. Removing renal stones can be painful.' He turned to her. 'We'll give you some painkillers to take home. Let me see the wound.'

Roughly, he rolled her towards him onto her right side and removed the dressing from her left flank to expose a drainage tube that I hadn't noticed. It was connected to a vacuum bottle on the floor that appeared empty. I had moved away from him to stand at the other side of the bed and he looked up at me, commanding, 'Why don't you pull that out? Good practice. Come on!'

I looked around the room but couldn't see sterile gloves or a dressing pack with forceps to use as clamps, all of which I knew were required for the procedure to remove this kind of drain. He couldn't seriously intend that I use non-sterile bare hands? I was saved by the door opening to admit a senior nurse carrying a steel tray with a packet of sterile gloves, a dressing pack and a bottle of antiseptic.

He glared sideways at her, demonstrating to me how bloodshot his eyes were. 'Who are you? Where is Samantha?'

'Your nurse is on a break, Dr Mendoza. I saw you come in and decided you'd likely need these.' She indicated her burdens. He tutted.

At the sink she quickly scrubbed her hands, elbowed the taps off and put on gloves. Even though the nurse was gentle in removing the drain, Carmela winced. In minutes, the nurse had swabbed the red tender wound and applied a clean dressing. Re-wrapping the instruments in the old pack for re-sterilization, the nurse discarded the used tube and soiled gauze swabs into a lidded yellow hazard bin and picked up the empty drainage bottle from the floor.

Mendoza stood silent and sniffing until she'd finished then turned to the patient. 'Right, you can go home. You may shower but not have a bath until your wound is checked next Saturday. That's it.' His hand was on the door handle when Carmela finally found her voice.

'Doctor, what about the money?'

'That's in hand. You'll be hearing from us. Full settlement.'

After he left, the nurse tried to make the patient comfortable back on her pillows, although I could see she anxiously looked from the door to the nurse and back several times.

The nurse patted her hand. 'He's gone. Don't worry, Mrs Gomez. Best you get some rest before I call your brother. I'll go get you some painkillers.'

Something about Carmela Gomez suggested to me she'd had a hard time, even before this surgery. The woman's chart said she was thirty-three but she looked older. There were many lines round her tired eyes and she looked as sad as she did sore. It wasn't for me to enquire into her story, although I wondered why, since she wore a wedding ring, her next of kin wasn't her husband but a brother? Was she a widow? And most curiously of all, what had Mendoza meant by 'Full Settlement'?

Intrigued, I went outside to the desk to look for her case record but couldn't find it in the trolley. I flipped through them all a second time.

'Where is Mrs Gomez's case sheet?' I asked.

'Dr Mendoza keeps some patient's case sheets in Dr van Lindholm's office upstairs. We mostly write in the nursing notes. If we need to add something to the medical records, we contact him or Dr van Lindholm. Or sometimes he sends the medical summer clerk Frankie. They've all got keys. It's something to do with his charity, I think.'

'What charity?'

'Sativa. It helps poor patients. Van Lindholm holds fundraisers for it. Most of Dr Mendoza's Sunday charity patients are only in for 48 hours—to keep down costs, I imagine. It's the same with his nurses, usually only on Sunday till Tuesday evening each week. Though as far as they're concerned...' She looked me in the eye and smiled ruefully. 'Stunning looking women they may be, and the

121

office assures me they are qualified, but frankly, I do wonder where he gets them! Anyway, in the main, the patients are Hispanics and Blacks.' Leaving her comments dangling as if their ethnicity explained everything, she busied herself logging Carmela's medicines onto the Kardex and dispensing pills from a trolley bottle into a little plastic cup. As she set off to deliver it, she started humming a tune. Odd. She didn't seem at all concerned by the irregularities of the practice of Dr Juan Mendoza.

But over the rest of the day, I thought it curiouser and curiouser. Dr Juan Mendoza looked to be as abruptly dismissive towards everyone as Dr van Lindholm. Neither looked like they cared whom they offended, staff or patient. Renal physician Dr van Lindholm aggressively took samples from the hospital's lab and sent them elsewhere. We'd also heard him demand that Medical Chief Dr Harper employ special nurses for his 'friend' Dr Juan Mendoza who admitted patients only at weekends, kept scant records and spoke to them like dirt. And as for Frankie, so often seen with van Lindholm, where did he fit in? But to my mind in all this, the worst offence was medallion surgeon Mendoza's disregard for sterility. Asking me to remove a drainage tube without asking if I knew how to or providing sterile gloves? Ye Gods, what was the story here? I definitely needed to pump Frankie.

Chapter Thirteen
Victims

Tuesday evening was spent in more pleasant circumstances: a drive-in movie. I doubted it'd catch on in rainy Britain, but sitting in a car with popcorn and a handsome young man's arm around you was fine by me. The movie was *Live or Let Die*. John said most summer drive-in movies shown were, like this Bond film, a few years old. But they still attracted many young folk to the field above the town. Though I'd gathered watching the movie wasn't the main purpose of the night out. That was making out. Understandable.

We did have some conversation. I chided John about his ignorance in thinking Sean Connery was Irish. And argued with him. He disagreed with my opinion that Connery would've been better sticking to selling milk in Edinburgh as he couldn't act himself out of a paper bag. But our squabble didn't last. There were more pleasurable things to do.

I suspect Laura and Coop, parked behind us, had a similarly good evening. We were home long before they were. I was still a good girl. But not as good as I'd been.

~~~

Back in the hospital on Wednesday morning we were in a now familiar routine: seeing patients, learning about procedures. An unremarkable day apart from the conversation I overheard in the Coffee Shop mid-afternoon.

Drs Van Lindholm, Mendoza and some other specialists were discussing the harassed nature of their lives. One doc complained he never saw his children except at weekends. Another moaned he couldn't find the time to enjoy flying in his new single-engine plane. Lindholm laughed.

'I've sold mine Wes. It's a waste of cash if you can't go up every weekend. You can hire great planes quite reasonably when you need them from Teterboro. I'll give you my man Dino's number. Dino Laurentis. Great pilot. Always has a couple of planes ready to go.'

'Wes' discussed types of planes that meant nothing to me. His voice was affected and drawling with a vibrating, irritating, nasal twang like Katherine Hepburn's. He eventually concluded, 'Yeh, maybe for us planes aren't worthwhile toys, Elias. But I see you've splashed out on new wheels. How's the Roadster?'

I disengaged from my eavesdropping at van Lindholm's detailed high tech bragging in answer to Wes which merged into a voluble criticism of Nixon's Gold Standard policy (whatever that was).

Turning to my student companions, I found Coop was on a more mundane subject: what would we do at the weekend? I was now up for most things. Though I'd probably draw the line at a flight in a plane piloted by van Lindholm...

~~~

On Thursday I surprised myself by brooding on philosophical matters. During term time at university, my every waking moment seemed to be spent worrying about getting through the work mountain. This summer gave welcome respite, time for taking stock. I came to realise that, despite amazing medical advances, especially in the States, doctors still faced many conditions we couldn't help. On the Floor that morning were two new arrivals from Intensive Care that Hiro had clerked in at dawn as the unit had been desperate for beds. He asked me to interview them and report my conclusions which were that in both cases, they needed cures that could never be.

The first was twenty-one-year-old Nick. He'd been at a weekend party in a friend's house without parental supervision. What happened reinforced my concerns about Coop's proposed gathering. Nick and his pals had been drinking all day and doing 'stuff' (unspecified, but according to him, "No worse than weed"). In the early hours, he'd dived into the pool, stoned. Sadly, he'd chosen the shallow end. The consequences were devastating fracture dislocations of cervical vertebrae five to seven. With the resultant damaged spinal cord, he'd initially required ventilation as his chest muscles couldn't function, but two weeks on, was miraculously breathing by himself.

Unfortunately, apart from slight tingling in his left little and ring fingers, he now had no sensation below the neck. And no muscle power apart from a slight ability to move one shoulder. He'd been transferred to our Floor to see if Dr Mendoza could do some procedure to drain his kidneys, which had also been damaged in the dive. I was surprised to learn Mendoza did occasionally see patients on weekdays. Nick's condition was seriously long-term, probably permanent. What kind of medical insurance, I wondered, could pay for indefinite twenty-four-hour care? And unlike Frankie's RTA woman (who at least had potential funds from a driver she could sue if found) this guy only had himself to blame. Unless he could sue his friend's family for having the pool? Or his weed supplier? I'd already sussed Americans were keen on litigation. It was a fairly frequent topic in the coffee room.

From reading Nick's case notes, I knew that he was unlikely to walk again. Yet here he was, joking crudely about the catheter in his bladder and the enemas he needed to "shit bricks!" as he chatted cheerfully to me about his family, his local league football prowess and ambition to be a lawyer like his "Pop". Although I thought this was surely a pipe dream now, I remembered Jon Baker's teaching in St Mungo's ITU back in Glasgow and didn't say what I thought. Nick still had hope and, ironically, a girlfriend with a degree in Physiotherapy. He was confident that between them they could conquer the world. I wondered if she'd last the duration.

While in my heart I was dreading the day I'd have to tell a patient there was no hope, I left Nick with a promise, vowing to source some of the Oreo ice cream he craved. I hadn't a clue where I'd get it but hoped Jess would know.

Next door to Nick was another tragic patient. She was lying in bed at an odd angle facing the window but turned on hearing me close the door. Despite being quite dopey, she greeted me with a broad smile and tried to sit up.

'Oh, hi, Scottish friend! Fancy meeting you here. Say, can you pass me a drink?'

With her bruised face and tangled messy blonde hair, it took me a moment to recognise it was Kitty from the local A&P store.

While filling a glass from the water jug at the bedside, I deduced the reason for her odd posture. I could only see one leg and foot under the bedcoverings: her left. Her right lower leg was absent. I knew immediately that Kitty must be the hit and run victim who'd been attracting so much attention in the hospital. To enable her to drink, I had to half-cradle her head and support her back: her bandaged right hand and lacerated arm were too shaky to hold the glass and her left arm and hand were encased in a plaster. After she'd drained the glass, I gently let her sink back onto the pillows.

'Thanks. I needed that. But God, I need my meds again too. The headache's back.' She raised her mobile right forearm to her brow.

'I'll go ask.'

'And could you tell them that if that nice policeman who came in before wants to come back, I've remembered something. And maybe could you also find out if Brad's phoned and when he's coming in?'

I assumed Brad was her boyfriend. She couldn't know he'd been arrested. Again, here I didn't say anything, only murmured reassuringly, 'Right. I'll go get you painkillers and ask.'

She closed her eyes.

Back out at the desk, the nurse was on the phone so I skimmed Kitty's case sheet.

Kitty Gerber, age 24, Shop Assistant and Fitness Trainer. Road Traffic Accident victim at Brunsfield Park. Suspected Hit and Run. Found 7am Sunday by dog walker. Unconscious. Massive blood loss. Hypovolaemic shock. Degloving trauma right leg. Severe compound fracture tibia and fibula with considerable bone and tissue loss. Poorly perfused with non-viable tissue below fracture site necessitating below-knee amputation. X-rays show minor skull, rib and left forearm fractures. Lacerations to right hand and forearm sutured...

When the nurse finished her call, I asked for Kitty's painkillers. She consulted the girl's med card and dispensed an oxymorphone tablet. Though I didn't know it by name, the suffix 'morphone' told me it was obviously an opiate. She had a junior nurse check the tablet and Kardex with her, then despatched the girl to administer it.

When Hiro returned from OR, I told him Kitty was asking to speak to the police again and he called switchboard to connect him to the police office. After a short chat, he hung up, telling me they'd be sending someone out after lunch.

'You won't believe it but they asked if we could manipulate the timing of Kitty's pain relief to make her more lucid than she was yesterday. As if! What do they think we are, magicians? She's suffered agony, poor girl. If I could get the guy who left her, I'd kill him.' He slapped his hand on the desk in emphasis. 'How could anyone leave a young woman at the side of the road like that to die like a dog—especially one bleeding out so badly?'

For English being his second language, Hiro's invective was eloquent and emotive. And I had to agree with him.

'I know. How could they not even have called an ambulance anonymously?'

Hiro took her records from me, added a few notes and sat back. 'Did you hear the story that she ran out of her house after an argument with her boyfriend and so he was arrested? Well, that police office just told me they're no longer holding anyone which suggests it wasn't him who did it. Must be that his car wasn't bloody and damaged. Guy on the police desk said they're looking into whether it was deliberate, though. Maybe there was something in that hint Nat got about drug dealing being involved? '

'Oh, surely not? Can't see her shacking up with a low life. She's sweet.'

'The guy hinted it was her Dad who was a dealer.'

'Oh? Anyway, is the guy they took called Brad? If so, she wants to know when he's coming in. I wonder if he knows what room she's in?'

He handed me Kitty's records. 'Why not ring him and ask? If he's next of kin, his number will be in here. I hope he stands by her.' He grunted. 'Lovely girl.'

~~~

In the afternoon, the floor was quiet, so I sat at the desk reading a textbook from the doctors' room. Brad appeared to sit with Kitty just before two policemen arrived who stayed around half an hour. As they came back along the corridor towards me from my left, I heard a noise from the right. Turning, I glimpsed a figure coming from the lifts that suddenly spun around abruptly, re-traced its steps and shot through the nearby door to the stairs. Bizarre behaviour. But then I wasn't that surprised. It was Dr van Lindholm.

'Weird fellow, isn't he?' I said to the scribbling nurse at my side.

'What?' She didn't look up.

'Dr van Lindholm,' I said. The policemen drew level. One nodded at the nurse. 'Thanks for calling us. Miss Gerber has given us valuable information. She's remembered some details about the car and driver.' Looking pleased, they left, hats tucked underneath their arms.

The nurse turned to me. 'What was that you said just now about van Lindholm?'

'Oh, about him being odd. He was coming along here just now but turned on his heel and ran back to the stairs. Funny how he makes me feel uncomfortable. Think it's the way he looks at you. Kind of odd. Creepy, almost.' I shivered.

'Maybe you scared him off!' She laughed. 'You sure it was him? We've no patients of his in here and as far as I know, and we haven't asked for a Renal Med consult today. Maybe he got off at the wrong floor, like he thought this was Med Floor Three?'

I doubted he'd be as daft. He'd know immediately he was on the wrong floor from the wall colours. On this Surgical Floor they were turquoise, on the Medical Floor, peach. I wondered if he had left because he saw me sitting at the desk? Or had it been because he saw the policemen coming? At that point, two patients arrived back simultaneously on trolleys from OR and I was given tasks to do. The rest of the day flew by.

~~~

At tea in the kitchen, I mentioned van Lindholm's 'turnaround' to Laura, who echoed the nurse.

'Well, don't you think he probably just got off at the wrong floor and went back to run down the flight to Medical? You got a thing about him, haven't you?'

'Och, I haven't really. But you've got to admit he's rude and weird. I'm bewildered why Nurse Makkonen fancies him unless it's raw brutality she goes for.'

Laura laughed. 'Some women like a bit of 'rough', I believe! I hear she is tutoring some nurses van Lindholm's brought in for Dr Mendoza. Maybe she'll get lucky by doing him a favour.'

'From the way he ignores her I wouldn't bank on it!'

'Right, Mhairi, tonight. You up for a walk after tea or will we just watch telly? I could do with some slobbing about if I'm honest...'

Before I could answer, Jess came in and I asked her about Oreo ice cream. Suffice to say we drove out to get some. There were hundreds of ice cream varieties in the parlour. After taking some ourselves, we bought several flavours for Nicky and the Medical Floor nurses, who were well chuffed. I agreed with Nicky: Oreo Cream was terrific. I wondered why we Brits hadn't tried putting our similar (almost) Peek Freen Chocolate Bourbons into ice cream?

~~~

On Friday morning when I arrived, there was a sense of unease pervading the Surgical Floor. Groups of nurses stood about whispering. A serious looking policeman was sitting with his arms folded outside Kitty's room.

There had been an intruder in the ward after midnight. They thought he'd been in a few rooms. One patient had reported a missing pocketbook, another odd US term. How had a handbag become a book over here? Another patient had reported a silent figure had opened his room door only to leave again immediately without a word. But when the intruder had entered Kitty's room, she'd been heard to scream. Luckily, a young nurse from the next room had charged in to bravely tackle the man who was forcing a pillow on her face. Succeeding in pulling him off Kitty, the girl had struggled with him but he was bigger and managed to thrust her off before escaping down the stairs. The police were called. Despite the theft from the other room, they'd concluded that it might be Kitty's hit and run driver trying to silence her. The duty policeman made a pout while emphasising the 'Hit' in 'hit and run' implying the road accident had been nothing of the sort but a targeted attack on her specifically.

I thought that stupid. Who'd want to kill a nice young shop worker? And anyway, surely they'd know that by now she would

have described the driver to the police? But the officer was adamant that there had been an article in the local paper about Kitty's
injuries saying that she was in Ellis Memorial. The police were
convinced she'd been attacked by the driver trying to finish her off.

The door sentry policeman stoutly defended this official line.
'Someone wants her dead, sure as Hell. Or at least the hit 'n run
guy has some big reason for not wantin' identified! The Boss's
decided this girl needs protection so we've to be on guard 24/7
till the bastard's caught.'

Rumours electrified the hospital. The commonest one was
indeed that the 'perp' of the smothering attempt was the hit and
run driver. And, in order to know exactly where Kitty was in the
hospital, he must be on staff. Or even be a policeman. Everyone
who'd been on call overnight was being interviewed. How he'd
got in was a big mystery too. Management considered overnight
security tight with all outside doors locked from ten o'clock.

The now well-sedated Kitty was moved to a different room
nearer the nurses' station with her seated guard. At noon I went
in with a nurse to check her obs. Fortunately, her BP, heart rate,
temp and blood pressure were all normal. As she was now wide
awake and keen to talk, I sat down.

'Are you okay?' I asked. Stupid. How could she be?

'Better now I've got a cop at the door. They think it was the
driver trying to finish me off, but I know it wasn't. They didn't
listen. The guy during the night was younger shorter, stockier. I
could see his big shiny white eyes above the bandana thing he had
over his nose and mouth. I never saw his hands but between his
hood edge and the bandana I could see his forehead was definitely
black. The guy that gunned me with his beat-up big car was white,
older and taller. I know I was pretty out of it after he hit me, and
it was very dark with the streetlight shining behind him, but I can
still see his outline walking over to me. He had an older walk, ye

know?' I wasn't sure I did. 'Admit that I didn't get a great look at the driver's face before I passed out, but I reckon I'd know it again.'

I changed the subject. 'How's your head?'

'Drugs are working. Head's the worst when it builds up. Funny jaggy pain in in my foot too, the one that's not even there. Phantom pain, they call it. Say, who'd a thought that, huh? Pain from a non-existent foot. Gonna be tough, but glad I've got Brad to help. He's a star. Poor thing's feelin' guilty 'cos we rowed the other night and I stomped out. Hey, I'll not be doing much of that again, will I, the stompin'?' She laughed almost hysterically. 'Stupid row too. Who cares if he doesn't put out the trash or help in the house?' She smiled sadly. 'He's a better man than my Pa ever was. Keeps better friends too, no low life hangers on, you know?'

Again, I didn't know. What would constitute a low life hanger on? Whatever else he was, my Dad definitely never had any of those! I responded simply. 'That's good.'

'Anyway, they'll get me a new one. Leg, I mean. They say that means a fitting for a mould soon to get a temporary 'prosthesy' thing, or whatever you call it, made. Then it'll be lots of physical therapy. Be back up and running in no time.' She smiled as she closed her eyes to drift off again.

In admiration at her acceptance, albeit likely opiate driven, I left wondering again about the financial implications for Kitty. I thought it unlikely she could resume her job as a fitness instructor, though maybe she'd manage the A&P store. I headed down to meet John in the dining room. It was full of fervent chatter. Nurse Makkonen had been found in a linen cupboard. She would swoon no more in ER.

Chapter Fourteen
ER Drama

At six o'clock in the evening, all the diners knew was that Nurse Makkonen had disappeared sometime after midnight during her overnight shift and her body had been found late morning by a laundry assistant returning clean sheets to an ancillary store. We were debating events with some nurses when Randy rushed in. He could add no details to Nurse Makkonen's death but looked very distressed as he sat down to gobble a plate of food at speed. 'Say, you guys, how'd you like to help out with a bit of clerking in ER tonight? Probably can get you some cash for doing it too. As if it's not bad enough we have police crawling all over us with a dead body in a cupboard, my fellow Resident has buggered off for a supposed family crisis. And seems he's on the police radar for Makkonen, so I guess she didn't die of natural causes. Can't find anyone to pitch in for the evening. I just need help till midnight.'

While shaken on hearing of a murder on hospital premises, John and I felt so sorry for him that we agreed to 'pitch in' from six till twelve. Randy was delighted. Soon however, he had to rush off to answer his pager, taking his can of Coke but leaving half of his food on his plate.

~~~

That night, we worked hard, following the nurses into treatment rooms, taking histories and relaying them to Randy for decisions on treatment or referral to specialists. We had the on-call Orthopaedic Resident trapped in ER practically all evening treating fractures from accidents and assaults. Apart from the police interviewing staff about the death, other officers appeared in a steady stream with victims or waifs and strays. It was jumping, making me wonder if Kitty's attacker mightn't have snuck in via the ER door the night before when it was similarly busy? And had he taken out Nurse Makkonen on the way up to the Surgical Floor? Without a time of death for her there was no way of knowing.

For Kitty, I didn't buy the gossip that it had to be a hospital employee or policeman who'd wanted to kill her. It would have been easy for any assailant to assume Kitty had needed surgery and find the well-signposted Surgical Floor and try a few rooms before finding hers. There was no way of knowing whether her hit and run been by chance or an intended murder by someone connected with her father. Or if Makkonen's demise was linked. We were so busy clerking in patients, running to fetch people and filing notes that we had no time to discuss any of it

Around eleven, the waiting room suddenly cleared and we managed a coffee break. We got ten minutes before a call came warning of a seriously ill patient en route. The minute the screaming ambulance drew up and the doors swung open, two nurses and Randy were up and running alongside the incoming casualty heading towards Trauma One. As usual, the paramedics relayed clinical stats on the patient's condition. The trolley was closely followed by a weeping girl who'd clambered out of the ambulance front seat. A nurse stopped her from entering the examination room.

I took her to a seat in the waiting area. Elena was sixteen and told me her mother had been unwell since hospital discharge three days ago: weak, not eating, fevered and vomiting. Though she'd prevented Elena from seeking medical help, when she'd started shaking and rambling, the girl had phoned 911.

'I'm sure you did the right thing. What was your mother in hospital for?'

She looked at me shyly before answering. 'Kidney stones. They were removed by the surgeon Dr Mendoza.' The girl stared. I realised my jaw must have dropped when she asked abruptly, 'What's wrong?'

'Nothing,' I replied, 'but I think I saw your mum upstairs here on Tuesday. Is Her name Carmela?"

The girl nodded, looking at me intently. 'You're foreign, aren't you?'

'Yes. I'm Scottish, over here working for the summer.' I patted her hand. 'Let me go see what's happening and then I'll come back and let you know, okay?'

'Thanks.' She sat back. Exhausted. And so very young.

I looked at her as I rose and had a thought. Where was her father tonight? Or the uncle whom I knew was to have been phoned to collect Carmela? I had a thought. I turned back. 'Elena, do you have your uncle's phone number?' Puzzled, she nodded and pulled a small diary out of her bag.

The inevitable clipboard woman from the desk was approaching. I hailed her. 'This young girl's mum's in Trauma One. I think she's quite sick. Maybe we should get a responsible relative in?'

'Of course, but first things first.' She sat to quiz Elena. 'Patient's name, date of birth, ethnicity?'

'Carmela Gomez. She was born in Mexico but now she's a US citizen,' answered Elena.

Mrs Clipboard asked, 'Next of kin?'

Elena hesitated. 'My father. Think he's in Ensenada.'

The woman jotted this info down before asking. 'Social Security Number?'

Elena started crying. 'I don't know!'

I put my hand on her forearm as she sat beside Elena. 'Whoa, enough! She's a child. Get the uncle!' I wrote down the number Elena showed me in her diary on a piece of paper as she sat sobbing and handed it to the woman. 'Here, go get him now! Any other details will be in Mrs Gomez's records. She was only discharged on Tuesday.' My heart was racing at my boldness but this child was being bullied and ready to break. But still the wretched Mrs Clipboard persisted in wanting the last word. It seemed forms must be completed at all costs.

'And what insurance does your mother have?'

From her bag, Elena produced a card with a polythene cover. Mrs Clipboard shook her head. 'That's not an insurance company, they're a charity. We'll bill you and then you have to contact them to see if they'll pay.'

Charming. Just what you need to hear when your mum's desperately ill. I now actually grabbed Mrs Clipboard's upper arm and repeated through gritted teeth, 'Get her bloody uncle!'

The woman took off, grumbling. Elena sniffed and managed a weak smile at me.

'Okay, Elena, I'll be back. Stay here.'

I slid into Trauma One where the team were busy. Drip up, EKG machine leads connected, a monitor showing low pO2, low BP and a high heart rate. Randy was issuing orders, bloods were being taken off by a phlebotomist and handed in a bag to John whom Randy addressed tersely, 'Full panel, let's check everything. results stat. Get them faxed.' Seeing me, he waved me over. 'Come. What did the daughter say?'

'Before that, I have to tell you I saw this woman, Carmela Gomez, on Tuesday on Surgical Floor. She's Dr Mendoza's. Was discharged on Tuesday after surgery for renal stones. Her daughter says she's been increasingly sick, fevered, incoherent and eaten nil since discharge.'

'Diagnosis, Dr MacLean?' asked Randy, waving at the beeping monitors. 'I'll add that she's collapsed and unresponsive now.'

'Septicaemic shock?'

'Excellent. Then what now?'

'Antibiotics, fluids, maybe dexamethasone...'

136

'All done. Next step.'

I looked around at the nurses, who'd all paused to watch me. 'Call Dr Mendoza?'

'Correct! Full marks. Hey, Helen, go phone him in. It's his mess. Not the first.'

I remembered the drain removal nonsense. 'And how's the wound? The drain site looked a bit red and she was in a lot of pain on Tuesday. Source of the infection?'

'Good thinking. Look.' He raised Carmela's newly acquired theatre gown and helped by a nurse, removed the dressing on her side.

'Jesus, what a stink. Anaerobic infection, bugs that can breed without oxygen, probably Peptostreptococcus and Clostridium.'

I knew of such bugs well from Glasgow Paddy.

'They can destroy tissues rapidly. Said to be the smell of the trenches in WW1. Oh, this definitely is one for Mendoza! There's a fluctuant abscess here but I'm not lancing it.'

After my experience of the kick-back from lancing a non-smelly boil, I was with him there. This one would need complete riot gear protection. A nurse sprang forward to take swabs and rush off with them. Another sprayed the wound site with antiseptic and put a light gauze over it. The smell of Paddy's leg wafted up again. And again, it stayed with me for days.

But now the door opened and in strode Dr van Lindholm, his usual brusque self, peremptorily demanding, 'What's the story here?'

Randy was bravely hostile. 'This is Dr Mendoza's patient. What's it to do with you?'

'I have his pager. He's in PV. What's the deal?'

Randy shrugged, presumably accepting Mendoza must be in PV, wherever that was.

'Carmela Gomez, 33, five days status post kidney surgery. Arrived via 911 thirty minutes ago. Septicaemic Shock. Lung creps.

Likely got pneumonia as well. She's a mess. Had dexamethasone and iv antibiotics. Bloods off. X-ray coming. Foul anaerobic wound abscess with spreading cellulitis.' Randy was standing erect, eye to eye with Lindholm, holding out his blue gloved, clenched hands in an almost pugilistic stance. He looked muscular, fit, imposing. And in my view was correct in glaring at van Lindholm and challenging him. 'She needs a surgeon, not a medical internist. I don't think Chief Harper would approve of you seeing this patient. Not sure it's even legal...'

I knew covering for a colleague in a different speciality wouldn't happen at home. Surgeons worked in teams, in rotas separate from physicians. But here I'd noticed specialists usually worked independently, every man for himself, only occasionally collaborating. Randy had told us they rarely took holidays or had friends to cover. Perhaps Mendoza had no surgical friends?

Van Lindholm's tone would have cracked ice. 'That, Doctor Resident, is none of your business. But if this woman has no insurance, as I suspect is the case, and needs surgery, I'll arrange transfer to St Thomas. It has a charitable critical unit. Sativa will help.'

Randy looked furious. 'I think she's too ill to move. We could get Newton...'

But the door had already swung to a close behind Lindholm. Randy was swearing as I sidled out to speak to Elena whom I found finishing an iced tea and a packet of sandwiches.

'I'm diabetic,' she said, as if in apology. 'I took my insulin just now as I missed it earlier and got these from the machine.'

If she was diabetic she definitely needed adult supervision. 'That's fine. Have they called your uncle?'

'Yes, but he'll be a while.'

'Okay, Elena. Your mum's holding her own but she's being taken to St Thomas hospital for an abscess operation and so they can look after her in a critical care unit if necessary. Dr Lindholm says some charity will pay.'

'Yes, Sativa. I tried to tell that woman we've been told they'd pay for care since...' She stopped, looking over at Mrs Clipboard, currently becoming increasingly voluble while speaking to a patently stoned young man with a bloodied hand. The waiting room was busy again. Elena stood up. 'Sorry, I need to go to the washroom. Do you know where there's a trash can for these?' She held aloft her drinks can and sandwich wrapper.

'Let me take them. You go on.' Walking across the hall to the bin meant passing the doctor's room. Through the partially open door came an unmistakable voice.

'It's a shit fest, Juan. You've fucked this one up. I'll get her to St Thomas's but you'll need to watch it...' He paused. Obviously, the other end was speaking. 'Goddam it you better! No wonder you lost your licence in Los Angeles. If the Board here finds out it's curtains for the whole caboodle. Pack of cards...' Another pause then, 'Damn straight, I was! Yeah, and I'll use my MRT ambulance.' He went silent for a moment before talking volubly, 'You're damn right, I'll fix it. As usual. Maybe I'll even end it. Enjoy your fuckin' vacation!' He slammed down the phone. I heard the clicks as he re-dialled and then his peremptory voice. 'St Thomas's? This is Dr Elias van Lindholm. I have a patient for you.'

I crept past the door to dispose of Elena's rubbish. On her return she told me about her other health problems including asthma, recently better controlled with new inhalers. But the diabetes was still difficult though she'd had it for four years. Watching her diet and checking her sugars she found irksome. And she hated needles.

After a long hour, a blue ambulance arrived at the ER door and its crew trundled a gurney into Trauma One. We'd seen van Lindholm return into the room after Randy and John left to attend a stabbing in Trauma Two. As he'd passed us, the specialist told Elena she couldn't go in the ambulance but could phone St Thomas's later to get her mother's room number. No explanation of her condition, no emotion showed, no consoling words. And ignoring my family's swearing taboo, I decided he really was a bloody bastard. No other word to describe him.

We followed Carmela out to the ambulance bay, watching two attendants collapse down her trolley for loading. Her drip bottle was set on a low stand that just fitted into the limited headroom. The ambulance looked much less practical and capacious than our UK ones. One nurse had to get into the front passenger seat. Suddenly, van Lindholm rushed past us to bend forward into the open ambulance door. I saw the drip tubing move as he spoke to the nurse, although his back was towards us. As he stepped back and straightened up, I noticed he had something in his right hand that he closed his palm over before putting it into his trouser pocket. Unlike other visiting medics in ER, he hadn't even bothered donning a white coat for his visit. He gave some final instructions to the nurse at the trolley, a pretty black girl who looked very serious. Dr Van Lindholm turned away to disappear around the corner, presumably to the doctor's car park.

The ambulance was a sleek, shiny dark blue vehicle emblazoned with a white MRT logo and caduceus on the side and a Red Cross with 'Medical Recovery Transport' underneath on the tailgate. As it sped off down the drive with blue light flashing, Elena started sobbing. I put my arm around her, uttering the timeless platitude, 'I'm sure she's going to be fine.' She seemed to droop as I squeezed her shoulders encouragingly. 'Come on, pet, let's go back in and wait for your uncle.'

Inside, the rest of our chat was revealing and poignant. Elena talked rapidly, sometimes lapsing into Spanish, about her home life and her mother's struggle since her father left with a 'puta' when she and her brother were only four and two. Her father had possibly returned to his hometown of Ensenada though there'd been no contact or financial support since. Her little brother, Diego, had died at eight after some gut infection that sounded like

E.coli. To make ends meet, her mum had three jobs, cleaning and waitressing. She and Elena sounded more like sisters than mother and daughter, doing everything together. Uncle Raoul was her father's brother, but he'd disowned his philandering sibling and had tried to take care of Carmela and Elena, even though he had a family of his own.

Raoul arrived. He was a medium height, edgy, thin Hispanic gentleman in a crumpled pink-striped shirt and the fashionable baggy ripped blue jeans I'd noticed a lot since arriving in New Jersey. He hugged Elena, listened to my story and said he'd take his niece to her home to collect her meds and some clothes before taking her to stay with him until her mother was better. I suggested he confirm his contact details with reception.

As they walked off to do this, I was struck by Elena's clothes and bag. In the heat of the drama, I hadn't taken in that they were spanking new. And expensive. White Ralph Lauren denim shorts, red polo shirt, pristine white soled sneakers and a swanky watch. I knew the logo. Were they from Uncle Raoul's generosity? But if so, why not pay for insurance for his brother's family? Hmm. Those bell bottom jeans of his might even be designer too. But what did I know?

I worked for an hour writing up notes and speaking to new arrivals. Then another Resident appeared to relieve Randy. And us. It was almost midnight and I was shattered. John walked me to the Home where we sat on the bench in the front garden for a snog: our routine now. I was definitely falling for John Coulter with a clatter. When we paused, I leaned into his left shoulder and started telling him about Dr van Lindholm's call with Mendoza.

'He actually referred to Dr Mendoza having lost his licence in Los Angeles. Can you be struck off in one State and work in another?'

'Well, if you don't tell them, maybe...I mean, I dunno what the comms are like between State Boards. But you'd need balls to pull that off. Would be a risky business.'

'And I don't understand why Lindholm sent that woman to another hospital. Is it true it's a charity one?'

'I think St Thomas's is heavily subsidised by donations. But it's away over at the State boundary. Risky trip for her.'

'Can van Lindholm do anything he likes? No one ever seems to challenge him.'

'Huh,' said John. 'He's certainly a bit of a loose cannon, just like his friend Mendoza.'

'And van Lindholm said he'd get one of 'his' ambulances, like it was his company. Could that be right?'

'Sure, many American docs have fingers in lots of pies. Ambulances, labs, pharma companies, elderly facilities.'

I was appalled. 'But isn't that a conflict of interest?'

'Well, I know you have to put your connections to pharma companies, for example, on research papers but don't think there's any law against running para-medical stuff. Never thought about it. Might ask Dad.'

'What does your dad do?'

'He's a DA in New York. A District Attorney.'

'Sounds impressive. I've only heard about DAs from Perry Mason! And another odd thing from tonight, that woman's daughter, Elena, was wearing new designer clothes, very expensive ones. Yet she said they were 'real poor'. How could she afford them?'

'Shoplifting? Wouldn't be surprised. Or knock offs, that's like, fakes. But hey, chill. That's enough thinking. It's late and you look shattered.'

'And Nurse Makkonen- I didn't like her much but it's awful. Who would kill her?'

'Enough. We can't do anything about it. Here,' he cupped my face in his hands to kiss me. Long and slow. My thoughts disintegrated into nothingness. Nuzzling my neck, he whispered in my ear. 'I wanna tell you something,' before moving back to face me.

I looked into his soft blue eyes and managed to mumble, 'What?'

He gave a huge smile, took my hand and kissed it. 'I love you, Mhairi MacLean. And I've never, ever, said that before to any girl in the whole wide world.'

I felt teary. There was more kissing. We went to bed very late. Separately, sadly.

Chapter Fifteen

Living it Up & Losing a Patient

On Saturday evening, John and I went for burgers with Laura, Coop, Jess, and Randy. To my delight, Jess and Randy had been on a couple of dates since the party. We heard lurid tales of High Schools in New York and Costa Rica. But eventually, the chat palled. John and I felt we had to bring up the *Carmela Affair* and its attendant *Incriminating Phone Call*.

Coop was horrified. 'Jesus, John, that's big league! Mendoza got the boot in California? Guess the Board doesn't know. What are you goin' to do about it?'

'I'll speak to the old man tomorrow night, seek advice. He's at the beach this weekend. Not sure I want to involve Mhairi, though. Remember we only know because she overheard the call through a door.'

'Wonder what he got done for?' mused Randy. 'Not washing his hands?'

Although everyone laughed, this was a deadly serious situation that we'd become embroiled in, one that could turn nasty and legal. John was quite right. I didn't want to end up being stuck with police statements or returning to the US for court appearances. Dad would be horrified.

'Who knows, Coop? But Mendoza does looks like a twitcher, doesn't he?' Before I enquired lamely what bird watching had to do with anything, John expanded his comment, 'I mean, sometimes he seems high, sometimes edgy—maybe coming down? I think he's defo a druggie. Wonder if the suspension was drug related? California is the strictest of Boards, I believe. But Dad can easy check. It's kinda 'watch this space' folks.' He tapped the side of his nose conspiratorially before giving me a quick kiss on the lips. 'Don't worry, babe. I'll fix it.' He squeezed me tight.

Coop looked at his watch. 'Right guys, we should get goin'. Are you gals all ready for tomorrow? Bathers of course for the pool. You'll get towels. Picnic from Ma should be ace. The dining room meals are pretty high end but mostly fancy shit. A picnic's the thing!"

With everything going on, I'd almost forgotten Coop's invite to the Country Club. 'Oh, yes, looking forward to it.' I really was. Everything had been a bit heavy. Except for John's declaration last night, of course.

Coop turned to Jess and Randy. 'You two want to come too?'

'Sorry, I can't.' Jess looked pointedly at me. 'Family stuff to-morrow.' I wondered if she'd pluck up courage to tell Randy about her little Barbara.

Randy also declined Coop's invitation. 'Be studying, sadly. Exams coming. Need to make use of every spare minute I can get.' At this, he looked shyly at Jess. I wondered if he'd decided any free social time he had would preferably be spent with her.

'Please yourselves, you'd all be real welcome.' Coop settled the bill. We contributed to a generous tip. The servers deserved this one. John and I headed for a moonlight walk in Brunsfield Park. Unlike our parks in the UK, it wasn't locked at night. There were several spaced-out residents already sleeping on benches, but we knew a secluded spot of our own.

Next day at one, following a loud toot outside the Home, Laura and I found John sitting in a splendid new car. As we appeared with our bags, he sprang out, threw them in the boot and opened the car doors for us with a flourish. 'What d'ya think?' Grinning widely, he waved at the shiny silver car with tail fins. 'Early birthday present from my wonderful Grandma Coulter. A Buick, no less!

She's a Women's Caucus star in D.C. You gotta meet the woman, gals, you'll love her!'

I knew about the Women's Caucus from Jess and was getting used to everything being abbreviated in the US but wasn't sure about the D.C. so asked, 'Sorry, what's D.C?'

John laughed as he turned a corner, alarmingly steering only with the palm of one hand. 'District of Columbia. Often used as abbreviation for Washington, our capital city.'

'Oh, right. By the way, another abbreviation I've heard but don't know what it stands for—P.V.?'

'*Per vaginam*.' He threw his head back to roar with laughter. 'D'you not know that stands for vaginal examination, baby?'

'I know *that* p.v., you idiot, but I want to know where the place PV is that Van Lindholm told Randy that Dr Juan Mendoza was. You were off with Carmela's bloods. Doubt he'd have said the surgeon was up a woman's ...'

'Jacksie,' finished Laura from the back seat, falling about with laughter.

John frowned as he turned into a long curving drive flanked by pristine lawns and well-trimmed hedges.

I wasn't being side tracked. 'But PV- where is it?'

'Probably Puerto Vallarta, it's a Mexican resort on the west coast. Might even be where Mendoza's from? I've heard a lot of folks have been buying high-end properties there recently. It's a cool, up and coming place. Good climate. Sunny but usually has a nice breeze, or so they say.'

He was now parking beside a Rolls Royce at the front of an imposing two-storey building of fine pink brick that had sparkling white paintwork. Dormer windows poked out of a slate-grey roof and a series of imposing white cement pillars ran along the front. Impressive. Coop was waiting to greet us at the top of the steps.

After signing us in at a desk worthy of a very top-notch hotel (or as I imagined one might be), Coop took us on a conducted tour. There were two restaurants, one casual, one smart, a bar, an indoor pool, gym, locker rooms, tennis courts, an outdoor pool with more changing rooms and two championship-level golf courses. Membership fees were eye watering. Coop's family had been members since its founding in 1886. He obviously loved the way everyone greeted him by name, clasped his hand and clapped him on the shoulder.

By the pool, he'd already selected space for us. Under a dazzling white parasol was a circular table with six seats fitted with comfy blue cushions. Nearby six loungers were already festooned with matching blue towels.

Laura looked round appreciatively. 'This is lovely Coop.'

The pool area was beginning to fill up with families and couples. Some left bags on the loungers and headed for the restaurant. Coop pointed to a wicker hamper and a lidded plastic chest with a handle. 'Lunch from Mum. I'll get us some drinks. How about fizz?' He waved a hand in the air. A waiter in a black T-shirt and shorts appeared wearing an odd little apron.

Almost before we sat down, other young waiters arrived with two bottles of sparkling Californian rosé wine, glasses and a tray of olives. One poured each of us a glass of wine, the other went off to return with ice buckets, a jug of water and water glasses. The wine pourer removed the first dead bottle and, acknowledging Coop's lunch paraphernalia (obviously, a regular feature of his arrival), asked if there was anything else we needed?

'No thanks, Marvin, I've got everything. We're good!'

We sat at the table and Coop served. I loved it: sun, pool, fantastic food and John at my side, sitting close. This was life as it should be lived!

We were served several things we'd never had before: bell peppers, roasted eggplant and avocado were what I remember. And discovering cilantro is coriander. On occasion, John fed me forkfuls of stuff that I was wary of—but all were delicious. Laura and I had never laughed as much. We ate mountains, drank copious amounts of rosé and moved on to white when the boys turned to beer.

Several times we had to stand up to be introduced to passersby and were urged to speak in order to demonstrate our 'cute accents'. But we didn't mind. Coop's friends and acquaintances were charming and polite. That especially struck me: the place had a marked air of sophistication, people in holiday mood, relaxing and chilling. Peaceful. Some laughter, no rowdiness. As the afternoon wore on, we were persuaded to go and change for a dip in the pool.

I came out wearing a loose white shirt over my new red M&S swimsuit—as chosen by Laura. I was wary of swimming as I'd eaten so much and decided I'd wait a bit before going in. Kids were frolicking in the smaller pool. Coop was already swimming up and down the main one. John appeared. My heart flipped.

How tanned and fit did he look in his neat, tight, blue-and-white striped swimming costume? I was feeling sensations of pleasure that were extraordinarily intense and unsuccessfully trying to convince myself it was the wine.

Laura nudged me and whispered. 'I see what Jess meant when she said John was "ripped". God, look at those pecs!' She winked and made a suggestive, very unfeminine face.

I watched him dive in from the side. Unbelievably, this was the boy who'd declared he was in love with me! 'He swam for his school,' was my only comment to Laura as I tore my eyes away to massage my pale flabby arms with suncream. I lay down on my sunbed, resolutely looking heavenward, and closed my eyes. But I could still see that body. And felt, what? God, it must be lust. I tried of think of something else but couldn't.

Suddenly it was raining. Opening my eyes, I discovered it wasn't rain, it was pool water. Being flicked over me by John. He pushed himself easily up out of the pool, knelt at my lounger and kissed me. I opened my eyes and melted into his. Then he spoiled it.

'Come on, lazy bones—get in that pool!'

Lifting me up bodily, he threw me in.

When we returned to the Nurses' Home in a cab, Jess was sitting in the kitchen with a coffee reading a nursing journal.

'Hi, guys! How was your day?' Noting Laura's silly grin, she laughed. 'Say, did I miss somethin' or what? You guys been on the liquor?'

Giggling, Laura flopped down. 'The Country Club was ace, Jess, you should've come.'

'Oh, well, had to take Barbara to the mall for shoes and stuff. When I was there I realised I haven't taken you shopping yet, have I? We should go up city soon. Howzabout next Saturday? I'm off. Hey, we could take Babs too. She loves the PATH.'

After PV, I was scared to enquire about initials but Laura happily asked, 'What path?'

'The train from Jersey stations into New York is the PATH, *The Port Authority Trans-Hudson* trainline. Around since the 1860s and called different things over the years. My Dad's the rail buff, he'll tell you proper. But recently they've knocked down the old Hudson Terminal and opened up a new station in Manhattan at the new-fangled World Trade Centre. Quite somethin', I hear. We should get off at it, have a scout round then head up to Greenwich Village. There's heaps to see in New York. You've been to Times Square, haven't you? But did you do Radio City? Or Filene's Basement for bargains? My fave store! Say, you guys down for this?'

Though I'd have said, 'up for this,' I assumed she meant the same thing. 'Grand,' I answered, slugging a glass of water and leaving Laura to hear about the joys of New York. From her glazed look, I doubted she'd recall any of it later.

I took a leisurely shower, not the 'lick and promise' quickie I'd had at the Club. After washing and conditioning with Sabrina's products, my hair was now a joy to deal with. (Apart from the home's temperamental hair dryer cutting out every five minutes). I was pleased John loved the shorter look, said I looked like starlet Ann-Margret. Ah, John. Sensual waves of pleasure were regular experiences now, even when he was absent. Totally amazing.

I wrote a dutiful 'Week Two' letter home about learning lots and meeting lovely people, flopped into bed and slept all night.

~~~

Monday morning saw me chomping Cheerios in the kitchen with Jess's *American Journal of Nursing* propped up on the milk jug. Two nurses rose to leave, abandoning their dishes on the draining board as Laura appeared in her dressing gown, hair wild, cheeks mascara-smudged and face pained. She groaned at the noise of my bubbling kettle.

'I'll never drink again. My head's exploding.'

Another young nurse arrived, added to the draining board mountain and laughed at Laura. 'Oh boy, you look like you need some Advil—heavy night? Been there, sister!' Opening a cupboard, she took out a packet of pills. 'Here, take some of these. A couple for later too!'

As Laura had her eyes shut, I took the packet. Advil, I saw, was Ibuprofen. 'Thanks. I'll get her to take one with some breakfast.'

'Yep. Good idea. Best taken with food. See you!' The girl left, banging the front door as she went. Laura winced and muttered, 'Jesus!' before sitting down with her head in her hands.

Taking a tablet out, I gave Laura one with water, replaced the pill box on its shelf and made her a cup of coffee with sugar. I'd read that hypoglycaemia exacerbated hangovers. She took it mindlessly and groaned again.

'I should've stopped when you did!' Exhaling deeply and melo-dramatically, she moaned, 'It was Coop going off to speak to that old girlfriend. I mean, he was gone ages and I got mad and swigged a couple of glasses in a hurry, that's all. Not sure I remember coming home, though.'

'Och, that girl didn't mean a thing. He's just a sociable lad. Coop was all over you later!'

'Oh, I expect you're right. But my, what about you and John!? Hey, I saw all that crackling sexual tension! It's getting hot, isn't it? You done it yet?' She squinted up at me.

'No, as it happens. But forget that. I woke up this morning thinking about that ER woman from Friday night, the septicaemic one. Can't get her out of my mind. Wonder how she got on.'

I've already recounted how I how I phoned St Thomas's about Carmela, and how they had no record of her attending or being admitted on Friday night and our conjecture about what might have happened to her. But after breakfast we had to go on up to the hospital for our weekly clinical talk and assembled in the Seminar Room along with our fellow externs.

While waiting on the speaker, we discussed our next placements. I was pleased to be going to Medical, where Jess worked. After our frenetic Friday night in ER, I hoped it would be less busy and said so. 'Mind you, I expect there'll be the odd "Dr Pacemaker" in Medical with heart patients and such.' I didn't say I was worried how I'd cope in an arrest situation.

Coop admitted, 'I haven't been at an arrest yet, have you?' He looked at Laura who replied enthusiastically.

'No. Actually, I haven't but I can't wait! It must be so thrilling to revive someone.'

Perhaps it was, but the responsibility was daunting. And my brain returned to the subject of Carmela. Had she arrested? I had to know. The only thing to do was phone Carmela's family if I could get a number. I knew ER had Uncle Raoul's: I'd sent him and Elena to the desk to confirm it. Stupid now I thought of it: it would be on her records from the ward where the nurse had intimated he had to be phoned about her discharge. But getting it from ER would be easier. I also decided there couldn't be any breach of confidentiality or ethical problem involved in what would only be a simple friendly inquiry to Elena. I saw no reason to ask Randy about it.

Thinking of the devil, Randy walked in and spied a fellow Puerto Rican Resident whom he greeted with a Spanish, 'Ola!' This triggered another memory from the Friday night about Elena and her uncle as they'd gone to ER reception to confirm his contact details. There'd been a brief, if heated, conversation in Spanish peppered with Elena's remonstrances. It now floated back into my consciousness. She'd said, '*Dinero es no más importante que mi madre*.' From my rusty Spanish O Level, I knew '*madre*' was mother and '*dinero*' was money. So, had she said, 'Money is *not as important* as my mother—or *not more* important? Wasn't '*mas*' 'more'? What did she mean? Had Uncle Raoul refused to stump up for Carmela's care? Or help with insurance costs? And on the topic of paying for her care, why had Mrs Clipboard dismissed the charity, Sativa, that Elena had thought covered her? Though I'd initially accepted van Lindholm had arranged Carmela's transfer because she'd no funds to pay for our posh hospital, I now doubted that. Dr Bobby Newman had said you were supposed to get emergency care where you were and sort out finances later. She'd been a serious emergency. I was lost in thought. Until John sat beside me and took my hand.

He smiled and said, 'Good morning!' Apart from the disconcerting fluttering behind my sternum, I felt safe and secure. Weird. But only for a few seconds. My preoccupation returned.

'John, you know that woman Carmela Gomez we saw on Friday night? '

'Yes?' he said, cautiously.

'She's vanished.'

'What d'you mean, vanished?'

'Gone. I phoned St Thomas's and have no record of her arriving, living or dead.'

John looked shocked. 'Gee, how come?'

'I'm going to ER to try to get a number for the daughter or one of the family and call her to see what's happened to her.'

'Good idea. I'll come with you. Let's go at lunchtime.'

At that point, a Final Year Resident arrived to deliver a talk on hypocalcaemia and chronic kidney disease. The lights dimmed as slides were shown. I tried to relax into the complexities of calcium metabolism, though by the end of the talk I was even more confused than I'd been before we started. But at least van Lindholm didn't appear.

Chapter Sixteen
The Missing Records

After the lights went up, we went to the Coffee Shop before I spent a couple of hours browsing case sheets at the Nurses Station on my new Floor. By one, John sought me out and before eating, we headed for ER where today Mrs Clipboard was replaced by a smiley young blonde Candy-striper that John used his charm on.

Leaning on an elbow, he smiled. 'Hey, didn't I see your picture in the Herald? You've won a scholarship to Yale—Jodie, isn't it?' As she nodded modestly (or rather preened flirtatiously) John grinned. 'I wonder if you could help us...' He recounted the story of Carmela.

She melted off to flick through a rotary card system on the desk. And frown. Then moved back to rustle though filing cabinet drawers. And frown. Finally, she sat down at a dark screen on the desk where she moved a microfiche frame from side-to-side over the light below. Gazing at the illuminated patient lists on her screen she chewed her lip. And frowned.

'Nope. Friday, you said? I don't understand it. She should be up on this list by now. We do have Friday night and Saturday morning attendances on here but there's no Carmela Gomez recorded as being seen, nor records being sent on up to a Floor for admission or to the Records Department on discharge either day. You sure that's the right name you got?'

John said, 'Definitely.'

'Then, I'm afraid I can't help. I've no idea where her notes are.' With an apologetic smile, she glided off to answer a persistently ringing phone.

'This is getting worse.' I was very cross. 'Come on, let's find Randy.'

He was in the ER doctor's room reading a thick case file.

'Randy, do you still have the records for Carmela Gomez? They're not out there.' I nodded back at ER reception. 'In fact, the girl says she isn't even listed being here on Friday.'

'You joshing me? Records go with the patient to a floor if they're admitted or round to records at the end of the session when signed off by the ER Chief. No one else should take them. Carmela must be on the attendee list at reception. Maybe you could check with Records then and see if they went by mistake without being logged. But God, we all saw the woman. Who could forget that transfer nonsense? But what d'you want them for?'

I explained about calling St Thomas's, Carmela's disappearance and my idea to phone the daughter.

He whistled. 'Something's not right here, guys. First someone tops a nurse then a patient disappears.'

Our helpful desk clerk, Jodie, now popped her head round the door. 'Say guys—and hi, Dr Ortez—there's defo something funny with the patient files from Friday night. I've noticed there seems to be a gap. No one's listed as attending ER between eight and ten in the evening. Was it real quiet?'

Randy laughed. 'Sure as hell, it wasn't, as these two know. They were here!' He flapped a hand at us and stood up. 'I'm going to see about this.' To Jodie, he said, 'Can you go get Hiro to hold the fort for a bit? bit? No-one should be able to fuck the records. The ER Chief's off today, but I think I'll go and talk to Dr Harper. Shouldn't be long.' He strode off purposefully.

We went to get lunch but I wasn't hungry and only managed a few mouthfuls of lasagne. 'What do you think's going on, John?'

'Dunno.'

'There's other odd things I've heard about records for Mendoza's patients. Do you know he keeps the doctors' records for his Sunday charity patients in Lindholm's room? The residents and nurses work only from Nursing Notes and have to get him or Lindholm or sometimes even Frankie to get the surgical records if they need to add something to them. Isn't that odd?'

'What? How's that even allowed?' John put down his fork. I'd noticed most Americans eat using a fork only. And prongs up. Disquieting for me, and totally against Una's table manner rules. The thought was abruptly terminated by John slapping his hand on the table. 'I bet that's where Carmela's case notes are—van Lindholm's room!'

'But it doesn't explain why Jodie found no record of Carmela's ER attendance at Ellis. Or why St. Thomas's has no trace of her. I can't imagine Dr Mendoza or Dr van Lindholm could fudge records over there.'

John tutted. 'As a charity funded facility, I doubt that pair would want admission rights to St Thomas's. Not rich enough pickings for them. Fees are reduced at that kind of hospital.' John picked up his fork and finished his lasagne.

Mine sat barely touched. Once I'd have worried about leaving food, but today I didn't care. Pushing it away felt like pushing away a part of me that was no longer relevant. If I ate, I ate. If I didn't, I didn't. And I didn't care who saw what I'd left. As if mind reading, John reached out to take my hand and squeezed it. I sipped my half tumbler of milk.

'Down that milk and let's go walk. I need some fresh air.' John pushed back his chair.

In our shrubbery behind the tennis court, I decided it was time to tell him all about me. The dubiety over Mum's death, my lying father, my wacky *Wee Free* Gran and my battle with anxiety. It tumbled out easily.

John was a good listener, better even than my old GP had been–in the days when I'd trusted him. I didn't tell John absolutely everything though, about Roddy for instance. I retained a pang of guilt about him. Closing my eyes I could see him brushing his long red fringe out of his eyes, that gentle smile lighting up his angular face. But he was a long way away...John was here and now. And life was for living, as my mother's death had taught me. I felt sad too about Nurse Makkonen. What had she done to deserve such an end?

I opened up more to John, telling of the night I heard about US summer clerkships at a dinner of my all-male tutorial group, comprising one student from each year of medicine, telling of my annoyance they were all obsessed with career ambitions and ladder climbing. Like me, John was more interested in helping patients. And he agreed with my feeling that not having medical parents put us at a career disadvantage. Lacking connections or system knowledge was a deterrent here too.

John leaned back. 'Have you thought what you'd like to do when you qualify?'

'I thought maybe Psychiatry but one boy, Simon, ridiculed me, saying I'd never make any money at that unless I got into one of the big London private clinics. But money isn't everything.'

'It is if you don't have any,' John countered.' Especially in the U.S.A.'

When I had run out of woes, he stroked my cheek saying he thought I'd come through all my trials admirably. In turn, he told me about his family who sounded solid and uncomplicated. We had a short embrace then parted with a long kiss.

'Don't worry about anything, babe. You've got me to support you now. And I'm going to call Dad tonight for advice. Lots of things to ask him. Right, back to work!'

He walked me over to the hospital and I returned to the Third Floor.

Unfortunately, Medical Third Floor had some patients of van Lindholm's. Mid-afternoon he arrived to see two of them. Neither was a renal case. One headed a law firm, the other was a PR executive. The lawyer had intractable high blood pressure, the PR man unexplained chest pain requiring a barrage of tests. I trotted dutifully after the Resident assigned to van Lindholm, trying to avoid engaging directly with the man himself, although I doubt he'd any notion what I thought about him. Even if he knew what had happened to Carmela, he was too intimidating to ask.

On his brief ward round, he did engage with these patients fairly well, debating management strategies, tweaking drug doses, ordering tests and giving sanctimonious reassurances. These high-powered guys, super-anxious about their mortality, hung on his every word. One said, 'I trust you implicitly, Elias. I know you know your stuff. No one better.'

Such faith in Dr van Lindholm was totally misplaced given what I'd seen to date. Finally, the specialist scribbled in their notably normal and present-in-the-trolley notes and left abruptly without acknowledging or thanking any medical or nursing staff like any normal specialist.

Jess wrote up his visit in the nursing charts and made out a pharmacy requisition form for the lawyer's new pills that she gave to our attendant Candy-striper, the ubiquitous, Ellie May. Lindholm had cursorily acknowledged her by name on arrival. She'd responded with coquettish eye-fluttering, embarrassing to watch.

Once Ellie May had disappeared into the elevator, Jess turned to me to say, 'You do know Lindholm's a wanker, don't you? And sorry to say, I saw Ellie May get out of his car last night in town. She's so trusting and young. Wouldn't like to see her hurt. Thinking I might warn her about his reputation. What d'ya think?'

I shrugged. 'Would she listen? And strictly speaking, Ellie May's an adult.'

'But he's an ace creep. Needs locked up,' Jess said fiercely. 'You know he had a thing with Makkonen? Dumped her as too clingy. Wonder where he was on Thursday night?'

I could see his point, she was over the top, and yet Laura had said he still asked Makkonen to tutor nurses? It was an enigma.'

I changed tack, telling her about Carmela's disappearance. I did suggest she kept it to herself, having a strange feeling we shouldn't broadcast the disappearance or the missing records around the hospital until more facts were known. She thought about a few other hospitals on the way to St Thomas's but couldn't think why they would have taken Carmela to any of them. None as far as she knew had a critical care unit.

Before dinner I popped in to see Kitty though didn't disturb her as she was sleeping. But she did look a bit better.

~~~

That night I went to bed early and started writing a diary. I had kept one after Mum died and had found it good to put my thoughts down and somehow get things straight in my head when stressed. But tonight, my exposition of the doings of Mendoza and van Lindholm, the demise of Nurse Makkonen and the disappearance of Carmela sounded like a film script with too many unknowns. None of it made much sense. Surely I was exaggerating? Doubtless there'd be prosaic answers to all the worries.

Around half ten, Jess fetched me to speak to John on the phone. Getting out of bed, I trotted to the hall.

'Hello darling. How are you?' He sounded so sweet.

'Fine,' I said, pleased to hear his voice but still feeling edgy and a bit down. There was too much going on. And perhaps I was a little anxious that I had told him too much about my weaknesses. But he sounded upbeat.

'I wondered if you would like to come with me to New York next Saturday and stay over? Mum would love to meet you. And we can ask Dad all that stuff together.'

'That would be great. I'd love to. Actually, I was going to go up to the city on Saturday anyway with Jess and Laura, but I'm

159

sure they'll enjoy themselves on their own. Jess was talking about some PATH train.'

'You can do that again. I'll drive us up on Saturday morning. The folks haven't seen Gran's present yet. Dad's very envious of the car. You might meet my sister too. She may be up from Harvard for the weekend.'

After exchanging a few whispered sweet nothings, I hung up and went to seek Jess to apologise about reneging on her outing. I found her sitting on her bed reading a textbook. She really did work hard.

'Sorry but I've been asked to visit John's family on Saturday so won't manage the trip to the shops. Maybe we can do it again before we go home?'

'Sure thing! My, my, staying with the folks. Hardly been a minute for you two as well. Serious stuff, Mhairi MacLean!'

I felt myself blushing.

Jess gave me a bear hug. 'Never mind. Another raincheck!'

Tuesday passed uneventfully. One of the few July days that did. But we were no further on in finding out why so many records could have vanished, where Carmela had disappeared to or why. And as for Nurse Makkonen? There was no news at all about her.

There was however, one cheering event. In the afternoon I helped Kitty take a first few tentative steps with her preliminary 'prosthetic' leg. She was a determined young lady though not yet out of the woods. I worried that the abrasions from gravel on her good leg were beginning to look inflamed. The nurse was going to request antibiotics. I hoped they would prevent her getting septicaemia. I felt I was becoming an expert on it.

Chapter Seventeen
The Thirteenth Question

Wednesday morning saw me now in a routine, following special-ists around the Medical Floor while they reviewed their patients. These specialists again included Dr van Lindholm. When I was asked to clerk in a new patient for him, I nervously followed the resident's stipulations about how 'VL' liked his notes: meticulous but succinct. It went without saying that what VL wanted, VL got.

I was itching to know what response Randy had received on Monday when he'd been to see Dr Harper about last Friday's fid-dled ER records and Mendoza's potentially dodgy status in the State of California, but since then, he'd been nowhere to be found. Jess said he'd taken a few days off and was expected back tonight. Infuriating. But John planned to tackle him in the Residence as soon as he reappeared. We were also not much further forward about Makkonen's death, though Jess knew one of the interviewing cops from school who'd disclosed she'd not been sexually assaulted 'only asphyxiated with a pillow' as if that was permissible. Inter-estingly, he said they didn't think her death was linked to Kitty's ordeal but were looking for a missing doctor, I reckoned Randy's Resident ER partner whom we'd filled in for. We were all on edge. It was disquieting working in a facility where doctors might be practising illegally. And killing. Not for inclusion in a letter home.

By half twelve I was hungry and headed for an early lunch in the dining room, where I took chicken salad and a Coke to an unoccupied table in the corner. I now ate my meals with a fork in my right hand US-style. It was surprisingly easy and felt seditious.

It's surprising how sometimes small acts of rebellion can be the most satisfying.

On the table I found a local paper dated Tuesday that had been discarded. *The Brunsfield Herald* was, I should imagine, like any local paper worldwide, covering road accidents, court appearances, miraculous triumphs of survival over the odds and photos of diamond wedding celebrations, though admittedly the shooting in a local store might be less likely to feature in a Scottish paper.

A few pages in, my eye was drawn to a half page of boxed 'ads' bordered by graphic curlicues, wedding bells and crucifixes. These were Intimations of Births and Marriages plus Notifications of Deaths and Funerals. One entry caused my chicken forkful to remain poised in midair in front of my open mouth.

Gomez
Suddenly, on Friday July 16th at Plainsfield District General Hospital, Carmela D'Angelo Gomez, beloved mother to Elena and the late Diego, dear sister-in-law to Raoul. Funeral Mass will be held at Our Lady of the Rosary Church, Brunsfield East at 3pm on Thursday July 22nd 1971 to which all family and friends are invited. Enquiries to Santorini's Funeral Parlor, Green Street, Brunsfield.
    'Come to me all who labour and are heavy laden and I will give you rest.'
                                 Matthew 11:28

Right, that was one mystery solved: Carmela had died in a District General Hospital in Plainfield. But why?

~~~

That night, Laura and Coop went to the cinema and John and I headed for a MacDonald's. Despite John's coaxing, I didn't fancy another beef burger.

'Get me something chicken-y,' I asked, even though I'd had chicken for lunch. Admittedly, I wasn't thinking straight. My brain was in turmoil pondering Carmela's death. I went to sit down and left him at the counter queueing to order.

Randy and Jess appeared. Giving Randy her order, Jess left him in the queue and came to sit with me. Quickly telling her about the funeral notice, I asked if Randy had gained any info from Harper about the missing records and whether the Chief had known about Dr Juan Mendoza's dodgy registration status.

'Huh. Only got a few words with him this morning before work and he's been ranting about other stuff on the way over here. When I asked what Carlton Harper said about the missing records, telling him you'd told me about Carmela, he blew up.'

'Oh dear. Sorry. I didn't think he'd mind me telling you.'

'It wasn't *that* he blew up at. No, it was what Carlton said that made him mad. Here they are. I'll let him tell you himself.'

The boys laid out our meals from the tray. But before even taking a bite, I had to ask Randy, 'Okay, so what did Carlton say about Mendoza's licence and the disappearing records? I've got news on the Carmela front, by the way.'

'Carlton's a fucking ass.' Randy grimaced, baring his teeth. 'So, first he says we must have 'heard wrong' about where she was heading. Fucking insult. Then he said 'glitches happen' with records all the time when you're busy and there'd be a simple explanation for the missing patient numbers and case sheets. And as for Mendoza? Carlton Harper said they knew about the L.A. suspension. That it was for some petty drug mix-up and was only for three months. Praised the pants off the guy for his 'numbers' and charity work and then hinted I should 'watch it' as Elias has reported me for

163

causing trouble for him with some nurse. Said I'd no idea what he was talking about and sadly felt I had to bite my tongue. I just apologised through gritted teeth for troubling him and left. It's too near to the Boards for me to risk a disciplinary. And van Lindholm can be vindictive. I already know how he thinks. Frankie told me. Hispanics shouldn't be senior medics in mainstream US hospitals. They're more suited to work 'down chain' in charity hospitals'

'What? How ridiculous!' I put down my chicken burger.

'Then, when I was halfway out the door, he called me back, turned on a smile, patted my fucking arm and said, "But I expect you meant well. You know my door is always open for staff who are worried about something. Feel free to come in if you have any more concerns about working practices. Never hurts to hoist a flag, you know." Total bullshit. Talk about a U-turn? Doesn't know which way is up. *Hijo de puta!*' He bit into his burger so viciously that pickle and cheese shot out the sides. A common hazard, I'd noticed. But not usually such an explosive one.

I changed the topic by delving into my bag to produce the announcement I'd torn from *The Brunsfield Herald* and set it down in front of Randy out with explosive pickle range.

'At least this answers one question—why Carmela wasn't in St Thomas's.'

John read over Randy's shoulder and exclaimed, 'So, she died in D.G.? I wonder what happened? Though I expect if a patient runs into trouble in an ambulance the rule might be to head for the nearest facility. Something I meant to say before, but not sure if it's relevant, I saw Lindholm going out to speak to the ambulance attendants as Carmela left. God knows why. And Mhairi, I did check after you mentioned about docs owning stuff—Dr Elias van Lindholm does own that local MRT ambulance outfit Carmela went off in. And a blood supply lab in NY. I was busy on Friday, but you know it occurred to me that there was no real need to wait on his special ambulance instead of the usual service, other than it earning him more money, I guess, from whatever charity he gets to eventually pick up the bill.'

Dismissing my unease about the ethics of medics getting involved in commercial medical services, I homed in on John's comment about VL going out of ER after Carmela.

'I was outside with Elena watching when Carmela went off and I saw van Lindholm up at the ambulance and wonder if he might not have given her a shot of something as she went into it?' I closed my eyes, trying to visualise the scene. 'He was fiddling with the drip and had his back to us but I'm sure there might've been something curled into the palm of his hand that he put it into the pocket of his trousers. He wasn't wearing a white coat.'

Randy's brow furrowed. 'Like a syringe? Really? Well, if he did give her a shot, what of? And why? There was nothing else indicated at that point.'

'I wonder what her death certificate says?' John looked pensive. 'And who signed it? Maybe Dad can get hold of a copy.'

'I'll find out that and what story the family's been given tomorrow afternoon. I've decided to go to the funeral and speak to Elena.'

'You're not going alone, babe. I'll take you.' John looked concerned. I was getting to like being called, 'babe'. John put his arm around me. 'It won't matter if we miss one afternoon in the hospital. We'll just tell our Residents we're going to pay our respects at a funeral.'

~~~

Next afternoon we arrived at the church early. Because John wasn't exactly sure where it was, he'd allowed plenty of time. Cars were already parked outside and people were milling about at the door, I presumed waiting on the coffin. But then, I'd only ever attended one funeral. My mother's.

John led me in to sit at the back from where we could see that many people were already seated, a few were praying in front of the altar and Carmela's body was already there. On top of her coffin, framed by a wreath of white roses, sat an elevated photo of her looking happy, smiling and beautiful. A rosary was draped over the photo, which was the same shot as the one on the Order of Service we'd been given on the way in. I felt tearful already.

'She'll have been here all night for the Vigil,' whispered John. 'That's what we do.' It was the first inkling I'd had that he was Catholic. We'd never had cause to discuss religion. My Presbyterian childhood indoctrination gave me qualms about our belief differences. But what did it matter? My heart thumped. I didn't see us going anywhere long term. But how I wished...

People trickled in to sit in huddling groups. The organist was playing a hymn I'd never heard before. The priest walked up past us to greet the funeral party at the door and led them back down to the front, Elena walking between Raoul and a woman whom I presumed was her aunt. They sat in the front row. The priest went forward to the altar and genuflected before turning to face the congregation.

As the Mass progressed, John whispered explanations and joined in the responses which were in English, not Latin as I expected. He went up to receive the sacrament when it was offered. The singing was very moving, the organ music adding to the atmosphere. It made me appreciate how much my church was missing by forbidding instruments.

The coffin was transported out by pall bearers who included Raoul and we joined the file wending round behind the church to the prepared grave in the grounds to the rear. I noticed a headstone beside us listed a Diego Gomez, aged eight: the son who'd died. After a reading, a prayer, a poem in Spanish recited by Elena and further blessings from the priest, Carmela was slowly laid to her rest. Earth was scattered into the open grave. Elena threw in a flower. Hankies were prominent. But I wasn't crying. I was consumed by anger. Why had this lovely woman died? Mendoza shouldn't be operating. He was incompetent.

As the crowds dispersed, I headed straight for Elena who was walking out slowly on Raoul's arm. When I touched her shoulder, she turned to weep on mine. Raoul hesitated, then walked on with his wife when Elena waved him to go on. She drew back and gave me a weak smile.

'Thank you so much for coming. You were very kind at the hospital.'

Aware of tears falling, I brushed my cheek. 'She was a lovely lady. I met her in the hospital after her surgery, you know, just before she was discharged.'

Elena looked surprised. 'Did you tell me that on Friday? I don't remember everything. It's all a bit muddled—such a shock.'

I decided this was not a time to ask for any details about her mother's death.

'Elena, I'd like to speak with you about something. Would you be kind enough to meet me soon, perhaps for a coffee? It's quite important.'

Her eyes flashed. I could see anger but knew it wasn't directed at me when she looked to the distance and immediately said, 'Yes, I would very much like to talk to you too. There is much to discuss.'

'Could you manage to come to the Coffee Shop at Ellis Memorial?'

'No,' she said firmly. 'Not the hospital. Please meet me at *Di Marco's* in Maple Street. Monday around four?'

I'd no idea where Maple Street was but vowed I'd find it. As Elena moved off, John was at my side. We stood watching her walk ahead, robotically accepting hugs from women and shoulder claps from the men. Among the dozens of mourners milling out from the grave side towards the exit, we stood out, especially tall, blond John. Almost everyone attending was Hispanic. It was an outpouring of love for someone valued in their community.

As the crowd thinned, John led me back to the car and we drove to the park where we went for a walk without saying anything. Eventually, sitting in the late afternoon sunshine with his arm round me, John said, 'You know, I think we have to find out what happened to Carmela. I wonder how much Dad can help?' He looked at me earnestly. God, the boy was handsome.

I pulled myself together. 'Maybe Coop should speak to his dad too? He'll know how the system works. I mean, why did Carmela end up at the District General and not St Thomas's?'

'We've got loads more questions, babe. And need a lot more info before we know whether this is malpractice. Number one, what was given as cause of death? Two, who certified her dead? Three, why *did* the ambulance end up in D.G. not St Thomas's? Four, who erased her Ellis Memorial Hospital attendance—and all those other patients'—last Friday at our ER and removed her records? Five, *why* would they? Six, *is* Mendoza responsible for her death? Seven, how come van Lindholm was treating a *surgical* case? Weird he was covering for Mendoza. Eight, what *is* the relationship There? Phew, that's a lot of questions.' John looked tired after just listing them.

I sat forward and turned to look at him. 'And we've got more. Like, nine, did Lindholm give something lethal to Carmela as she left our ER? Ten was she a liability for his friend Juan Mendoza? And from way back, think I told you, question eleven, what did Lindholm tell Carmela was 'Settled in full' when I saw her before discharge? Then twelve, there's that Spanish conversation I heard between Elena and her uncle. What was that all about? Those mentions of 'the money' and her mother being 'more important'? And we haven't even begun to discuss Frankie! I mean that's question thirteen. Where does Francis Cooke Junior fit in? I know he's racist from what Randy says, but why is he so cosy with van Lindholm? And why would he be asked back as intern for a second year?'

'Oh God, Mhairi, so much we don't know! But question thirteen and its ramifications are the only ones we can deal with till we see Dad on Saturday and you see Elena next Monday. Let's get Frankie alone tomorrow.'

As a treat, John took me for tea to the Bohemia restaurant downtown. He had never been but knew Laura and I had enjoyed our meal there on the Fourth of July. Our discussion and surmising about van Lindholm continued over the meal. When Gretel came to ask how our food was, she overheard his name and made a face. 'Oh, you've met the famous Dr van Lindholm, have you? Huh, he used to come here when his wife was away. I'm glad he no longer comes. He is not a nice man.'

As she moved off to greet new diners, John looked after her and shook his head. 'As if it wasn't bad enough, there's another question to add to the pile. Now, what on earth did Elias van Lindholm do to upset your friend in here?'

~~~

Next day in the dining room, Frankie found himself surrounded by John on his left, me on his right and Coop and Laura sitting opposite. We had got them up to speed in the serving queue.

'Hi guys!' He looked at each of us in turn as we sat down with our trays. 'So, am I flavour of the month, or what?'

'We've just got a few questions.' Laura gave him one of her irresistible smiles.

Frankie seemed to relax. 'Really? Okay, shoot.' He wiped his greasy mouth with a paper napkin.

'We were wondering about the research you're doing with Dr van Lindholm. What's it about?'

He flushed. 'What's it to you?' With four pairs of eyes staring intently at him, he realised he had to answer or cause a scene. 'Oh, it's just, you know, stats and assessments.'

'Stats of what? And what are you assessing? We're interested.' I was feeling bold. 'And why have I seen you quite often going in and out of Finance next door here?'

John looked at me in surprise. But then it had only occurred to me at that moment how often I'd seen Frankie coming out of the department. And I remembered Helga from Finance. Her clipboard, seen when I'd been with Coop's Dad, had had yellow sheets under the white one she'd torn off as bills for patients. I pushed on. 'I mean, they don't keep patient clinical records in Finance, but they do have patient invoices and other bills. Are the yellow sheets you give to van Lindholm copies of patient bills?'

Frankie shuffled in his chair and looked towards the exit. I'd block him if he tried...

'Er, no. Yes. I mean, well I look in Finance for patients who've been in—or are in—debt and have run up big bills but can't pay. I borrow the records for him to review.'

'Okay, but how is that research, exactly?' Coop pressed him.

Frankie didn't like it. His hands were shaking. 'Cool it, guys. Like, Elias only wants to find people in trouble and help.'

'So, how's that 'research'? I mean is there a paper in it? What's the remit?' John glared.

At this Frankie squirmed and his voice rose an octave. 'Hey, guys what's with the inquisition? So, VL's got a charity thing goin' on. He helps folk out. I just give him names and details then he checks their records and I take the yellow accounting sheets back when he's done.' His eyes flicked round the room. 'It's legit. His charity's called Sativa. There's a fundraiser next month. You should come. I'm gathering info on medical debt and patient's circumstances for a paper he's going to get into the *Milbank Quarterly* for me. About how hospitals can find funds for debtors, especially those with no relatives. No big deal. I gotta go.' Grabbing his obligatory bottle of Coke, he jumped up and ran out.

Coop looked at Frankie's tray on which lay half a burger, most of a carton of chips and two chocolate brownies. 'Hey, I think we spoiled Frankie's appetite!' No one laughed.

'So, Frankie only 'borrows' yellow papers and Elias van Lindholm is Saint Theresa?' I shook my head.

'My ass, he is,' said John. 'And that research sounds bullshit. Right, I'm off to make a list of questions that need answers for Dad. And sorry, babe, got something I need to do tonight. But I'll pick you up at ten tomorrow if that's OK?'

I nodded. He gave me a kiss on the cheek and left.

Sitting playing with my food in the manner of my old trick i.e., chopping up and moving it about, I sat on for a bit. Frankie wasn't the only one with a spoiled appetite.

Laura looked at me, concerned. 'You mustn't worry about all this, Mhairi. It isn't really our responsibility. If John wants to pursue it, let him. But don't make yourself ill over it. We need to just concentrate on learning as much as we can while we're here and most of all, going out to have fun.'

'I know,' I said, pushing my plate away. 'This fish isn't nice anyway. It's overcooked.'

'And think on the coming weekend up in Manhattan. It's exciting! You're "meeting the folks", darling. Now that's a serious business!' She elbowed me and winked.

God she was as bad as Jess, making too much of this visit. It was just a fact-finding chat with John's father.

Coop got up to go. 'They're good folks, the Coulters. I met them the day John came over. And their apartment sounds real swell. It overlooks Central Park.'

'Swell' or not, I just hoped Mr Warren Coulter, D.A., might be able to find us some answers to our questions. But I doubted he'd could determine exactly what had gone on in Carmela's ambulance last Friday.

But I doubted he'd could determine exactly what had happened to poor Nurse Makkonen. Or Kitty Gerber, whom I'd found scared, weepy and tearful on a visit earlier, upset that no witnesses to her 'accident' in the early hours of last Sunday had come forward.

And as for what had happened in Carmela's ambulance last Friday? That was anybody's guess.

Chapter Eighteen
Catastrophes

After the Residency Party, early hours of Sunday 11th July 1971

He loves Saturday nights when Ava's at her mother's. Out on the patio, Dr Elias van Lindholm takes a long, satisfying drag on his joint before snuffing it out in a plant pot. Good stuff, this last batch from Eduardo. He'll keep more than usual. Should be time for another smoke once he's got Ellie back to her car at the Nurses' Home.

It'd been a bit risky, picking her up at the back of the Home at Ellis Memorial, but it was convenient to save time. Anyway, it was late enough, with few folk about and safer than letting her drive here. His old neighbour next door, Randy Ramsay, was probably still on alert. Bloody nosey guy. Eyes like a hawk. Prone to wander over for a chat with Ava in the afternoons. After one incident, thankfully successfully explained away, he'd decided it was best on pick-up nights to take out the old Ford with its darkened windows and speed back in under the carport before opening a door. No point in exposing girls to Ramsay's lenses, whether binocular or camera.

This Ellie's a smart kid. Complied to the letter with the note he'd palmed at the Resident's party. Assured him she left the shindig without telling anyone where she was going. Was ready and waiting in the carpark bang on midnight. All it had taken to reel her in had been one grope in a side room and two Coffee Shop flirts over the last couple of weeks plus some discussion about helping her into a career in nursing. But she was easy meat. And had proved a satisfying and undemanding ride. Unlike that off-the-wall ER nurse. Something might have to be done about her.

Frankie, too, was on his mind as he waited on Ellie getting ready. He'd been useful for all the paperwork trawls and home visits, sussing outs safe bets and potential targets. But he was becoming annoying and tiresome. Asking too many questions. Perhaps the boy had served his purpose. He'd find another sucker. Next week he'll tell Frankie the fund's dried up. Recite the mantra, 'You've learned all I can teach you.' Not that anything he's learned will help him pass exams. Huh, but if he fails, it might help him become a private dick!

Through the open doors he hears the shower is still running. What do broads do in bathrooms for so long? He'll have to scrub it when he gets back, of course. And get the towels and bedlinen washed and dried before tomorrow afternoon. Admiring his new Audemars watch, he sees it's now one thirty a.m. Time he got her back.

In the bedroom she exits from the ensuite, towel draped casually below nipple level for maximum titillating effect. He feels hardening begin, but there's no time for a third performance. The second had been vastly better than the first: she'd obviously lost her virginity to a green frat boy, maybe even only done it once. But now she's had proper tuition in pleasuring a man. Especially how to put a condom on without using fingers and stay down there longer than many.

He smiles at her. 'Come on, darling, gotta get back for your car.'

She blows him a kiss and dresses. That doesn't take long. Lace thong. Minuscule brassiere. Turquoise silk shift, barely fanny length. She tosses aside the shower cap he'd urged her to use. 'Don't want to get that lovely hair wet. It'll take too long to dry!' really meant, 'Don't shed long blonde hairs in my wife's shower.' Age may have dimmed Ava's sex drive somewhat but it hasn't impaired her snooping ability. Sad her blonde hair needs encouragement from a bottle now. Time marches.

They're now in under the porch. His keys are in the ignition. She is moaning. 'Oh, Doctor Elias sweety, why are you using this old heap—can't we go in the Lincoln? Everyone drools over it in the carpark. I love it!'

And there she has it: the Lincoln's conspicuous. Reversing out of the drive, he speeds off while saying, 'Oh, this is here and ready. Let's just go!' He blows her a kiss.

On the way back, she laughs, her hand kneading his crotch. Now, hasn't he awakened something in this Candy-striper? Stopping at the rear of the downtown park, he accepts a swift blow job perfected in rhythm and direction by his hands. And then they're off again.

At the foot of the hospital drive, he parks away from the street lights and caresses her thigh upward. Leaning in, he gives the usual, 'You're amazing, darling! One of the best nights ever!' before kissing her passionately. 'But we must be discreet. I'll let you know when Ava's away again.'

'Couldn't we go to a hotel or something?'

God, she's so into him! It's a turn on. He pats her hand. 'No, best not. Trust me. Be in touch.'

Ellie gets out, all tanned thighs and a flash of side pubes from those ridiculous pointless thongs. She blows a kiss. Scampers off. Oh, to be eighteen again! He drives away.

Tomorrow he gets the long-awaited new car. Ellie will love the new Boat-tail Buick Riviera, full spec: air conditioning, power windows and front disc brakes, six-way power seats, tinted glass, cruise control, 5-spoke chrome wheels, AM/FM stereo. Colour? Red. What else? Ava doesn't know he's bought it. But it's a status symbol, so she'll love it to.

Back home, within ten minutes he's wiped the shower, hoovered the bedroom, and tossed towels and sheets into the top-load washer in the basement. He then sprays the bedroom with a freshener. Scent lingers and Ava has a nose like a pig sniffing for truffles. And a bad-ass lawyer brother. Back downstairs, he lights another joint and pours a whiskey. Time for some erotic movies until the wash cycle ends and the tumble dryer has spun. Everything must be cool, clean and replaced by noon. He needs to encourage Ava to go visit her mother more often. He has barely sat down when the phone starts ringing. Shit. It's bound to be the bloody hospital. Who else?

'Yes?'

It is. So, a patient is fitting and that stupid boy, Horowitz, can't decide if it's safe to repeat the anticonvulsant he's administered? That Second Year Resident is a jackass. Such a pity his father survived Auschwitz. Carlton had ignored Elias's objection to the appointment. That was in the 'BP' time Before Photo, before Dr Carlton Harper, the renowned Ellis Memorial Chief of Staff jumped when asked. Infuriatingly, the way Resident Rotas worked meant Horowitz occasionally had to cover Elias's patients. He must think of a way to get him fired. But now he's been called in, there seems nil to do other than go see this patient himself. He'd suggested she had Dialysis Disequilibrium syndrome. Horowitz has never heard of it. Could that be a lever for firing- incompetence?

Chewing strong mint gum, he jumps back into the Mustang. No blue movies tonight. Oh, the sacrifices required to save lives! The car backfires. He must get the Lincoln plates swapped onto the new car: New Jersey, MEDIC 1, The Garden State. Then everyone will know it's his. It'll be a guzzler, though. Nixon better fix the rising gas prices.

At the hospital, the patient is sleeping. He makes a cursory examination of her, speaks to the nurses, and writes up a change of drug before tersely dismissing Horowitz. Returning to the Mustang he speeds out of the carpark and turns up the radio.

'Fuck! What the hell?' A sickening thud accompanies a red-dressed body rolling over his hood. It falls off to the side, long blonde hair fanning wide. The car bucks and jerks before he can brake to a stop. Where the fuck did she come from? He has just turned the corner before the parking lot that'd seen his last climax of the night. OK, some park shrubbery does obscure the road here, but she should have heard his engine. Why the hell was she walking here at one a.m. anyway? Must be a hooker.

Before getting out, he looks up and down the street. Deserted. No nearby homes. The girl lies on her back on the grass verge, golden hair spread out. No sign of blood and brain spillage but spikes of bone are visible through an injury on her lower leg. A serious compound fracture. She's moaning. Alive. Maybe not for long. Blood is pumping out of the wound.

He inspects his car. A cracked headlight, still in situ. No identifiable debris on the road. No dents he can see on the impact side, though the light is poor. Blood spatters are visible on the wheel arch and hubcaps. Snatching Kleenex from inside, he wipes what he can see and gets back in. The engine's still running. Calling anyone would be career curtains. He doubts he'll pass any drug or liquor test. It's an easy choice.

Five minutes later, he is inside his three-car garage, its electronic doors closed. The strip light shows fresh blood on the fender, grill and tyre sidewalls. It hoses off easily at normal pressure. Turning the power up, he jets under the chassis. The residual pink water drains over the cement floor to ebb down the metallic grill at the entrance. By the time he's finished, it's after three. Too late for setting up the screen and movie projector. Time for a short sleep.

At the top of the stairs, he swears. 'Shit!' He's forgotten the laundry. Returning to the garage, he removes the linen from the washer and crams it into the dryer. Then, remembering the soiled Kleenex on the passenger seat, he retrieves it, flushing the evidence down the toilet amongst a pile of unsoiled tissues.

In the guest room he strips naked, sets his alarm for six thirty. He will have to rise early to fix the marital bed and phone Hubert to come for the car first thing. It will definitely need a new headlamp, the scratches on the bonnet and wing repaired, and a complete valet, of course. Hubert will accept his prepared story. "Goddammit, would you believe I killed a deer on the way home? Haven't seen one for years, have you?" Perfectly plausible.

Always obliging, Hubert. As owner of a small tyre and auto repair shop he's between the devil and the deep blue sea: just making ends meet though unable to afford full med insurance. And as he is working, he's ineligible for Medicaid. The hospital debt from his wife's illness is substantial. Patient debt is useful in many ways. As a clinician, he can claim patient debt against tax bills. Or waive it and claim payment in kind. Like car repairs. He also decides it might be best to get Hubert to say he's had it all weekend.

He sleeps soundly, confident no one saw him hit the girl and that any evidence otherwise will soon be no more. He was getting good at covering his tracks.

~~~

Five Days Later, the Night of Carmela's Transfer, Friday July 16th 1971

They'd come to a stop at a red light. The nurse in the passenger seat turned to the driver, 'Don't you think we should go through, Desmond?'

'I wasn't told this was an emergency, babe. Just a patient transfer. No siren.'

From the back came a command, 'I'd step on it, Desmond. Think this is an emergency now!' The nurse was crouching in the back holding the patient's wrist. 'Jesus, Bessie, her pulse has rocketed.'

Suddenly the patient started shaking and making choking noises. The alarmed driver set off his siren and shot through the red light.

'So, what exactly is the story here, Faith?' asked Bessie, turning to face her in the back. 'I didn't hear the specialist brief, just took the paperwork from that blond student guy.'

'Septicaemic shock, five days status post kidney surgery. They said she was stable when we got her but God, she's gone real cold.' Faith bent over to lift one of the woman's closed eyelids. 'Pupils dilated as hell now! She was talking only a minute ago, if a bit drowsy but she's out now.'

Grunting, she started rubbing Carmela's chest with her knuckle to rouse her. 'Hey, Carmela, stay with me! Hell, she's completely unresponsive. What the fuck? Pulse is thready. It's a crash. Think she's no chance if we go for St. Thomas. Too far! Step on it, Desmond. Let's do the D.G. It's nearer.'

The ambulance driver swiftly turned a corner and put his foot down. In minutes they had pulled up at the door of Plainsfield District General Hospital ER and Bessie had flown out of the passenger seat to open the rear door of the ambulance and help Faith get their patient out. As they rushed through the doors they shouted 'Emergency' at the reception desk and an orderly and nurse appeared. While calling out details of Carmela's condition at them, the girls propelled their inert patient up the corridor as directed..

When the gurney reached the first free consultation room, Bessie whispered, 'I think I should go call van Lindholm.' Faith nodded and moved her burden on into the room alone.

Bessie was lifting the public wall phone when she heard the Tannoy system announce, 'Dr Pacemaker to Room One'. She felt her own heart race. This wasn't good. A second patient in a month collapsing en route to St Thomas's? A second almost identical story.

Inside the assessment room, Faith was giving the attendant doctor the patient's story. Slightly modified. Somehow she decided to hold back from mentioning van Lindholm's parting 'antibiotic' shot. Like hell it was a sulphonamide! Her mind now raced.

That woman who died a month ago, had also been operated on by Dr Juan Mendoza. The situation here was so similar, even though tonight it was Dr van Lindholm who'd sent her off with an injection, not Mendoza. Faith had heard from her Operating Room orderly brother Winston that van Lindholm and Mendoza worked a lot together. He thought they were doing some experimental research. What fucking experiments had they been doing to these women? She felt a chill as she watched the District General ER staff try to resuscitate Carmela. Winston said the word on the street was that Mendoza had drug cartel connections. But even if that was not true, she felt he was bad news, not to be crossed. Her worry was that for these two odd patient transports, she'd been singled out. Neither she nor Bessie were officially on the rota tonight. Or last time. They'd been specifically phoned. And frankly bribed by a substantial sum.

Something smelled here. Faith did not trust van Lindholm one whit. She was also uneasy about how much Winston idolised him. Her brother loved the Triumph Tiger motorbike van Lindholm had given him for his other job as a weekend despatch rider with that New York City lab, but she feared he was being led astray. Those bruises and scratches on his face that he came home with in the early hours yesterday? No way did he get those from falling off his motorcycle! More likely fights or tussles with someone. God knows what kind of 'favours' he occasionally did for van Lindholm. Often during the night. Might be time for new jobs for both of them. Winston would do what his big sister said. He'd promised Mama before she went that he always would.

At least from tonight there'd be another bonus, quiet a substantial one. Maybe enough for a deposit on a decent apartment back in Brooklyn? With her qualifications she should land a good job uptown. And she'd ensure she got a good reference from van Lindholm, hint at her discretion. She knew a lot and suspected much, much more.

Carmela's attached monitor bleeped for the first time. Faith calmed a little. It isn't showing regular sinus rhythm but there has been some electrical activity from the cardioversion. Maybe Mrs Gomez could make it. As they shocked her, Faith closed her eyes and started praying.

Chapter Nineteen
The High Life

Saturday 24 July 1971

By ten to ten on the next Saturday morning, our third weekend in the States, I was at the front door of the Nurses' Home waiting for John. As usual, he was exactly on time. This journey up to Manhattan was going to be the longest journey I'd made in in his splendid new car and he'd warned me he'd have the top down. I'd borrowed a silk scarf from Laura to preserve my hair. It was wild enough. Goodness knows what it might be like after driving up to the city in an open-topped sports car.

I sat in down in the car, musing on this "going to meet the parents" thing that Jess and Laura thought such a big deal. We were only going because we needed to ask John's Dad if he could throw light on some of the troubling things we'd uncovered about some of the hospital staff, not because we were getting engaged or any other such nonsense. Though I had to admit to myself, I was pretty shocked at how quickly I'd accepted that John and I were a couple. This relationship was so much more intense than any previous one I'd had, even with Roddy back home.

As we moved off, I looked across at John. He had an amazing, handsome face. Was he really 'mine' in the way all those pop songs warbled? Might he be, *The One*? God, I'd become like a soppy Austen heroine within a month of meeting the boy!

We travelled up the very congested Interstate 78 East Highway. Its multiple lanes moved painfully slowly. Our spells of immobility gave John time to treat me to a lowdown on the US highway system and turnpikes, which I quickly gathered meant toll roads.

He was particularly adamant that the authorities were 'nuts' for a recent decision they'd made to double the tolls going into New York City via something called the Holland Tunnel but abolishing any payment going out. He pronounced it nuts. It hadn't helped traffic flow at all. Our journey was meant to take about fifty minutes but instead stretched to over two hours. It looked to me as if everyone and their granny had a car in the US of A but I realised that didn't necessarily guarantee they'd get anywhere fast.

At one point when we were immobile for twenty-five minutes with the sun beating down, I was glad I chosen a long-sleeved shirt or my pale freckled red-head skin would have been burned to a crisp. It was as hot as I'd ever experienced and I was tempted to ask if we could put the roof up. With difficulty, I held my tongue. John loved it down. He was like a child showing off a marvellous new toy: his 'roadster' was not for hiding in. But I couldn't help asking, 'Wouldn't it have been easier to go in the train?'

John patted my knee. 'Sure, but as I said, I want to show this beauty off.' Since he removed his hand from my leg to pat the dashboard while saying this, I realised it wasn't me he was talking about. 'Besides, Grandma hasn't seen it either—she just got it brought over to me.'

It was almost noon when we exited the Holland Tunnel beneath the Hudson River. We then wound our way northward on Manhattan Island where, after much crawling through streets and stopping for red lights, we ended up on the East Side of Central Park. Beside a smart Art Deco marble building of immense proportions, John suddenly indicated right and shot down into a subterranean carpark where he parked beside some of the largest and swankiest examples of automobiles I'd ever seen. Pulling on the handbrake, he grinned. 'Welcome to the East Side!' After replacing and securing the Buick roof, he grabbed our bags from the boot, locked the car and guided me to the car park elevator.

It opened inside the building at street level in a high-ceil-inged and impressive lobby where John was greeted effusively by the uniformed doorman who helped us with the bags and hailed another, posher, elevator to take us upstairs. It was shiny polished steel with a fully mirrored interior and carpeted floor that rapidly transported us to the twelfth floor where John let himself in to flat Number 12C with a key.

In an instant, he'd elbowed the door ajar and thrown our bags into the hall, before putting his arm around my waist and rushing me inside all the way to the lounge window where he stood saying, 'Ta Da!' and throwing his arms out like a magician. The view from the full height window over Central Park and the city skyline was breathtaking. As was the apartment.

Looking about, I tried to avoid gawping like a country bump-kin. The carpet was cream, as were the linen sofas. Piled up cush-ions were gold and lemon. Brass and glass tables held china bowls I thought were possibly Chinese. Several large crystal vases held the palest of pink lilies. On small marquetry tables were many little ornaments like porcelain dogs and silver framed photos. Every wall held several large, mainly landscape, oil paintings. It was like a movie set.

John waved at the stunning view and grinned. 'Welcome to the Upper East Side—don't you love it?' I nodded briefly before he grabbed me for a twirling hug that ended in a kiss before we were interrupted by a voice.

'Put her down, John. Let the poor girl take a breath!'

I'd have known she was John's mother, slim, same blonde hair and warm blue eyes. Jacqueline Coulter was tall and athletic, in an outfit of wide navy slacks and casual lemon silk sweater with pearls that shouted class. She grasped my hand in hers and gave me a close one arm hug.

'Welcome to New York, Mhairi. I'm Jaqueline, but please call me Jackie.'

I was overwhelmed. And delighted she knew how to pronounce my name properly. I wondered what else John had told her about me. She put her arm through John's and led him to a sofa, waving at the others for me to choose one.

'Come on, you must tell me all about Ellis Memorial, Johnnie. And we're dying to hear about Scotland, Mhairi.'

Overwhelmed by the luxurious surroundings, I sat grinning like an idiot. I had no idea how much a DA earned, but this home spoke of serious wealth—although it was very comfortable and welcoming, not merely ostentatious.

'We weren't sure how long it was going to take you. The traffic's been particularly awful today, according to Magda. So, how's the car, Johnnie? Dad's dying to see it.'

'It's terrific, Mom. I love it!'

'I've arranged early lunch, then I thought you'd probably like to take Mhairi to see Central Park. You hungry?' John nodded, but then, like Laura, he was always hungry. 'Your dad's on the phone in the study. As usual. God knows how long he'll be but come on through and we'll just start.'

A young woman in a pretty summer dress (addressed as Magda) served us delicious cold tomato soup. So, the Coulters had a maid! I'd never met anyone with servants. I was served white wine in a crystal glass.

John's mother started telling me about her ancestry research on the Coulter family. She'd discovered they'd originated from Aberdeen, then for some reason had travelled to County Antrim in Northern Ireland to farm in the late eighteenth century before emigrating to America, settling in New York in the early 1800s.

'Gosh, that's interesting. I only know about a few generations back of mine. Both my parents' families are from the Western Isles, Lewis in particular, although they didn't meet there but in Glasgow as students.'

'Genealogy is fascinating, Mhairi. You'd be amazed at what you can find.'

At that point, John's father arrived.

'Hi Mhairi, great to meet you!' Squeezing my hand in both of his he said, 'Call me Warren,' before sitting at the head of the table. On being presented with his soup by Magda (who had arrived without a summons), he thanked her, exclaiming, 'Great, Gazpacho, my favourite! Now, John, tell us about this ridiculously extravagant car that my mother has given you.'

Smiling broadly, Jackie offered me more garlic bread and shook her head. 'I don't know about you, Mhairi, but I think there's nothing worse than two men talking about cars.'

I laughed. 'There's also football, of course too...'

'They'll be on to that next!' She offered me a plate of neatly cut sandwiches, saying, 'Keeping lunch light. Big dinner tonight.'

'Oh?' I asked. 'What's happening?'

'I have a little celebration planned tonight for John's birthday tomorrow.'

'It's tomorrow? He never said.' I wondered why he hadn't.

'I've booked us dinner at John's favourite place, Delmonico's. Their steaks are legendary. And Grandma Coulter is coming along. She's very intrigued. John doesn't often bring girls home.'

'It all sounds lovely,' was my bland response. Grandma Coulter sounded quite a formidable character from John's description. Anxiety rose from my stomach as I munched slowly on an egg sandwich, feeling sorry I'd taken a cheese one as well. Warren nodded over at me.

'John said you two had something you wanted to discuss. Some trouble at the hospital?'

'Em, I think John might be better at explaining. It's quite complicated. A lot has happened.' I couldn't think where to start.

Jackie looked at me intently, raising a well-manicured eyebrow. I felt my face warm.

'Right. Sounds serious. Hey, Warren?' She tapped a fork on her wine glass to get the attention of the boys at the other end of the long mahogany dining table. 'Let's finish up in here and take the sandwiches through to the lounge. Magda can bring the coffee in there. I sense these young people need our help with something.'

Ensconced back in a deep cushioned sofa, I was tense. Never mind my anxiety about meeting Gran Coulter, there was the worry I might spill coffee on this pristine sofa. And I was now concerned that we might be making a mountain out of a molehill where Ellis Memorial Hospital was concerned. Surely Dr Mendoza must be legitimately registered to practise, or such a prestigious hospital would not have employed him? They must have done checks. In truth, all we had was the notion that he'd lied about being struck off and a series of odd happenings, a few missing records and a patient who'd temporarily vanished but turned out to be dead. And of course, there was poor Freya Makkonen.

But John waded straight in. 'Dad, can you check whether a doctor in our hospital, a Dr Juan Mendoza, had his license revoked in another State? He's weird. Operates alone with personally chosen staff, keeps records separately out of the ward and a patient of his disappeared, then we found out she'd died.'

'That doesn't make a lot of sense, son. But sure. Checking someone's registration is easy. What State do you think he was censured in?'

'California. Possibly Los Angeles itself.'

'Surely the hospital would have verified his licence?' John's mother shook her head.

'Well, you'd think so, but the Chief of Staff, Dr Carlton Harper, seems scared of another doc, a nephrologist guy called Dr Elias van Lindholm. We've seen Harper jump to do his bidding. And this van Lindholm sure is very 'in' with Mendoza, even covers for him, yet Mendoza's a surgeon.' John shrugged with his hands out. 'A poor one too, according to Mhairi. She saw a really infected wound in a patient he was discharging and I saw that woman re-admitted to the ER with septicaemia. She's the one who died.'

'Phooee! Dodgy docs, separate records and careless surgery? Highly irregular. I smell malpractice suits here.' Jaqueline set her cup down forcefully.

Seeing my puzzled look directed at his mother, John patted my hand. 'Mum's a lawyer too, darling. Medical malpractice a speciality.'

Warren looked up to the ceiling, obviously thinking. 'But just how does this affect you two? I mean they haven't involved you in anything illegal, have they?'

'No, not directly. A nice Fifth Year resident called Dr Randy Ortez told Dr Carlton Harper, the Med Chief of Staff, that 'someone' overheard a conversation calling into question Mendoza's licence to practice. He didn't say it was Mhairi who eavesdropped. But Harper didn't want to know. Nor about that patient, Carmela, we mentioned that I saw with septicaemia in the ER who'd gone missing on transfer. Moreover, the woman's ER records can't be found and the listings for other ER patients that evening—Friday July 16th—have also vanished from the system. Harper just shrugged it off, even when told there were no hospital admission records on file anywhere for Carmela despite her having been earlier operated on by Mendoza. And Randy thought the Chief was so disinterested that he even decided not to say how bad Mhairi thought Mendoza was, that he was rude, had an awful bedside manner and appalling attitude to sterility.'

I nodded in agreement at this.

On the edge of her seat, Jacqueline leaned forward. 'What exactly was wrong with this Carmela woman?'

'As I said, I saw her in ER with septicaemia, five day status post renal stone surgery. We called Mendoza in, but van Lindholm came instead and sent her off in some irregular ambulance service I've since discovered he owns. He insisted she go to a charity Special

Care Unit at a hospital across State as she'd no insurance. But when Mhairi phoned St Thomas's, she was told the woman never arrived.'

Warren frowned deeply. 'This all sounds deeply disturbing. The registration status of Mendoza may be the least of the problems in this story. Have the police been involved? What do the woman's family say happened to her?'

I answered this time. 'Well, we haven't spoken to them yet, but by chance I saw Carmela Gomez's death notice in the local paper. She died in a different hospital. John and I went to her funeral where I spoke briefly to her teenage daughter, Elena.' I felt emotional and couldn't hide it in my voice. As I wavered, John reached out and took my hand. 'I've arranged to meet Elena on Monday to find out what she's been told and what her mum's death certificate says.'

Warren looked over at his wife. 'Is that wise, Jackie? What do you think?'

John's mother made a face. 'If it's just Mhairi and Elena and there's no one else present, it's probably okay. But you can get a copy of the death certificate as well as checking up on this Don Juan guy too, Warren, can't you?'

'It's outside my jurisdiction, strictly speaking, but I can make a few calls. Have you seen any other patients Mendoza's operated on?'

I shrugged. 'A few. While I spent a week in the ward he admits patients to, he had a couple of patients on the floor. I was not asked to see any of them. They were cared for by designated nurses. I believe he only does charity cases, operates on a Sunday morning and has them out by Tuesday. Lot of them seemed renal, I think.'

Warren waved a finger at John. 'Something stinks here. You're right, Johnnie. My advice is that you stay well away from him. And this van Lindholm—he German?'

I answered. 'No. I believe his family were Swedish. They came over after the war.'

John let go of my hand, put his hands behind his head and leaned back, stretching out his long legs before crossing them at the ankle. 'So, Dad. Ideas?'

'Think this Mendoza sounds incompetent at best and illegally practising at worst. Even though it's Saturday, let me make some calls. I've a few favours to call in.' Warren left for his study.

Jackie turned to me. 'It also sounds like the Ellis Memorial Hospital President and Board of Governors need to be informed of the missing records and this woman's treatment. Do you think the family will want litigation?'

I shook my head. 'Elena's never mentioned that as her intent but I can't be sure. She seemed cross about whatever happened. They don't look like they'd have money to engage lawyers, though there was a thing Mendoza said to Carmela after her surgery, something about her getting 'full settlement', whatever that meant. Also oddly, for the daughter of a poverty-stricken charity case, Elena Gomez was wearing new designer sneakers and clothes. John thought they might've been fakes but I'm not so sure.'

Jackie looked surprised. 'Hang on, did he mean settlement of his fees? Why would a surgeon be settling his own bills? Was the woman well at that point?'

'Yes,' I replied. 'Well, actually I saw she had a bit of an inflamed wound even then so should have been kept in for a few more days. Another thing we know about is that a charity called Sativa is involved. Elena had a card in ER that she offered as insurance. But the finance lady dismissed it as no use. I'd forgotten about that.'

'Curiouser and curiouser. I thought I knew all the medical insurers and health charities but I've never heard of Sativa. Or I wonder, might the 'settlement' be a payment not to sue for something else? This intrigues me. Might get one of my investigators onto Sativa to see how it functions. Write down the full names of these two clowns please, Johnnie.'

'Thanks, Mom.' John fetched a notepad from beside the phone.

"I'll get on it on Monday. But nothing we do tonight is going to bring back this poor woman, is it?' Jackie topped up her coffee.

'No.' I sighed heavily.

When John went off to speak to his dad in the study, I told Jackie about Nurse Makkonen's death. She was appalled but quick to move over beside me and pat my hand. 'Let's forget all this for the moment. Tonight at Delmonico's. What are you going to wear?'

I had to smile sheepishly. 'I'm afraid I didn't know about the dinner. John never said...so, I haven't brought any dresses. I've only got jeans and a spare top!'

'No worries. Let's go see what Monica has got in her wardrobe. John's sister is about the same size and height as you. Such a pity she couldn't get over from Yale this weekend. She'd have loved to meet you.' Jackie rose and held out a hand for me to get up from the low sofa.

We went into Monica's bedroom, at least double the size of mine at home with an ensuite bathroom. 'Gosh, this is such a lovely house.' I said, standing transfixed at another window overlooking Central Park.

'It's old money, Mhairi. Warren and I are comfortable but we couldn't afford a house here on the East Side without the Coulter legacy. It's all from railroads, believe it or not!' She swung open the doors of a double wardrobe and pulled out half a dozen short dresses. 'How about this green? Great with your red hair. Or the blue silk with striped bodice? If you need a slip, you'll find one in those drawers.' She pointed at a chest under the window. 'And I can give you some new pantyhose if you need them. Those flat white pumps you're wearing will go with anything. That's lucky—Monica has tiny feet.'

Jacqueline left me to do a solo fashion show in front of the double wardrobe mirror. The emerald green dress with silver edged neckline fitted best. My legs, I decided, were looking a bit tanned and I reckoned I could dispense with her offered 'pantyhose' (which I assumed were tights). I found John to ask his approval of the dress. His answer was a kiss. It must have been all right then.

Chapter Twenty
Climaxes

After I'd changed back into my jeans and T-shirt, we went for a stroll in busy Central Park. Eventually, we found an empty bench seat at a quiet spot by the lake and John told me about his Friday night chat with Frankie.

'Once I'd sowed the seed that Lindholm and Mendoza might be up to something illegal, Frankie became real worried because he's actually taken money from van Lindholm, though I'm not entirely clear for what. He didn't need much prompting from me to agree to find out whatever else he can but I hope he's careful.'

'Careful about what?'

'Sneaking into van Lindholm's room tonight. After I told him about the missing ER records, he said he'd go have a look around it in case any of the missing records from the Emergency Room are there, especially Carmela's. And he intends to dig out some of Mendoza's past Sunday patient case sheets which he thinks are likely kept in the room long term. While admitting he'd never actually looked at what these patients were in for, he suddenly got agitated, saying he was a fool and that some of the names of recent ones might be people he'd identified last year for Lindholm as being in big debt to the hospital. He wondered if Mendoza and Lindholm were paying folk to take part in experiments about some odd blood products from Lindholm's NY lab. But since the patients had surgery, I didn't think that that likely. To be honest, I have the impression Frankie isn't that bright. Not sure I'd like him as my physician. If he qualifies, that is…But he also insisted he was going to tackle van Lindholm on Monday for an explanation about Carmela. I told him I didn't think that was a good idea.'

'Oh, neither do I—brave boy! Think I may have maligned Frankie. I wouldn't be brave enough to go and rummage in Dr Elias van Lindholm's room.' By the way, we mustn't forget poor Freya Makkonen. Jess told me van Lindholm actually had a fling with her, did you know? Yet despite being dumped she was still making a play for him every time I saw them in a room together.'

'No, I hadn't heard that. God, I wonder if he had anything to do with her murder? I doubt that Randy's disappearing Resident Doberman was the type to murder. Quite wimpy, according to him.'

~~~

Later, we went in a taxi to Delmonico's, heading south along Fifth Avenue and wending our way down to Beaver Street in the Financial District. En route, Warren recounted the history of Delmonico's, started in 1837 by Italian-Swiss immigrants to serve French cuisine to dignitaries visiting New York. Since then, it had fed US Presidents, titans of industry and the rich and famous from Mark Twain to Dickens. I heard there were several branches, but we were heading for the original one, the Coulson's favourite.

It was very grand. I chose Caesar salad to start (though still have no idea why it's named after a Roman Emperor). For main course, I had my first lobster—and champagne. It was one of my happiest evenings ever. I ate everything with relish and drank more than I should.

John's diminutive Grandma Coulter was delightful and interesting. Now retired from law practice, she'd been high-up in the State Department and was still active in the Women's Political Caucus that Jess had told us about. She felt strongly about women's equality in rights and pay and wanted a big push to get more women into political office. Her attainments were long. She'd even worked on JFK's presidential campaign. And raised four boys. I was full of admiration for her.

We were late home. In the hall, John's parents hugged us good-night before heading to bed. As their room door closed, we were standing obliquely opposite outside Monica's room which was mine for the night. John's good night kiss seemed especially electric. I felt weak and dizzy and knew it was more than the effect of the champagne. Sitting with him and his family tonight I'd come to an inescapable conclusion: I was definitely in love with this lanky, sensitive boy. Yet it was only weeks since we'd met. And tonight, I did not want to go to bed alone. He stepped back to hold my gaze. And read my mind.

Opening my door and nodding into the bedroom, he whispered, 'Would you like me to stay?' He caressed my cheek with the side of his hand. I nodded and closed my eyes as he clasped me to him and started kissing my neck. My heart pulsed to my ears as previously unexperienced tingles reached upwards from my pelvis. John's substantial male arousal was pressing into my lower abdomen. All amazing but, oh God, what was I doing?

I whispered, 'I'm not on the pill, you know. We can't take any risks.' I closed my eyes and saw my mother's face. My heart skipped a beat.

John whispered back. 'Two ticks. I'll be back.' He went next door to his room.

Rushing in, I shut the door. Almost in one movement, Monica's dress was unzipped and cast over a velvet chair at the window. I closed the drapes (formerly known as curtains in my limited world), discarded my knickers and bra on the floor and pulled on the short white broderie anglaise nightdress I'd left laid out on the bed. Chosen by Laura from M&S, it was strappy and thankfully lacier more than utilitarian. Leaping into the big soft bed (lucky old Monica had a double all to herself), I pulled up the covers just as the door opened to reveal John, standing flushed and adorable and clad in cotton shorts.

Softly closing the door, he flipped the lock. As he slid into the bed, he pulled off his shorts, tossed them to join my underwear on the floor and lay back, smiling his boyish smile.

'I haven't done this before, you know,' I mumbled between kisses.

'And I haven't done it before with anyone I feel for like I do for you,' he said.

'Not sure that's grammar,' I said laughing.

'Who gives a fuck!' was his answer.' I do think I love you, Mhairi MacLean.' He held my face between his hands, kissing me slowly and gently as our bodies came up against one another in a warm and gloriously tactile experience of youthful hedonism. His hands moved, I responded. Conscious of his parents across the corridor I found it very difficult not to cry out. But we didn't need words. He knew exactly how to pleasure me. With tenderness, slowly, anxious not to hurt me, we gloriously became one. I melted into bliss.

For the first time I understood my mother and father. This was how I was conceived. They'd 'got ahead of the wedding' but hopefully John's 'prophylactic' would prevent me having to give up medicine like my mother because a baby was on the way. Me.

We fell asleep curled tightly together but I woke at seven in an empty bed. Propriety, of course: John had returned to his own bed. I stretched out, luxuriating in life and nakedness. Now I was a sinner. And with a boy I'd only met weeks ago. The goading Simon Winters from my university tutorial group would have been proud I'd taken his advice; I'd got laid.

~~~

A few hours earlier the same night, Ellis Memorial Hospital

Frankie passes no one as he walks down the stairs from the Residency to Floor Three. On the way, he wonders why few specialists take offices in the hospital. As far as he can see, only the Chiefs of Medicine, Surgery and

Obstetrics have them. And Dr van Lindholm. Most other specialists only have their private offices in the town.

He is a bit scared about what he might find in van Lindholm's room, or VL as the nurses called him. And worries if he does find the missing records, how is he to say he found them? Frankly, he can't see why anyone should have taken them from ER in the first place. But all of John's info was disturbing. Made him doubt the wisdom of aiding VL. He had been flattered to be recruited for 'special' tasks and be asked back for another summer here—but has he been naïve? Has VL had some hidden agenda? Had patients identified as being in need not just benefited from his charity but had to enrol on some studies for the money? Then there's Mendoza. It is odd how he works in isolation and is as friendly with van Lindholm as he is. They don't appear to have anything in common. Are they fiddling Medicaid? But he's only been asked to collect data on impoverished indebted patients, not Medicaid or Medicare ones. Surely nothing he's done for VL has been illegal? But what he's about to do tonight might be.

He's prepared a story in case he's discovered. If it's by the night-time cleaner, he's collecting something for VL he forgot earlier. If by VL, though why in God's name he'd be in at this hour, the story is he's looking for a precious pen from his late grandfather that he remembered last having in the room days ago. Not the greatest excuses, but plausible.

Letting himself in with his key, he closes the door quietly and locks it from the inside. He looks at the different filing cabinets. The single grey one on his right he knows holds records for Mendoza patients recently in hospital or down for admission this weekend. His smaller second key unlocks it and reveals three case sheets: one for a cholecystectomy, two for nephrolithotomies. One is a name he recognises: a Sativa patient he's interviewed about overdue hospital bills. Amazing how so many poor people have kidney stones. He must look up why.

To his left is a two-drawer blue cabinet he's never accessed. Unsurprisingly, his key doesn't fit its lock. Thinking about James Bond films where they do clever things jiggling paperclips, he reaches for the top drawer of the desk to look for one. Conveniently, he finds it open, key in its lock. Two spliffs lie inside. My, my, Elias. Naughty boy. It also holds a notebook, several pens, two paper clips and, he can't believe his luck, a keyring. One of the keys opens the blue cabinet.

Its top drawer has casefiles arranged in alphabetical order. Skimming over them, he finds one for Carmela Gomez. With racing heart, he opens it. On top, it has loose papers for her final ER visit and a carbon copy of a scribbled St Thomas transfer document signed with van Lindholm's manic scrawl. Properly secured together in the folder are Ellis Memorial Hospital in-patient records detailing her surgical admission. Under these, loose at the back, are two more sheets of paper. One, instantly recognisable by its thin blue paper, is a Theatre Procedure slip stating she'd had a 'partial left nephrectomy'. The other is a signed Patient Permission slip for a 'total left nephrectomy'. What the fuck? And finally, at the very back is a large unsealed brown envelope.

Frankie opens it with shaking hands and pulls out the contents. His brain races, trying to grasp the significance of its contents. The first document is a report from a New York Laboratory Service called MLS. It shows blood grouping results and other 'compatibility tests' including human leukocyte antigen ones that he's heard of but in his current stress, cannot remember what they mean, apart from them being used by some bloke called Teriyaki or Terasaki or something to assess transplant donors. The patient name on the result sheet is Carmela Gomez.

Next come three sheets clipped together. The first has a name at the top, Yahir Abbas and one halfway down, Gabriela Burgas. Handwritten below each is a doctor's name and a phone number and below this information, a line of increasing amounts of dollars. Large figures. From the area codes he guesses the first phone number is in New York and the second, Boston. The largest sum is the one at the end of a line under the NY doc. The winner of a bidding war? The underlying two attached sheets are laboratory results from the same NY lab as Carmela's: one for Yahir and one for Gabriella. They look remarkably similar to Carmela's.

Frankie sits down. The penny drops. Of course—they are selling kidneys to the highest bidder! Okay, the donors look like they're being given incentives by having their hospital debts paid off, but from what he sees, he's damned sure there's a shedload of profit being made here by van Lindholm and Mendoza.

He flicks through multiple other sets of notes, all with similar inserts and envelopes, all with signed consent for kidney removal though official 'blue paper' surgery notes listing ops as lithotomies or only "partial" nephrectomies. Each case sheet holds at least one potential kidney recipient's compatibility results, a doctor's name and East Coast phone number. A few, like Carmela's, have two patients listed with escalating payment proposals, likely garnered from phoning each doc in turn. Essentially, VL and Mendoza are stealing from the poor to save the lives of the rich.

The amounts paid indicate the 'needy' kidney failure patients wanting new organs are indeed rich. Might many of these recipients be from overseas? It's always difficult to know in the States, such a melting pot of immigrant names. At the back of the drawer are slim files containing single sheets of Ellis Memorial Labs' patient serology results: presumably, potential donors for whom VL is seeking buyers. Frankie quickly refiles everything.

The lower cabinet drawer holds financial paperwork he can't make head or tail of. Several folders are for the charity Sativa. Multiple statements going back several years show deposits from various sources including NY clinics, payments to individuals of sums in the low thousands and to numbered accounts (doubtless VL and Juan's) for much, much higher amounts. Additionally, there are folders containing patient invoices and settlements. One for Carmela Gomez shows another patient called Gomez has had an outstanding hospital bill paid by Sativa.

Right at the back of the drawer sits a thin, drawer-width red folder and a bulging smaller blue one. Opening the red one, he nearly faints. It contains two large colour photos that wouldn't have been out of place in the hardest gay porn magazine. The naked Dr Carlton Harper is in ecstatic flagrante delicto with a guy Frankie recognises as one of last year's residents, a Second Year who, oddly, isn't around this year. The photo, he guesses, has been taken by telephoto lens through a window but the resolution is excellent. He remembers hearing Lindholm bragging about his fancy cameras and winning some wildlife photo competition. This is certainly 'wild' life'! How Harper must regret not closing the curtains. Certainly, he must know these photos exist—it explains Lindholm's strutting behaviour in the hospital. Harper had much to lose: a nice wife and two boys.

But the smaller blue folder shocks him more. It holds nude photos of young women. Lots of them. Taken on a bed with a red velvet headboard. All from the same elevation. A hidden camera? These photos look like they've been kept for vicarious pleasure rather than blackmail—but who could tell? He recognises several of the young women. Nurses. Candy-stripers. He pockets one for which he sees there are several copies, thinking that with Lindholm having a wife, it might be a useful bargaining tool if things go wrong. But this gives him a pang of shame. How could he start thinking like him? Squinting at the pics he decides they were likely taken in a marital bed, for that over-the-top padded red velvet board and the quality nude oil painting hanging above it weren't the stuff of a hotel.

By now he's had enough. Moving quickly, he restores the contents exactly as he's found them, locks up everything and replaces the keyring in the drawer. Peering out of the door, he tentatively looks up and down the corridor. It is as quiet as a grave.

He creeps back upstairs to his bedroom and puts the photo inside the thick pages of his Harrison's Principles of Internal Medicine before pouring himself a large bourbon. When he eventually lies down, sleep eludes him. At six a.m. he gets up to make a strong coffee and curses himself: he should have asked John for his New York home number. It's almost unbearable not knowing how soon he'll be able to divulge his findings.

Another niggle eating away at him is what he saw in the hospital carpark in the early hours last Saturday when Nurse Makkonen had been murdered. He had paused in the tennis court shrubbery to snog a nurse he was walking down to the Nurses Home when he heard van Lindholm and Makkonen arguing. How often had van Lindholm professed to be annoyed by her irritating crush on him? Yet he'd heard Makkonen swear and threaten to tell his wife something. Had they actually had an affair? She had stormed back over to the hospital and van Lindholm had screamed off down the drive in his car but it had preyed on his mind all week. Had van Lindholm come back and silenced her? Frankie had decided not to tell the police and become involved. He felt afraid. Very afraid. What had he become embroiled in?

Chapter Twenty-One
Early Birds

Sunday 25 July 1971

A few hours later, probably around the same time that John had slipped out of our bed of sin, Laura went for an early morning run. In Fourth Year, she'd given up running for the University team due to work pressure, but while in the States, had vowed to train in the cool of the mornings. Today, she was intending to run up the hill to the hospital and down the other side. No one was about as she jogged through the doctor's car park to the right of the building, almost empty at that time in the morning with only a couple of big cars obviously belonging to specialists and one battered Resident's Cadillac. She saw no one until she spied a figure languishing against the side door beside the parking lot. Unlikely to be a patient this early.

The dark-skinned loiterer wore a navy New York Yankees baseball cap pulled down low over his face. She recognised it because her cousin always wore one. The young man was wearing a denim shirt and jeans with a leather waistcoat hanging loose. While she watched, he took a drag from a cigarette and leaned on a sign that said *Laboratory Deliveries*. Not that he looked like he was delivering anything, though a powerful-looking, dark blue motorbike was balanced at his side. Laura jogged on, veering off to the right towards the tennis courts. Pausing for breath, she looked back through the bushes and saw the door laboratory door opening. A blonde nurse in scrubs came out. She recognised her as one of van Lindholm's 'Blonde Bunnies' (as Jess called VL's special nurses). With a cheery, 'Hey, Winston!' she handed over a sizeable blue container, which he stowed into the box at the back of his bike. After clipping the box securely, he sped off with a roar on the one-way hospital drive, passing ER around the back.

Laura thought that the crack of a Sunday dawn was an odd time to send off packages from a hospital. Blood specimens, most likely. To another lab? Wondering what the bike's logo MRT stood for, she jogged on.

Once back home, she showered and spent some time dithering about what to wear for her Country Club lunch with Coop and his parents. She'd had a letter from boyfriend Greg in Glasgow and felt a bit guilty she hadn't written. He was sweet. But Coop was so much more. And last night he'd been spectacular in bed.

~~~

An hour before this

Dr Elias van Lindholm emerges from his car in the doctor's car park. This is his favourite time of day, a time when it's possible to work without interruption or distraction. And to take advantage of the quiet 'work lull' on Floors to have cosy chats with the latest nubile young pretty things. But in truth, he's becoming tired of the Candy-stripers, feeling a need for some more mature cooperation and experience. That tall Scottish intern, Laura, for example, has a confident look. Unlikely a virgin. Going up in the elevator, he considers how best to approach her. But in his room, thoughts of seduction take a back seat. He's after the Carmela Gomez files.

With her death, it's always possible a coroner might come sniffing. No autopsy has been mooted, thankfully, but might be best to modify her inpatient notes and return the ER ones to Records. Misfiled of course, like those of Elizabeth Adams from last month. Unlikely to be any pushback from her: non-paying patient, no relatives, no questions, simply certified Dead On Arrival at D.G.H. Thank Christ he had taken admission rights at the District General. It had proved useful, even if he rarely put a patient into its rooms, his clientele preferring a more upmarket hospital. Few of the Ellis staff knew he had privileges there: no prestige, not worth trumpeting. But he'd made sure the employees at MRT knew, and to phone him if they ever ended up in D.G in an emergency.

As for Gomez, the plump little daughter will now be in funds so it's highly unlikely she'll try suing Mendoza. And the uncle's been spoken to. Having the odd cop on the payroll is always worthwhile, something his father learned in Sweden during WW2. By now, Officer Charlie Schwartz will have made it clear to Raoul Gomez that drug running doesn't make you an upstanding citizen and planning a lawsuit against the hospital might make you liable to police scrutiny you'd prefer to avoid.

Right. First the top desk drawer to remove two reefers he'd left last time he'd been in here. That had been with that nympho nurse from Dialysis. They'd been chiefed, topped up with bourbon, after her night shift. And done it on the desk. Twice. As he smiles at the memory, he notices there's also a small key ring lying loose in the drawer. How on earth...? He had thought it amongst the several he usually kept on his person, in his pocket. Shaking his head at his absent-mindedness, he goes to open the blue filing cabinet.

The Gomez case file is not there! An unusual panic seizes his chest like a vice. For seconds. But no worries, it is in the drawer, misfiled under 'F'. That can't be blamed on any cannabis confusion on his part. He didn't touch the files while Dolly was on him. And in any case, he would never file Carmela Gomez under anything other than 'G'.

A quick check shows nothing else out of place. Still. Someone has been in here. Sitting for a few moments, he considers the implications. If someone has read the files, particularly the insertions, the scheme is compromised.

He'd changed the lock a year ago to ensure the cleaners' master keys didn't work, telling the supervisor he'd do his own. And the door has not been tampered with. To get in, someone needed keys. There are only three sets of keys. One, his. Two, Dr Juan Mendoza's, though he's beyond caring what's in any records; the crack's catching up with him. And the third set are with that thick Cooke lardo. Okay, as he keeps telling himself, Frankie's been useful gathering debt data, interviewing potential Sativa 'beneficiaries', sussing out relatives and any additional financial debts they may have for leverage. Stupid son-of-a-bitch even believes he'll help him get a paper into The Milbank Quarterly. As if anyone was interested in the research findings of 'Debt Accrual Factors in Working Poor Patients Ineligible for Medicaid' or whatever nonsense title Frankie had planned. But if he's been the one snooping, why? Or might someone have badgered him for the key? Unlikely to be a fellow student. He's observed that they despise him. Frankie-boy's going to need a serious word. It's a crucial time. Potential recipient numbers are climbing, the wealthy overseas market is expanding through the NY specialist clinics. Now isn't the time to risk having his system trawled over by the Hospital Board or AMA.

Quickly, he fillets all the records, stacking the incriminating flimsy blue true Theatre Notes and Patient Permissions surgery slips along with the brown envelopes into an empty box file. The incriminating blue girls' photo folder and oh-so-useful Harper red one he stuffs into his briefcase. But the bottom drawer, the Sativa and payment data files, he'll leave and collect later. They're satisfyingly obscure and muddied anyway.

Finally, he takes today's three patient files from the cabinet, locks up his desk and door and runs up the stairs to the theatre suite. Juan has just finished the first kidney case but by God, he looks rough. Needs a shave. And likely a detox. Sighing, he returns to his car. If he can't find another cheap replacement surgeon, one not too picky about morals, the scheme may fold—or at least be less lucrative.

On the way home, he calms himself. No need to panic. Nothing has been taken. The scheme is likely good for another year. Then he can wind up Sativa and head for Mexico. The house will be finished. And spectacular. Ava will approve. If she doesn't, there's the divorce ammo: photos of Ava and her golf pro. The kids will be at college by then. Perfect timing.

He decides to slip Carmela's files back into the Hospital Records tomorrow. These other babies he's removed will find a home in the useful wall cavity at his pool house.

But the solution for Frankie Cooke will need some thought. Should it be definitive? Might be less of a worry overall. Adrenaline had eased out Elizabeth Adams and Carmela Gomez fairly efficiently. It had been necessary. He couldn't risk St Thomas's doing X-rays or scans and finding that they'd not had the surgery they were listed for at Ellis Memorial but nephrectomies. And find that the kidneys had been removed for no good reason. Well, not for them.

Turning into his driveway he decides it might be timely to 'borrow' some of Juan's drug supplies to solve his problem.

Chapter Twenty-Two
Murder, Malpractice & Road Runner

Sunday 25th July 1971

After a birthday brunch (cake for breakfast) with John's parents, we ran around the nearby Metropolitan Museum of Art and skimmed the Museum of Natural History before driving back to Brunsfield. Although I'd had trouble looking John's Mum in the eye before we left, if she'd any suspicions about what we'd been up to in Monica's room, she showed no sign.

This time, our only delay travelling was caused by a parade of shaven-headed, orange-robed *Hari Krishna* devotees weaving and chanting as they spilled out of Central Park. Popularised by the Beatles' George Harrison, John said the Hindu sect was springing up all over the place. Despite them, we arrived back in Brunsfield by six. To be met at the door by a flustered Laura.

'What's wrong?' I asked.

'Frankie's been over, twice, looking for you, John. Says he knows what Lindholm and Mendoza are up to. And I saw something this morning that fits his theory.'

'What?'

'Think he should tell you himself. It's quite complex.'

'Okay, let me go get him and Coop and we'll do a pizza.' He looked at Laura intently. 'How bad is it?'

'Jail bad, mibbe?'

John sped off. Dumping my bag in my room, I joined Laura in hers. She looked calmer.

'How was your weekend, Mhairi?'

I blushed. 'Well...'

'You did the deed? Atta girl!' She hugged me tightly, whispering, 'Me too.'

I smiled, but countered with, 'But now I feel it's all spoiled. I hope we're not getting caught up in something that'll end up with us having to appear in court.'

'It's kidneys, Mhairi.'

'Kidneys?'

'Yes. Looks like van Lindholm and Mendoza sell them to the highest bidder. He finds patients needing money. Or rather, he had Frankie doing Finance Department digging for him to find folk in debt to cajole and test to see if they are a match for anyone whom he could find was in the market for one. The bold Dr Elias got him on board by convincing him he could publish a paper about patients in hospital debt with social problems that would help lobbyists to improve Medicaid provision, but really it was about finding folk who'd let Mendoza pinch a kidney in exchange for settlement of their debt by his so-called charity, Sativa. Frankie reckons they're making a fortune. I think I saw one speed off on a bike this morning. We know Mendoza operates early on Sundays and at seven today, when out running, I saw a biker scream off from the labs with a cooler kind of thing a nurse gave him. Fits, doesn't it? Time is of the essence to keep kidneys viable for transplant. I think they are only viable for a few hours even chilled.'

'Ah, this might also explain those samples I saw van Lindholm taking from the lab girls here for 'outside tests at another lab' and Carrie's ER fridge samples for him. I thought the extra samples were about helping him sell blood—as the Lab guy told me VL does—but they might well have been from 'charity cases' he's selected as prospective kidney donors.'

'Sure, Mhairi, there're *lots* of things that fit. Let's go out and see if the boys are back.'

In minutes, we were squashed into John's car and headed for Pizza King.

~~~

In the fast food restaurant, Frankie looked ill as he slowly explained his findings: the case sheets, loose 'real' theatre records, permission slips incompatible with what was done, brown envelopes of lab details, names he presumed were recipients with increasingly large sums alongside doctors' phone numbers.

'It's big business. I can't believe he took me in—he wasn't in this for charity. God, he even had me visit patients at home to suss their circumstances, debts, home troubles, job security, details of relatives, next of kin. Took me for a fucking fool! Presumably, he wanted folk as desperate and isolated as he could get. Or maybe even other relatives who might be a better match for one of his rich foreigners.' Frankie looked tearful.

I reached over to pat his hand. 'You weren't to know, Frankie. And remember when you were away at college, he'll have been paying someone else to do it.'

'Huh! And probably a lot more than you got.' John shook his head. I glared at him. His comment would hardly help poor Frankie who already felt exploited and foolish.

Frankie cleared his throat. 'But that's not all. He had other things in his cabinets. Like this.' From his pocket he pulled out a photograph of a completely naked Ellie May lying seductively, legs apart, on a bed with a red velvet headboard.

'Jesus,' said Coop, 'she's fuckin' fit!'

John was more measured. 'She's Nat's cousin, did you know?' We didn't. 'But look how she isn't looking at the camera. I bet she didn't know it was being taken. But why keep a photo like that in his room?'

Frankie shrugged. 'Same reason as he took it—a trophy or memento? Or to take out, ogle and jerk off over? There were a few dozen of them, named and dated on the reverse, going back a few years. What a scumbag. He even had himself in some of them, leering nakedly at the lens pretending he's Rock Hudson or something. Gross. All taken from up high. He's a camera buff, you know. Must've rigged up a delayed action set up on the wall or a wardrobe.'

A customer sidled by. Frankie put the picture back in his pocket.

'Who were the other women?' asked John.

'I recognised some Candy-stripers and nurses but many I've never seen. Mostly blonde. Always a single girl in the frame.'

'So, not an orgy then? But still, it's sick. Especially if they're all young and didn't know they were being photographed.' Laura looked disgusted.

'But the best photos were too big for my pocket.' Frank smiled ruefully.

'What? Why were they the best?' asked Coop, leaning forward.

'Well not best technically as photographs, but because they explain why van Lindholm has Harper round his little finger.'

'Ah, so he's been at van Lindholm's orgies too?' Coop narrowed his eyes.

'Nope.' Frankie settled his mouth in a tight, grim smile. 'He's a Mary.'

I had to say, 'A what?'

'The guy's a cocksucker, sorry ladies.' He nodded at Laura and me. 'There he was, in full glorious technicolour, and not bad focus considering it was obviously through a window, doing the business on a Resident I knew last year who's now left.'

'But Harper's got a wife and kids! Has their photo on his desk.' I put down the pepperoni pizza slice that I'd been greedily chomping. It seemed all my appetites were voracious this weekend, for more than pizza I realised, as John slid his arm around my back.

'Like, that matters?' said Frankie, properly laughing for the first time. 'Loads of gay men marry for respectability, especially in the medical profession. No one gives a fuck, except maybe the Catholic hospitals, as long there's no in-your-face publicity. God, Lindholm's photos sure were in Harper's face! Reckon they were taken at the Ramona Motel. It's got blue shutters.'

John wiped tomato off his chin. 'So, VL must have been following him and lucked out. Risk of exposure would be enough for Harper to allow VL a free hand and let Mendoza cut up innocents in the Operating Room early on Sundays as well as get his chosen band of staff employed, likely ones who won't spill any beans. Wonder if he pressurised them with naughty photos too? Chancey, though. Wonder how many kidneys he did?'

'Loads in the files.' Frankie shrugged. 'It looks very lucrative.'

'So, knowing what we know, what should we do about it?' Coop sat back.

I piped up. 'Well, John and I told his parents about Mendoza's possible licence loss and the missing records.'

'Dad's looking into that. And when we get back I'll phone him about this.'

I added. 'And Mrs Coulter is getting an investigator to look at Sativa. She's a lawyer and wondered if Elena Gomez might want to sue Mendoza about his shoddy treatment of her mother. And that was before we knew about the organs for sale. I'm seeing Elena tomorrow.'

Coop put his hand out flat on the table and tapped once forcefully. 'Now, I think we all agree this is about bad medicine, exploitation, horse-trading kidneys, money-making and so on. But is it all illegal?'

John blew out slowly. 'Well, if Mendoza is working without a licence, that is. But paying for organs? Dad will know. Then this charity might be illegal if it's a fake, in reality only a smoke screen for Lindholm's payments in and out, but that needs specialist investigation. To me though, the worst thing is coercing these poor folk to donate kidneys. Even if it's not illegal, it's certainly immoral. And the hospital's unlikely to be pleased at a dubious money-making enterprise such as this under their roof.'

'Isn't preying on young women and taking photos against the law?' I asked.

'Doubt it.' Laura almost snorted. 'I bet the police won't care about that sort of thing. They'll likely argue the women were above the age of consent. I know someone at home who reported an assault and got humiliated with no follow-up. Even if they know they were being photographed, would these girls come forward, especially if any were blackmailed? Doubt it, too embarrassing. In any case the police might decide it's not worth court time. But at home, if any were patients of a doctor, the GMC wouldn't like it. Probably strike him off.'

There was an interlude for our explanations about the General Medical Council.

Frankie looked interested. 'Right. So, it's a national regulator you have, not State Boards like the US?'

As I nodded, John touched my arm. 'Hey, Mhairi, what was your idea about what VL was up to at Carmela's ambulance? Have you told the guys about him fiddling with her drip and maybe pocketing a syringe? After hearing Frankie's stuff, I wonder if he might've finished her off in case she told someone what they did to get her so sick or in case her next hospital might discover she was minus a kidney, not just stones. If he did, that's plainly murder.'

I sat back. 'Gosh. That's an idea. On the other hand, she did have serious sepsis, probably caused by Mendoza being slap-dash with sterility. He's at least liable for manslaughter.'

Coop looked worried. 'Right. So, Lindholm might be charge-able with homicide and Mendoza with manslaughter. If we can prove it. But they've got high stakes here. And they seem pretty ruthless. We need to be careful.'

Laura started collecting up our pizza rubbish. 'In amongst all this though, I can't understand why they didn't do a postmortem for Carmela. At home, if you die soon after surgery there has to be one.'

'You mean an autopsy?' John answered. 'It's up to the coroner or medical examiner and someone has to report it.'

Laura sighed. 'And Lindholm would know the right people to lean on to accept his version, I suppose. What can we do?'

John took charge. 'Let me speak to my father and we'll meet again tomorrow night after Laura's seen Elena. Once we know what she's been told and if she wants to take things further, we can decide whether to involve the police or the Board of Governors or both.'

Back at the Home, John and I briefly hugged and kissed at the door. Then Laura and I sat in the kitchen drinking wine. It had been a long day. And a whirlwind few weeks in America. Already I'd learned more than I wanted to. Not just about US medicine and surgery but about medical malpractice, the law and sexual antics. Mine included.

Light relief came in the form of a present from Laura and Jess's visit to Filene's Basement: short, pink baby doll PJs with a *Road Runner* motif. Off the shoulder top and scant shorts—what would Una say? I'd forgotten Laura had been up in the city with Jess. Laura proudly showed me another purchase, bell-bottom trousers covered in hundreds of faces from the famous 1969 up-state New York Music Festival at Woodstock. As Jess had actually been there, we peered at them for ages looking for her face, while we finished a bottle.

To my surprise, I heard that our waitress friend, Gretel, from the Bohemia restaurant had gone up to New York City with them. She'd phoned after I'd left asking if we'd like to go there with her this weekend and had happily tagged along with Jess and Laura. Seems Gretel had got on like a house on fire with Jess. I wouldn't have thought they had much in common. Later, I was surprised to find out there was a surprising amount. None of it pleasant.

Chapter Twenty-Three
Macey

Monday morning found me in Obstetrics. Apart from knowing where a baby came from, I knew nothing about childbirth. At Glasgow, Obstetrics and Gynaecology were subjects we didn't do till Sixth Year. The Senior Resident handed me an illustrated diagram of the stages of labour and sent me off to shadow an Intern called Sol who was the most recently qualified doctor on the floor. I discovered that for patients without insurance who had, nonetheless, to be given acute care, he and I were 'It' in the delivery suite.

It was so busy, I had no time to think about taking a break. I discovered childbirth was a messy, bloody, painful and at times brutal business. Although I was told strong opiate painkillers should be withheld in later stages of labour for fear of depressing a baby's breathing, I was shocked at how infrequently they were actually given to women in severe pain, even in early labour. "Let's see how she does," was Sol's parting shot to most patients after doing a pelvic check to see how far the womb neck had dilated and thus how far along towards delivery they were. I slowly got the impression that Sol's comment was especially likely should the panting, suffering, woman be coloured.

Sol let me examine some of the women myself. After deciding one woman was only a few centimetres dilated and nowhere near ejecting her child, I lost it. The heavily built black girl was sweating profusely and crying out in agony with every contraction, pleading for help. I turned on Sol and fiercely muttered, 'For the love of God, she's nowhere near delivering—you must give her a painkiller!'

Looking hurt and indignant at my challenge, he waved me outside before speaking. 'Okay, if you insist, she can have some Demerol. But you'll have to go and get it. You'll need to find two nurses to sign for it and you can give it. Lateral thigh, intramuscularly. I'm off for a smoke.'

With difficulty, I found a Junior Nurse to get what I realised later was pethidine from the locked drug trolley and a Senior one to sign sanctioning its use. When I asked if I could personally give it, she shrugged and started to walk off. Flicking the charts, I could see that all the women looked like they'd been written up for pain relief on admission. I had to ask,

'Excuse me, but why do you give Demerol to so few women, and especially as I see it, to so few Black ones? Or am I wrong?' I tried not to sound too critical, but it was hard.

'Oh, the Blacks have a lower threshold for pain. You get used to their dramatics.' With that, the nurse sat down to resume her monologue on last night's hot date directed at another bored looking, heavily 'made-up' nurse unprofessionally chewing gum. I sighed, thinking here were many differences between UK and US medical personnel, not only the language they used.

I took the jab, administered it myself into Macey's lateral thigh (probably illegally as I wasn't qualified) and sat with her for a while. She dozed off. Reluctant to go and look for Sol, I stayed until she wakened with a smile.

'It was real good of you to go get me something. You've got a cute accent. Where are you from, Ireland?'

'Scotland.' I said. 'So, is this your first baby?'

'No. I lost a baby girl last year.'

I was incensed. Even without obstetric training I knew from first principles this patient needed monitoring. Or at least occasional midwife visits, yet all morning it looked like Macey had received only one check, from Sol. But I only asked her, 'What happened last time?'

'The baby got stuck. Never breathed. My last doctor said I should have a C-section this time, but Eddie lost his job. And our insurance. And this doc's just said, "Let's see how you do."'

'Is Eddie coming in?'

'They sent him away. Said they'd call him later. I heard the nurse mutter husbands were a 'fuckin' nuisance.' Killed me a bit. Huh, shouldn't think it happens along the corridor. Reckon it's only poor folk's husbands that clutter up the place.'

I was inclined to agree. Leaving Macey Baker to doze, I went for lunch, promising to return later.

~~~

The US had expanded my vocabulary as well as my experience. My lunchtime conversation with John was full of expletives. We stole a few minutes of privacy with a short walk through the grounds and a kiss before I returned to Macey who was now contracting every minute and amazingly, had a midwife in attendance who'd just done a vaginal exam.

'Nine centimetres. Time for the Delivery Room.'

I pushed the trolley along the corridor, assisted Macey up onto the delivery couch and helped put her feet into the stirrups, the awful demeaning things used to elevate them out of the way to allow medics access to the perineum for delivery. They looked very uncomfortable. I thought they must make it harder for women to push. Macey looked terrified. I took her hand. Her pulse was like an express train.

'She's crowning,' said the nurse unemotionally. 'Get the pack.' She waved at a trolley bearing a linen-swathed theatre pack which I rolled over beside her. After she'd kicked up a stool to sit on, I headed for the sink to start scrubbing up in the hope that I could help.

'No time,' shouted this sharp-nosed nurse, already unstrapping the sterile instrument pack with gloves that had opened doors and pushed a trolley. Sterility? Out of the window! As I quickly dried my hands and donned some sterile gloves from a pack, a voice in my head questioned, "Would this happen with an insured patient?"

'Come on, girl, get pushing!' The orders came fast and thick for Macey. 'Again. More. Stop now! Feeling round the baby's neck for the cord.'

'That's what happened last time,' panted Macey, staring to pray. 'Dear Lord please let me be safely delivered! Our Father who art ...'

'The Lord's got nuthin' to do with this, girly. Maybe out in the fields, but in here it's you and me, right? Okay. Now push some more.' After further exhortations and much groaning, the baby's head appeared, then its shoulders, before eventually it plopped into the midwife's hands. She scooped the blood-stained sticky baby up onto its mother's abdomen, on which she had at least draped a sterile green linen sheet. Handing me the scissors, she said, 'Okay, Miss Scotty, you wanna cut the cord? Those clips there,' she pointed at the trolley, 'put 'em on the cord an inch apart and cut in between. About here.' She stretched out the umbilical cord.

I complied, then placed the now separated baby further up into Macey's arms. She was crying with joy. I wasn't far behind. The midwife continued on to deliver the placenta, which she tossed into a stainless-steel dish. 'Looks intact. Always check no raggedy bits, Scotty. They play havoc and get infected if left behind.' She cleaned up Macey's vulval area and swabbed her with antiseptic. 'You got a little tear, honey. But I don't think we need to bother the doc with it. Sure, and it'll heal up fine.'

I wasn't so sure. But she wasn't insured.

Pushing back her stool, the midwife elevated the lower end of the bed that had been dropped for delivery and showed me how we should bring Macey's feet down together from the stirrups.

'She'll be sore enough for a day or two. Don't want to add a hip injury.'

After this sole concession to humanitarian care, she handed me a towel for wrapping the baby and left.

I was flabbergasted. No, 'Well done,' to Macey. No, 'Goodbye and thanks,' to me. What about giving the baby a bath? Or showing Macey how to breastfeed her? Or all the other things I'd seen in movies? Then the door opened and a nursing assistant came in. John later told me that US graduate nurses, like midwives, don't do menial tasks, such as bathing babies.

'Hi, time to get you back to the ward, honey, and bathe this babe!'

At least the nursing assistant who came in next smiled at the new arrival. She was the only coloured employee I'd seen in Ellis Memorial apart from an elderly male cleaner in the ER.

The assistant lifted the baby and smiled at her. 'So, who is this then?'

'We haven't picked a name. Didn't want to test fate.' Macey said apologetically before looking at me. 'What's your name?'

'Mhairi MacLean.' I spelled it out for her.

She mouthed it back but obviously wasn't keen. 'You gotta middle name?'

'Margaret, after my mother.'

'Yea, Maggie! Let's do Maggie. Hello little Maggie, isn't your daddy goin' to be pleased to meet you!'

As they set off down the corridor to a postpartum room, I noticed it was almost three. I had to meet Elena at four! I didn't bother finding Sol to tell him I was off. As if he'd care. But in case he did come looking, I told the girl at the desk I was off to an appointment. It was Candy-striper Ellie May, who seemed to be popping up in a different hospital department every day.

Rushing down to the Home to discard my white jacket, I phoned for a cab. I hadn't a clue where Di Marco's was. But a cabbie would know.

Chapter Twenty-Four
Di Marco's & A Death in the Residence

Maple Street was on the east side of town in an area we hadn't yet visited. It consisted mainly of small shops and eating places with flats overhead. When dropped off by my taxi at the corner, I walked past a clothes shop, an electric goods store and a grocer with window notices in Spanish about a missing child. Next door was Di Marco's, a single-fronted restaurant whose doorway and window could have done with a fresh lick of red paint. Its gilded window arch declaring 'Di Marco's' was also worn away in several places. Inside, at the front was a bar seating area with small leatherette chairs. To the rear, large tables covered by red checked cloths were set for dining, separated from the bar by an old battered mahogany waiter's station flanked by sad-looking potted palms.

Elena was sitting at the front window with a cup of coffee and a pastry. She looked to be the only person in the whole place. Seeing me, she rose with a smile.

'Hello, Mhairi. Glad you made it.' I got a warm hug before she called to the rear of the restaurant, 'Nico!'

A handsome olive-skinned boy of about eighteen appeared, wreathed in smiles. He obviously adored Elena, who smiled back at him.

'Can you get my friend a coffee, Nico? Or would you like something else?' Elena stretched out a palm towards me. This seemed a very different girl from the one sobbing on my shoulder in ER that terrible night. More assured, grown up. Was this for the benefit of Nico or had something happened to make her so?

'Coffee's fine.' I sat down with my back to the window and watched Nico scurry off with a wink and little air kiss.

'So, Elena, how are you?'

'I am sad, of course, because my mother has gone, but mostly now I am angry, thinking about what my mother was made to do.' She breathed in slowly through her nostrils and exhaled forcefully. 'I do not think it was right. That is why I wanted to speak to one of the doctors, like you, who saw her at the hospital.'

I'd assumed she'd twigged I wasn't a doctor. 'Sorry, Elena, I'm not a doctor yet. I'm just a student. But what do you think your mother was forced to do?' I decided not to disclose what I knew until I'd heard her story.

'To sell a kidney to pay my medical bills. Oh, you will not know but I have been admitted many times with my asthma and diabetes. My mother was much in debt. We have no care cover. She agreed to give Dr Mendoza and Dr van Lindholm a kidney. He promised that if she did so, a charity would pay off all our debt. But why was selling a kidney necessary if it was a charity? Sometimes my mother was too trusting. And now, since she died, I believe they have paid a lot of money to my uncle, supposedly for me. Though he has not told me how much he got. Oh, of course, Uncle Raoul has bought me presents, says he will open an account for me to use—but I don't trust him.' She rolled her eyes. 'How can I trust a man whose business is death?' She paused at this enigmatic comment because some diners came in, waiting until they had passed, before adding in a low voice, 'He is a drug dealer. Thinks this new cocaine will make us very rich. My mother told him she disapproved.' Elena sat up defiantly. 'As do I.'

'Oh! A new kind of cocaine?' I didn't say I knew nothing about the old kind.

'It's called Crack. They boil it with baking soda or some such. It is more addictive, good for business. But anyway, as for my mother's death, Raoul doesn't want me to make a fuss. He says her death is God's will. My ass!' She spat out the words. 'She did not die of pneumonia. It was that man Medoza who killed her. Her wound was a mess. He is a butcher! Dios Mio, the death certificate did not mention her surgery at all. That was what killed her, them taking her healthy kidney.'

'How do you know she gave them a kidney?'

'She told me after the operation. Said Dr van Lindholm told her you only needed one, it would not affect her life, the operation was simple and she'd be back at work in days. All lies. I think she became so ill because the operation was done badly. And then at the ambulance, did you see? I think Lindholm gave her something. What? Why then and not when she was still in the ER? Madre de Dios—did he kill her as he was afraid she would say what they had done?'

My flesh crawled. Elena was confirming what Frankie had suggested and I thought I'd seen outside ER. She was looking at me so earnestly and distressed that I had a lump in my throat. For a few seconds I worried that agreeing about van Lindholm might add to her grief but decided truth is truth.

'Yes, I suspect that too. I think we should expose these two doctors. What they did was immoral. I expect they got a lot more money for your mother's kidney than they gave her.'

'But do you know how much lawyers cost? Raoul will not pay.'

'I don't know. But I do know one who will help us all she can.'

'Raoul will not be happy. But it is important to find out why mothers die, is it not?'

My heart somersaulted. More than anyone, I knew this was true. 'Could you maybe come up to New York with me on Saturday? If I can, I'll arrange for you to meet a good lady lawyer. At least you need advice. I've already told her about your mother.'

Elena looked astonished. 'Fantastico! Thank you, Mhairi. I am afraid I must go to get ready to help in the restaurant. I do it several nights a week and at weekends and cannot let Nico and his father down.' Her smile was warm, genuine and innocent. I truly liked this girl and hoped she'd find some peace.

My own peace was still some way off. Walking west to the hospital guided by the setting sun, I eventually found a street I recognised and headed home on foot, thinking. So, Elena did want to sue, but at sixteen, she was surely still a minor. If Raoul were her guardian, could he stop her demanding an investigation? But on the other hand, should she be forced to keep living with him, a cocaine dealer, against her will? At least when my mum died, I'd had Dad, my brother Archie and Gran Una, who apart from her killjoy beliefs was kind and caring. Elena's situation was all so dreadfully sad.

At the Home, Jess was waiting in the kitchen with more horrific news.

'You'll never believe it, Mhairi, they've found a dead body in the Residency!'

~~~

I grabbed a few Oreos and headed up to the hospital to find John. Although we'd planned to meet tonight for a Council of War, the time and location had been left vague. I couldn't wait for him to contact me.

Several police vehicles were parked out in front of the hospital and in the lobby an officer was taking notes from the Candy-striper at the desk. Looking at her pretty face, I wondered if she'd featured in Lindholm's porn gallery? When I came out of the elevator on Sixth Floor, I was confronted by another policeman. He barred the way into the Residency.

'I'm sorry, honey, but you cannot enter this area. It is a crime scene.' He put a gentle arm on my elbow to direct me back towards the elevator.

'But I have to see my boyfriend. Please officer.' My batted eyelashes were useless.

He shook his head and repeated, 'This is a crime scene. Please leave.'

At that point John appeared from behind the striped tape slung across the Residency door. He was ghostly white and drawn. I wondered even if he'd been crying.

'It's alright officer, I think Detective Burr will want to speak to this lady.'

The cop was unconvinced. Exasperated, John retreated to return with a middle-aged crewcut guy in plain clothes wearing an armband that said 'Police'. John introduced me and I was taken under the tape down the corridor.

'What on earth is going on? I asked John as he took my hand to follow the detective. In the sitting room we passed Coop, Nat and a few Residents. The TV was on with the sound turned down. Detective Burr took us on into a small office that I'd never been in. He sat on a padded seat at the desk and gestured us to sit on two plastic chairs at the opposite side. Leaning back, he scrutinised me.

'So, Miss MacLean, I hear you and this young man here have turned detective?'

'Och, we didn't intend to. It's just that odd things have been happening. Like, a patient vanished. We were puzzled. And worried.' But I could contain myself from asking, 'Who's dead?'

John answered. 'Frankie.'

'Frankie? How? When?'

Detective Burr answered, 'We think in the early hours of the morning. The cleaner didn't do the room as usual at noon as a 'Do not Disturb' notice was hung on the door. She thought someone had come off a bad night. But at five o'clock this afternoon your friend here realised he hadn't seen Mr Cooke all day so went to his room. And found him dead.'

'How?' I was shocked to my core.

'From an overdose of intravenous drugs, it appears.'

'Drugs? Frankie doesn't take drugs. Well, I think he might have had some cannabis at...'—I caught Johns's almost imperceptible shake of the head—'...in the past. But not serious potentially fatal drugs. What d'you think he took?' I was still trying to get my head around this.

'He had a used syringe beside him and there were other signs of drug use in his room. We thought that perhaps it was accidental or a bad batch until John here told us about the interesting time you've all been having with a certain...' he flipped back his notebook, '...Dr Elias van Lindholm and Dr Juan Mendoza. I'd like to hear what you know, Miss MacLean.'

We then spent the best part of an hour as I detailed what I'd seen, what I'd heard, the news fresh from Elena and that from our pizza evening at which Frankie had dropped his bombshell about kidney transplants and false records. I told him everything I could think of and was surprised how much better I felt once it was all out. John sat beside me silent but with a reassuring arm around my waist, nodding when I recounted incidents at which we'd both been present. I finished off by telling the detective that we had told John's parents everything, except for yesterday's revelation, in the hope of getting advice on what to do.

John added, 'My father is on his way now from Court in the city. I called him.'

'Is he a lawyer?' The detective continued to scribble without looking up.

'He is District Attorney for the Southern District of New York. His jurisdiction is up to our county border, I believe.'

That made Burr sit up. 'Well, guys, seems you have a heavy hitter on your side.'

'We don't need anyone batting for us, we haven't done anything wrong, detective. In fact, due to our efforts I think you'll shortly have a lot of information on these two doctors and the death of the poor woman whose death triggered our interest.'

'I didn't say you had done anything wrong, Mr Coulter.' The detective was running a finger around inside his too tight collar. The small room was warm and windowless.

'I need to get a glass of water, if you don't mind?' I rose and made to leave.

John stood with me adding, 'If Frankie Cooke killed himself, I'm a monkey's ass. I suggest you speak to Dr Elias van Lindholm or Dr Juan Mendoza and find out where they were overnight.' He followed me out.

Fetching a glass of water from the kitchen, I returned to sit with John, Coop and Laura, who'd managed to fight her way in helped by Coop. Nat was pacing about the sitting room, very edgy and shaking. He whispered to me he had some hash in his wardrobe and didn't know what to do. Panic was written all over his face. He was sure the police were going to search all the rooms. I reassured him with a hug that they showed no signs of doing that. He started to sob. Poor Nat. He seemed very sensitive and I wondered if he had what it takes for medicine, though admittedly this current stressful situation was out of the ordinary. While the others were engrossed in a discussion about drug use amongst medics, he suddenly whispered to me.

'I'm gay, Mhairi. I can't help it, it's who I am. But I've been foolish in allowing myself to be led on.' He looked around the room and leaned closer to my ear. 'I've been 'intimate' with a senior staff member, he pressurised me.'

Why he decided to tell me then I have no idea. I didn't say I already knew about his sexual inclination from a comment by Randy, just shushed him to stop worrying and gave him another hug. He couldn't stop shaking.

It was now John's turn to get agitated. 'You know it's all my fault Frankie's dead? If I hadn't pushed him, he'd never have gone into Lindholm's office looking for stuff and he'd still be alive. I reckon he must've disturbed something and van Lindholm decided it had to be him as he had a key.'

'But we don't know for sure it was van Lindholm who killed him, do we? It could be someone else involved. And it wasn't *you* who gave him a fatal jab.' I wasn't having any of this. 'It is not your fault!'

Randy and Sean were also trying to convince John he shouldn't blame himself when Warren and Jackie appeared at the door. We stood to receive warm hugs before they asked us what was happening. As John had become too upset to speak, I told them about Frankie. 'We've already been interviewed by the police...' I paused in my explanation to Jackie as an impressive tall figure wearing an expensive suit and silk tie strolled in through the door.

John spoke to his father at my side before sinking back into the sofa. 'Hey, here's the Hospital President, Mr Charles Schieffer. Didn't think he ever came out of his lair.'

Warren Coulter strolled over to greet the man as Lieutenant Burr appeared from the far side of the room. Seeing his Police armband, Warren turned his attention to Burr. 'Are you the officer in charge of the investigation?'

Burr replied. 'I am.'

Warren then pointed at us. 'Lieutenant, if my son and his girl have given statements, can they go now? I reckon they need to get a drink.' He looked at the detective expectantly.

'So, who exactly are you?' Burr asked, frowning.

'Warren Coulter, New York District Attorney. His father.' Warren nodded towards John.

Burr looked at the sofas of Residents and students and shrugged. 'Sure. The ones who've given statements can go, the rest please wait, my deputy will get to you presently. But no one leaves town.'

Warren came over and squeezed John's arm. 'Okay, John. Why don't you go and take Mhairi for a coffee now then come over and meet us in the Marriott Bar in a couple of hours to eat and debrief? Lots to tell you. Mom and I have booked in there since we thought it would likely be too late for driving home tonight'

Schieffer, whom I'd gleaned was in overall administrative charge of the hospital, not just the medics that were Dr Harper's responsibility, had a brief discussion with Burr then suggested Warren and Jackie join them in the Director's Office.

I was relieved to be off the hook for now and I thought going for a coffee an excellent idea. In fact, going anywhere away from the Residency was attractive. With difficulty, I pulled a morose John to his feet, said some goodbyes and followed Burr, the Coulters and President Schieffer out of the room. We let them take the first elevator down to Level Two where the Director's Office lay, then called another car for ground level. But I was barely in it when I couldn't suppress a totally inappropriate giggle. John looked at me bewildered.

'What's with you? I sure as hell see nothing to laugh at.'

'God, it's just I never believed I'd hear anyone say that to me!'

'Say what?'

'Burr. You heard what Burr said, "Don't leave town."'

John had to smile. 'You're crazy, you know that? Not sure why I love you. Let's go and get a proper drink. I've never needed one more in my life. You got ID with you?"

I hadn't, so we walked down to the Home to fetch my passport. While there, I quickly changed into smarter trousers and a lace top, picking up a cardigan for possible restaurant air conditioning (I'd been frozen in Delmonico's). In the kitchen, John gave Jess the lowdown. She got upset.

'Frankie? Oh dear. He was a bit of a dickhead, but no one deserves that.'

'I expect Coop will be let out shortly and be right down here with Laura and Randy. Better have some of that Tennessee Whiskey of yours at the ready.' He hugged Jess and turned to me. 'You know, I'm not up to driving. Let's call a cab.'

It arrived promptly. We left Jess sniffing into a kitchen towel. I felt torn, but knew we had to get away. In the cab, John hugged me close. 'You know, babe, I think we should get a room for the night.'

'But I don't have any night things.'

He looked at me tenderly and whispered, 'You don't need any night things for what I have in mind.'

The male libido is remarkably resilient. Whatever dreadful circumstances its owner faces it seems it can rear up and revitalise.

~~~

It was late when Warren and Jackie finally found us in the Marriott Bar. I was on my third drink—but not of wine. Daringly, I had gone a step further than the Martinis on the plane and ordered a Manhattan. And thereafter, two Tom Collins cocktails, John's prescribed remedy for perking us up. They did. We'd also polished off massive hamburgers with bacon, cheese and pickles plus obscene piles of 'French Fries' and some New York cheesecake. John's parents followed our example (without the cocktails) and then sat listing everything they had found out about Elias and Juan. And Sativa. And much more.

But our pressing worry was what had actually happened to poor Frankie. Had he been murdered or had he felt so despairing that he'd taken his own life?

Chapter Twenty-Five
Disposal, Disclosure & Danger

Early morning the same day, Monday July 26, 1971, Ellis Memorial Hospital Residency

This one he has to do himself. Delegating the last disposal to young Winston was a disaster. How hard could it be to silence a fucking injured whore? He'll not try fixing her again at present. Not completely sure she got a look at his face in any case. And with the extent of her injuries, and he's sure, a head injury, she likely has post traumatic amnesia. He couldn't do for her himself on a surgical floor, too risky. He's a distinctive figure, easily recognisable, who'd have no plausible excuse for creeping around a surgical floor out of hours. But this potential victim resides in a non-public area. And is a more imminent threat to the survival of his lucrative activities. It's a no brainer.

Dressed in unaccustomed dark sports gear, sneakers and baseball cap, he ascends the five flights two at a time. He's chosen the time well and meets no one on his way. With Monday mornings in the hospital always busy, he's banking on the fact that on overnight Sundays no medic stays up. It's now two-thirty a.m. on Monday. Few residents are likely to be wandering around the corridors or stairs. Any staff on night duty will be on their Floors or in ER.

He enters the secure Residency using a master key acquired during an amorous fumble with a nubile Hispanic cleaner. From the recent party, he knows exactly which room is his destination: first on the right through the lounge. The target door is unlocked. With a gloved hand, he turns the handle to open it. There is no creak. The room is as messy and disorganised as its owner.

The task is easily accomplished without sound: a pillow held down by his left elbow: a generous bolus of opiate administered through a neck mole rapidly takes effect. Initial resistance wanes allowing an immediate venous brachial puncture that gives obvious bleeding in front of the elbow before circulation ceases. Then a syringe and tourniquet are suitably discarded around the left arm. Done.

A swift check of the room yields no recognisable documents or papers of note. He distributes the incriminating objects he has brought around the available surfaces and behind some books. A small packet of Juan's crack cocaine, small leaves of foil, a silver spoon, matches, a used candle, some reefers, an empty heroin sachet. Enough.

Opening the door gently, he pauses to listen and freezes. A toilet is being flushed up the corridor. Padding feet approach. His heart misses a beat until he hears a nearby door softly close. The muffled footsteps cease: the owner must have returned to his room. Reassuring. If they had continued along to piss while he's been doing his deed, they cannot have heard a thing.

In seconds, he is back out into the corridor, through the lounge and out of the Residency door. Peeling off his gloves as he runs down the stairs, he allows himself a smile of satisfaction. Killing is easy. And students kill themselves all the time with drugs.

Later that morning, Dr Elias van Lindholm is on the Third Floor, standing in front of an exasperating patient. He imagines silencing him the same way as France Cooke Junior. But the nurse at his side reminds him of the matter in hand.

'Has Mr Delgado to return for review, Dr van Lindholm?' she queries.

'Yes. Three months.' He nods and leaves while the whiny patient is still complaining about being no better. There's fuck all wrong with him, the asshole. But he might as well milk him. His next bill will be loaded.

Elias walks back down the stairs and out through the lobby, surprised that as yet, there is no police presence. Shows how slack the cleaning staff are.

His car purrs throatily as it accelerates out onto the main road and he ponders the decisions he has to make.

Firstly, in light of a possible disclosure of his enterprise, what to tell Ava? Little as possible, he thinks. Previously, as long as she's had funds, she's never once asked where they've come from.

Secondly, best to take off for a short period. But where to go? Next weekend is their wedding anniversary, although for the last few years he's never acknowledged it. This one, however, usefully provides an 'in' for a break. Yes. Feigning apology for his recent 'neglect,' he will sweep Ava off to Paris. And she'll not object to a trip away, being usually compliant with his choices for vacations as long as they necessitate expensive additions to her wardrobe. Besides, since she can still be 'up for it' with coaxing, jetting off to Europe might light a bit of fire.

He suspects that flak may be about to ricochet around Ellis Memorial. Best to be off grid for a while, even though he doubts the Gomez daughter will stir any lawyers over her mother's death; money is a powerful silencer. And he has hidden all incriminating documentation. Plus, Lard Boy's death can't be connected to him. He wasn't seen and jogged over to the hospital from his car that he'd left some distance away. If asked about Frankie, he has of course, comments ready: "Such a waste. A bright boy. Been helping him with a social research project. Drugs have a lot to answer for. The government needs to do more." My ass.

The hospital legals are bound to move in to suppress the story. Any drug death on hospital premises is not good for business: the press won't distinguish between a student intern and a hospital staff member. President Charles Schieffer, his Board of Governors and Chief of Medicine Dr Carlton Harper will have their work cut out.

Regarding the transplant investment program, he's made decisions already. In a call first thing, he's got Juan Mendoza to agree to work his way through the remaining pro bono cases subsidised by the hospital and Sativa. He's told him all patient records remaining in his office now look legit and that the 'official' logged and laundered Sativa accounts are in the usual drawer just in case they're requested. He has mentioned possibly taking a short trip away.

Before going to the office, he deviates to the bank to make a few transfers. Nothing too showy. The manager, Wilmington, is on the Sativa books and will disclose as little as possible should it be necessary for the van Lindholm finances to be scrutinised. Fortuitously, the trails to the Mexican and Panamanian accounts are bafflingly tortuous.

Once at the office, he parks across two spaces. Today, no one is going to park too closely beside him. That asshole who had stopped him getting into his car last week should have been charged. Twenty minutes he wasted raging around the other offices to find the driver and get the car moved so he could drive home. Asshole police wouldn't get it towed.

This morning, he has only two patients waiting in his rooms. He despatches both with a battery of prescriptions and over-detailed advice that should keep them occupied for a while. At his desk, he briskly dictates two letters for his secretary, Jordan, to type then puts on his jacket, aligns his cuffs exactly and goes out to reception to issue some orders.

'Now, Jordan, I plan to spend our wedding anniversary on Sunday in Paris. I'm taking Ava as a surprise.'

'Oh, Doctor, how romantic!' The secretary tucks a wisp of over-bleached hair behind an ear. God, she needs a decent hairdresser. Ava had chosen the bitch herself, no doubt thinking that her plainness would dissuade him from temptation. It hadn't. He'd had Jordan anyway simply because he could and reckoned he was probably the best fuck she'd ever have.

'Can you block off appointments until next Tuesday? Anyone objecting, direct them elsewhere.'

Jordan nods furiously. 'Of course, doctor. My, a week in Paris. How lovely!'

He doesn't mention Ava will be at her mother's for another two nights and that he has plans of his own meantime.

At home he packs a bag and makes three calls. The first is to book two First Class plane tickets to Paris for Wednesday evening. The second is to Ellie May, currently at home: he's checked the Candy-striper rota. His invitation time means she'll arrive well after him. Third call is to the Marriott manager for the usual suite. Not for him Harper's skanky motels. The Marriott's elevated position at the western edge of town and its spacious deluxe suites with large double baths—and even bigger bouncy beds—make it perfect. Especially as he can use a false name. He's ceased using the family home. Why risk being spotted—or have the hassle of cleaning up afterwards? And the photography has lost its appeal. 3D sex wins hands down. And he's never short of partners.

Arriving just after five, he books in without removing his sunglasses. Payment is in cash. In his suite, he discards his tie and starts on the mini bar. It's now six p.m. There's nothing about Ellis

Memorial on the TV news. Nothing to worry about. Fuck. He's for-
gotten his reefers. He lights up a Marlboro.

~~~

As John and I sat in the Marriott bar with his parents, I thought
how impressive they were. Although Warren had a folder of notes,
he hardly referred to them as he took us through their findings.

'My investigator Danny has had a field day. Mendoza did have
his licence to practise revoked for six months in 1965 in California. And in January 1968, it was completely revoked in Kentucky.
He certainly got around with serial jobs and is still listed as being
licenced in New Jersey and New York. Obviously, he didn't report
his Kentucky revocation. The Californian censure was for 'drug
irregularities, though he found no record of any drug charges being
officially laid against him in the courts. The Kentucky revocation
referenced drug and alcohol issues and a serious assault on a fellow
surgeon in Louisville, but again there's no police record.'

'How come?' I asked.

'That's not unusual,' Jackie said. 'Hospitals don't like adverse
publicity. It's often low-key civil suits and direct-to-the-Board
complaints which cause doctors to lose their licences. And State
Boards, strangely, have no obligation to tell other Boards who
they've bumped off. Incidentally, I haven't told the Ellis Hospital
President this yet. I wanted some physical paperwork in my hand
before approaching him.'

Warren now flicked through his notes. 'Before all this, Dr
Juan Mendoza was a high-flying scholarship student at UCSF in
San Francisco, completing specialist surgical training—general
and urological—with flying colours before being assimilated as
a junior partner into a surgical multi-specialist practice in LA.
He was there till the mid-sixties when, for no discernible reason,
he left to work on staff in a series of Los Angeles hospitals, then
a private clinic in New York for eighteen months before taking

off to Kentucky where he only stayed for eight. Danny found a gap in records then until he found him practising in Brunsfield in 1968. He set up offices and obtained admission rights to Ellis Memorial and the Plainsfield District General Hospital. Today, the Ellis Memorial Hospital President, Charles Schieffer, told me his Board were taken with Mendoza's willingness to perform elective surgery at reduced cost for the uninsured. They felt that this was good for their image. Mendoza's referee was van Lindholm by the way, but curiously, we couldn't find any connection between them prior to this. Juan Mendoza has no marriage recorded but he does cohabit with a much younger Latino girl whose family are known felons. He himself has no police record.'

'It's quite a chequered career,' commented John.

'Now, one thing I found particularly interesting after you phoned telling me about the kidney transplant set up, was that Danny says the private clinic in New York where Mendoza previously worked is now making a name for itself with them. The Prestige Clinic in Manhattan has links with a Boston Interhospital Organ Bank that's been around for a few years. This Manhattan Clinic attracts a lot of foreigners—Arabs and wealthy Europeans in particular.'

'So, that's probably where they were sending the kidneys?' I asked.

'Perhaps. I'm told that once out of the body and chilled, kidneys are only good for about six hours so that'll be his radius of supply. The police aim to speak to Mendoza tomorrow and get a warrant for the files Frankie told you he'd found. As for Elias van Lindholm,' Warren turned a few pages to read out, 'He's a grad of Columbia. I know a professor there, Richard Delacroix, who told me van Lindholm did all his renal med training in his faculty and was well thought of clinically though known for being taciturn and impatient with colleagues. Bit of a wild card. He wasn't hugely popular.

Dicky couldn't understand why he'd ended up in what he called 'a backwater' down here. Last he heard, Lindholm was working in some up-market facility in New York City. We've yet to confirm where, but I do wonder if it was the Prestige Clinic Mendoza served in? As for personal life, van Lindholm is on his second marriage. He wedded his secretary, Ava, after a divorce twelve years ago that got publicly messy, which might be why he left New York. Danny suggests his Catholic Hospital Board in the city might have quietly denied him admission rights. He also notes Lindholm lives in an extremely expensive house he thought well above his pay grade. I have forensic accountants trawling his finances—and that of the charity you mentioned, Sativa. It is registered.'

At this point I drained my fourth cocktail like a zombie, aware I was cognitively shutting down. My eyes were open but my ears and brain felt disconnected. John looked at me and said to his parents, 'That's all great info Dad, but I think I need to get Mhairi to her bed. She's wasted. Could we continue tomorrow—say at breakfast around eight?'

'Sure. You booked in, son?' asked Warren. John nodded as he helped me to my feet. His dad shook hands and Jackie hugged us. I felt so grateful that they had actually suggested themselves we stayed over and made no comment on us sharing a room, although I did catch Warren whisper to John as we passed about 'prophylactics'—another new word I'd recently added to my ever-growing US vocabulary. The Coulters were lovely people. Warren even insisted on paying for our stay.

Up in our first-floor room, while John went to the loo, I threw off all my clothes and, realising I had no nightie or PJs, just laughed and slid under the sheets. A naked John appeared to join me with a cuddle. His advancing hands were irresistible and certainly wakened me, although I had to ask between lingering kisses, 'I heard your dad muttering about prophylactics! I hope you have...I mean,

you weren't allowed back to your Residency room and we're nowhere near a chemist.'

'Chemist? D'you mean drug store?'

I slapped him gently. 'You know what I mean.'

'If you mean rubbers, they're everywhere over here. I got them
in the Men's Room!'

Resourcefulness in a man. I like it. We eventually got to sleep.

~~~

There is a state between sleeping and waking where you're sen-
tient but unable to move or speak. I'd first noticed it when quite
a young child. Often accompanied by a feeling of mild anxiety. I
think it might be a kind of Neanderthal throwback, an autonomic
nervous system initial 'adrenaline' state of alert allowing you to
suss out danger before you leap up rashly into full 'flight or fight'
danger response when disturbed in the early hours of your cave
by the smell or growl of a sabre-toothed tiger. Hardly relevant in
a Marriott, but around five a.m. I woke like this.

Anxious. I looked around the room but had no idea where
I was. The clock with glowing hands was not mine. The room
curtains weren't blue, like my Glasgow bedroom ones, nor peach
like the Nursing Home drapes. I took in a whole wall of curtains
with a gap which shed a strip of light on a blanket and coverlet
heaped on the floor. And I was naked (naked!) on a huge, crumpled
bed. I managed to turn. And relaxed. Beside me lay John, on his
handsome back, lying modestly under the single sheet and snoring
softly. The events of the last few weeks flooded my brain along
with a throbbing headache. My overriding desire was for water.

Feeling self-conscious in my nakedness, I slipped on one of the
towelling dressing gowns we'd found on the bed and tossed aside
with the coverlet as we'd made love. Creeping into the bathroom
and filling a glass, I emptied it several times. I noticed a basket of
toiletry 'goodies' on a shelf with a welcome disposable toothbrush
and microscopic tube of toothpaste. My teeth, glutinous from

sugary cocktails, were glad. Back in the bedroom, I felt wide awake and had no desire to lie back down. Instead, I walked over to peer out between the curtains.

Sitting on the crest of a hill to the west of Brunsfield, the Marriott had a curving drive sweeping down to the tree-filled streets of the town. The view stretched past it to the distant hill on which Ellis Memorial Hospital stood. To the left was a squiggly lake, silver and glistening under a full moon. As I watched, the sky on the horizon was gradually lightening. A new day was coming. It was a pretty and peaceful sight. Until a car drove up the driveway. A taxi.

Directly below our room, from the front entrance of the hotel, came a female figure. She walked unsteadily towards the cab. Young, blonde, tall and slim, in a silver mini dress with showy, sparkly, high-heeled sandals that matched a small shoulder bag. As she recovered from falling (less than gracefully) into the back seat, she flicked back her curtain of long hair, exposing her face. God, it was Ellie May. What on earth was she doing in the hotel at this time in the morning? Or rather, who?

From behind came a sleepy voice. 'What are you doing, babe? Get back into bed!'

I went to stand at the bedside. 'Ellie May just got into a taxi. I wonder if Lindholm's here?'

'What? Oh, no, I think he entertains at home. Those porno pics were domestic.' He'd raised himself up on one elbow for a few seconds then fell back, closing his eyes.

'I'm going to scout out the carpark and see if his car's here!'

John sat up properly. 'What? Why on earth...?'

But I was already collecting my scattered clothes. My bra had inexplicably fallen into the litter bin at the dressing table.

As I dressed, John swore and leaped out of bed, starting to pull on his jeans and T-shirt. 'God, you're not going out there alone.' He shoved his bare feet into his loafers and picked up the room key. 'Come on, then.'

As we passed through the lobby, the reception girl didn't look up from her book. Outside, the small side car park held four cars: none Lindholm's. To the rear was the main carpark. And in the third row, there was no mistaking the flashy monster Buick and its plate: Medic 1. We stood and stared at it.

John sighed. 'Well, he's here. So what? The police will be wanting to speak to him today. OK, I'll tell Dad at breakfast and ask him to phone that detective and say he's in the Marriott. Now can we go back to bed?' He took my hand to lead me back up to our room where he fell asleep again. I didn't.

Chapter Twenty-Six
Elena's Story

By eight on Tuesday morning, John and I were enjoying mounds of blueberry pancakes in the Marriott dining room with Warren and Jackie. As John's dad had had to return to the city for a court case, the plan was for John to go get his car from the hospital car park and take his mum to the police station with Elena. I'd telephoned her last night to get her to come over, thinking that if Jackie were in Brunsfield today, it would be easier for them to meet rather than have Elena trail up to the city.

After Warren left, Jackie chatted on in the dining room for a while about Scotland, my family and my career plans (such as they were). I had the feeling she'd sensed my anxiety at finding van Lindholm's car and was trying to distract me. I was reassured that Warren had phoned Lieutenant Burr's office to say that Dr Elias van Lindholm could be found at the Marriott Hotel, though I was keeping half an eye out on the door, expecting him to appear any minute.

While Jacqueline went off to her room to pack, John took a cab to get his car and I used our room phone to try to reach Laura at the Nurses' Home. I'd already called last night to say we were staying over at the Marriott but in case she was worried, thought I'd let her know I wasn't coming back till later.

Jess answered the hall phone. 'Hey, Mhairi. It's Jess. What's up? You sound tired.'

'Well, I didn't sleep great. It's all been a bit much.'

'You don't say? We've had half the police department up and down the drive already today. No idea what the heck's goin' on.

But I'm on a day off and got Babs later. School's out. Sleepy Laura's just up. Might get her to play hooky with us and go up to Lake Hopatcong. Lots to do up at the lake. You could come too if you like? We can wait.'

'That sounds great, but not sure when I'll be back. I'm going with John and his mum to speak to Elena then they're going to see Burr. Can you tell Laura I should be home for tea.'

'Okay. I'll take care of her. She'll love the lake.'

I thought how great it would be to go and wander beside a lake, beneath the trees...But there were other things that needed done.

When John returned, we went down to the lobby together and commandeered a set of sofas in the corner with a coffee table sitting between. Jackie arrived, left me with her overnight bag and went to check us all out of the hotel.

On her return, I thanked her for her kindness, still silently marvelling that she or Warren hadn't objected to us sharing a room. Her eyes locked mine. As if reading my innermost thoughts she said, 'It's no problem. I love seeing John so happy and I thought last night you needed to be together and away from the hospital.' She turned to her briefcase for a notebook and pen in preparation for her chat with Elena. 'Now, what age did you say this girl is?'

'Sixteen,' I answered.

'And is this Uncle Raoul her legal guardian?'

'No idea. I just know she's staying with him. And here she is.'

A smiling Elena was coming towards us, hand in hand with Nico. 'I hope you don't mind,' she said to me, indicating the boy. 'Nico has a car so it was easier to come with him. But he has to be back at the restaurant before twelve.'

Jackie shook hands with them both and sat beside John. Elena sat with me, facing the main lobby, with Nico on a single seat to her right. Jackie started by saying she was happy to help in any way she could and if Elena wanted to pursue the hospital or individuals she'd act for her on a pro bono basis. Seeing her puzzled look, she added, 'I mean without upfront fees. Though my firm might take a percentage of any damages you're awarded.'

Elena looked thoughtful. 'It is not about money. It is about truth.'

We then moved step by step through the story as Elena knew it. Nico obviously knew most of it too as he nodded at intervals, occasionally emphasising a point with, '*Si!*'

The thorny topic of her age came up. She would be seventeen in September.

'As the law regards you as a minor, Elena, I need to know your official next of kin.'

Elena looked disconsolate and shrugged. 'Not sure. I live with my Uncle Raoul now.'

'Where's your father?'

'Ensenada, I think.'

'And were your parents married?'

'I don't think they were, you know. I've never seen marriage papers in the box with our official documents.'

'And what is Raoul's exact relationship to your mother, is he her brother?'

'No, my father's. I know Uncle Raoul does not want investigations into Mother's death. He dislikes the police. I am not happy with him. To be honest, I'd prefer to stay with Nico's family. His mama says it would be fine.'

'I'll get in touch with Welfare to ensure that's okay It's more complex lately since The Children's Bureau was changed, but I'll get someone to come and see you.'

Elena smiled. 'Anything you can do...'

Nico looked at his watch, kissed Elena and rose. Accepting that John would bring her back later, he went off to drive back across town.

After a short further chat, Jackie put away her book and pen and stood up.

'I think I've got the picture, Elena. Next, we should go downtown to the Police Department to see a Detective Lieutenant Burr, who's very interested in what happened to your mom. He's expecting us. I'll be with you all the time and my advice is to tell him what you've told me and be completely frank, even about your uncle. You do realise that if we move you from his care it may mean you become estranged—are you prepared for that?'

As Elena replied 'Yes', I looked from her face to the lobby behind and froze. A figure stopped in his tracks to stare directly at me. His eyes flickered in recognition before registering fury as he took in Elena beside me. I'd never previously seen anyone whose eyes 'blazed' as they say in books, but his were as hot and evil as it got. In seconds, he was out of the hotel entrance and practically running past the window at our side. I hoped to God that he was going to be arrested soon.

~~~

John drove us to the County Police Headquarters. Since there was no public parking to be had, we dropped Jackie and Elena at the front door and headed for the shopping mall opposite, where John suggested we might find a coffee shop. The plan was to sit near its door and if they hadn't come to find us in an hour and a half, we'd walk back over to the swish modern police building and wait in the lobby.

Successfully bagging a parking space close to the shopping centre entrance, we wandered in. The place was impressive, with one shop of every conceivable kind from shoe shops to jewellers. Not far inside, we found Dinah's Coffee Shop. While I went in to order, John disappeared into an adjacent supermarket. I took ages to choose from the vast array of cakes and pastries on offer and was just sitting down with my plates of donuts and flaky things when John re-appeared with a bundle of magazines.

'Thought since we'd be here for a bit we could do with some distraction. Take your mind off things.' He laughed as he placed the first one down. 'Or maybe not...'

Considering our current preoccupation with events in casualty departments, the first wasn't exactly diverting. Its headline blared, '*60,000 Citizens Die Yearly Because 60% of ERs Lack Equipment and Personnel*'.

My comment was heartfelt. 'And some die because of greedy, careless doctors! I wonder if we'll ever see that as a headline?'

'That'd be a bit too serious for *The National Enquirer*. It's one of the top US magazines. Bit more likely to run stuff about aliens or crazy celebrity antics.'

Magazine two was *Reader's Digest*. I'd read it at home in the dentist. I browsed some short articles on advances in birth control, drug use in GIs in Vietnam and a curious article labelled, '*I am Joe's Intestine*'—one of its autographical articles 'by' body parts. John had also bought me a woman's magazine, *McCall's*, much like one of ours at home, with recipes, fashion and articles on home décor. But I thought its advice on how to get divorced unlikely in a mag at home, divorce still being kind of taboo. John admitted knowing many divorced folk. I knew none.

He had two 'serious' magazines. *Scientific American* thankfully had nothing on transplants but led with an article about corn, which apparently lacks vital essential amino acids that 'single-stomached' animals (us, pigs and chickens) need. Mankind was doomed unless we could breed more nutritious crops. *Time Magazine* was less gloomy, with funny political cartoons and book reviews, although John lambasted one item on Nixon's plans for economic growth. He thought planning to end the Vietnam War and the Draft more important.

We skimmed them all and had a second coffee. Without pastries. I looked at my watch. 'How long do you think they'll be?'

'Depends on what Burr asks, I suppose.' John shrugged. 'He grilled me for an hour yesterday, but I think Elena's got more to say. Mom'll be keen to get back up to town. She had to do a lot of diary pushback to get here.'

'It's good of her to take on Elena.'

'That's Mom. Like Gran, support women. Once they've finished with Burt, I'll drop Elena off first, then Mum at the station before then we go back to the hospital. But gee, you look real tired, babe.' He gently stroked the bags under my eyes with his thumb. As if on cue, I yawned. Seeing it was almost ninety minutes since we'd left them, John suggested we start walking back. Halfway across the car park we met Jackie and Elena coming over. The girl looked a bit happier and a smiling Jackie put an arm round her.

'It's done. Elena was great. Let's take her home.'

'Not home. Can I go to the restaurant? I'm going to stay with Nico.'

'Sure, I'll drop you wherever.' John opened the back door for Elena to get in.

Over the roof of the car Jackie frowned at him. 'I wonder if we shouldn't take her to get her stuff first? Raoul may be angry when she tells him she's been to the police.'

From the back seat Elena was adamant. 'No, it's fine. I'll not tell him. And Nico can take me for my things after the dinners are served. Raoul is usually out in the evenings anyway.'

John dropped Elena off in Maple Street and at his Mum's insistence, me next at the Nurses' Home. As he came out to give me a brief kiss, Jackie moved into the front seat for the ride to the station. It was now after five. Her diary for the day was completely screwed.

Inside the Home, Laura and Jess hadn't yet returned from their outing. I passed a few nurses watching TV, with a cursory, 'Hi!', went to my room and flopped on the bed. Next thing I knew, Laura was shaking me.

'Hey, Mhairi! It's eight o'clock. Have you had any tea?'

'No.' I tried to focus as her questions bombarded me.

'So, what's happening now? What did John's father find out? How was Elena?'

'Stop, Laura! I need food first! All I've had all day is a pastry. Well, and a donut. Think though I did have breakfast. Anyway, come talk to me while I make an omelette.'

While I whisked, I talked. Laura listened. I recounted Warren's info on the past history of our two troublesome docs, Elena's complaint to the police and Jackie's acceptance of her case to prosecute if necessary. 'Elena's determined to get justice for her mother and prevent anyone else going through what she's suffered.'

Pouring my egg froth into an omelette pan, I threw in grated cheese, reckoning I needed all the energy I could get. Distractedly I told Laura about corn's shortfall in nutrients. 'But you know, cheese must be the perfect food, mustn't it? Like eggs. Must have all the essential amino acids if they grow baby cows or chickens.' My brain sprang into a mental recitation of a list of the essential amino acids memorised for Biochemistry Finals. A bewildered Laura stared as I parroted, 'That's histidine, isoleucine, leucine, lysine, methionine, phenylalanine, threonine, tryptophan, and valine. God, I'm surprised I remembered that!' Unfortunately, it started repeating endlessly in my head like one of those songs that you can't get rid of. It had happened before when I was over-tired. Which I was. Very. I was aware Laura was trying to tell me something but didn't take it in. 'Sorry, Laura, what did you say?' I flipped my omelette onto a plate.

She repeated her words, separating them distinctly as if speaking to a child, 'I said, there is another Carmela, well, a woman called Eizabeth Adams, who died a couple of months ago after Mendoza operated on her.'

'What?'

'Yes. Today, after I'd got him up on everything that's happened, Hiro remembered about a patient of Mendoza's he saw in ER not long ago with a severe wound infection and who was transferred away like Carmela. Hiro had to leave Mendoza alone with her when a serious RTA came in. Remembering it was a day the New York Yankees got beaten by the Cleveland Indians 2- 1, he worked out the date and went to check the details only to find Elizabeth's case records, both ER and Admission, missing. And there's another two-hour gap in the afternoon ER records around the time when he thinks she was in. One of the ER nurses remembered her and agreed it was that day. Elizabeth was a septicaemia case after renal 'stone' surgery. Sound familiar? She also went off in a blue ambulance and he phoned St Thomas's who didn't get her. Pretty identical. By the way, Hiro reckons our Dr Juan Mendoza snorts, he's seen stuff he's left in the Gents. Foil and stuff I expect.'

'Snorts?'

'Cocaine, dummy. Explains why he's either morose or twitchy.'

I thought back to the morning that he'd asked me to pull out Carmela's drain without sterile gloves. His flippant cavalier attitude might well have been from being high. My amino acid recitation ceased. I was now wide awake. 'So, has Hiro told Lieutenant Burr?'

'Yes. When he found no record for Elizabeth Adams, Hiro phoned him.'

Jess arrived, wearing shorts and a *Looney Tunes* T-shirt, and wielding a bottle.

'Hi, guys! Anyone for a bourbon?' She produced three glasses from the cupboard.

She didn't need to ask. Bourbon was better than Scotch. But I wouldn't tell my father.

~~~

It was midnight the day after Frankie's death. Burr was at his desk with his chin in his left hand and a glass of whiskey in his right. He didn't often resort to the bottle in his drawer, but there were times when you needed a break and some alcohol to calm the 'busyness' in your mind and let the dust settle. He tilted the bottle. Only enough Jack Daniels left for one more. It had been an intense few days.

He stared at the two State of New Jersey death certificates that had just arrived on his desk.

The first was for an *Elizabeth Adams*. **Date of birth April 22nd 1939: Color, White. Cause of death, Pneumonia, duration one week. Date of death May 22, 1971. Place of death, Plainsfield District General Hospital. Certified by Dr Elias J van Lindholm, M.D.**

The second was for a *Carmela Gomez*. **Date of birth December 24 1937. Color, White Hispanic. Cause of death, Pneumonia, duration one week. Date of death July 17, 1971. Place of death, Plainsfield District General Hospital. Certified by Dr Elias J van Lindholm, M.D.**

Two unbelievably identical certificates issued eight weeks apart.

He also had in front of him depositions from two Senior Residents in Ellis Memorial Hospital ER that these women had not actually had pneumonia at all but septicaemia following renal surgery. And the Ellis Memorial Japanese Resident, Dr Hiro Wantanabe, had testified that Dr Juan Mendoza, the renal surgeon, was alone with Adams for a time immediately before transit. Plus, two credible witnesses had alleged seeing van Lindholm fiddling with the i.v. drip of the second victim, Gomez, at an ambulance prior to her transit and pocketing a possible syringe. One of those, the juvenile daughter of the second patient, was adamant her mother had told her she'd been coaxed into 'selling' her kidney in return for debt clearance.

Burr had been surprised to find that there was no law on the statute book making the selling of kidneys illegal but there was, for sure, a law that made killing troublesome witnesses to a secret enterprise a major felony. Must be big business if it meant eliminating women whose condition might potentially expose they had been harvested for organs, not treated for any medical condition.

As for the Cooke boy's death. God, it couldn't be worse. His senator father was as rich as Croesus, thick with the Commissioner, and had behaved like a bat out of hell when he came into the precinct. Though the death had initially presented as a straightforward drug overdose, Burr had rapidly concluded that it wasn't. Apart from the fact that the student's family, tutor at college and his colleagues at the hospital here all denied he took any Schedule 11 drugs, he had no scars from shooting up, only that one puncture wound at his left elbow crease. Since Frank Cooke was left-handed, it was extremely unlikely he could have injected anything into his left arm. A further confounding factor was the pathologist calling today to admit they had just found a puncture wound in a mole on Frances Cooke's neck. A jab there would have knocked him out instantly. And could never have been self-inflicted.

No, Frankie was murdered. And the motive for his death? He had heard clear testimony from several students that the boy had disclosed finding incriminatory evidence in van Lindholm's office last Saturday night. Had the doc somehow got to know about the break-in and killed the boy to silence him? On searching Lindholm's room tonight though, there had been none of the patient records or lab reports Frank Cooke had reported. Nor anything else incriminating.

Three murders, then: two women patients, Carmela and Elizabeth, and a male student, Frankie Cooke. But there was also the problem of the suffocated nurse that everyone thought a histrionic lovesick busybody. Her passion was van Lindholm. Had Makkonen known something she shouldn't? That missing doc Doberman had turned up with an alibi. What a red herring: he'd been at his pregnant girlfriend's flat the night of the murder and they'd fled to Vegas to tie the knot and avoid his furious future father-in-law. Now the van Lindholm connection deserved attention.

Then Hospital President Schieffer had also mentioned the attempted murder of that Kitty hit and run woman on the surgical floor…Might they be connected? Had the hit and run perp simply tried to silence her or had she been a target for some other reason? One of the boys thought her father had been put away for drugs but it seemed too long ago for any possible gang retribution. No, he would discount the nurse and the hit and run victim from the equation at present. There were enough unknowns already.

Was it time to bring in Doctors van Lindholm and Mendoza and grill them? An arrest warrant for the women's murders was premature as most 'evidence' regarding them was hearsay. Still, he was justified in asking if Mendoza and van Lindholm could account for their movements early in the morning the Cooke boy died. And what they had to say about the patients Elizabeth Adams and Carmela Gomez. They had a lot of explaining to do if nothing else.

Odd that van Lindholm had certified both deaths, surely? And both in the same hospital, one he did not usually work in. He looked at the clock. One a.m. Time for sleep. Best to go home and be back fresh at seven to start phoning. He emptied his glass and returned it to the desk drawer.

In the car on the way home he resolved to warn the Prosecutor first thing about the cases so far, though likely D.A. Warren Coulter might have already done so. He also needed to get search warrants for Mendoza and Lindholm's homes and external professional offices and exhumation orders for the bodies of Elizabeth Adams and Carmela Gomez. Thankfully, neither had been cremated. Most importantly, he needed to bring in van Lindholm and Mendoza. He passed a liquor shop. Long closed. Might be some at home. No wonder so many cops had problems.

Chapter Twenty-Seven
The Marvellous Rory, Flying Off & Throwing Up.

On Wednesday morning I was back in Obstetrics early and made my apologies to the Chief for being absent the previous day. He was quite the thing about it under the circumstances. To my delight, today I was assigned to a different Resident.

Bruce was much nicer to the patients than my last mentor. He talked to them, examined them thoroughly, made proper notes, ordered blood tests on all patients, private or not, and issuing cautions to midwives in the delivery rooms if he saw a potential need for intervention. Today, I saw no women labouring on their own and we'd efficiently completed a tour of the whole floor before the specialists started arriving to see their patients.

The first visiting specialist was a handsome cheery chap with bushy grey-brown hair and eyebrows. In red shirt, tartan tie and exuberantly flared pants, Dr Rory Donald welcomed me as a compatriot from the 'Home of his Ancestors' as he considered Scotland. He reminisced fondly on the year he'd spent in Glasgow when training and, after his round and a delivery, invited me to his offices downtown for the afternoon.

These were stylish, carpets, chairs and exam couches being in complementary shades of grey and pink. His pride and joy was his state-of-the-art ultrasonic machine. Scanning babies in the womb, he told every patient, was the brainchild of a Glasgow professor, Iain Donald, whom I suspect patients thought he was related to. They loved him, one even whispering an 'Isn't he marvellous?' at me behind his back. I loved his *Advice Pack for Moms* which included a sheet for grandparents: *Don't Give Advice Give Money!* Patients left wreathed in smiles.

I spent a lovely happy afternoon swept up into Donald's world of excellent empathic doctor-patient communication. After making notes on his last patient, he put down his Dictaphone and smiled at me. 'Apart from being here and Ellis Memorial, Miss MacLean, I do a free weekly clinic over at St Thomas's. There's one tomorrow with a scheduled C-section after. Would you like to accompany me?'

'I would, very much. Thank you.' I was genuinely keen but admitted to a pang of guilt, recognising that one reason was that I wouldn't mind being away from Ellis Memorial for a bit. It was so full of tension.

His Chief Nurse drove me back to the Home, kindly arranging to pick me up at 7.30 a.m. next morning to take me to St Thomas's before she went on to man Rory's office phones.

At the Nurses' Home, Laura was making a chicken casserole. From the hall, I phoned the OBS Floor, leaving a message for Bruce that I'd be out with Rory in the morning and went to my room to write home. To Archie, Dad and Una, went a letter that was bland bar my exciting delivery of 'Maggie'. To old school friend Aileen went a narrative that would have done a Hollywood script proud. Writing it down heightened my anxiety. These docs were dangerous people.

~~~

That Wednesday evening, July 28th, the Van Lindholm Residence, Brunsfield

Ava is still packing. His Piaget tells him she needs to get a move on. He calls up, 'Come on, honey, the car will be here soon. Anything you forget we can buy in Paris.'

This surprise Paris trip has gone down well. Ava's never been. They've screwed twice since he told her. Cheque book waving always gets a girl in the mood.

He hasn't told Juan he's going overseas. Pity Sunday's kidney was non-viable: it should have made it to Boston within the timeframe but for that truck fuck incident on the freeway. He's demanded his cut anyway. Luckily, the donating guy had needed a relatively modest sum. He looked okay on Monday. Should be home now. Fingers crossed that two septicaemias had made Juan more careful.

But Dr Juan Mendoza has become increasingly unreliable and his attempted curtailment of his personal opiate consumption has failed miserably. He has another guy in mind for the future nephrectomies, but meantime Juan has to go. After a bit of thought, he's left an anonymous note for Charles Schieffer, suggesting the Hospital President should be aware of the bold Doctor Juan Mendoza's Californian and Kentucky licence revocations. A drug test will finish him. Shame. He was a fucking hot shot in his day. God knows what he's done with his money: perhaps it has all gone up his nose? Pathetic to see him now. Drives a wreck of a car and his supposed 'wife' looks like she's been dressed from a whore's emporium!

Ava appears. Now her short Chanel above-the-knee silk dress and edge-to-edge cream jacket with fine black trimming are class. And those red shiny stilettoes are always a turn on.

The taxi is hooting. As they leave, he spies Randy Ramsay the nosy neighbour at his fucking window and gives him the finger.

Leaning back, he accepts Ava taking his hand, barely containing her excitement, chattering about the places she wants to see. But his mind strays to the sight of that Gomez brat at the Marriott with that Scottish girl. He wonders if the redhead has received his present yet. It had been a melodramatic long shot at curtailing her interference, but amusing. He'll be legitimately well away if the police come calling. The gift couldn't possibly be attributed to him.

In truth, the police will have trouble charging him with anything. Selling kidneys isn't illegal, despite recent rumblings that legislation is needed to stop them all going to the rich. There is no proof whatsoever that Juan or he eliminated those two women who were transferred. They were necessary and legitimate collateral damage to prevent a shitstorm that Schieffer and Harper wouldn't have been able to contain and the Board wouldn't have tolerated. Running over the girl in the red dress couldn't be pinned on him either. No witnesses and she can't have given any description to the cops or they'd have been at his door. Snuffing out the blackmailing Freya couldn't be pinned on him either. No one saw him in his cap and tracksuit disguise when he slunk back into ER via the lab door. He had the lock combo.

Ava is nudging him. He reconnects with the present as she snuggles into his shoulder.

'What do you think, darling? Should we go to Chanel first?'

'Of course, babe. This week's all yours.'

~~~

On Thursday morning it had rained overnight. Brunsfield was comfortably cooler. But the hospital was a hotbed of speculation. It is amazing how quickly titillating news travels in small communities or work environments. By noon, everyone knew police were investigating Carmela's dodgy death and that van Lindholm and Mendoza were wanted by the police in connection with something. Everyone also knew van Lindholm's Third Floor office had been searched, though details as to what the police were looking for were sketchy and highly speculative. Apart from the police however, only John, Coop, Randy, Hiro and us girls knew the details. Jess was in on some of it.

Just after seven, I was eating breakfast with Laura, Jess and her friend Belle, when the doorbell rang. Being nearest the door,

Jess went out to return clutching a large bouquet of flowers and a be-ribboned parcel.

'Who are they for?' I asked nodding at her burdens.

'Why, you, girl!' Belle melodramatically bowed and presented me with the trophies.

At the sink, after drying her hands on the wrong tea towel (we'd given up on Mrs Heinz's lists), Laura came to peer over my shoulder. 'Who are they from—John?'

I read the little attached card. 'No. It says, "With grateful thanks from Macey Baker, XXX".'

'Who's Macey Baker?' Laura looked puzzled.

'She's the woman who named her baby after me, well, gave it my middle name. Nice of her to send a gift but she shouldn't have wasted money on me, her husband's only a jobbing builder They've no insurance and she gets by earning pennies doing hair for friends.'

Jess was fixing on her white cap at the mirror the nurses kept propped up in a corner of the kitchen for that very purpose. 'Sometimes it's those with the least who are most generous. What's in the parcel?'

It was a fancy box of Swiss dark chocolate creams. I was a little disappointed. 'That's a shame. I don't like dark chocolate. Have some if you fancy, girls.' I put the box beside the mirror and unwrapped the tall flowers. 'Oh, lilies! How unusual.'

'But pretty nice. Spicy scent too.' Laura sniffed appreciatively.

I stuck them in a jug of water before following Laura to get our jackets and notebooks. By the time we left, the kitchen was empty. Jess was over at work and Belle in the bubble bath she'd promised herself before a day of lounging on the sofa with popcorn watching TV. It sounded an appealing day off. But for us, duty called.

~~~

Up on the Obstetrics Floor, there was a lot of activity: two sets of twins were in progress. One was being delivered by my Dr Donald, so Bruce sent me into Delivery One.

The first baby was ''crowning' as I arrived and was delivered with ease. Like most twin pregnancies, this delivery was early. Mum was 35 weeks pregnant and the babe was quite light, only five pounds eight ounces. The contrast to Maggie's birth was striking. Donald kept up a running commentary of encouraging banter directed at the patient. A paediatrician stood by at a trolley topped by a small mattress. The minute the cord was cut, the little boy was handed to him for a comprehensive check and whiff of oxygen. "Apgar 9 at one minute," he announced. The nurse swaddled the babe in a blue blanket before handing him to his dad, sitting beside his mum's head.

Donald prodded the mother's lower abdomen. 'One down, one to go, Nancy. Don't worry if Baby Boy One looks a bit sticky, we'll bathe him when you're finished.'

'What's Apgar 9?' The dad looked worried.

The Paeds guy answered, 'Anything above 7 is great. It's a way to measure how well a babe is on arrival, like his colour, heart rate, response to stimuli, movements, breathing and so on. You grade them as zero, one or two and add them up.' He smiled reassuringly.

Donald added, 'And for the benefit of our overseas guest student here, we have to proudly tell you that this internationally adopted Apgar System was developed by anaesthesiologist and first woman Professor at Columbia, Dr Virginia Apgar, who was born not five miles up the road in Westfield, New Jersey.'

It was obvious from the looks on the faces of the attendant nurses and Paediatrician that was news to them, although, as I've commented before, it's often difficult to assess a person's true expression if half their face is under a surgical mask. Jerking his head

257

towards me, Donald joked, 'You should be thinking what you'd like as *The MacLean System*, Mhairi!'

Baby Two was breech. 'Little fellow here's coming out the wrong way round but not to worry. Here we go. One foot, two feet, two nice little legs, now we're talking turkey! Big push with this contraction, Nancy!'

It was a few contractions more before infant Number Two was safely delivered. She was quiet, sleepy and floppy, not moving her arms. 'Apgar 4' came quietly from the paediatrician as a suction tube went down the babe's throat and an oxygen mask was applied to her face while he vigorously rubbed her chest and behind an ear. Fortunately, she quickly gave a few strangled sobs, yelled loudly and waved her arms about indignantly. After a quick listen to her chest and check of her limbs and back, Babe Two was swaddled and presented into her mother's eager arms.

Donald was merrily whistling while neatly sewing up the episiotomy cut he'd made in Nancy's perineum to get the second babe out quickly. The twins were now crying in competition, as were mum and dad. I slunk out in search of the other twin delivery.

I was beginning to agree with Donald that delivering babies was "an awesome profession" and wondering if it might be for me. Although its associated Gynaecology speciality involving abdominal surgery for the likes of hysterectomies and tumours held less appeal. Doubtless Simon Winters back home would dismiss Obstetrics as having no money in it since few UK women had babies privately. But in New Jersey, I realised OBS and Gynae was a gold mine. Despite his altruism, Donald had admitted hysterectomies were his bread and butter. 'What woman doesn't want the baby basket removed once her family is complete?' But to me, if you didn't have a disease, it seemed a drastic alternative to the pill. If lucrative for hospitals and specialists.

Once disrobed and washed up, I met John for lunch, after which he suggested a walk in the grounds. But I 'took a raincheck', feeling lower abdominal cramps and suspected 'the time of the month' was on hand, albeit several days early. Stress, I knew could disturb menstrual cycles. (There'd definitely been a bit of that lately.) Apologising, I headed back to the Home to take precautions.

Coming out of the bathroom in our corridor, I found Belle leaning against her room door, shivering and looking ghastly pale. She rushed past me to vomit violently in the loo.

'Think I've got a stomach bug, Mhairi,' she moaned.' Been vomiting all morning.'

'You don't look well at all. I think you should go over to ER. Come on!'

I half carried her out of the building while clutching a stainless-steel bowl from the kitchen. We managed to stagger up the drive to the lobby, where a Candy-striper fetched a wheelchair. Through in ER, Randy was at the desk and looked curiously at my patient, head in the bowl.

'Another one?'

'Who else is being sick?' I asked.

'Jess. She's up in 308 on an i.v..' He looked at Belle filling my bowl. 'She was vomiting violently too. Anyway, let's get this young lady into Exam Two. What's her name?'

'Belle.'

I wheeled Belle in and waited while he examined her. She was now lying back, grey, retching, drooling and weeping, with hands and feet intermittently twitching. Randy pulled up her eyelids to shine his little torch into her eyes. 'Strange. Tiny pupils. Have you taken any meds or used any eye drops today, Belle?'

Belle shook her head and slumped back, eyes closed. Randy moved into ER doc mode, commanding the attendant nurses. 'Okay, guys, let's get bloods—a full 18 set and a tox screen. Put up an i.v. stat, Normal saline.

Belle was now muttering about wanting to go for a swim, the hotel was too hot. Then she was talking to someone over my shoulder. I looked round. There was no one there. Alarming.

Randy left the nurse setting up the drip and a First Year Resident taking bloods for quickness and nodded for me to follow him out. I seemed to be spending my life having heart to hearts in corridors!

'Not sure what's going on here, Mhairi. This is worse than salmonellosis or any food poisoning I've seen. She's toxic and confused—yet she's got no temperature. Any clue what she's been doing today or what she's eaten?'

'Well, we all had the same breakfast of cereal and tea. And then she had some toast and butter, but Jess didn't.'

'Could you please take a minute to go up ask Jess if she's had anything else today too?'

'Sure.' I headed towards the elevators.

Chapter Twenty-Eight
The Chocolates Did It

Up in Room 308, Jess was lying pale and tired but looked miles better than Belle. My attempt to joke that it was "amazing what some folk would do to get out of working" fell like a lead balloon. Quelled by her glare, I moved swiftly on.

'Randy wants to know exactly what you've eaten today. Belle isn't well either.'

Jess pushed herself up with her non-drip right arm. 'Eat? Cheerios and milk same as you. A banana. Oh, and some of your chocs. Though I spat one out as it had a funny aftertaste. Still kinda got it.' She smacked her tongue on the roof of her mouth.

I was sitting slouched on her bed but suddenly sat straight up. 'I am a fool! Jess, what do white lilies make you think of?'

'Funerals?'

'I don't think those flowers and chocolates that came for me this morning were from Macey at all.'

Jess perked up a bit to say, 'Why? Then who sent them?'

'I wonder if they were from Van Lindholm and he spiked the chocolates with something for spite because I'm helping Elena Gomez. Wouldn't put it past him...'

'Jesus, you think? Suppose you could check with the Macey girl whose name was on them. She'll be home by now but Admissions will have her number. Unless of course VL's fucked up her records too?' She lay back exhausted, sighing heavily, lids drooping.

I reckoned she'd had a shot of promethazine or some other strong sedative antiemetic and decided I should let her doze. Giving her a hug, I headed down to Admissions, got Macey's number from her records and phoned.

She was delighted I'd called. No, she hadn't sent me gifts. And yes, the baby was doing great. She started on about how grateful she'd been for my support but I guiltily cut her short, breaking off the call and wishing her well. Back in ER, I sought out Randy. He scoffed at my suggestion the gifted confectionery might be to blame for the girls' GI upset.

'Poisoned chocolates? Are you pullin' my chain? This Ironside or a murder movie we're in?' He laughed.

'Well, those chocs were the only thing Jess and Belle both had that Laura and I didn't. We're not sick. And the woman Macey, whose name was on the card, someone who named her baby after me, knows nothing about them. I really wouldn't be surprised if van Lindholm didn't send them via a courier. You've no idea how furious he looked when he saw me with Carmela's daughter.'

'Bit nuts. And how could he know about Macey?' Randy was struggling with disbelief.

'God knows. Though the baby naming was big hospital gossip that day.'

He held his hands up in surrender. 'Okay, go fetch the suspect candies if you can. But be careful, don't even touch the box. Take gloves, put it in a plastic bag, seal it and bring it over.'

'I think I'll phone Lieutenant Burr too. Just in case he wants it.'

Randy nodded. 'Police number is up beside the payphone on the wall.' He pointed.

'It's okay, he gave me a card.'

'And I'm going to phone the Poisons Bureau with Belle's symptoms.' Randy left.

I practically ran back to the Home. The chocolates were where I'd left them in the corner beside the propped-up mirror. Donning the blue rubber gloves I'd brought from ER, I opened the box to check what had been taken. There were six empty spaces. Jess said she'd had one and spat out another, which meant Belle must have had four. Perhaps her choices were a different fondant flavour, better able to disguise the aftertaste Jess complained about—or simply some by chance had received less poison, perhaps injected into them? What a thing. A shiver went up my back. No one had ever wanted me ill or dead before.

I closed the box, took out a bin liner from under the sink and started wrapping it up, at which juncture, Mrs Adela Heinz appeared on one of her random sorties into the Nurses' Home. Jess said she liked to check up on us, see we were behaving ourselves properly.

'Mis MacLean, isn't it? Now why are you in here wrapping things up in trash bags instead of working up in the hospital?'

I didn't take this well. Someone had attempted to kill me. My reply was cross. 'This bag contains a potentially poisonous box of chocolates that I have to take for analysis by the police. It might be best if you got someone professional in to thoroughly clean the kitchen in case it has been contaminated. Already two nurses have been admitted with signs of poisoning after eating some.'

As I wound Sellotape round my package, she stood, mouth open, bewildered and speechless. I found it peculiarly gratifying.

Sadly, I couldn't find Burr's card in my room, so had to go up to ER to phone the general police number. It took them ages to locate Burr, who listened quietly to my story and suspicions that I suspected were due to the incident at the Marriott. He didn't laugh.

'Where are these chocolates?'

I told him I was standing in ER with them, all wrapped up and sealed.

'Leave them at the desk. I'll get an officer over to pick them up for our lab to analyse. And I'll come down to take statements this afternoon. Are the young women in danger?'

'I'm not really sure. One's quite ill.'

'Now Miss MacLean, these suspect items were addressed to you specifically. I advise you to be careful. Although I can tell you Dr van Lindholm is in Paris today. His secretary tells us he flew out last night with his wife. And in strict confidence, I can tell you that during a search of his property this morning, documents of varying kinds were found hidden in the wall of a pool house that support Frances Cooke's statements to you. Dr van Lindholm has a lot of explaining to do. We, however, do have Dr Mendoza at the precinct presently. I cannot say more at this time, as I'm sure you understand.'

'Of course.' I felt my anxiety drop a notch or two. But still, I did not know for certain whether VL had sent the dangerous presents.

'I will be in touch.' He rang off.

Over at the desk. I sealed my binbag into an outer yellow Biohazard one and sellotaped on a label saying, 'Evidence for Detective Lieutenant Burr.' I wasn't taking any chances it might wander or be binned.

In Room Two, Randy was administering something to Belle, who still looked clammy and pale if more alert and 'with it'.

'Hi, Mhairi. Belle's BP is better.' Randy patted her hand reassuringly. 'We're on this. No worries.' She gave him a wan smile. Progress.

I went over to sit with her. 'I'm sorry, Belle, but I think it was something in my chocolates that made you ill. How many did you eat?'

'Three, I think. The fourth I spat out. Supposed to be vanilla on the box pic but it tasted funny.' Randy had popped out and returned. I told him Jess said the sweets tasted funny and that she'd had four.

He nodded sheepishly as if admitting defeat. 'Okay, it likely is them. Madre de Dios, chocolates as poison! ¡qué ridículo! Stupid idea. You told Burr?'

'Yep. He's sending a guy over to get them for analysis and coming himself later to speak to the Belle and Jess. What did your Poison Bureau suggest it is?'

'One of several things.' He nodded at the nurse standing by. 'Let's get Belle upstairs.'

Outside he looked serious. 'They suggest nerve agents, insecticides. Our lab here can check for some, others need the county lab at District General. 'You never took any?' he asked, looking concerned.

'No. I hate dark chocolate.'

'Me too. Give me Hershey's every time!' Randy licked his lips. I didn't say I hated gluey US chocolate even more than *Bournville* but he must have misread my disgusted look as anxiety since he clapped my arm affectionately saying, 'Hang in there! We'll get this sorted.' He left for the next patient.

As Belle now came past on a gurney, I quickly asked, 'This morning, the guy who delivered the chocolates—what was he like?'

She had perked up a bit and her eyes were much clearer. 'He had a flashy blue motorbike with kinda sticky-out Harley mirrors, was wearing a leather waistcoat and a baseball hat. Black, young, nice looking. Big eyes. Bike had a square trunk like pizza delivery guys have. Why?'

'Just curious. They're analysing the chocs. Lucky you didn't take more.'

'Kinda old-time trick, sending someone poisoned candies, isn't it?' Belle sighed. The nurse squeezed her arm in reassurance.

'Yes. Spiking food was the thing in ancient times. I once wrote an essay at school about the French Queen Catherine de Medici. She was a nasty piece of work, supposedly eliminated loads of enemies with poisoned stuff and even had her own daughter kidnapped...'

'Jesus, you don't say? You know any wicked queens over here in Jersey?'

I smiled despite feeling grim. 'No, but van Lindholm is my best guess as the villain.'

Belle's attendant snorted, 'God, you should ask the girls about him. Complete sleazeball! Well, the only one who considered him a catch was poor Nurse Makkonen. Didn't get her far, did it? Right.' The girl nodded towards the elevators and I got the message. They had things to get on with. A porter helped her trundle Belle into the lift.

I went to the Coffee Shop for a drink and pondered about Belle's description of the chocolate courier. He sounded very like the MRT biker Laura had described at the lab door on Sunday morning. I realised that just because Lindholm left for Paris last night didn't mean he couldn't have instigated the delivery. Who did he think he was? Acting like he was some crime lord in a TV drama or something? Randy had brought up Ironside, but my favourite was Perry Mason whom I used to watch with Mum. His side kick was the dishy Paul Drake, who, now I thought of it, bore more than a passing resemblance to my John. I switched off carnal thoughts and returned to my OBS posting.

On the Floor, I wandered around for an hour or two 'observing' but my heart wasn't in it. The minute it turned five, I went back to the Home for tea after which Laura and I checked on Jess who was feeling considerably better, had a brief encouraging gossip with Kitty on the Surgical Floor then watched some TV with John. He left at the 'legal' eleven and I gratefully sank into bed. It had been quite a day.

Friday was nice and uneventful. We hoped our troubles were over and van Lindholm would return to end up in police custody.

Saturday was August first. We had now been away a month though it seemed much, much longer. John decided we would have a mini party in the Residency with some expensive wine his Dad had sent to cheer us up. Jackie had also sent me some special chocolates from a Californian Company called *Ghirardelli* that was her favourite. I expect they were better than *Hershey's*, but I declined to try them: I was off chocolates.

Satisfied that Jess was now out, better and safely tucked up back home with her Mum and Babs for a few days and that Randy said Belle was making progress, Laura and I joined Coop and John to party. They ordered burgers and fries to be delivered which we washed down with copious glasses of Warren's best Californian wine. It was great to relax, albeit with pangs of occasional guilt that Frankie was no longer with us. And sadness that Nat had felt the need to phone his father and disappear off home with him in a nervous state. But none-the-less, we were young, healthy and liberated from the worry that lives in the hospital might depend on us solving mysteries or doing something. The police were on the case and we could leave it to them. We let off steam playing loud music, singing and talking nonsense.

Eventually, when I noticed on the wall clock that it was past midnight, I suggested we should probably go back to the Nurses' Home and bed. But the boys continued on, teasing Laura, larking about, talking animatedly about films and TV series that we'd never heard of but must see. Eventually I stood up and dragged Laura from her seat on Coop's lap. Declining the boys' kind offer to walk us back down the hill (I wasn't entirely sure Coop could stumble that far and John wasn't far behind him in the inebriation stakes) we kissed our goodbyes and left the residency.

Outside at the lifts I had a daft idea. We should go to check on Belle before turning in. I felt incredibly guilty that this poor innocent girl was ill from poison intended for me. She'd been in hospital now for two days and I hadn't visited her. Laura agreed it was a good idea and we pushed open the door to the stairs instead of calling for the lift. A fatal alcohol-fuelled decision.

We were giggling like schoolgirls as we teetered unsteadily down the stairs heading to her room on Floor Three. Once there, I was poised on the landing in front of the door when Laura said something funny and I turned to her to laugh. My right hand was already on the doorhandle, and I was about to pull it inward when, suddenly, the door developed a mind of its own and burst open with a jerk. My wrist was bent back acutely. In pain and startled, I yelped, overbalancing and grabbing Laura to steady myself. She had been standing immediately behind me, perhaps a step or so to my left. The door opened wide to reveal the last person I expected or wanted to see.

How in Hell's teeth had he got here? Wasn't he supposed to be in...

Chapter Twenty-Nine
Morning in Paris, Midnight in Brunsfield

11am the day before, Saturday August 1st, The Ritz Hotel, Place Vendome, Paris
She turns her head from side to side deciding her hair isn't quite as good as when Eduardo does it, but then a hotel hairdresser, even in the Ritz, could never match a Fifth Avenue stylist. It's the one thing Ava feels they do less stylishly in France, hair. Her bob is cut close to her jawbone and the colour is holding out: a nice golden blonde, very similar to her original natural colour. Well, it had been a more peroxide-aided shade when Elias fell for her. There are no roots showing. Any hint of silver is so ageing. And she is now aware of being the age his first wife was when he left her.

She sits at the dressing table applying her new Chanel make-up and wonders where Elias has got to. Strange. On her return, she'd expected to find him lounging on the bed watching crappy TV. As far as she knows, he knows no one in Paris. It is unlikely he has gone down to meet anyone. It's too early for a drink, even for him.

The priority this Saturday is her appointment with the small atelier recommended by that English starlet in the lounge yesterday. How lucky she was able to secure an appointment for noon today. Seemingly, this dressmaker has a growing reputation for excellent cut, especially for slacks. The hairdresser today had recommended another smaller house with a designer trained at Guerlain who specialised in ball gowns. On Monday she'll make an appointment there. With those two Sativa Benefit galas next month she needs something new and classy. Glancing at the clock, she decides that if Elias isn't back soon, she'll simply have to get reception to call a cab and go alone to today's appointment.

In the ensuite bathroom, with some irritation, she checks her make-up under the brighter light. If these classic European hotels won't have overhead lighting at their dressing tables, the least they can do is put stools in their bathrooms in front of the mirror. She is sure that Coco Chanel, rumoured to have been a frequent guest here, did not crouch down and peer in the mirror to perfect her 'look'. Today, her own isn't too bad but the bright light does accentuate some eye wrinkles. Camouflaging them is beginning to take a little more effort. Finally, she downs her sponges and brushes and smiles at her reflection: still pretty damned good for forty-two!

Washing her hands free of make-up involves reaching for the soap in its pretty dish. As she does so, she pauses. This bathroom only has one basin: so passe in the US. But something is missing. Where is Elias's toothbrush? Come to mention it, where is his razor? Looking round, she notes his leather Hermes toilet bag is also nowhere to be seen. After checking inside the bathroom cabinet and finding it empty, she slams its door and almost explodes with anger.

In the bedroom, she flings open the ornately carved wardrobe. One dinner suit, two pairs of grey pants and a raincoat still hang, but the shelves of shirts and underwear are much depleted. His suitcase remains on the rack at the side, but his Pan Am flight bag no longer sits in the bottom of the wardrobe. His passport is no longer in the bedside drawer. Who the fuck does he think is? Taking off without a word.

But why has the bastard done a runner? This trip was his idea! Might it be connected to the call he took last night before dinner? Hmmm. He has been pre-occupied since. She had answered the bedside phone and spoken to a female caller with a thick accent that had asked to speak to Elias. He had spoken briefly to her in incomprehensible Spanish before hanging up abruptly. When challenged, he'd dismissed it as a colleague's wife wanting advice about lawyers as her husband was in some trouble with the police. He'd been dismissive when she asked him what for.

'Forget it, Ava. It doesn't concern you.'

But this absence does. Big time. How dare he abandon her in a foreign city? First thing this morning she'd been delighted he'd been so supportive when she'd complained about needing to wash her own hair. He'd phoned down to get her an appointment, saying a hotel of this calibre would have a stylist on call 24/7. Then they'd made love. Supportive? My ass! Likely he'd thought it a godsend to get her out of the way to let him pack up essentials and run.

She thinks of previous pivotal moments in their fifteen-year marriage. As a young medical secretary, she'd been swept off her feet by the handsome blond doctor. How thoughtlessly she'd ended his marriage, ignoring the hurt she'd caused to the family he left behind and now rarely saw. He hadn't wanted more children and she'd happily complied with his wishes.

Over the years, she's put up with some fairly blatant extra-marital liaisons, accepting them as a price to pay for the lifestyle she enjoyed on her generous allowance. But this desertion? The ultimate insult! He thought he could get away with a quick tumble, not even much of a performance truth be told, and abandon her in a Paris hotel room, creeping off like a fucking criminal? Unacceptable!

For too long she's ignored his rampant escalation of infidelity. The prints from the film inside that camera Maria found on top of the wardrobe had been hard to take but she'd merely replaced it and decided to gloss over it; boys will have their fun. However, it had meant that she now ensured she was always partially covered on the rare occasions they had sex in the bed. And she now had regular

271

gynaecology checks in case she might catch anything from his whores. There had been one disturbing photo though: the girl was very young and looked possibly drugged. Oh, yes, she has plenty of proof of infidelity. And for collaboration, there is always Mr Ramsay next door. In the past, she's dismissed his insinuations about Elias entertaining female 'visitors' when she's been away. Out of sight, out of mind. But now? This is an insult too far! That Ramsay would testify, she has no doubt. She knows the sad, be-wigged divorcee fancies her.

Time to take back control of her life. She strides over to the phone and dials reception.

'Good morning, this is Mrs van Lindholm in the Dauphin Suite. Can you make a Person-to-Person call for me to a Mr Wesley Naismith in New York City? The number is...'

Wesley's Manhattan firm, Aster and Naismith, Attorneys at Law, have terminated several friend's marriages with excellent results. Pre-nup agreement or not, she'll sue the fuckin' ass off Elias, make him cough up big time. She will use Aster as they are bigger divorce court combatants than her brother's firm though she'll ask him to help clear the house when Elias is out.

As she waits, she tallies up other ammunition she has. A few months ago, she'd overheard Elias jibe to the accountant about how easy it was to fool the IRS. It had made her snoop, following her thrice-married mother's advice on navigating marriage. Ears open, Eyes open. Assemble evidence. Prepare for any eventuality, expect the worst. Well, this desertion was her final straw. The photos she'd taken in his study of 'duplicate' investment accounts, captured while he was at a Vegas conference last month (likely really a 'fucking-off' weekend) were further bargaining tools. He might think she's a dumb blonde, but she's always known he hides his desk and filing cabinet keys in his father's old cigar box.

The phone rings. 'Mrs van Lindholm? I have your call to New York.'

Ava smiles. She knew Wesley would take her call even at 6 am, Eastern Time in New York on a weekend morning. He'll love taking the case. She knows his detestation of Elias as an arrogant arriviste is one of the reasons he's bedded her several times. But she doesn't mind. A girl deserves some fun. And he's great in the sack. Much better than Elias, the little prick.

~~~

Next day, Sunday, August 2nd, 1 a.m. Eastern Time, Level Three, Ellis Memorial Hospital

In the doorway, Elias van Lindholm's bushy blonde moustache was level with my eyes and for the first time, I noticed it covered an ugly jagged purple scar on his upper lip. Despite my shock and fear at the door bursting open on me, I fleetingly wondered how he'd got the wound? A fight? He exhaled in a snort of rage, his breath reeking of smoky whisky. The worst kind.

As I tried to step back, the tall physician raised the bag he was carrying to clutch it with both hands and smash it into my face with grunting strength. The force cannoned me back into Laura and knocked us both back down the flight of stairs. Though the right side of my body was free to fall, the weight of my left fell heavily onto Laura, propelling her backwards and causing her to bump repeatedly against the railings before we tumbled in a heap onto the half landing. We crashed down twelve steep steps that were covered in a shallow pile coarse carpet but had hard metal edges. Before my head made contact with the floor, I heard Laura's hit it with a sickening thud. Mine coasted on more slowly, rolling over her right shoulder before bumping down. Neither of us made a sound. No time to scream or cry out. As I lay awkwardly on top of my friend, winded and momentarily confused, I tried to focus

273

and summon some breath to yell at the tall cursing figure as he ran past, treading on my left leg and kicking Laura's arm out of the way before sprinting down the second flight. I only managed a feeble whimper that I doubt he heard as he took the stairs two at a time before vanishing.

Trying to rise was difficult and I was concerned about hurting Laura further. She lay lifeless, twisted and silent, eyes closed. I looked down at my right arm and realised that not only was my wrist unresponsive to any movement I tried, but it was also excruciatingly painful and swelling alarmingly. My left ankle was probably also broken and wouldn't take my weight. I managed to gently roll off Laura, who was unconscious and made no response to my urging and gentle shaking. Hearing the thud her head had made coming into contact with the landing, I knew it would be a miracle if she hadn't fractured her skull. In tears, I screamed, 'You bastard!'. A complete waste of energy. What Laura needed wasn't anger but medical attention: asap.

Helped by my one good (left) arm and injury-free right leg, I attempted a sort of crab bottom shuffle laboriously and painfully upwards, one step at a time, to the Third Floor door from where we had started our crashing descent. Knowing the Second Floor only held the now-closed dining room, seminar room and admin offices, I was compos mentis enough to know no help would be available there. I had to go up.

My head was bursting with a headache that had gone from dull to splitting in seconds and I could now taste the blood pouring copiously from my nose. Agonisingly slowly, I reached the door, but it took several attempts to open for its design meant it came inward and its handle was well above my head. Everything I needed to put weight on for purchase was excruciating but eventually I managed to manoeuvre my good hand up, grasp the handle, pull in the door and crawl around it. Rolling rather than crawling, I was making my arduous way across the Floor Three lobby when Clayton appeared.

'What the fuck?' was his comment as he looked down in horror at my battered face and the writhing contortions I was attempting in order to progress.

I cried out, 'Clayton, please go get Laura. We fell. She's bad. On the stairs out there.' I nodded at the door which had closed back on itself.

Hearing my shouting, a nurse appeared in the corridor and Clayton called to her, 'Can you get a chair asap, Margot?'

I sobbed, 'Forget me, Clayton, Laura's worse—got a skull fracture. It was Lindholm. He pushed us.'

'Lindholm? But he's in France!' Clayton put an arm under each of my armpits to bodily haul me into the newly arrived chair.

'No, he's not, he's here. But never mind—get Laura!' I sobbed. 'Please go to her!'

Clayton ran out to the stairwell, returning in seconds to dart into a room off the hall and emerge with a trolley which he propelled to the stair door with one hand, while in the other, he held one of the wooded boards with cut-out carrying handles that we slide under cardiac arrests. He shot through the door as the nurse retuned with another Resident who followed him into the stair well.

Margot turned to me. 'Let's get you down to ER, my girl.' She gave me a towel to staunch the copious flow from my nose and spun the chair round to pull me backwards into the elevator.

'Did I hear you right—Lindholm did this?'

I nodded.

'Fuckin' prick that guy. Cuttin' his balls off without anaesthetic is the least I'd do to him. Saw him a few years ago get it in the face from a girl. A broken glass stem. Opened up his lip. Great party!'

So, that explained the scar I'd never noticed it until I was up close and personal tonight. I was peculiarly delighted to have had the answer to a question answered almost immediately after I'd encountered it, a first during this summer saga. I tried a smile. But it hurt. As did my chest. Especially taking a deep breath. I decided I had broken ribs. God knows what my face was like: it felt like it'd been flattened. What had he intended? Just to get away- or to kill us?

This summer was turning out to be a complete disaster. I should never have persuaded Laura to come on this ridiculous trip to this damned hospital. Coop had told us it had been endowed by a millionaire WW2 arms dealer, Hopgood Ellis, whom he reckoned was trying to atone for his fortune amassed from death and destruction. This place was surely riddled with evil. Yet here I'd been, urging Laura to wander about at night in a mental 'lark' to visit Belle.

Laura was likely dead. And I was responsible. How could I ever face her mother? I buried my face into Margot's towel, adding copious tears to the scarlet blood that already sullied its pristine whiteness.

Chapter Thirty
Bruised & Battered

It was peculiar being on the opposite side of the consultation situation in ER, lying on an examination couch being prodded and poked by a nurse, having BP cuffs and thermometers thrust at me. Hiro was the Resident on call overnight and examined me to pronounce confidently that in his opinion, I'd broken my right wrist and possibly my nose, but only badly sprained my ankle. The other good news was that I was going to have two black eyes.

Within half an hour, X-rays did confirm an un-displaced crack fracture in my wrist, but intact bones on my left ankle and to my surprise, no obvious broken ribs. My chest was only bruised. But painful at every breath. My nose was deemed '*gladimansta*' (by Hiro. Seeing my horror and incomprehension, he laughed. 'Sorry, that's Japanese for, 'bashed in.' Very technical.

A disconcertingly cheerful orthopaedic guy arrived with a technician to plaster my wrist and strap up my wounded ankle. He also cleaned up my nose. The latter involved some quick but agonising manipulation with a metal instrument of torture followed by uncomfortable packing, but as I'd had a shot of something, by that time I no longer cared. Much. Just as the doctor was writing up details of his tortures, John arrived, remarkably sober considering the state we'd left him in. Ambitiously trying to stand up from the exam couch in my opiate confusion in order to hug him, I promptly fainted into his arms.

A few moments later, I came back to reality on the couch feeling like a weak Victorian damsel, cradled in John's embrace (painful though it was). They then wheeled me off into the elevator and upstairs to an Orthopaedic Surgery room on Fourth where I fell asleep after another mind-numbing shot.

When I woke a second time, I was totally panicky, heart racing, chest aching and crying, worse than anything I'd experienced after Mum's death. It was bad enough having hurtled backwards down the stairs and suffering the distress of hurting Laura (whom I'd been reassured was actually alive) but despite being calmed temporarily by a visit from the Floor Resident, I got stressed again as I was being disturbed at frequent intervals by nurses taking my blood pressure. At the fourth assault I complained bitterly. 'What's wrong with my blood pressure? I'm not feeling faint now.'

The diminutive nurse who looked like she'd just left primary school gave a tinkling laugh. 'Oh, don't worry. Your blood pressure's fine.'

'So why am I getting so much attention?' My head and arm hurt like hell again. Obviously, my bliss-inducing jab was wearing off.

'Oh, it's your accent. It's so cute. We all wanted to come and speak to you.'

From this I gathered that tonight's shift was comprised of nurses we'd not yet met. Cross, I said, 'Well, tell them if they want to chat they don't need an excuse. Take the bloody sphygmo cuff off my arm and go get me some painkillers!'

The blonde doll-like nurse inclined her head towards her shoulder to regard me like a rare medical specimen. The manoeuvre made her cap now look vertically placed on her head instead of at the rakish angle it was in reality when she was upright. Even in extremis I couldn't help noting details. But after I'd blinked a couple of times I saw not one, but two caps. On two heads. And the room was in motion. I panicked again. Was this double vision and vertigo from a head injury? Had they missed a skull fracture? Had I had an X-ray of my head? The girl's insane grin wasn't helping me. Nor did her comment.

'Say, you speak English real well, you know. Though they say you've only been here a month. Amazing!'

That bombshell was the final straw. I shouted at her, 'For God's sake, of course we speak bloody English! Painkillers- I need painkillers! And please find out how my friend Laura Ellis is!'

Fortunately, my vision seemed to have corrected itself and I could see only one hat with a single blue stripe indicating her juvenile position. It bobbed rakishly as she nodded and left. I sank back. God, the girl was as insulting as van Lindholm. What bloody language did they think we spoke in Scotland? Okay, we had Gaelic, but it was spoken by only a tiny minority. Granted, that included my gran, though despite her best efforts, Archie and I never learned anything bar counting to ten. Oh, God, that reminded me: home. If the hospital phoned Dad about all this, he would be incandescent and feel all his worrying was justified.

I turned over and groaned. It seemed as if there wasn't any part of my body that didn't hurt. Yet at least I was awake and could feel pain. But Laura, how was she? I was sobbing when John appeared at the door but still managed a barrage of questions.

'How's Laura? She was bleeding from her ear—doesn't that mean a serious middle skull fracture? How bad is it? I mean, was she just unconscious or did she arrest? Or is she...'

John sat on the chair at the bedside, picked up my free hand and held it tightly.

'Hey, Mhairi. Cool it. She'll be up here soon. While you were sleeping, I went down to see what was happening with her. She's had X-rays and a scan, has definitely got a broken arm and some expert's looking at her skull X-ray. They had a Neuro guy in as she woke and she was pretty muddled. He thinks she's definitely concussed but her bloodied ear was from lacerations sustained from ricocheting down the stair railings.

'The Plastics guys are stitching her up and Coop's with her. I reckon she'll be fine. Don't worry. Apparently her first words—'God my head hurts!' made Hiro counter with, 'Pain is good!' She then came out then with lots of swear words that Hiro says were new to him. Mind you, she did ask me what day it was and wondered whether she'd missed some plane, but they don't seem to be too worried. Just concentrate on getting yourself better. She's in good hands with Hiro and Clayton and three specialist guys!'

'Thank God! I thought I'd...I thought she'd...' I sobbed again. 'I thought she'd died. I didn't think she was breathing. Then when Clayton took a Resus board out to her...'

'Well, if you told him she was unconscious, it's what I'd have expected. Haven't you seen boards used after accidents to stabilise someone's neck if there isn't a neck brace to hand? It's not perfect but putting a neck and head carefully on one is better than risking a cord transection if a patient's neck is broken. Clayton sends his regards, by the way.'

'But how is her neck? I'd have thought it must be broken. She fell with such a clatter.'

'They're saying she's only got whiplash. Her injuries, I think, could've been worse.' He squeezed my hand. 'Much worse.'

'God, if I could get my hands on van Lindholm's bloody neck!'

'Think there might be a queue! By the way, Burr's coming in to speak to you around eleven. While you were having your ortho treatment in ER, I phoned the police department about Lindholm's assault.'

'That's good,' I said. My head was starting to thump again. 'But please, John, can you go and get me some painkillers?' Thankfully, at that point a nurse appeared with a little plastic cup of tablets. John poured me water from a jug at the bedside and I swallowed them hungrily, never even asking what they were. I'd have taken anything.

John looked at his watch. 'Okay, that's eight now. I'll let you rest after the meds, go grab a shower and then come back. I'll see where they're putting Laura and maybe we can get a chair and take you in to see her.' He stooped to kiss me, gently touching my cheek and whispering, 'Your poor face. Looks like you've done a few rounds with Joe Frazier! But it'll heal. I love you, Mhairi MacLean.'

I lay back, drifting off into a pharmacological euphoria thinking I should've told him I loved him too. And vaguely wondering who Joe Frazier was.

~~~

Detective Lieutenant Arthur Burr arrived accompanied by another detective, a woman with magnificent mahogany skin and a gentle smile whom he introduced as Officer Celia Damon.

I tried to smile. I wasn't sure if it was successful. My face didn't seem my own. They pulled up chairs to sit beside the bed and Burr started.

'Good morning, Miss MacLean. You up to some questions?'

'I'm a bit woozy, and sore, but fine, go ahead.'

'So, can you tell me what happened last night?'

Giving an account of our encounter with Lindholm, I realised it had lasted only seconds. Burr looked puzzled when I said I'd been hit in the face with a Gladstone Bag.

'A what?'

Celia saved me the trouble of explaining. 'It's a leather portmanteau bag. Opens up at the top.' She demonstrated the shape and opening of one. 'You see them in western movies.'

I'd only seen my old GP, Mannie Cosgrove's. Suddenly on the grey wall opposite I saw his face beside that of my father. In panic, I closed my eyes. When I opened them again a few minutes later, our old GP and Dad had thankfully disappeared. My clinical interest was piqued: an opiate hallucination? Burr was repeating some question.

'Are you okay, Miss MacLean?' He looked concerned.

'Sorry, just a bit doped up. What did you say?'

'Right. So, after he hit you in the face, what happened, Mhairi?'

How nice, he'd started using my first name, and remembered how to pronounce it.

'Yes, he hit me hard in the face with his bag. He'd taken it in both hands and turned it—maybe so that the metal frame would hit me harder full on? I don't know. The bag did look heavy, like it had stuff in it. Never seen him with one before, nor anyone else here, for that matter. We were on the third floor, outside on the stairwell landing by the way, did I say? That's the floor with his office on it.'

'Yes, we're on Fourth, the Surgical floor. You're in 402 in case you don't know. We had his office searched the other day but no one reported a bag. Suppose he brought it into get something, perhaps? Burr turned to his assistant. 'Maybe go take a look down again at his room, Celia. It has his name on it, room next but one to the elevator. See if anything's disturbed or looks odd. Reckon he must've been in it.'

Celia closed her notebook and left to do his bidding. Inexplicably, I started crying.

Burr smiled kindly. 'I'm sorry, Mhairi. This has been an ordeal for you. I hear your friend is making good progress. It was a wonder he didn't kill you both.'

'I just wish you'd get him.' I tried to pull myself together.

'We're on it. At least we know what car van Lindholm's driving. A few hours ago, a German lady, a Gretel something, called the station to say he'd bullied her into giving him hers.

'Oh, Gretel Neuberger? She's lovely. Works in the *Bohemia* restaurant downtown. She mentioned knowing Lindholm. I wondered how well. Thought maybe they'd been close...'

'I'll leave her to tell you about that but she called him lots of things in German, none of them I reckon, complimentary. Love affair gone sour or maybe worse? Hinted he'd had a hold over her. She mention that?'

'No, but I wonder if the hold concerned photos of her un-dressed on a bed? We should have told you about the ones Frankie found in van Lindholm's room. Loads of them. But I didn't think they were relevant. Poor girls. Some very young. Awful.'

'Well, it's due to you telling her that Dr van Lindholm was up to no good 'big time' that she plucked up courage to call us. And of course, she was mad he'd gone off with her car. Confidentially, we've already got those photos Frank told you about. They were hidden with accounts and patient papers behind a false wall in the changing room at van Lindholm's pool. And other photographs were still in a dark room in the attic of his house. I've locked the girl pics in my drawer at the station. My girl's eighteen and I know how I'd feel if someone had taken photos of her.' He shook his head. 'Probably why I'm tellin' you all this. Keep it to yourself.'

'He certainly seems to be an all-round callous rat.'

'Jesus, Mhairi. You've certainly had an education about the sleazy side of life in Jersey. I reckon there's likely loads of guys like him all over but he sure is one particular right son of a bitch. 'He coughed, looking sideways at Celia who'd returned and grinned at his comment. 'I mean, he's some piece of work.'

I smiled too. He was right, Dr Elias van Lindholm was a right S.O.B.

Celia reported, 'The room's not locked. There's a grille loose on the desk that likely came from a ventilation duct high up in the corner. A chair was underneath it. Maybe he could've had that bag, or whatever it was that he had in it, hidden up there?'

Burr looked furious. 'It wasn't checked when they did the search? Jesus. what are they teachin' these guys at police college?' He turned back to me. 'Okay, girl. You just concentrate on gettin' better and we'll catch the devil. Your friend Gretel gave us a good photo of him so that's out to all units, what we call an APB, along with the licence plate and model of Gretel's Chrysler.'

'What about Dr Juan Mendoza? He's got a lot to answer for as well.'

'Oh, we have him. He's a lulu, Mhairi. Don't mind saying he's been very cooperative. Blames Lindholm for pressurizing him. Admits the Sativa setup was a charity scam laundering monies from the kidney buyers. They spirited off most of it for themselves, with smaller amounts going to the donors. Mendoza had his money in cash but says Elias has accounts in Panama and Mexico. He complained Elias dished him out peanuts compared to his own cut. When thieves fall out it's a good day for us. But he's not talking this morning. He's in a bad way. Had to move him into the prison hospital...'

'Rumour has it he takes cocaine,' I said.

'Shouldn't say but reckon it'll be out in the press soon, anyway. They reckon he has a big problem with the nasty stuff. Worse shakes I've seen.' He looked from Celia to me. 'Right. Anything else to tell me, Mhairi?'

'I don't think so.' I only wanted to sleep.

Burr patted my hand and stood up. 'We'll be in touch.'

~~~

After a snooze I managed soup for lunch, although with my sore jaw, the crusty bread was impossible. John returned with a wheelchair to take me along to see Laura, now in 409. I was thrilled to find her propped up in bed and grinning (if weakly), a bandage stretching from her right temple over to her poor left ear. A plaster encased her left wrist. Looking at my right one she grinned and weakly raised it. 'Snap!'

'My wrist's fractured,' I said. 'Got a sprained ankle too.'

'Bet my wrist is worse—it's fractured in two places!' She looked pleased, like it was a competition. Morphine does funny things to your rationality.

Sitting at Laura's side was a handsome man in his fifties. He looked prosperous despite only wearing slacks and a polo shirt, might be the suntan and the serious watch. She introduced him as her Uncle Vincent. I should have known who he was, as tall and blond as his sister Grace, Laura's mother. The New York banker rose and came forward with hands outstretched to clasp mine.

'How are you, Mhairi? This has been some situation I'm hearing.' He sat back down and took Laura's good hand, explaining, 'When Grace got the hospital call that Laura and you had been in an accident she, of course, phoned me and I shot over. Thank God you are both on the mend!'

I reserved judgement on Laura, who looked far from the mend with her head bandages and alarming neck brace. Coop arrived, kissed Laura on the forehead and came over to give me a gentle hug.

'Oh, hi, Mhairi! How are you? Sorry, I had to go grab a sandwich. Have you spoken to Burr? I just saw him getting into the elevator.'

I nodded.

'He's been in here too,' said Uncle Vincent. 'Only stayed a few minutes, asking Laura to confirm it was van Lindholm who pushed you two. Said he'd be back for a proper statement in the morning.'

'Do they know where van Lindholm is now?' Coop frowned. 'I'll be happy when he's in custody.'

'They don't, but they know he's in Gretel's car and they have a good photo of him that she gave them. It's out to all forces, apparently.'

'Gretel?' Coop looked puzzled. 'Your waitress friend? What's she got to do with him?'

'Old flame apparently. Went sour,' I said, with an effort, thinking my painkillers didn't seem to be lasting long enough.

Vincent confidently asserted, 'I'm sure they'll get him.'

'And Mendoza?' asked Coop, looking from Laura to me. 'How about him?'

I shrugged. 'He's in custody but in drug withdrawal in a prison hospital. Burr admitted he was talking, thinks there's no love lost between him and Lindholm, money arguments for one. Burr says they've got lots of the stuff Frankie saw. Found it hidden in his pool house. Photos and everything. Burr was surprisingly frank with me, said Lindholm had some hold over Gretel. Likely photos.'

'Funny Gretel didn't say she knew him that well when we spoke about him in the restaurant.' Laura frowned.

John grunted. 'But she was uncomfortable one night I took Mhairi for dinner and we spoke about him, wasn't she, Mhairi?'

I nodded.

Laura sighed heavily. 'Well, right enough, would you likely say, "Oh, Him? Yeah, we 'got it on' for a while but like, I was an ass and he's got naked photos of me." Come on!'

This was reassuring; Laura obviously had her humour cortex intact. She was going to be fine.

'Huh, sure as hell don't think I'd have admitted what happened.' said Coop.

'Mhari, did Burr tell you what Mendoza's admitted to?' Laura asked.

'Only about the charity money that was from kidney-selling. And he blamed everything on Lindholm.'

Looking at all the dejected faces in the room, I decided I needed to lighten the mood and turned the conversation to the ditzy nurse who'd been impressed at me speaking good English for a Scot. It gave us our first proper laugh for a while.

'Guess I can expect a few curious nurses in here too, then. Now that I'm awake!' Laura made a face.

Seeing I was flagging, John wheeled me back to my own room. I was beginning to feel exhausted and happily let John lie on the bed beside me. I fell asleep before any nurse came to object.

Chapter Thirty-One
Klusterfuck, Confrontation & Confession

Earlier the same day

To quote his old Captain from military service, the situation is no longer a salvageable SNAFU (Situation normal: all fucked up) but a complete Klusterfuck. He might've delayed bailing out but for those fucking Scots girls being on the stairs knowing he was back. He couldn't risk lingering and finishing them off.

He'd already tried to silence that red headed MacLean one who was whipping up the Gomez brat. Since, even for a more substantial payment, Winston had refused to attempt another pillow silencing gig on her, he'd had to resort to the clumsy poisoned candies idea. He had managed to persuade Winston to deliver them but didn't tell him anything about the contents. His always-willing secretary, Jordan, had ordered the chocolates and he'd spiked them with the weedkiller himself, hoping that if the nosey MacLean girl took even a couple, she'd be out of commission for few days. Ideally after four or five she'd have had a nasty GI storm, with wretched vomiting and horrendous diarrhoea, rapidly segueing into seizures and a 'Schmerzhafter Tod', or painful death. How he loved those capitalized and dramatic German nouns. He'd learned more than just German words from his father. Steig was full of aphorisms: adapt; always be prepared; never admit to anything. Policies that had worked well for the old man during and after the War in Sweden when he collaborated big-time with the Nazis. How he'd manged to flee to the States with his questionably acquired gold was extraordinary. And it was now safely legitimatised in property deals.

Like Steig, he has developed police informants and has had a heads up about the pool house discoveries and Mendoza's disloyalty. He knows things are getting tricky. This fucking country doesn't respect entrepreneurs seeing a need and reaping a profit! He's checked the law. It's still hazy about negotiating transplant deals and he knows he can run with that no problem but if his man Charlie's right about the plan to exhume those two women, forensics might confirm their ends were not due to natural causes. No point in taking the chance. Lucky that Resident has taken off and they're pursuing him for Makkonen. She was deranged and out to get him. Stupid broad.

Acquiring serious ready cash for immediate expenses without attracting the attention of the authorities is tricky nowadays within the US. Thank God he'd kept that cocaine stashed in the office. And thank the Blessed Virgin those search cops were assholes who never looked up.

In exchange for the drugs, Pilot Dino has agreed to mount a flight to Mexico and provide a float of readies. Unbelievably, considering his South American drug trade, the pilot boy's a stickler for filing flight plans. But Dino fucking better leave his name off today's manifest. He's been assured it will all be sorted by the time he gets to Teterboro. All that remains to be done is to phone Old Steig from the private terminal to tell him where the papers are giving him the right to the house and to urge him to change the locks before Ava returns. She can fend for herself. Bloody women are the source of all the major aggravation in the world. But he smiles at how easy it was to persuade gruesome Gretel to give him the car keys. Jesus, she's let herself go. He hadn't even been tempted. Time for pastures new.

He turns off the Freeway into Teterboro.

~~~

By ten on the Monday evening, I'd convinced the Senior Resident on call that I was compos mentis and capable of walking on crutches. To my delight, he discharged me. But not Laura, whom they'd decided did have a small skull fracture and needed kept in for observation. The nurse gave me a bag with meds and some instruction sheets and left me to dress. John went for a wheelchair. But I wasn't to be left in peace. I had just struggled one-handed-ly getting my bell bottom jeans over the ankle bandage when in walked Dr Carlton Harper.

The Medical Chief of Staff stood fidgeting, clasping and un-clasping his hands in front of his ample stomach. He awkwardly shook my good hand and cleared his throat several times before saying, 'I am so sorry you have had this little accident on hospital property. I hear you are making a good recovery. And of course, you must take off all the time you need. Do not feel you have to hurry back to your placement. The hospital will continue to make your payments...'

As if I cared about his puny 'pocket money'. It was his stupid-ity in bedding a junior and getting caught that underpinned this whole thing. For without the traction of the photos, van Lindholm's scheme might never have left first base (after a month I'd adopted many of Coop's baseball metaphors). Something in me snapped, maybe triggered by opiate disinhibition. My usual timidity and respect for seniors vanished. I let fly.

'How dare you come in here apologising for a 'little' accident! Some 'little' accident! You well know, Dr Harper, this 'accident' was actually a wilful assault on two innocent young women by Dr van Lindholm in his eagerness to evade the police. It may not be *directly* your fault that my friend and I were injured, but none of this would have happened if you'd stopped van Lindholm's schemes. I'm sure there will be questions to be answered about how long he was al-lowed to practice here considering the irregularities in his conduct, professionally and as an assaulter of women, shortcomings that have been obvious to us even in our short time at Ellis Memorial. And as for the standard of care given by Dr Mendoza—the legality of whose registration is also doubtful—it absolutely beggars belief! I wonder how many have died in the wake of these two evil men...'

Harper's face couldn't have become redder as he stood trembling before me, his mouth forming words that never made it to his tongue. While I was yelling, John had arrived to stand quietly behind him at the door. The man hadn't heard the door softly opening and jumped violently when John spoke.

'Dr Harper, you must realise the hospital will be liable for the dreadful events of today. You do know my parents are both senior in the legal profession? In fact, my mother is an attorney specialising in medical malpractice.'

Harper gave a squeak of horror and rushed out.

John looked pleased. 'That's told him!'

I was surprised to feel a wave of pity. 'Och, I almost feel sorry for him, I mean, van Lindholm only got away with his schemes because Carlton's gay. But he can't help that.'

'But he could have helped by not pretending he was straight and duping a poor woman into marriage. And he could have decided not to hit on junior staff and bully vulnerable students like Nat, who's still reeling from his enforced encounter with him. Anyway, here.' John handed me my new crutches from the corner. 'There you go, hop into this carriage and I'll wheel you to freedom!'

He sped me down the corridor towards the elevator.

~~~

Back at the Nurses' Home, Jess was in the kitchen with ice cream and an open textbook. She jumped up to greet me like a long-lost sister. Though I could have taken a lighter squeeze. Ordering John away, she said she'd see me settled. He agreed to go, after a chaste kiss. I wasn't up to anything else. But having dozed under the effects of pharmaceuticals most of the day, I wasn't ready for bed. Jess provided more ice cream and we chatted until midnight. She was a late bedder anyway. And, I knew, a poor sleeper.

After appraising her of the sorry details involved in our 'little accident' and Harper's feeble apology, I decided van Lindholm was taking up too much of my life and moved on to ask after Barbara.

Jess stared into space for a few moments, before looking at me intently. 'After everything that's happened, I think it's time I should tell you the truth. But you must swear for Barbara's sake, never to tell a soul.'

'Of course,' I replied, intrigued.

'Barbara's father is Dr Elias van Lindholm. He raped me one night in an ER storeroom when I was a Candy-striper. In fact, it might be the one they found Freya Makkonen in. Her death sure gave me shock. There but for the grace of God, and all that...'

'Oh my God! Did you go to the police about the rape?'

Jess laughed. 'You reckon that'd have been an idea? You obviously don't know how women are treated over here for reporting rape! A naïve, blue-collar family, seventeen-year-old girl accusing an eminent hospital doctor? Who'd have believed me? And if it did get to court, I'd be labelled a whore. I saw the media bloodshed at school when a girl took on a teacher for assaulting her. I couldn't expose my parents to all that.'

'But still, he should have had to pay.' My mind was reeling, trying to appreciate the physical and mental trauma she'd suffered.

'Oh, I got him to pay. Though furious that I wouldn't get an abortion, he did give me money, enough for the house deposit and Babs' schooling. All via a third party of course and after I'd signed an NDA. But I know he was heck of a pissed off that I stayed on here to do my nursing training. I didn't see why I should go away. And, huh, maybe I subconsciously wanted to be a constant reminder to him of his brutality, you know? But how naïve was I! That struttin' highfalutin bastard doesn't give a fuck. But I have kept quiet about it. I'm even civil if I have to meet him on the Floor but I'll never forget what happened. I decided not to tell anyone Barbara is mine—and his—child as I don't want her to grow up knowing her father's a rapist. And worse now, probably is a murderer.'

We talked about fathers. Hers was terrific. I told her all about mine: his lies, my worry about exactly how Mum had died, whether he'd contributed to her death or even killed her. Despite the distractions of the recent drama, that uncertainty still festered in me, though in reality, I was struggling to understand what his motive might have been. By the time Jess helped me into bed at two a.m., I felt as though we'd been through the Blitz together, sharing traumas. Yet I'd only been here in New Jersey five weeks.

Chapter Thirty-Two
Lakes, Mountains & Gulfs

There's something about contemplating water that's very soothing. Peaceful Lake Champlain was a perfect antidote to the chaotic events of the previous weeks. Its distant mountains were shades of dusky blue. The lake itself was silver and smooth, with flocks of birds flying low across the water or bobbing in groups beside the pebbled shore. Coop's parents owned a lakeside lodge in the Adirondack Park and once Laura was released after two nights in hospital, Brigitte Mayfield had persuaded Uncle Vincent to let us recuperate here rather than at his place in the busy city. On the Thursday after the stairs incident, Coop's sister Suzi joined his Mum, Laura and I to set off for the four-bedroomed wooden lodge which had a large garden, boathouse and personal jetty. Coop and Michael Mayfield were to come over with John at the weekend.

The drive up was scenic. Coop's mother gave us a running commentary on the places we passed through, lacing it with stories about the importance of Champlain in American history. Sadly, however, being still dopey from hefty painkillers, I was asleep by the time we reached the Civil War.

Come Saturday morning, apart from a dark purple line under my right eye, my face was looking much better, well on the way to recovering from its battering. My nose had been unpacked and was again usable as an organ of breathing and my wrist and ankle were hurting less. Now I could get by with one crutch, although Laura still needed two and was taking regular analgesics for her fracture headache.

The lodge was a magical place and the Coulters very welcoming. We felt surrounded by kindness and spoiled rotten. The living areas had shelves and shelves of books of all kinds: fiction and non-fiction, US and European. One volume Brigitte gave me to read was particularly intriguing. *Aerobics* was about the benefits of exercise and had become Brigitte's bible in recent years, responsible for her early morning runs. Laura was envious: the trails looked amazing. But it would be a while before we'd be running anywhere.

Late Saturday morning the boys and Michael appeared bouncing up the track. The car had barely come to a halt when John rushed out waving a newspaper.

Stopping in front of my garden seat, he held up the front page with a grin.

'Looks like he's had it!' The paper front page bore a large old photo of Elias van Lindholm in his white coat with a drug company logo behind, presumably talking at some pharma sponsored conference. Above his arrogant face ran the headline, *Fugitive Doc Dies in Plane Crash.*

'Say, what d'ya know?' said John. 'The article says van Lindholm hired a private plane from Teterboro Airport outside New York to take him to Mexico. But glory be, seems like divine intervention had it hit by lightning and falling near the shore of Lake Douglas north of the Great Smoky Mountains National Park. The plane was severely burned out and the two charred bodies discovered are said to be the pilot and Elias. That's it. All over.'

I felt strangely cheated. 'Okay, he's gone. Not sure anyone will miss him, but this isn't how it should've ended, John. Wouldn't it have been better justice if Elena could have had her day in court and he and Mendoza could be stuck in jail for the rest of their lives?' Part of me, however, acknowledged that there was one beneficiary of this outcome: Jess. Now that Elias no longer walked the planet, she could stop worrying that he was a threat to her or might contact Barbara with the truth of her paternity.

Michael Mayfield came up. 'And by the way, Dr Harper has resigned as Chief of Medical Staff. I believe the President was about to sack him for his corruption, or rather coercion into shady practices by van Lindholm. Easier all round for the hospital. But the staff know what went on.'

Brigitte sat beside me. 'Well, Mhairi, at least his death means that you and Laura won't have to come back across here to testify at a trial. Though they might need you to speak against Mendoza, I suppose. But I do hope you'll come back to stay with us, whatever happens.'

'I'll second that!' John stooped to kiss me and sit on the end of my long wooden steamer chair. Coop sat on Laura's chair at my side. Suzi appeared with a tray of coffees and cookies, Coop reached over to snatch one, dunking his biscuit in a coffee before making wide eyes at Laura and I and dropping another bombshell.

'Hey, and do you know it wasn't just patients and the girls that Elias van Lindholm tried to kill? Burr was back in ER yesterday quizzing Randy about that woman who lost a leg in the hit and run coupla of weeks ago. Remember her? Turns out she finally got home and saw a *Brunsfield Herald* article about Elias being wanted by the police. She phoned them to say the guy in the newspaper article photo was the one who ran her over and left her for dead, the bastard.'

'Oh, Kitty? That's the girl we met at the A &P when we arrived. We've been visiting her on the Surgical Floor. She's had such a hard time. God, that was van Lindholm too?' Laura exclaimed.

'I wonder what else he did?' I sighed as John reached out and squeezed my hand.

'Nurse Makkonen they reckon,' Coop frowned. 'They've closed the case according to Jess's cop friend.'

I reckoned so too but didn't mention Jess's own awful experience in the linen room.

'Guess we'll never know all of it. Not sure I'd want to.' John looked at me with that puppy look that I found amazing. Though my heart missed a beat: how would this end? An ocean would soon separate us.

We had a barbecue of sweetcorn, steaks and salad washed down by beer and wine. I opted for alcohol rather than my pills but Laura felt she had to stick to her painkillers and took soda.

The sun was setting. I felt very safe and content in this remote lodge, injuries notwithstanding. An owl hooted in the woods beside us. The moon flickered through tree branches swaying in the breeze. The dusky silhouettes of the hills reminded me of Loch Lomond.

'This could be Scotland, you know,' I said to John as we sat side by side on my long wooden chair. 'Well, mibbe the trees look a bit different, except some of them are very like Scots pines.'

'But there's a place called Essex down the road—and it hasn't rained this week. It couldn't possibly be Scotland!' said Laura, laughing.

'You girls wanna come fishing tomorrow? I can lift you into the boat.' Coop pointed at a decent-sized dinghy tied up at the jetty that stretched from our foreshore.

'You never know, you might get to see Champ,' said Suzi, winking at her brother.

'Who's Champ?' asked Laura, looking expectantly at Coop.

'Right, so like, you know how you got a Loch Ness Monster? Well, we've got Champ the Lake Champlain monster. Though he must be pretty long in the tooth as he was first seen five hundred years ago.' Coop emptied his beer bottle and went for another.

Laura impulsively decided to risk a glass of white wine, reckoning that we had a doctor on hand (though Coop's dad was now on his third whiskey). She raised her glass. 'Let's have a toast to our hosts! A big thank you to the Mayfields for all their support and generous hospitality.' She raised her glass. 'To the Mayfields!'

John and I raised our glasses. After taking a gulp, I raised mine again. 'And here's to Simon Winters!'

John looked worried. 'Who's he? Your boyfriend back home?'

'No, that's Roddy.' I said for devilment but noticing John looking upset, I quickly added, 'No, Simon's the pompous twit I told you about who's responsible for us being here.'

'I'll drink to him then.' John raised his glass again. 'Simon Winters!'

'And absent friends,' said Coop. 'Here's to Frankie.'

Joining him in this toast, I silently added one to Carmela, and Elizabeth and the countless other women still alive who might have suffered emotional damage caused by van Lindholm with his seduction and seedy photography. Like Jess and Gretel.

I'd grown very fond of Jessica Heffernan. And her bravery. I'd finally come to the decision that she was probably right to keep Babs in the dark; lying to a child can be justifiable in some circumstances. Nothing but distress could be gained by telling a child she was the result of a rape.

In this peaceful place with a protective arm and laughter round me, I had another epiphany: perhaps my father had been right to lie too about the circumstances of my mother's death. As children, the truth would have been impossible to comprehend. And now, deep in my heart I couldn't accept he had really wished my mother dead. This week during my soporific brush with opioids, I'd had different flashbacks of my childhood. Not this time of my parents arguing, but of my mother's sorrowful face brightening into a smile when Archie and I appeared. Of her running along a beach in Lewis laughing with him, throwing stones in the water. Of them collapsing into one another's arms on a blanket in the sand, singing. They had surely been very much in love. They had been happy a lot of the time. He couldn't possibly have wanted her dead. The likelihood was that indeed, she had only sought short-term escape from torment, hadn't really intended to leave young Archie and I permanently. Or Dad.

God, Dad! I'd been told the hospital hadn't phoned him as I wasn't as badly injured as Laura and Brigitte had left it to me to contact him. I couldn't face phoning. A letter would have to do. Despite my promise to write regularly, we were now week six and he'd only had two short, bland pages of rubbish. I had to rectify that in the morning

Gradually the others drifted off to bed leaving John and me alone in the moonlight. An elegant bird swooped over the lake beside us. John thought it was an Osprey. He kissed my neck, one of the few places not hurting. Sadly, wine wasn't as good a pain-killer as codeine. He whispered his annoyance that I was sharing a room with Laura.

'Never mind,' I said raising his face and gently kissing him.

'So, this Simon guy, I mean, how did he get you here?'

'Well, it was a dare in a way. But I've managed to follow his main advice for the summer.'

'What was that?' John frowned.

I whispered, 'Didn't I say? To get laid!'

John roared with laughter. 'Anything else he advised?'

'Learn about the world of medicine. It is very different in America. I think it would suit Simon to work here. You make more money. He likes money, almost as much as sex, I think. It's all he ever talked about.'

'So, never mind the sex, we know about that.' He kissed me on the nose. I'm pleased to say I had healed enough to take that...'What have you learned about America? I mean apart from the van Lindholm and Mendoza nonsense.'

'Yes. Here it's all about birds. Clinically, I've learned I prefer seeking sparrows to rare hummingbirds. I like treating common sparrow conditions and I'd hate to have to work while worrying all the time in case I'm sued for missing something as rare as a hummingbird. And morally, I hate vultures like Juan and Elias who chased dollars, but I love docs who are clucky ducks like that OBS guy, Rory Donald. And above all, I think medicine, money and murder are a hateful mix. Having free medical care paid for by the state must be fairer and better.'

John looked confused but completely adorable, not a word I'd ever previously considered applicable to a male. I was about to say, 'I love you,' but a long and passionate kiss got in the way.

I knew I was going to enjoy the remaining weeks of our US summer, yet underneath was a layer of sadness. Having discarded the sorrow of doubt about my mother's passing, I had acquired a new one: the fate of our relationship. I knew the gulf between John and me was wider than the physicality of the Atlantic Ocean. Our natural habitats of commercialised and socialised medicine were as profoundly different as those of hummingbirds and sparrows. And probably as incompatible. And even though I was probably unlikely to encounter more actual murders in a US hospital in the future, I wasn't sure I could ever work in a country where money affected clinical decisions.

As I sat in John's arms, I realised the Mhairi going home in September would be very different from the one who'd left in July. Suppressing a sigh, I wondered if my newfound confidence would be enough to give me the strength to write a *Dear John* letter when I went home.

But for now, the passion at hand eliminated all rational thought.

Epilogue

It is three weeks before Elias van Lindholm knows he is officially dead. When he calls his mother, she is overjoyed to hear he is actually alive. His father Steig is less so; he has paid to bury a stranger.

Elias tries to explain away his tardy attempts at contact by the pressure he's endured and the complexity that's been involved in the re-arrangement of his life in Coronado. Steig is unimpressed, ranting about the furore created by the Ava's irate demands on returning from Paris. She had kicked up a great fuss, wanting to know where she could send divorce papers. And lawsuits, as she hotly disputed his sole ownership of the Brunsfield mansion, and insisted it could not be legally transferred to his father.

News of Elias's 'death' in the plane crash had made her completely incandescent. She'd refused even to organise the funeral. But as resourceful as ever, his clever father had assuaged her by revealing the large van Lindholm accounts in Mexico, now her due as a widow. Well, she wasn't a widow, but she need never know she wasn't. Anyway, according to Steig, she'd taken off to the Puerto Vallarta house. Good riddance.

Shame about Dino Laurentis dying, but on balance, by obsessively leaving the van Lindholm name on his flight manifest, the pilot had done him a favour. Though Elias had pulled out of the Mexican plan in favour of South America, thinking the authorities were less likely to pursue him there, the filed paperwork had still shown the pilot of the crashed plane as 'Dino Laurentis' and the passenger as 'Elias van Lindholm.' God knows whom poor Dino had died with. But luckily, light planes do not withstand lightning well. The two bodies must have been well charred and the autopsies must have been cursory for him to have been declared a fatality. He's happy to stay dead, though.

Steig's other news, that Juan Mendoza is dead does not surprise him. Was only a matter of time before the drugs caught up with the surgeon. Likely he'd have confessed to the cops that he'd killed Elizabeth Adams but for the Gomez woman, he had a sound alibi of partying in Puerto Vallarta. Elias sighs. On balance, Juan's family over there were another good reason for him to have fled to Panama instead. He's met the Mexican Mendoza Clan. The kind to bear a grudge. Drug runners were not forgiving people. No, Panama was a good decision. He'd made no secret of his palatial Mexican home. Everyone would expect him to go there

Steig could not enlighten him about the situation concerning those interfering Scottish bitches. No poisoning cases at Ellis Memorial had hit the press nor word of any mishaps involving overseas students. Given more time, he'd have found a more efficient disposal method than poisoned chocolates. He still has friends in Jersey. Might they be able to pursue those students in a more final way? It might be entertaining if nothing else. But would it be worth it? He's at no risk now: the police can't pursue the dead!

He assures his father that he has enough funds to ensure his new life can be a good one. The monies from the timely sale of the MRT ambulance and MLS lab companies just prior to the final shit-fest are substantial, and now accessible here. In his Nilsson 'alter ego' accounts.

Hanging up on Steig, he relives his escape and the details he has not shared with him. The personally hailed cab from Teterboro to John F. Kennedy in a newly purchased baseball cap, jacket and stylish Ray-Bans. The last minute purchase of a Business Class ticket to Panama using his Swedish Nilsson passport, that byproduct of his teenage snooping skills. What a surprise to find a Swedish birth certificate naming him as 'Jorge Elias Nilsson' of 'Father unknown'. Over the following years, his dilettante mother never mentioned its presence or acknowledged its disappearance. He has kept a copy of the other certificate citing his birth six months later as 'Elias van Lindholm', the one used for registration at college and obtaining his first passport as a US citizen. Doubtless, there was a story there. But he hasn't asked his mother. He doesn't doubt his paternity. He is Steig's double anyway.

As 'Nilsson', flying down here to Panama City Airport and renting this beach property has been easy. Sipping beer, he watches the blue waves lap the salt and pepper sand of the Bay of Panama. The new, permanent house he's commissioned will be further out, have a larger pool. Panama has it all. Sun. Sand. Sea. Palms. Flowers. Willing women.

Amongst the garden orchids and blossoming bushes, a tiny hummingbird hovers, precariously feeding on nectar before swiftly moving on. He wishes today's girl would do the same. That fucking shower's been running for twenty minutes. Disappointingly, she's not a natural blonde: her pubes gave her away. But there'll be better women for a prosperous man about town to find. Coronado is growing. Who knows what opportunities may arise? For business as well as pleasure.

ACKNOWLEDGEMENTS

No book is actually the work of one person. I am indebted to the many medical friends who contributed stories of their time in the States as students, and in particular, to my ex-classmate Dr Douglas Lees. M.D, now an eminent Michigan Cardiovascular Surgeon and Dr Laurence A. Kirwan, M.D., F.R.C.S., F.A.C.S. in Connecticut who kept me right about the day to day workings of a US hospital that I had long forgotten (if indeed I ever noticed them myself as a student!) Any mistakes are my own.

Thanks must also go to the beta readers, especially Polly Beck (Lawrence's sister) and Grace Shaw with their eagle eye for errors, to my Uni tutor Dr Cathy MacSporran and her Garnethill Writers Group for ongoing encouragement and Greenock Writers Club without whom I would never have had the courage to submit anything for publication.

Thanks are also due to the lovely staff of Sparsile Books - Stephen Cashmore, Jim Campbell and the redoubtable Lesley Affrossman who fearlessly deals with everything from smouldering computer meltdowns (literally) to garbled confused emails from me. The book would not be what it is without their editing input.

But most of all, thanks to the readers who buy and review my books and in doing so, help the work of the charity PlanUK to better the lives of children worldwide.

Follow Anne Pettigrew:

Website:	http://www.annepettigrew.co.uk
Facebook:	@annepettigrewauthor
Instagram:	anne.pettigrew.author
X (Formerly Twitter:)	@pettigrew_anne

About the Author

Glasgow-born Anne spent 32 years as a Greenock GP and is a graduate of Glasgow (Medicine 1974) and Oxford (MSc Medical Anthropology 2004). Worked in psychiatry, women's health & journalism (Herald, Pulse, Doctor etc). In retirement took Glasgow University Creative Writing tuition to pen books about women doctors, rare in novels except in Mills and Boon or cast as pathologists. Runner-up in Scottish Association of Writers Constable Silver Stag Award 2018. Chosen as a 2019 Bloody Scotland Crime Spotlight Author - 'one to watch.' Member of several writers' groups. Short story competition winner. Lives in Ayrshire and enjoys good books, good wine, and good company.